the
Keeper's
Defiance

THE KEEPER'S SAGA: BOOK THREE

the Keeper's Defiance

Kelly Nelson

WALNUT SPRINGS PRESS

For Greg,

who believed in me and encouraged me to pursue my dreams.
Without his unwavering support, I wouldn't be where I am today.

Walnut Springs Press
110 South 800 West
Brigham City, Utah 84302
http://walnutspringspress.blogspot.com

Text copyright © 2013 by Kelly Nelson
Cover design copyright © 2013 by Walnut Springs Press
Interior design copyright © 2013 by Walnut Springs Press

ISBN: 978-1-59992-896-8

This is a work of fiction. The characters, names, incidents, and dialogue are products of the author's
imagination and are not to be construed as real, and any resemblance to real people and events is not
intentional.

The Keeper's Saga

The Keeper's Calling

The Keeper's Quest

The Keeper's Defiance

The Keepers' Council (coming in 2014)

Acknowledgments

First, thank you to all of my readers. It is exciting to have so many people delve into the world of the Keepers with me. I love your excitement and enthusiasm over Chase and Ellie's adventures. Without you this book wouldn't be possible. Thank you to my husband and children for their love and encouragement. I wouldn't be where I am today without them. Thank you to Linda and Garry at Walnut Springs Press for their continued support of my writing career as well as their friendship. Thank you to Tracy Anderson of Anderson Photography for the graphic-design work on the front cover. Thank you to all the folks at Brigham Distributing. Finally, a special thanks to the Costco managers who have opened their doors and welcomed me into their stores for book signings. But most importantly, I am grateful for a loving Heavenly Father who hears and answers my prayers.

Characters

Chase Harper—the Protector; the Protector's Keeper (born Feb. 17, 1994)

Ellen (Ellie) Elizabeth Williams—Chase's girlfriend (born May 28, 1845)

Jessica Harper—Chase's twin sister

Joe and Jennifer Harper—Chase's parents

Adam Harper—Chase's cousin

Amanda Harper—Chase's cousin

Steve and Marianne Harper—Chase's uncle and aunt

Randy Jones—Hilhi football quarterback

Kim Stanton—Chase's ex-girlfriend

Walt Griffith—Ellie's ex-beau in Boston

Mary—Ellie's great-aunt's live-in servant

Garrick Eastman—the Guardian; the Guardian's Keeper (born Oct. 8, 1944)

Rose Adams—Garrick's deceased wife; Davy's mother (born Sept. 16, 1791; died Aug. 24, 1818)

Davy Adams—Perception's Keeper; Garrick's adopted son (born Jan. 6, 1812)

Master Archidus—the Master Keeper; king of Algonia

Lord Arbon—king of Shuyle; Archidus' older brother

Legard—a Sniffer; Lord Arbon's second in command

Captain Marcus Landseer—Algonian soldier who reported the destruction of Radnor

Wickliff—an old elf; father of Creation's first Keeper, Courtenay

Segur—Algonian soldier

Aiton—only soldier of Barculo's to survive the attack on Radnor

Falon and Pellyn—twin brothers; Algonian soldiers

Barhydt—Algonian soldier who is part sorcerer

Azalit—daughter of Archidus

Mud—head guard in Arbon's dungeon

Bartimus—assistant guard in Arbon's dungeon

Brierly—Marcus Landseer's younger sister

The Mortensons—neighbor to Garrick and Davy in 1829 Ohio

Carol and Lyman Gibson—owners of the mercantile in Vandalia, Illinois

Millie and Benjamin Johnson—neighbors to Ellie's grandfather in Hurricane, Utah

Places

Algonia—kingdom of Master Archidus

Cadré Unair—fortress city of Algonia

Shuyle—kingdom of Lord Arbon

Valley of Tierran—entrance to Shuyle

Susack Plain—grassy plain in the center of the Borderlands

Saddle Pass—gap in the Shuylian mountain range

Dragon's Lair—portal between the old world and Shuyle

Witches Hollow—portal between the old world and Algonia

Prologue

Until this particular night, Joe and Jennifer Harper never had a cause to search their son's room. Chase had always been respectful and trustworthy, but his senior year at Hillsboro High School in Oregon had been difficult. At times moody and secretive, their son was often aggressive and had developed a sudden interest in fencing, leaving his parents baffled.

Joe's jaw about dropped through the floor the night Jennifer announced that Chase had been in a fistfight with Randy Jones over a girl—Ellie. Come to think of it, all these bizarre behaviors started around the time the family met her. It was no secret Chase liked her—any fool could see that—and Joe found himself resenting Ellie and her intrusion into his relationship with his son. Joe missed the weekend fishing trips, watching late-night SportsCenter on ESPN together, and their one-on-one basketball games in the driveway. Lately, Ellie had Chase wrapped around her little finger. He was at her beck and call day or night, and Joe felt slighted.

He stared at the locked door in front of him. Unless his son was hurt, he expected to find the room vacant. A wave of anxiety washed over Joe as he inserted the narrow screwdriver into the knob and sprung the lock. He threw open the door and strode into the empty room.

His wife Jennifer followed. "Where could he be?" she asked. "It's nearly ten o'clock. He's never come home from school this late without calling. It's not like him."

"I'll bet he's with that girlfriend of his," Joe said.

Jennifer picked up their son's cell phone, wallet, and keys, and then pointed to the pile of clothes he'd worn to school that day. "Why are these here, if Chase isn't?"

Since their twins, Chase and Jessica, got cell phones for their fifteenth birthday, Joe could count on one hand the number of times they were without them. It was both a blessing and a curse. How often had his kids failed to hear him because they were wrapped up in texting their friends? On the other hand, he could always get in touch with them—until now. He frowned. "I don't know, but that explains why he didn't check in."

Jennifer left to make a call as Jessica leaned her head into the room and said, "Hey, what's up?"

"Do you know where Chase is?" Joe asked.

"No. Why?"

"He's missing."

"Have you tried Ellie's cell phone?"

"I didn't know she had one."

"Chase got her one for Valentine's. I'll call her."

Jessica proceeded to call the number while Joe shook his head. "Chase got her one for Valentine's," he mimicked, his voice heavy with sarcasm.

"There's no answer," his daughter said as she made another call. "Hey, Adam, do you know where Chase is?" A hollow silence filled the room as Jessica listened to Chase's cousin and best friend's answer.

Once she slid her phone closed, Joe asked, "Well, what did he say?"

Jessica bit down on her lower lip. "Adam doesn't know, but the weird thing is, Chase skipped track practice today without telling anyone."

Jennifer appeared in the doorway, her eyes dark with concern. "They found Ellie's door locked and her clothes and cell phone in her room as well. How can both of them disappear like this?"

Jessica's mind churned through the strange things she knew about her brother as she debated what, if anything, she should say to their parents. She knew how he'd left, but had no idea where he'd gone or why he hadn't returned. She watched her father pull vintage clothes and various weapons from her brother's closet as her mother thumbed through the pages of an ancient, leather-bound book.

"This is a journal belonging to Ellie's grandfather," Jessica's mom said.

Jessica's dad picked up a black trench coat and ran his thumb over the Nazi swastika affixed to the sleeve. "Is Chase in the school play *The Sound of Music*?"

"No. They aren't even doing *The Sound of Music* this year," Jessica replied.

"Hmm." Her dad pulled a handful of ammo clips from one pocket and a Luger pistol out of the other. As he looked closely at the weapon, his eyes widened. "Chase has a loaded gun in his closet. And these are mint-condition antiques. They're probably worth a small fortune." Jessica's dad slid his hand over the stock of a muzzleloader rifle and glared at her. "How did Chase get these? Did he steal them?"

Without thinking, Jessica jumped to her brother's defense. "No, Dad. Not exactly."

"Jess, what do you know about all this?" her mom asked.

Jessica shook her head. "It's supposed to be a secret, and I don't think you'd believe me anyway."

Her dad stepped closer, raising his voice to say, "I don't care. If you know something, young lady, you'd better start talking."

"Okay. It started last summer when Chase went for a bike ride in Zion National Park. Both Adam and I got text messages saying he was lost. By the time I returned his text, Chase said he was walking back. When he got closer he called and asked me to bring a change of clothes—girl clothes—and meet him near the park entrance. He walked into camp with Ellie a few minutes later. She looked like she'd come out of an old western movie. Then Chase told me this crazy story about finding a gold counter buried in a cave—"

"What's a counter?" Jessica's father interrupted.

"Dad, just listen. I'm getting to that. When he touched one of the buttons inside, he went back in time, where he met Ellie. The men who owned some of those clothes had captured her and were trying to get the counter. Chase rescued her, and since her grandfather used to have the counter, she knew how to use it and helped him get back here.

"I didn't believe it at first, but I felt sorry for Chase since he looked beat up. I know he has a weakness for cute girls, so I thought Ellie had tricked him or something. I took her in the girls' bathroom to change clothes, and she was either a really good actress or she wasn't from our time. She didn't know anything. I thought maybe she was Amish or something, and I figured Chase's time-travel story was bogus."

Jessica paused for a moment, then continued, "Remember when Ellie went back to Boston for a while? Well, Chase told me he left her in 1863. And then later he said he spent six weeks in the year 18–something or other, digging the Erie Canal with another Keeper. That's what Chase calls himself—a Keeper. I still didn't believe him, so when he was moping around about Ellie being gone, I dared him to go back to 1863, if he could. I hoped he would snap out of it and admit it was all a big lie, but it wasn't. He really did it—he put on some old-fashioned clothes and left. I stood right here and watched him turn a dial on the counter and then vanish. I walked through where he had stood seconds before, and there was nothing. He had promised he'd be right back, so I waited. A minute later, he suddenly appeared, only he was shivering and his hands and feet were ice cold. After that I had no choice but to believe him."

Jessica paused again. "So I'll bet Chase came home from school today, changed into his old-fashioned clothes, and used his counter to take Ellie to another time and place. But what I don't know is what happened to keep him from coming back home."

Jessica's father raised his eyebrows and shook his head. "That is the most ridiculous explanation I've ever heard. And I thought Chase came up with some whoppers."

PART I
Chase

ONE
The Borderlands

Wickliff's sharp whistle pierced the air. "Dragons!" he yelled.

My head shot up. "Ellie, over here." I jumped to the ground, grabbed both horses' reins, and pulled the animals into a thick stand of willows. Ellie burrowed through the twisted branches ahead of me. Everyone in our group scattered, finding cover beneath the trees and brush lining the river's edge.

I sat on my heels next to Ellie and looked at the two horses. Their ears drooped and their lathered bodies quivered. We had ridden them hard through most of the night and into the morning, and they'd been on the trail for days before we'd stolen them. I grimaced as I realized we were going to push them to their limits and beyond. There was no way around it.

My heart raced as the familiar snap of the dragons' wings grew louder. I knew Ellie and I were hidden from their view, but I wondered about our horses—all twelve of them. They were harder to hide. But the dragons passed by at a leisurely pace, and I repositioned myself to watch them leave. They followed the river until they were nearly out of sight before angling north and fading into the horizon over the rolling plains.

I released a deep breath. *That wasn't so bad.* I looked at Ellie. "Are you all right?"

Her head was buried in her hands, her shoulders shaking. Convinced our horses weren't going anywhere unless we made them, I dropped the reins and wrapped my arms around my girlfriend. "It's okay. They're gone now."

She leaned into me and rested her head on my chest. Slowly I stood, pulling her up with me.

"I'm scared. I'm exhausted," she said. "And I don't see how we're going to get back home."

She choked back a sob, and I could tell she was making every effort to be brave. Seeing the fear in her eyes made my heart constrict. All I ever wanted was to keep her safe and make her happy. Right now, I was failing miserably. Our rescue party had freed Ellie and Davy after the Sniffers abducted them and brought them to the new world, but we were far from safe. The rival countries of Algonia and Shuyle were on the brink of war, and we were smack-dab in the middle of it.

"We'll get back home," I said more confidently than I felt. "We've just got to take it one day at a time."

Ellie wiped her eyes and squared her shoulders. "Yes. I mustn't let my fatigue get the best of me. Yesterday, I held out no hope of ever seeing you again. And yet here you are."

"Harper?" yelled Garrick, who was also a Keeper—known as the Guardian—and Davy's adopted father. "Let's go."

I led both horses into the open, then held Ellie's stirrup while she stepped into the saddle. The other riders moved away to the east.

"Hang in there," I said to Ellie. "Soon we'll be in Algonia. You'll be safe there—I promise."

She gave me a halfhearted smile. I mounted my horse and nudged it forward to follow the rest of the group.

"I thought dragons existed only in fairy tales," Ellie said after a while.

"Yeah, they do. But we're in the fairy-tale world."

"What do you mean?"

"Wickliff explained it as an alternate dimension of Earth. Sometime during the Dark Ages or the Middle Ages—I don't know exactly—a group of sorcerers split off from Earth and created a new world. They took everything magical with them and left the regular people in the old world, where we're from. All that remains of their magic on our world is folklore and fairy tales."

Ellie sighed. "Why did those Sniffers take us? I mean, I know they want the counters, but Davy didn't have his counter with him. And why take me?"

"They laid a trap for me, and you were the bait."

"I'm sorry."

"Don't be. I shouldn't have left you alone."

We caught up to the main group, and I overheard Garrick say, "Those dragons didn't put a lot of effort into looking for us."

"I don't believe they were looking for us . . . yet," Wickliff replied.

"What do you mean?" Garrick asked.

"Considering the state in which I left Legard, and the condition of his cavalry, it may take them awhile to return to Lord Arbon. It will be Arbon who communicates our presence to the dragons. Believe me, Guardian, you will know when they are looking for you."

Marcus cleared his throat. "We follow the river until it turns south. I'm predicting we'll arrive by midafternoon. After that it's a hard ride over the Susack Plain before we reach the forests on the Algonian side of the Borderlands. We'll rest at the bend in the river until nightfall. With the dragons around, it won't do to be out in the open during daylight."

The rest of us voiced our agreement and urged our horses into a trot to keep up with Marcus and Garrick.

With the sun directly overhead, Ellie shaded her eyes and turned to look at me. "How are you feeling?"

I grinned. "I'm doing a lot better. That nasty liquid energy of Wickliff's did the trick."

Her eyes twinkled as she smiled back at me. "I'm pleased it helped."

When the riders ahead of us moved their horses into a slow gallop, we followed suit. All of our mounts were nearly spent.

Suddenly, the horse belonging to Segur, the largest man in our group, stumbled on the uneven terrain and went to its knees. The animal tried to regain its footing, but collapsed to the ground. Segur rolled clear of the sprawling horse and came to a stop in the grass. The man staggered to his feet, favoring his broken arm.

Ellie and I veered to the side to avoid trampling the downed horse and rider. I pulled my mount to a stop and turned to face Segur. "Are you hurt?" I asked.

He waved his good arm and hobbled toward the horse. "I'm fine."

The animal's eyes rolled back, showing the white around the edges. Except for the rise and fall of its chest and an occasional moan, the horse lay still. I dismounted and walked to the animal's side. When Segur bent to untie his pack from the saddle, I reached in front of him. "I can do that."

The big man's lips turned up. "Thanks, lad. Me arm's not workin' too well yet."

I removed the pack and stood. Garrick and Marcus rode back, their horses' flanks covered in white lather.

"We'll need to double up," Marcus said. "We've got to keep moving."

"Take my horse," I told Segur. "I'll ride with Ellie." I carried his pack to where my exhausted horse stood, dripping sweat and barely able to hold his head up.

Marcus turned his horse sharply and galloped away. Garrick and most of the others followed. Davy paused, furrowing his eyebrows as he studied Ellie for a moment. I removed my pack and tied Segur's behind the saddle. He got on and rode away. Ellie dismounted and walked slowly toward the suffering horse. With my pack fastened to her saddle, I mounted and rode between her and the dying animal.

"Ellie, come on. There's nothing we can do for him."

Without saying a word, she turned and took my outstretched hand. I pulled her up and she seated herself behind me, with her arms around my waist.

Marcus eventually slowed his horse to a walk, and when I reined in my mount, Ellie leaned her head against my back. Soon her body relaxed in sleep. When she started drifting to the side, I put my arm behind me and wrapped it around her back to keep her from falling.

Once the horses caught their breath, Marcus again picked up the pace. I inwardly groaned at the thought of having to wake Ellie. Everyone else moved ahead of us, forcing me to speak or be left behind. "Ellie, wake up. We've got to go faster."

She lifted her head and tightened her grip on me. I let go of her and urged our reluctant horse into a gallop. The afternoon sun baked the grasslands in the distance. Yet where we rode near the river, everything appeared moist and green. A cool breeze wafted along the riverbank, and the towering trees provided relief from the blistering sun. If we weren't dead tired and running for our lives, it would have been a pleasant horseback ride.

"Dragons!" Wickliff yelled with even more intensity than before. A moment later the airborne reptiles' screams echoed across the plains.

My heart pounded as I steered the horse closer to the river. I swung my leg over the animal's neck and hopped off, then helped Ellie down. Pushing her ahead of me, I pulled our horse into the thick brush along the riverbank.

Hideous screams burst from the dragons' mouths as they followed the river toward us. Beads of sweat trickled down my forehead. I glanced back and forth between Ellie and the horse, wondering if everyone else was hidden.

Crouched on the ground, I held the horse's reins in one hand. The beating of the dragons' wings grew louder, and the smell of smoke drifted on the breeze. A deafening roar sounded as one of the enormous creatures spewed fire above us in a rush of hot air.

The horse pulled back, fighting to escape the fiery inferno raging overhead, and I toppled forward onto my hands and knees. The frantic animal dragged me across the ground as I fought to hold on to the sweat-covered reins. When he stopped for a moment, I scrambled toward him. "Whoa there, boy. Shh."

I glanced up and gasped at the sight of a dragon's dull, gray-green scales through the leaves above me. The lush foliage sputtered and sparked as the fire fought to take hold, but the flames soon dwindled, leaving smoking branches.

The dragons heaved their next wall of fire into the trees above where I'd seen Wickliff and Marcus disappear. The squeal of a terrified horse mingled with a dragon's scream as the reptile bombarded the treetops with flames. Suddenly, I heard the thundering of hooves— one of the horses had escaped. The dragons veered off the river and gave pursuit.

With the monsters preoccupied, Wickliff, Marcus, and Barhydt moved closer to Ellie and me. After calming my horse, I shifted positions to get a clear view. Wickliff's mount was missing, and from the sound of it there wouldn't be anything left when the dragons were through. Soon, they turned their bloody snouts toward the river and spread their wings. I retreated into the brush next to Ellie and tightened my hold on the reins. Both dragons breathed fire onto the trees where Wickliff's horse had been hidden. Within seconds, smoky flames licked the sky. The dragons moved on, methodically searching the river ahead.

"Spread the word. We move out, but hold close to the trees," Marcus ordered.

I emerged from my hiding place and walked over to Segur's. "Move out, but stay close to the trees. Pass the word along."

Wickliff climbed onto Azalit's horse. The elf girl's once proud and fearless expression was now one of humility and terror. I watched Ellie emerge from hiding, her face full of the same fear. Anxious to be moving, I mounted our horse and offered her my hand. As soon as her arms circled my waist, I urged the horse downriver.

Ellie shuddered as we passed the smoking trees. Flames engulfed the surrounding bushes, but I expected the fire would quickly burn itself out. We searched the grassland for Wickliff's runaway horse. Ellie hid her face against my back when we saw the animal's mangled carcass in the distance. Without some good luck, that would likely be the fate of us all.

An hour later, Wickliff raised the alarm. "They're coming back."

We scrambled for cover. When a ball of flames erupted overhead, our horse again struggled to run free. Ellie lowered her head and clapped her hands over her ears, but nothing could block out the dragons' haunting shrieks. With all their ruckus, at least they didn't hear the commotion my horse made. Once the danger passed, the animal stood quivering, whether from fatigue or fear, I didn't know.

We rode until late afternoon before Marcus called for a halt at a sharp bend in the river. It almost doubled back on itself before meandering south. Far to the east, the forested hills of Algonia were barely visible across the open plain. The dragons' fury had left singed treetops all along the river. In places, tendrils of smoke reached into the sky.

"Spread out and take cover," Marcus said. "We rest here until nightfall."

I scanned the tree line and saw a large stand of willows just past the bend in the river. I slid off the horse and walked closer. In the midst of the trees was a level patch of ground. It looked well hidden and large enough for two people to lie down comfortably. I kicked a few stones out of the way and returned for Ellie.

She slid off the horse into my outstretched arms and I whispered, "Let's get you into bed."

A smile flitted across her face. "Oh, you found a bed in there?"

I grinned back at her. "Not quite king-sized, but you'll be in the lap of luxury, my lady. I'll show you after I tie up our horse."

After watering the animal, I led him to a small cottonwood tree surrounded by larger trees, with a patch of grass at its base. I tied the sweat-soaked reins around the trunk and hoped the knot would hold up under a dragon fly-by. I untied my pack and slung it over my shoulder.

"This way." I took Ellie's hand and led her into the willows. "It's not a bed, but it's the best I could find."

"I don't care," she said. "I'll take any place as long as I can lay my head down."

I pulled the blanket out of my pack and spread it on the ground. Once we sat, I handed her the water flask. "You should drink a lot. You don't want to get dehydrated, and I don't know where our next water stop will be."

She took a drink and tried to hand the flask back, but I told her to finish it.

"Do you want to see if we have anything to eat in our pack?" I asked as I climbed to my feet.

Before she could answer, I slipped through the willows to the riverbank and stepped into the water. My boots from Cadré Unair were the ultimate in comfort and completely waterproof. I filled the flask, raising it to my lips several times in the process. I wasn't the only one topping off his water supply before we left the protection of the river. Downstream, Marcus and Aiton stood knee-deep in the crystal-clear water.

I drank my fill and washed the sweat off my face and arms. From Marcus's description of the Borderlands, I hoped to be in Algonia by tomorrow night, although I didn't know if that necessarily meant we'd be safe. According to Segur, it would take another day or so to get from Algonia's border to the fortress city. After that, it would be mere hours until Master Archidus could send us home via Witches Hollow.

I threaded my way through the willows to where Ellie had laid out a flat loaf of dark bread and two pieces of jerky. I sat across from her as she tore the loaf in half. Famished, I ripped off a chunk of bread with my teeth. The loaf was half gone before I thought to slow down and savor the meager meal. The bread was dense and filling, with a touch of sweetness to it. I was sick of jerky, since I had eaten little else for the past three days.

I finished eating and rolled my nearly empty pack into a pillow. I lay down and began to relax for the first time in days. The gurgling of the river behind me, and the canopy of curly willow leaves overhead, made for a deceptively serene setting. We were far from safe, but I had my girlfriend back and we were together.

When Ellie finished eating, I whispered, "Come here." I stretched my arm out and she rested her head on my shoulder.

She brushed her fingertips over the stubble on my chin and smiled. "This place is beautiful, except for the constant dread I feel regarding those dragons."

"Yeah, it is." I exhaled and closed my eyes.

She shifted positions before the evenness of her breathing told me she was asleep. I settled my hand on the hilt of my sword and drifted off.

TWO
Susack Plain

Sleeping didn't end up being all that restful for me. The dragons' roaring combined with the thundering of hundreds of horses' hooves nearly paralyzed me. The whole of Arbon's army was bearing down on us. Fire lit the night sky like fireworks, and I realized none of us would escape. We couldn't outrun an army. The snap of a dragon's wings drew closer. Razor-sharp claws clutched my shoulders and yanked me into the air. "No," I yelled, grabbing for my weapon. I heard the scrape of metal as my sword slid out of its sheath.

"Chase, darling, wake up," Ellie said, her hand pressed against my chest. "Lie down—you're only dreaming."

Breathing heavily, I opened my eyes and wiped at the sweat on my forehead. I slid my half-drawn sword back into its scabbard. The sky wasn't quite dark, and only the rustle of the breeze through the trees filled the air. The peaceful gurgle of the river welcomed me back to reality. There were no dragons, and there was no army. It had been only a dream.

I shook my head in frustration. "I'll never be able to sleep right again." Wrapping both arms around Ellie, I buried my face in her hair.

She caressed the back of my neck and spoke softly in my ear. "All things pass with time. The nightmares won't stay with you forever."

I collapsed onto my makeshift pillow and covered my face with my arm. Feeling Ellie's gaze on me, I asked, "Were you already awake?"

"I heard you talking in your sleep and woke up."

I opened my eyes and looked at her. "Sorry."

She shook her head. "Don't be. What were you dreaming about?"

"Dragons."

She smiled. "That's not a bit surprising. I fear those frightful creatures will haunt my dreams for years to come as well."

I glanced away. "It's getting dark. I bet we'll leave soon."

"I suppose so." She paused, looking behind her. "What a lovely place this is. If only it weren't so dangerous."

There was something soothing about engaging in small talk. It calmed me after the disturbing nightmare, allowing the thudding in my chest to settle to a normal rhythm. "I'll feel a lot better once we make it to Algonia."

"I'm going to get up." Ellie stood and straightened her skirt. She walked away with a slight limp, massaging her lower back. After as many hours as we'd spent in the saddle, I didn't blame her.

I rolled over and climbed to my feet with a groan. I definitely felt the effects of running for two days, topped with fifteen hours in the saddle. But I didn't like letting Ellie out of my sight, so if she got up, then I got up. After stuffing the blanket into my pack, I went to look for her.

Marcus walked up the river, rousing everyone as he went. "Segur, Falon, Pellyn, time to move out." He didn't sound as optimistic as he had before, but maybe it was just fatigue I heard.

Garrick walked in the opposite direction. "Wickliff, Barhydt, Azalit—let's go."

Ellie had untied our horse and stood letting him graze near the others. Davy held the reins to Garrick's horse and his own. As an apprentice blacksmith, it was obvious he was comfortable around horses. Where I could hold my own and get by, Davy exuded confidence and easily excelled. He stood close to Ellie—too close for my liking—as he reached in front of her to check the cinch on our horse.

He picked up her free hand and laid his reins in her palm. "Can you hold these for me? I should tighten this cinch for you." When he smiled, holding her gaze and her hand longer than necessary, I hurried forward.

I flung my pack on top of the saddle and shouldered my way past him. "Don't worry, Davy, I got it. Looks like Garrick's ready for his horse."

Davy backed away and took the reins from Ellie. "Thank you, Davy," she said.

I tightened the cinch, then took the reins from her and mounted. I couldn't help but notice her amused smile.

She slid her foot into the stirrup and grasped my arm so I could pull her up behind me. "What's so funny?" I asked.

Her lips brushed the back of my neck with a kiss as she leaned forward. "You . . . Davy. He was only being nice, you know."

I doubt it. Davy annoyed the heck out of me, but I forced my lips into a smile and agreed with Ellie anyway. After all, she was sharing my horse, not his. Feeling threatened by him was stupid, really. But if Davy wasn't so dang nice, and if he wasn't always sporting that frontier look I knew turned Ellie on, it might be less intimidating.

Marcus circled his horse in front of us as the last of the sun's light painted the clouds a kaleidoscope of oranges and pinks. I could barely make out people's faces in the approaching darkness. Marcus cleared his throat and said, "Tonight we'll be in the open. Dragons are visual hunters. When Wickliff sends out the warning, dismount and get away from the horses. Spread out, drop down, and lay flat. If the grass catches fire, hold your position until the last possible moment. If you must move, crawl. Once the dragons leave, Wickliff can turn the flames. But remember, as long as they're overhead, you've got to stay low and be still. Understood?" The urgency in Marcus's voice was unmistakable. I hadn't missed the fact he'd said *"when* Wickliff sends out the warning" instead of *"if."* Undoubtedly, Marcus expected company before the night ended.

We all nodded our heads. Falon, Pellyn, and the rest of the soldiers looked bored with Marcus's speech. It must have been given for the benefit of us foreigners, and maybe Azalit.

Marcus raised his arm. "Follow me." He wheeled his horse around and galloped onto the Susack Plain.

The half moon rose above the eastern horizon as we left the peaceful river bend behind. The wind rippled the grass like waves at sea. Our horse made a heavy swooshing sound as he ploughed through the chest-high stalks. I was grateful this horse we'd stolen had an easy, comfortable gallop, like a rocking chair.

When Marcus slowed to a walk to rest the horses, most of us dug through our packs to find something warmer. Darkness had brought the chill of night. Ellie leaned against my back, her arms wrapped tightly around my torso as she tried to stay warm. I pulled out the elfish cloak and said, "Put this on. See if it helps."

I turned and watched her pull the long cloak over her shoulders and fasten the clasp beneath her chin. She pulled the hood over her head and let out a contented sigh. "How delightfully warm. Thank you, Chase. But what about you?"

"I'll use the blanket," I said as I pulled it from the pack.

When her arms circled my middle, I felt the warmth emanating from the magical cloak. I kicked my feet out of the stirrups and massaged my aching knees. After this long in the saddle, they were acting like those of a retired old geezer waiting for knee-replacement surgery.

Ellie again rested her head against my back. This would be another long night. The few hours of sleep I'd had in the past twenty-four hours weren't cutting it. My eyes blurred and played tricks on me in the moonlight, making me think the Shuylians were watching us. When my chin bobbed onto my chest, I jerked my head up. In front of me, Davy was slumped over in his saddle, and I wondered if he could sleep like that.

We walked long enough for our mounts to catch their breath before again pushing them into a gallop. Several horses stumbled, including ours, and we were lucky none of them went down. They were as dead-tired as we were. Marcus's plan, although necessary, was cruel. We would run these horses until they dropped or we were forced to abandon them to satisfy the dragons' appetites.

When the moon sat directly overhead, it happened. Wickliff pulled his horse to a stop and lifted his eyes to the sky. "Dragons," he yelled.

Azalit slid off, followed by the old elf. A crack of his staff across the horse's rump sent the animal galloping into the night.

I kicked my feet free of the stirrups as Ellie hooked her arm through my elbow and jumped down. "Go, Ellie," I whispered. Once my feet touched the ground, I grabbed my pack and turned to follow.

As I ran, I stuffed the blanket into the pack and slung it over my shoulders. The cloak Ellie wore rendered her nearly invisible, except when the hood bounced down and revealed her golden curls. I caught her within a few strides and grabbed her hand, then looked for Wickliff. He would know when we had to hide. Once I saw him drop into the grass, I stopped. "Lie down, quick," I told Ellie.

Across the plain everyone disappeared, leaving only the horses visible above the sea of grass. The last thing I saw as I dropped next to Ellie was our horse, doggedly following us.

"Dang it," I muttered, settling myself next to her.

"What?" she whispered.

"Our stupid horse is following us."

I repositioned her hood, covering her hair, and realized it probably would have been better for her to be by herself. She would have been perfectly hidden in the chameleon cloak. I pulled my arm off her back and tucked them both under my body, then turned my face to the ground. I couldn't afford to have my pale skin reflect the moonlight and attract the dragons' attention.

"Whatever happens, Ellie, don't move, okay? Even if something happens to me. Promise me," I said as firmly as I could in a whisper.

"Chase?"

"Ellie, promise me."

"All right," she finally said. "But don't let anything happen to you."

I risked a glance. Her head was angled slightly and we made eye contact before I turned away.

The two dragons roared toward us across the plain. Every horse leapt into a gallop as a burst of orange flame lit the night sky. The thundering of hooves vibrated the ground beneath my cheek. I figured we were directly in the path of our horse, so I moved on top of Ellie, covering both of our heads with my arms. If it stepped on one of us I didn't want it to be her.

The horse must have seen us at the last minute because he jumped, grazing my pack with his hind feet as he fled. One dragon swooped toward the horse. A burst of fire exploded overhead, sending flaming spittle raining down. Drops of the burning liquid pelted my arms. It hit my skin like acid, leaving bleeding holes in my flesh. To keep quiet, I bit my lip so hard I tasted blood.

The squeal of our dying horse compelled me to look up. The dragon looked like something out of *Jurassic Park* as it shredded the animal's flesh with its razor-sharp teeth. But it wasn't eating. It hunted for sport—Lord Arbon's sport. A deafening roar erupted, fanning me with hot air as the beast scorched a swath of grass in front of him. With a scream the dragon took flight, its scales reflecting the orange glow of the burning grass below.

The cries of other dying horses surrounded us as the roar of the dragons faded into the night. The wall of burning grass spread, but the wind was in our favor, driving the bulk of the flames away from us.

"Ellie, follow me. But stay low," I whispered.

Slowly, I crawled in the direction I'd last seen Wickliff. With caution, I rose to my knees and looked. Large patches of grass burned across the Susack Plain. The expanding rings of fire left black holes in their wake. The dragons flew in the distance, chasing down our scattered horses. I lowered my head and kept crawling.

A moment later, the call of a night bird pierced the air. I had heard that sound the night before we attacked the Shuylians. I jerked my head up and scanned the horizon. Wickliff stood waving his staff for us to follow. All twelve of us jumped to our feet and ran.

Soon the burning in my lungs matched the throbbing pain of my seared skin. "Chase," Ellie called from behind me. I stopped. She was bent over, struggling to catch her breath. "I can't . . . run all night. I'm sorry."

I turned back. "Don't give up. You can do it. One step at a time." I wrapped my arm around her and pulled her alongside me. Gradually our group spread out. Ellie and I walked a track farther to the north than anyone else and a little behind. I had become so numb to my surroundings, I didn't notice a horse lying in the grass in front of me until I nearly I stepped on him.

I let go of Ellie and inspected the animal. Lathered sweat caked his entire body. He lifted his head when I touched his neck. I saw no sign of injury and tugged on the reins. He moaned once before reluctantly scrambling to his feet. Nothing seemed to be broken. I smiled at Ellie. "Looks like you won't have to run all night after all." I loaded my pack onto the horse and helped her into the saddle.

I dragged the weary horse behind me, eventually catching up with our group. Shoulders were slumped forward, and heads down. If the others felt anything like I did, there was no energy for anything except getting one foot in front of the other, so Garrick startled me when he said, "Little brother, you found my horse."

I turned and looked behind me. Until that moment, it hadn't crossed my mind which horse I'd found. My sleepy brain was slow to respond. I said the first thing that came to mind. "Well, finders keepers, losers weepers."

Garrick must have been as tired as I was because he didn't have a good comeback, just let out a tired chuckle.

Everyone had stopped to listen to our exchange, and Azalit dug a small container from her pack. "Give me your arm," she ordered.

I extended both arms, and she smeared a cool, dark salve on my burns as she whispered an incantation. When she finished with me, she moved on to someone else.

I took a drink from the water flask Ellie and I shared, and then we were moving again. We ran when we could, but the walking time between running steadily lengthened as the night wore on.

Eventually, the first hint of light appeared over the hills in front of us, and the forest gradually came into focus. "Let's hustle. I want to be in those trees before day breaks," Marcus yelled.

Again we ran. Every time I jerked on the horse's reins, it felt like a knife going through my shoulder blade. I swear I put more energy into getting that stinkin' horse into a trot than I did running myself. He now carried both Ellie and Azalit, who at sixteen had most likely never pulled an all-nighter, let alone two in a row. As we approached the trees I prayed we were close enough to walk. I was about to collapse. I'd already retched once during the night. It happened after a particularly long haul of running, shortly after we'd found the horse. I had pushed my tired body to the point of being sick.

But the sensation I now felt not only involved the gut-wrenching nausea I'd experienced earlier, but included my head and everything else. I wasn't the only one struggling, either. Nearly every man had stumbled and fallen at least once. Only the threat of the horse trotting on my heels had kept me on my feet. I couldn't fall, I reminded myself. I'd be trampled for sure.

At the moment I felt I could go no farther, Wickliff's weary voice called out the one word I'd come to despise. "Dragons!" There would be no rest. There would be no stopping to walk. It was now a dead run for the trees.

Sunlight seeped into the valley. The foliage was sparse at first—it might be enough to hide a single man, but not a horse and three people. Farther ahead, I spied a stand of large, sprawling trees of a variety I'd never seen before. I veered in that direction and didn't stop running until I reached them.

Azalit and Ellie slid off the horse's back and darted for cover. The low-hanging branches brushed the saddle as I pulled the horse into the grove and dropped to my knees. Both girls stood watching me. My labored breathing matched our horse's heaving sides.

I turned my head away from them as my stomach churned. I doubled over, dry heaving twice before Ellie's comforting hand touched my back. I forced myself to swallow the excess saliva and take a deep breath. As I slowly stood, every inch of me hurt, from the cramped muscles in my legs to the burning blisters on my arms.

The dragons' screams echoed off the hills in the distance. Ellie covered her ears and clamped her eyes shut. I pulled her next to my chest with one arm, my other hand squeezing the reins. Azalit sat on her heels, leaning against the trunk behind her. I listened as the dragons flew up the tree line, spewing fire at random intervals. We must not have been seen because they paid no particular attention to our hiding spot. Once they disappeared, we ventured out. A path of fiery destruction marked their passing, and funnels of smoke curled into the sky. The breeze had died with the rising sun, leaving the morning eerily still.

We knew the drill, and without a word we fell in behind Marcus. He angled to the north, heading into the woods. An hour later he stopped and looked at the bedraggled bunch. "It's at least a full day's march between here and the safety of Algonia's border," he said. "I don't know that we can make it that far without rest. Garrick, what is your voice in the matter? Rest now or push on?"

Garrick looked at each one of us. In the light of dawn, I glanced at the others. We looked haggard—eyes glazed with fatigue, hair matted with sweat. And I wasn't the only one with ugly, blistering burns from the fiery spittle.

"Let's take a short rest, then push on," Garrick said.

Marcus nodded. "I know a place to make camp. It's not far from here."

He led us to a large stand of trees. They were like the ones we'd hidden beneath during this morning's fly-by, but Ellie and Azalit didn't need to dismount as we entered this grove. Marcus dropped his pack next to the charred remains of an old campfire ringed with blackened stones. I turned to help Azalit and Ellie from the horse's back. The men collapsed to the ground in exhaustion, many not even bothering to use their bedrolls. I tied the horse near a patch of grass and took my pack.

While I drank water from the flask, Ellie spread our blanket on the ground and lay down. I settled in behind her and slipped my arm under her head. Rolling on my side, I draped my other arm across her shoulder. Instantly, I fell asleep—the deep, dreamless slumber that only comes after extreme exhaustion.

Wickliff's shocked voice rang out, barely piercing my sleep-drugged mind. "Legard!" I wanted to ignore what I thought I'd heard. But an ominous dread filled my soul, and my body responded with of surge of adrenaline. I opened my eyes as Legard raised his hand and sent a pulse of crippling magic across the campsite into the old elf. At Wickliff's cry of pain, the camp came to life.

Garrick, used to fighting the Sniffers in our world, drew his sword and rushed forward. Without batting an eye, Legard flicked his hand and shot a pulse of magic into Garrick, whose body flew back fifteen feet, slamming into Falon and Pellyn. The three of them tumbled into a heap of bodies and swords. I dragged Ellie to her feet and pushed her ahead of me toward the horse.

"Run," I urged.

Azalit beat us there and untied the reins. I drew my sword, but had no intention of fighting Legard as long as the possibility of escape existed.

After I'd taken only a few strides, his crippling pulse hit me squarely in the back. I flew forward, and my shoulder slammed into

Ellie, sending her sprawling onto the dirt next to me. In paralyzed agony, I looked for help. Barhydt had his hand raised, creating a warped space in front of him. Aiton was behind Barhydt's magical shield as they both ran toward Ellie and me. Legard threw a pulse at Barhydt, but he deflected it. Aiton bent and pulled Ellie to her feet and behind Barhydt.

"No, let go of me," she screamed at Aiton. "Chase!"

My eyes met Aiton's. "Get her out of here," I pleaded.

Under Barhydt's protection, Aiton dragged the struggling Ellie across the camp. He threw her on the saddle behind Azalit, and with a hard slap on the rump, he sent the horse galloping into the forest.

Davy dashed behind Barhydt, asking what he should do. Aiton pointed and yelled, "Follow them." Garrick's son glanced at his pa and then at me, as Aiton gave him a hard shove. "Clear out. There's nothing you can do here."

Davy darted through the trees and out of sight. Falon and Pellyn detangled themselves from Garrick and took a defensive stance in front of him. Segur, still nursing a broken arm, stood hunched over Wickliff. Legard raised his hand and blew Falon and then Pellyn out of the way as he advanced toward Garrick. From behind the cover of a large tree, Marcus sent a barrage of bullets at Legard. Since the bullets weren't forged with magic, they clattered to the ground at Legard's feet. Aiton drew a dagger from the sheath at his waist and stepped from behind Barhydt to throw it at Legard.

Writhing on the ground in agony, I watched the futile battle unfold in front of me. Maybe Legard sensed the dagger coming, because he suddenly disappeared. Aiton's knife ricocheted off the branches behind the spot Legard had been standing a moment before.

An iron hand grasped my shoulder. "Hello again, Keeper."

He had reappeared above me. Weakly, I swung my sword, but Legard stomped my arm to the ground with his heavy boot and stood on my wrist. He wrenched the weapon from my hand and tossed it out of reach. Like the dragon's claws in my nightmare, Legard's hand seemed to pierce my skin. I struggled as he dragged me across the dirt toward Garrick. We were nearly there when Legard paused and jerked his head to the side. I followed his gaze.

Segur stepped back and corked Wickliff's flask. The old elf raised his staff and attacked. A pulse of electric energy shot through Legard and into my shoulder. At the moment it hit, my captor disappeared, taking me with him.

THREE
Captive

The impact of Wickliff's blast threw Legard onto the ground. But instead of sliding across the dirt in our campsite, he tumbled through waist-high grass, dragging me beside him. The Sniffer had transported to the Shuylian side of the Susack Plain. I looked up. Lord Arbon's army surrounded us. Once Legard released me from his talon-like grip, two soldiers took me into custody. They searched every inch of my clothing, undoubtedly looking for my counter. I had no strength to resist, and with hundreds of bloodthirsty soldiers surrounding me, it would have been pointless anyway.

One of their leaders stepped forward. "Where are the others?"

"I was able to take only this one," Legard said.

"Will you go back?"

"I haven't the strength to fight Wickliff alone. He is stronger than I anticipated, and he carries a supply of liquid energy. But, Captain Rawdon, you may yet catch them. They are only a day's ride ahead, and in the state I left them, they'll move slowly. Make all haste. And do not fail me."

I stood between two soldiers, feeling like my legs might give out at any moment. Periodically, the soldiers jerked on my arms. Legard sat, hunched over on the ground, a short distance away. His soldiers came to his aid, offering him food and drink.

Captain Rawdon mounted his black steed and raised his arm. "Move out."

His horse thundered onto the Susack Plain, followed by a wave of mounted warriors. The sight would have been awe inspiring if I didn't know they were hunting Ellie and the others. My chin dropped onto my chest. What chance did any of them have, with one tired old horse against this mounted army of hundreds?

The remaining soldiers watched the procession disappear over the rise. Legard motioned for help, and a soldier pulled him to his feet. "Secure the prisoner and return us to Shuyle," Legard commanded.

The soldiers dragged me to a fully enclosed wooden wagon. They threw open the door, and four guards lifted me in. One slapped an iron manacle on my left ankle, and then the heavy door slammed shut. After the guards turned the rusty lock, they banged twice on the door. The wagon lurched forward. I lay flat on my back, too weak to move. The floor stunk like old urine and sweat. I would have vomited at the smell if there'd been anything left in my stomach.

I groaned as the gravity of my situation crashed over me like a tidal wave. I saw no way for my beleaguered friends to outrun that army. I figured it was only a matter of time until they joined me. We had failed. On the brink of success we had come up short.

One day. We had needed only one more day to reach Algonia.

There were three small windows with iron bars in the wagon— one on each side, and one in the door. The painful, paralyzing effects of Legard's attack, plus the part of Wickliff's attack I'd absorbed, left me unable to do anything but stare at the dim interior for hours on end. During the jolting ride, I slipped into a welcomed but fitful sleep. Later in the afternoon, the scream of a dragon woke me. Wide-eyed, I scrambled to my knees, searching for a place to hide. Then it dawned on me—within the clutches of the enemy, I was perfectly safe from the dragons.

The exertion of getting up left my head ringing. I lowered my aching body onto the rough planks and escaped again into the oblivion of sleep. Night fell before I awakened. Still weak, I pulled myself to my feet, grasping the iron bars on a window to keep my balance. With my six-foot-one-inch frame hunched over, I moved from window to window, surveying my surroundings, my head banging on the ceiling when the wagon lurched. It had to be the middle of the night. Everything hurt, and I longed for a drink of Wickliff's nasty-tasting liquid energy. But I knew there wouldn't be any of that where I was going.

I sat down, leaned back against the wall, and drifted off again. When the rocking motion of the wagon stopped, I awoke and forced my heavy eyelids open. The light of early dawn filtered into the wagon. My tongue felt parched from thirst. With the pain of Legard's attack still tormenting me, it was several minutes before I could stand. How long would it take for this to wear off without Wickliff's medicine?

The rusty chain attached to my ankle was bolted to the floor and clanged as I shuffled from window to window, peering between the bars. We were inside the walls of a small fort. While I'd slept we had entered a narrow valley, and jagged mountain peaks towered above the wagon. A few of the soldiers exchanged their mounts for fresh ones, but the bulk of the company left, and a new squadron of cavalry fell into position around my prison. The large draft horses pulling the wagon were unhitched and replaced. Within minutes we were moving again.

If I understood Marcus's description of Shuyle correctly, we had entered the Valley of Tierran, so I was now in enemy territory. I lowered my head. Master Archidus' words echoed through my mind: *No one ever returns from where they are taking her.* Dejectedly, I sank to the floor, expecting to be dead within a matter of days, if not hours. How would Ellie cope with losing me? How would my parents handle my mysterious disappearance? And when would they finally resign themselves to the fact I was never coming home?

Perhaps Jessica, who knew about my secret life, could shed some light on it. There were so many questions I would never know the answers to. In a rush of anxiety, I realized I wasn't as brave as I'd thought, and I didn't want to die. Hot tears filled my eyes. All I wanted was to be home again.

All day the prison wagon rumbled up the Valley of Tierran. The sun transformed the wagon into a sauna, and my thirst became unbearable. I pulled myself up to the window. We had stopped in a small village. Wary mothers herded their children into thatched-roof houses as the mounted soldiers circled the square. Garden plots filled the space between the houses, and chickens roamed freely. This new world looked like it was stuck in the Middle Ages. The Industrial Revolution and the light of invention had yet to reach Shuyle and Algonia.

The brutish soldiers drew water from a well and filled a wooden trough, then led each horse to the water. The sight of all that water was too much. *It couldn't hurt to ask, could it?* "Hey," I called, waving to the man by the well. "Can I please have a drink over here?" He glanced once in my direction. A haughty smiled curved his mouth as he carelessly dumped the overflowing bucket of water onto the ground. I sighed. "Oh, come on."

The sharp crack of a whip striking my forearm sent me scrambling backward. "Get yerself back inside," shouted the driver. I wanted to yell, kick the door—anything but sit here quietly and die of thirst. But I was too weak to put up a fight. Leaning against the inside of the wagon, I slid to the floor and watched as a long red welt formed on my arm.

The simple effort of trying to get water had sent another wave of paralyzing pain through my system. I lowered my head and waited for the agony to pass. My dry tongue irritated my cracked lips, and the grumbling of my empty stomach would have to be ignored.

There was nothing I could do about any of it. In that moment of suffering, my view on life shifted and my opinion of humanity forever changed. Never before had I been so blatantly abused. They had denied me something as simple as water, when there was plenty of it to go around.

I pressed my fingers to my eyes and talked myself out of sobbing like a baby. I would most likely die before I saw another sunrise. What did it matter if I went out of this world hungry and thirsty, or satisfied? Perhaps if I felt miserable the dying would be less painful. It was certainly bound to improve my attitude toward the whole thing. Master Archidus had been right. This was a suicide mission, at least for me. My only consolation was the hope that Ellie and the others would somehow elude the massive army tailing them.

As the wagon rolled out of the village, I wondered about Legard. Every time I'd looked out the window he wasn't within sight, and I hadn't heard his voice, either. Where was he? Had he gone to follow Garrick? He had made it only too clear that he wanted Davy and Garrick. Nearly every man in our group had been stunned by a pulse of the Sniffer's magic. If they felt anything like I did, they would be hard pressed to travel anywhere. They would be sitting ducks for Lord Arbon's cavalry.

My weary body couldn't keep pace with the rampant thoughts running through my mind, and I surrendered to a restless sleep. The jarring of the wagon on the rutted road must have woken me a hundred times. At some point during the night, the driver again pulled the horses to a stop. Assuming it was another water break for the animals, I didn't move. Curled in the fetal position and chained to the floor, I waited.

FOUR
Lord Arbon

The stamping of horses' hooves drowned out the click of the lock, so it surprised me when the wagon door opened on its squeaky hinges. The guard with the key ring grabbed my ankle and unlocked the iron band.

"Get out," he growled.

I sat up and slid to the opening. Two guards yanked me onto the ground amid a circle of soldiers. One of them slapped my wrists into thick metal handcuffs. I raised my eyes to see Legard supervising from his perch next to the driver. Thankfully, he hadn't gone hunting for Garrick. I smirked to see that he appeared a bit haggard as he climbed down.

The prison wagon rolled away into the night, leaving me facing Legard in the middle of a large courtyard. Behind him loomed a sinister-looking castle. A shudder ran up my spine as several large bats swooped through the moonlit sky and past the turrets.

"Lock our prisoner in the dungeon. I'll deal with him on the morrow," Legard ordered. He turned and walked toward the castle door.

Watching him leave, I missed seeing the movement of the guard. He cuffed me on the side of the head. "You 'eard what he said. Get movin' 'fore I hit ya again."

I took two steps forward before another guard shoved his club into my chest. "Dungeon's not that way, you fool. Around back." A rough push sent me stumbling in the right direction. A series of pushes and slaps upside the head kept me moving across the courtyard and behind the castle. The guards led me down a narrow flight of stairs. The scurry of rats underfoot left me little doubt regarding my accommodations for the night.

I walked down a dimly lit corridor lined on one side with cells. By torchlight, I saw they were occupied with raggedly clothed, hollow-eyed prisoners. After glimpsing a decaying corpse, I couldn't bear to see anymore and stared straight ahead. At the other end of the corridor was a second staircase. It was to the cell across from those stairs that the guards took me. One final cuff to the side of my head and a shove in the back sent me sprawling onto the dark floor. Through the ringing in my ear, I heard the heavy door slam shut, and I was alone.

For a time I didn't move. *What's the hurry? I'll have the rest of my pitifully short life to explore this cell.* When a rat gnawed on my pant leg, I kicked it away and finally got up. The torch at the base of the stairs sent a rectangular beam of flickering light through the iron bars of the door and into my cell. The extent of my furnishings included a bucket in the corner, the smell of which indicated its use, a tin plate, a straw-filled mattress, and a scratchy woolen blanket. I estimated the cell to be no wider than fifteen feet in any direction. My only link to the outside world was one small window near the ceiling.

The mumbled calls of prisoners rippled down the corridor toward me. With trepidation I watched the barred entrance. A man hunched with age and moving with a distinct limp approached my door.

"Bread? Water?" he said.

My voice sounded more like a frog's croak when I said yes. I snatched the metal cup and drained it dry before he could change his mind. The water slid past my tongue, leaving a foul aftertaste. I didn't care. "Thank you. Can I have some more?"

Twice more he filled the large cup from the bucket of water he carried, and I guzzled it down.

"That's all," the old man said. He dropped a hard loaf into my hand before he left.

The chains between my wrists rattled as I tore into the bread. Even though it tasted days old and bordered on stale, I finished it in record time. The food took the edge off my hunger, but it far from filled me. I longed for some of the jerky I had complained about only yesterday.

Rats cleaned up my crumbs while I slumped against the wall and listened. Occasionally, the neighboring prisoner would moan or cry out between fits of coughing. For the rest of the night I didn't sleep as I wondered what Legard's idea of "dealing with" me on the morrow entailed. Hot tears burned my eyes as I contemplated the future I would forego. I wouldn't be taking Ellie to the party at Kim's house next weekend like she'd wanted. There would be no high school graduation for me. I wouldn't even do something as simple as eat dinner with my family again. And Ellie would never get to hear an official proposal from me, either. I was sitting on death row.

Shortly after dawn, the same old man pushed a creaky cart down the corridor with more food and water. He passed me another hard loaf, and I was lucky to get four cups of water from him before he left. I finished my meager breakfast, grateful to have something for my stomach to work on as I passed the time. After relieving myself in the bucket, I sat down to wait for Legard.

I resolved to go out as dignified as possible. If they wanted information, I'd keep my mouth shut. Regardless of what they did to me, I wouldn't talk. They would offer me empty promises, and I couldn't allow myself to give in to their demands. At the height of my pep talk, a rush of boots sounded in the stairwell across from my cell.

The two guards who'd locked me up the night before unlocked the door and entered. One was tall with a barrel chest, the other shorter with a generous paunch. A man in lavish robes swept into the cell after them, followed by Legard. One look at the new guy told me it was Lord Arbon. With sharp, high cheekbones, an angular nose, and slate-gray hair, he resembled Master Archidus. However, the similarities stopped there. Lord Arbon's look bordered on sinister, if not cruel, his black eyes hard and calculating. His air was one of superiority and domination, while Master Archidus, although a bit stern at times, had compassionate and understanding eyes. Even though Archidus carried himself with dignity and grace, he had never come across as arrogant or condescending, like his older brother.

"Well, my young Keeper, we meet at last," Lord Arbon said.

The fat guard grabbed a handful of my hair and hauled me to my feet. "Where's your manners, boy?"

The tall guard slammed his fist into my gut. "You stand when the lord enters. Then you kneel in respect."

Before I got my bearings, the fat guard let go of my hair and cracked his club across the back of my legs, dropping me to my knees in front of Arbon. "That's more like it," he said, watching me gasp for air on my hands and knees.

"Protector, where is your counter?" Arbon demanded.

I ignored him, staring at the toes of his shiny black boots until the barrel-chested guard threw his oversized fist into the side of my head. A flash of anger shot through me, and I scrambled to my feet. "I don't know. Maybe if you had a better Sniffer he'd actually bring you a counter."

Legard threw up his hand and sent two deadly pulses into my chest. I flew backward across the cell and slammed into the wall. My head made a sickening thud against the stones as I crashed to the floor in a heap. Warm liquid seeped through my hair, and my body throbbed, but the pain only intensified my anger. Grimacing, I glanced up at Legard. "You've got to do better than that to get me—"

Another pulse from Legard hit me. This one rolled my body back against the wall, completely silencing me. My breath came in quick gasps, and my heart rate accelerated as I realized he'd paralyzed me. I couldn't move a muscle—couldn't even speak.

Lord Arbon raised his hand. "One more and you'll certainly kill him, if you haven't already."

"Is that not our goal, milord?"

Blood ran behind my ear and down my jawline. It tickled my skin, but I was helpless to do anything about it. Every effort to move failed. I could blink my eyes. I could swallow. But that was all.

"You there," Lord Arbon said.

"Yes, milord?" a feminine voice answered.

"Keep this prisoner alive or I'll have your pretty head on the gallows come morn."

"Yes, milord."

Lord Arbon spun on his heel and left the cell. By the sound of the retreating footsteps, I guessed everyone had followed him up the stairs, but my cell door hadn't closed.

The blood pooled next to my face, covering my eye. The only thing worse than the excruciating pain of Legard's attack was the uncomfortable heap he'd left me in—my arm twisted beneath me at an awkward angle, my neck in a kink, and the length of chain between my wrists jabbing me in the hip. I blinked, trying to get the blood out of my eye. Why had Arbon stopped Legard? Why didn't they end it and be done with me? If they wanted to use my counter, they had to kill me eventually.

The hem of a tattered gray skirt appeared in front of me. I closed my left eye and stopped blinking my right one so I could see. *Please move me,* I thought, willing her to read my mind. She stood there for what seemed like an eternity. Maybe she was afraid to touch me. The blistering burns on my arms probably made me look diseased. Finally, she took hold of the iron chain between my wrists and pulled my arm out from underneath me. She rolled me onto my back, and my split head rubbed against the rough stone. *Oh, that kills, but thank you.*

She gasped. *Yup, I most certainly looked hideous.* With the cell spinning around me, her face wouldn't come into focus. Legard's attack had left me struggling to maintain consciousness. Within seconds I lost the battle and passed out.

When I eventually came to, I had no idea how much time had gone by. My pains were too numerous to count. I moved my eyes from side to side, searching for the woman but seeing nothing except the walls of my cell. I closed my eyes again. The throb in my head was excruciating, and it took every ounce of willpower I had, just to cope—to not go insane.

The touch of a cool hand on my bruised cheek sent my eyes flying open. The woman in the gray skirt knelt next to me. She was young, but maybe a little older than me. Her clothes looked like those of a servant or slave. A long braid of auburn hair hung over her shoulder, and her brown eyes looked on me with compassion.

She dropped her gaze and fetched a cloth from the bucket by her side. After wringing out the excess water, she began to clean my wounds. Her hands were gentle, and the cool water soothed the heat in my skin. She worked her way from my face down both arms. Lastly, she rolled me onto my side and cleaned the dried blood out of my hair. Then she tucked the rag under my head and left.

When she returned, she wrapped my head with a cloth bandage. I tried to speak to her, but nothing came out. I wanted to thank her, ask her name—anything.

"Time's up. Gotta lock down," a gravelly voice called from the doorway.

Smiling, the girl gave my hand a squeeze and whispered, "I shall return." Then she was gone. The door clanged shut, the click of the lock guaranteeing I wouldn't be going anywhere.

The minutes dragged into hours. At times I dozed. Sometimes I'd simply stare at the sliver of sky I could see through the barred window. The opening was near the ceiling, but even without the iron bars a man couldn't fit through it. I watched storm clouds gather in the fading light and heard thunder rumbling in the distance.

When I heard the man with the cart working his way down the corridor, my stomach growled at the thought of food, even the hard, stale kind. But with my next breath I felt bitter disappointment. Lying paralyzed against the wall of my cell, I couldn't get to the door to collect my bread and water. Even if the food was in front of me, I couldn't get it to my mouth. So that was Lord Arbon's plan—death by starvation.

"Good evening, Bernard," the woman called. My attention riveted on her voice.

"Evenin'," the old man replied. A moment later they were in front of my cell. "You want in?" he asked.

"Yes, please."

"You gotta hurry. I can't wait long."

"Lock up behind me. You can let me out first thing on the morrow."

"You gonna stay in there with 'im all night? You sure about that? Mud won't like it if he finds you in there."

Her voice was surprisingly cheerful, and I could imagine her smiling at the old man. "We'll have to make sure he doesn't find me then, won't we? I expect you'll be here before Mud even wakes up. And yes, I'm quite sure. The prisoner's harmless enough. You know as well as I that the rats will eat him alive, since he can't move a muscle. It'll be my head on the gallows if that happens, so never you mind about me, Bernard."

Without another word he opened the lock.

"I'll take that for him," the woman said. "Why don't you leave the water bucket in here for tonight?"

"Night, missy," he called as his cart moved down the corridor.

Lightning lit the sky, and a crack of thunder sounded. What a relief to know I wouldn't face the long, dark night alone.

The woman stood near my head and pulled a shawl off of her shoulders, revealing a cat in the crook of her arm. The small black animal hopped onto the ground next to me and sniffed my face. "There you go, Twila girl. Hopefully you'll do your job tonight and I'll get some rest."

Soft whiskers tickled my cheek, and the cat brushed against my shoulder as it walked away. I tried to smile. My lips moved a fraction of an inch, which was more than I could do this morning.

The woman leaned down next to me and asked, "Can you speak?"

"No," I tried to say. But of course nothing came out.

"Can you do anything?"

No, isn't that obvious? Only a complete imbecile would lie here unmoving all day long. To show her the extent of my abilities, I blinked my eyes.

She smiled. "Well now, that's something. I've got it. Blink once for yes and twice for no. Do you understand?"

Now we we're getting somewhere. I deliberately blinked once.

"Good. Are you thirsty?"

Yes, thank you! I thought you'd never ask. I'm dying of thirst. My tongue is so parched it feels like sandpaper in my mouth. I blinked one time in response.

"Let's get you upright then." Sitting up was even more of an ordeal than I'd imagined. She was a petite little thing, and I was dead weight. "My, this is proving quite difficult," she muttered. After tugging and pulling on my arm, she got me propped against the wall. The cat sat and watched the whole event. By the time the girl raised the battered metal cup to my lips, she was breathing heavily from exertion. The tepid water dribbled down my chin as I tried to drink, and only half of the liquid made it into my mouth. But I was relieved to find I could swallow.

"Is that enough?" she asked me.

No, I'm suffering from dehydration here. I need to drink the bucket dry. When I blinked twice, she raised another cup to my lips. I hated wasting so much of the precious liquid. Perhaps if I waited a little while, more of the feeling would return to my lips.

"Is that enough?" she asked again.

For now, I thought as I blinked once.

"I brought you something soft to eat." I watched her return to the doorway and pull a small pot out of a basket. "We'll need to share, though." She raised a spoonful of liquid to her mouth. "At least it's not cold yet. Here you are." She filled the spoon again and wiggled it between my uncooperative lips. It tasted like beef broth with small chunks of potatoes and carrots.

She ripped the bread from Bernard into small pieces, dipped them in the broth, and set them on my tongue, one at a time. Eating something close to a real meal was divine. For days I'd survived on either jerky and bread or nothing at all. When the small loaf was half gone, I closed my eyes. She hadn't bothered to take a bite of bread yet. I was still hungry but couldn't imagine she had enough to eat after sharing her dinner with me.

"Are you finished?" she asked.

I blinked once.

"Should we save this for later?"

No, you should eat it. You're too thin. I blinked twice and gave her my most intent look.

"Should I finish it?" she said.

Of course, after all you've done for me, it's the least I can do. I blinked once. It satisfied me to watch her savor each morsel of bread. The shuffling of the rats in the corridor brought a low hiss from the cat. Surely the rodents had smelled the savory soup and come to investigate. In the fading twilight, I watched the cat settle down on her belly at the edge of the shadows, her attention riveted on the doorway. Although still in constant pain, I felt a measure of comfort at having food in my stomach and companionship.

After the girl finished the last of the bread and took a drink, she asked, "Are you thirsty?"

Yes, I definitely need to drink more. I blinked once, and she held the cup to my lips. I was happy to find I had some control of my mouth and spilled far less than before. Four more times she asked if I wanted another drink. Each time I blinked once and downed another cup of water. When my stomach felt like a waterlogged boot, I blinked twice.

"My, you're a thirsty one," she said cheerfully.

She pulled her shawl around her shoulders and leaned against the wall next to me. Two large rats sniffed their way from the corridor into my cell. Confident in their supremacy among the prisoners, they didn't bother to look for danger. The feline's lethal pounce brought a high-pitched squeal from one of the rodents and sent the other scurrying away. The small cat dragged the rat, nearly half her size, into the corner.

"Good girl, Twila. What a good huntress you are," the woman said.

The dungeon needed about ten cats. A flash of lightning illuminated the cell and the blessed cat—hunched over the dead rat with her head buried in the meat.

"I should try to sleep," the girl said. "Would you care to lie down?"

I wanted to stand up and walk around, to move my cramped, aching, paralyzed muscles. But I reluctantly blinked once. I'd have an awful kink in my neck if I sat in this slumped position all night long. A low groan escaped my lips as my head hit the floor. Surprised by the first sound I'd uttered all day, I moaned again. She frowned. "Did I hurt you?"

No, you didn't hurt me. It was Legard who hurt me. But, yes, you did bang my sore head on the ground, although I don't care about that. Ecstatic, I blinked twice. I had finally made a sound. Maybe by tomorrow I could speak. Then I could begin to ask her some of the questions rapidly accumulating in my brain.

She laid my arms across my stomach and adjusted the iron shackles so they weren't pinching the raw flesh on my wrists. She touched the stubble on my cheek, her lips turning up in a smile. "Are you comfortable?"

Her reassuring touch made me wish I could smile back at her. *Absolutely not, but I can't think of anything more you could do about it.* I blinked once. "Well, good night then, Keeper," she said tenderly.

Wait! How do you know? What do you know? Who are you? I tried to say "wait," but only the faintest sound rattled in my throat as she walked away.

FIVE
Dungeon

Another flash of lightning lit my cell as the woman got a blanket from her basket and put away the empty soup pot. She positioned herself in the shadows by the wall next to the door. Anyone walking down the corridor and casually looking in would only see me. *What danger is she putting herself in by staying here?* Surely, Lord Arbon's threat to her wasn't meant literally. Then again, old Bernard had bought her line of reasoning.

I listened to the woman moving in the darkness, probably trying to get comfortable on the hard floor. When she finally slept, the evenness of her breathing soothed me, and for a long time I simply listened, pretending it was Ellie.

The death squeal of another rat falling victim to Twila's claws brought a satisfied smile to my lips. The smile itself was satisfying as well, and I felt the grin spread across my face. If I was lucky, by morning I could say thank you.

While the thunderstorm danced across the night sky, I tried speaking. After failing, I went back to the basics. "Mama" and "dada"—weren't those the first words out of a baby's mouth? After croaking out a few "mama"s, I slowly expanded my vocabulary. Sometime after Twila's third kill of the night, I faded into a peaceful slumber.

The jangle of keys and the echo of boots descending the stairs sent my eyes flying open. "Hey," I called to the woman.

She bolted upright, fear flashing across her face. She kicked a half-eaten rat carcass against the wall, scooped up her cat, and hid herself in the corner of my cell. I looked away from her, not wanting to draw the guard's attention.

The fat one paused at my door. "You there."

Surprisingly, my head turned slowly in his direction, but I held my tongue. I'd rather they didn't know my speech had returned.

"So, you survived the night, eh?" He laughed. "Good thing. Woulda been a waste to lose that girl to the gallows. I got plans for her." His haughty laugh echoed back to me as he lumbered away.

Bernard's timid voice greeted the guard at the other end of the corridor. "Mud, you're up early this mornin'."

"Get to work!" Mud yelled.

The prisoners' complaining cries followed the creak of Bernard's cart down the hall. "Startin' at this end today," the old man said. He stopped in front of my cell and fumbled with his keys. "Missy, you in there?"

"Yes, thank you," she answered. Stepping out of hiding, she put the cat into her basket and folded the blanket.

Bernard opened the door and waited expectantly.

"If I take your cart down and deliver breakfast could you please help him with the bucket?" she asked.

The old man grumbled something indiscernible, then nodded. The woman disappeared down the corridor with the food cart. When Bernard hauled me to my knees so I could relieve myself, I discovered my muscle control was coming back. "Thank you, Bernard. That's a relief," I croaked out.

He grunted his acknowledgement and left me slumped against the wall. He slammed the door shut and locked it.

"Great," I said to myself. "I get my voice back and I hardly get a chance to use it." With my stomach growling and my throat dry, it would be a long day.

That morning a flock of crows serenaded me with their nonstop cawing, and I wondered what had them excited. A few hours later the woman returned with bread, water, and a fresh bandage. Bernard let her through the door.

I smiled. "Hey, you're back already?"

She hurried to my side and straightened me against the wall. "Yes, but I'll need to hurry."

"What's your name?" I asked before she lifted the water to my mouth.

"Brierly."

I knew I'd heard that name before, though I couldn't remember where.

She put the cup to my lips and I drank it dry, then asked, "How did you know I was a Keeper?"

"I overheard Lord Arbon talking with Legard about a missing counter. A logical guess, I suppose, that you would be the Keeper they referred to." She ripped off a piece of bread and stuffed it in my mouth while she spoke. "Plus, you don't look Shuylian. And although you're dressed like an Algonian warrior, you don't look like you're from Algonia, either."

She put another piece of bread in my mouth, but I pushed it into my cheek so I could keep talking. "What else did you hear from Arbon and Legard? Did their army catch the other Keepers or a girl?"

"I know of no other prisoners being brought in since you. All of Shuyle is gathering for an attack on Algonia. Lord Arbon has summoned all the chief sorcerers and called for every man to take up arms and destroy Master Archidus and Algonia, once and for all."

My jaw was working overtime chewing the hard crust. Around a mouthful of food, I mumbled, "Why are you here? Are you a servant or something?"

A sad look darkened her expression. "During a raid on my village in Algonia, a group of Shuylian soldiers took me captive. I'm little more than a slave. But I've resigned myself to my fate, and at least I have my cat." A smile curved Brierly's lips as she gazed back at me. Her voice was cheerful again when she questioned, "How did a fine fellow like yourself come to be captured, anyhow?"

"Legard set a trap for me and another Keeper by stealing my girlfriend and his son. A group of Algonian soldiers brought us to the edge of Shuyle to rescue them. We almost escaped, too. We were one day's ride from the Algonian border when Legard attacked our camp. I need to find out if he caught the rest of them."

Brierly changed the dressing on my head while I talked, then helped me drink two more cups of water. As she gathered up her things, she said, "I'll see what I can find out. I promise to return later tonight, if I'm able."

"Bernard?" she called.

The old man returned to unlock the door, and she left.

All day I thought of Ellie. Could she possibly be safe in Algonia by now? Or was she sitting in one of those wretched prison wagons on her way to Shuyle? I slept for several hours, grateful to have the time pass. In the afternoon, my thoughts wandered to Brierly. Where had I heard that name before? After wracking my brain over the mystery, it came to me. Marcus. His sister had been taken the same way Brierly had described, and I could've sworn that was her name. Had I found Marcus's sister? Or was Brierly as common a name in Algonia, as Jessica was in America? I waited for the girl to return, dying to ask her if she had a brother named Marcus.

As the afternoon wore on, I thought I'd go crazy. I had to do something. This straitjacket of a body would drive me insane if I couldn't start moving soon. If I relaxed, I could tune out the ever-present pain. However, when I toppled onto my side and attempted to roll across my cell, it flared up with a vengeance. I maneuvered myself to the middle of the floor before resting on my back. Sweat covered my face, and my breathing sounded like it belonged to someone finishing a marathon. Staring at the sliver of blue sky through the window, I waited for the throbbing pain to subside.

Bernard eventually made his nightly rounds. Thankfully, he opened my door and brought me the bread and water.

"Where's Brierly?" I asked.

"Not here tonight. I expect she'll be 'round in the morning." When he helped me use the bucket, he grumbled, "Can't believe I'm doin' this for a prisoner who's bound to be dead soon, but I'd not hear the end of it from that girl if I didn't. Don't you go lettin' her get sweet on you, ya hear, boy? It's too dangerous. I'm warnin' ya, Lord Arbon won't bat an eye at killin' her if it means gettin' you to talk."

"I understand," I said.

"Do ya now? Do ya really understand the awful wickedness he's capable of?"

Not knowing what to say to that, I glanced away. Bernard propped me against the wall and held the cup for me to drink, then ripped my bread into manageable chunks. He set one in my mouth and another in my hand.

"You work on gettin' that to yer mouth. I'll bet by mornin' ya got it all ate up. If not, the rats'll clean it up fer ya." He gave a hearty laugh as he walked out and slammed my door.

The pile of bread chunks lay in my lap, tempting me. For what seemed like an eternity, I struggled to move the piece in my right hand to my mouth. The exertion left me sweating, but I finally got it there. After swallowing, I stopped to rest. The shuffle and squeak of the rats let me know they were starting their nightly foray. I'd be hard pressed to keep them away from me with a pile of bread on my lap.

My hand reminded me of the claw machine in the arcade at the bowling alley as it flopped onto my leg to pick up another piece of bread. Thankfully, that second piece made it to my mouth faster than the first.

The onslaught of rats didn't materialize as I'd expected. Maybe the cat's scent lingered in my cell, or perhaps the rats remembered her attack from the night before and were simply wary. Whatever the reason, I was grateful. My coordination improved with each morsel of food I got into my mouth, and eventually I finished the bread.

I couldn't help but think of my mom and dad. I felt bad for them. Dad would be mad at first. My poor mom would be sick with worry. I wouldn't have left without saying goodbye, if I had known I'd never come back. I could only pray that Jessica would be able to explain what might have caused my disappearance. I'd already spent countless hours worrying about Ellie. I couldn't keep my mind off her for long. Perhaps Archidus would return her to 2012. Then she could explain my fate, and there would be closure for my parents. But what would be best for Ellie? Maybe Archidus would send her back to 1863.

With a grunt I rolled myself onto the ground. There was nothing to do except sleep, but that should be easy. I was so dang tired all the time—the only bearable symptom of this whole mess. I cleared my mind of worries, burying them under the unrealistic thought that everything would work out in the end, and slipped into sleep-induced oblivion.

I jerked awake once, when Legard raised his hand to shoot me with his magic during one of my nightmares. Heart racing and breathing heavily, I turned over and eventually found my way back to sleep. The jangle of keys woke me early the next morning as Bernard unlocked the door for Brierly. She carried a water pail in one hand and a basket in the other.

"How are you feeling today?" she asked.

"I'm good," I answered. "Where were you last night?"

She averted her gaze and didn't make eye contact. "I brought you some hot porridge this morning."

"Hey, are you okay? Did something happen?"

She sat down and began spoon-feeding me the warm porridge. "I'll be fine, thank you, but I'd rather not speak of it."

Other than being in a bad mood, she looked okay, so I dropped the subject and savored the next bite of food.

"Keeper, may I inquire as to your name?"

"It's Chase Harper."

She furrowed her eyebrows and scooped up some more porridge. "Chase? What a peculiar name."

I smiled, hoping to ease some of the tension I saw in her. "I suppose Chase would sound funny to a girl named Brierly."

Her face softened as a smile appeared. "What is that supposed to mean? Brierly is a fine, respectable name. Quite common in Algonia, actually."

"Well, Chase is common in the old world."

She stopped feeding me and stared into my eyes.

"What's wrong?" I asked.

"I always thought the tales of the old world were just that—tall tales old men passed along because they couldn't think of anything interesting to say about our world. Are you telling me you're from another world?"

"Yeah. There's no place like this where I come from. Master Archidus brought me here. Why are you so surprised when you knew I was a Keeper?"

"I knew you weren't from Shuyle or Algonia," Brierly said, "but I never dreamed there was really a Keeper in the old world. I suppose I never gave much thought to all the folklore."

I had almost forgotten to ask her my question. "Do you have a brother named Marcus?"

She leaned forward with a twinkle in her eyes. "Yes! Do you know of him? Is he well?"

"I know him. He was fine the last time I saw him. He led us from the Dragon's Lair to where we rescued my girlfriend and the other Keeper."

She rested her hand on my arm. "Please tell me everything from the moment you met him. I'm so starved for news from home."

I started with the first time I'd met Marcus—the night he'd reported on the burned village. Then I told of our journey, paying careful attention to include every detail of my conversations with Brierly's brother. I described what I could remember of our attack on Legard. She smiled smugly at the news of our victory against the cavalry. I praised Marcus's leadership in evading the dragons and getting us across the Susack Plain. I admitted we should never have stopped in the woods to rest. We should have pressed on at all costs. We hadn't anticipated an appearance by Legard, and as a result, our group had been incapacitated within seconds. Lastly, I told of the massive army sent across the Susack Plain to hunt them down.

"That's it, I guess," I said. "Every day that passes without that army returning with my friends gives me hope they may have made it to safety."

Brierly's eyes brimmed with tears as she smiled. "Thank you, Keeper. You have no idea how much it means to me to hear your tale."

She sniffed once, then wiped her eyes on her apron and offered me water. I drank my fill and let her leave without saying more. Bernard's warning weighed heavily on my mind. It would come to no good if anyone saw us talking like that.

SIX
Evil Intent

The days blurred together. When I was able to crawl, I searched every square inch of my prison. I found something useful near the doorframe—a jagged piece of loose stone. I worked at freeing it until my fingernails were in shreds. When it finally broke away, I scratched a small mark in the grime-covered wall for every day I could remember being locked up.

Now that I could care for myself, I didn't see Brierly as often. One day she was sent to empty the buckets for Bernard. As she stepped into my cell, she smiled. "How are you this morning, Keeper Chase?"

With a straight face, I folded my arms and watched her dump my bucket, wondering how she got stuck with such a disgusting job. Beneath the glare of one of Arbon's guards, I didn't dare answer her. After the guard locked my door and left, I jumped to my feet. "Brierly?" I whispered.

She turned back, the hurt expression on her face changing into curiosity. "Yes?"

Keeping an eye on the guard's back, I motioned her closer. "It isn't safe to be seen talking with me. I don't want you getting hurt. You should act like you hate me." Frowning, Brierly stepped away and nodded once, then hurried down the corridor.

As the days turned into weeks, I missed Brierly's company and her food. I had lost weight, and the Algonian breeches hung on my hipbones. Despite my warning, once or twice a week she would stop by with an extra piece of bread or fruit. She never stayed to talk, just dropped the food through my cell door and left. Those breaks from the traditional prison fare were heavenly.

When I couldn't move, Bernard and Mud had basically ignored me as they unlocked my cell door to empty the refuse bucket. That all changed the moment I could stand again. As my strength returned, Bernard began treating me like a dangerous criminal. He insisted I set the bucket by the door, then move into the opposite corner. His assumption was right—I was dangerous. While recovering, I had studied my options for escape, all of which would cause bodily harm to the old man.

Now that I was healthy, I planned to overpower Bernard when he turned his back to dump my bucket. I'd steal his clothes, gag him, and leave him locked in my cell. As long as no one heard the ruckus, I'd have a decent chance of pushing his cart out of the dungeon. If I got out of there alive, I'd work out the next phase. Unfortunately, the opportunity to put my plan into action hadn't presented itself yet. Bernard was always careful.

It had been so long since Arbon's visit, I figured they'd forgotten about me. He'd probably decided to let me rot in his dungeon. Therefore, I wasn't expecting company when I heard the sound of booted men descending the staircase. I stood counting the tick marks on my wall and considering an alternate escape plan, when I heard the click of a key in the lock. I spun around. Behind Mud was an angry-looking Lord Arbon, flanked by four of his personal guards. My heart skipped a beat at the sight of them. The only consolation was the noticeable absence of my nemesis, Legard.

Lord Arbon stepped through the doorway. "I see you're back on your feet, Keeper."

I stared at him, saying nothing as I tried to calm my racing heart.

"Perhaps now you will be inclined to answer me." He paused. "Where is Protector's counter?"

"I told you. I don't know." I justified my answer by convincing myself that although I'd given the counter to Archidus, I truthfully didn't know what he'd done with it.

"Certainly, with your connections you have some idea where it is." After a moment of silence, a crack sounded behind me. I cried out when a sharp pain seared my back. Mud, Arbon, and his guards still stood in the doorway. I wheeled around in shock, surprised I wasn't alone in my cell. My eyes went wide. There was nothing there. On the second crack, I recognized the sound of a bullwhip. I turned, frantically looking for the source of my pain. Another crack sounded, this one drawing blood from my shoulder and leaving my skin feeling burned.

My hands were still chained, and hard calluses had formed around my wrists from the friction of the iron bands. I whipped my head around as the next snap of the invisible whip raked across my cheek. My cry of pain echoed through the cell, not even sounding like me. When I touched my face, my hand came away slick with blood. My eyes watered and I gritted my teeth as I moved warily in a circle. The next strike tore through my vest, stinging the skin on my back. Enraged, I faced my tormentor.

"Tie him up. I grow tired of a moving target," Lord Arbon said.

Mud and two of the guards advanced toward me. I stepped back, but there was no place to go. Although I put up a fight, Arbon's guards dragged me to the wall, and Mud attached the chain between my wrists to a hook above my head. Arbon's sinister laugh mixed with the crack of his invisible whip. Within minutes he'd shredded my vest. The ooze of warm blood running onto the waistband of my pants left me no doubt my back would look like hamburger when he finished. I gave up trying to be brave as tears coursed down my cheeks and I groaned in agony.

When I collapsed, the weight of my body hung from my chained wrists. After a moment of silence, Arbon stepped closer. "Now, where is Protector's counter? I can remove the pain as easily as I gave it."

My mind warred with itself, tempting me to say something, even if it was a lie. The silence stretched between us as I debated. I thought I could hold out awhile longer and began counting each pulse of my heart as my body throbbed with pain.

"Since you are disinclined to cooperate," Lord Arbon said, "I will tell you what I think. You had two options. Either you hid your counter in the old world, or you left it with my brother. You are young and most likely impulsive, so I doubt you had the foresight to safely hide it in the old world before seeking vengeance on Legard. Hence, it must have traveled to the new world with you. Since you attacked my cavalry in the company of Algonian soldiers, I know my brother condoned your actions. Although he is a fool, he isn't foolish enough to allow you near Shuyle with his precious counter. Therefore, I conclude that you must have left it with him in Algonia. Am I correct?"

I held my tongue. He'd guessed correctly, so nothing I said could save me now. A wave of nausea sent my nearly empty stomach into convulsions. I spit out a mouthful of foul-tasting bile. My head spun and I wondered if I'd pass out. "Why don't you just kill me?" I asked finally.

"Where's the fun in that? If you're dead, Archidus is free to find another Keeper. If you're alive, your counter will be held captive in Algonia. Surely you know it's easier to find a stationary object than one on the move. We've launched a full-scale attack and have broken through their southern border. If all goes well, we'll overrun Cadré Unair by the week's end. Once I have Protector's counter, you may get your wish. But rest assured, Keeper, I don't intend on killing you . . . yet. Not to mention, this has been quite enjoyable. We should do it again." Arbon chuckled as he turned to leave.

I listened to the sound of retreating boots and the creak of my cell door closing. I thought the men were gone until I heard Arbon's voice from the corridor. "Keeper, should you grow tired of these games and wish to join me, you're always welcome."

I spit a mouthful of saliva on the ground and raised my head. "Never!"

He laughed. "We shall see. You may change your mind once Legard has your girl. With the right leverage, you'd be surprised what a man will do."

His words were like a knife to my heart, and I clamped my eyes shut. What would I do if Ellie was at the receiving end of Arbon's torture? I couldn't watch her suffer. I'd break for sure. How deep was my loyalty to Archidus? Right now I honestly didn't know. His cause had robbed me of the innocence of youth, and now it demanded I forfeit my life.

The pain was becoming too much to bear, and having my arms locked above my head only made it worse. When I looked up the room was spinning. I wondered if I was going into shock. From the stairwell Arbon's voice drifted back to me. "Mud, get him down and patch him up. I might kill him next time, but for now I want him alive."

"Me? I don't wanna touch 'im."

"Then find someone else to do it, but I expect him to be breathing the next time I come down here," yelled Arbon.

Mud unhooked my chain, and I slid down the wall in a bloody heap. He stomped out and slammed my cell door as I sank into unconsciousness.

Through the fog, I soon heard Mud barking orders, his voice sounding distant and muffled. My cell door opened and closed, and then I heard Mud retreating down the corridor. I thought I was alone until a cool hand touched my cheek.

"Keeper Chase? Can you hear me?" Brierly's voice cracked with emotion.

I moaned in response.

"I hardly know where to begin with this mess." She peeled strips of the shredded leather vest out of my skin, and the resulting pain sent me plunging back into unconsciousness.

I awoke to a pungent odor. I was lying flat on my stomach with my cheekbone on the stone floor. I couldn't remember where I was or what had happened. I moved my arms to get up, but the jangle of chains brought me back to the horrible reality.

Brierly's hand touched my head. "Lie still. I've set an herbal poultice on your back. It will ease your pain and speed the healing. Are you thirsty?"

"Yeah." I lifted my head and drank the water she offered.

"You've slept for hours. That's good."

"You should go. It's not safe . . . for you to be around me."

"I can't. I've been locked in for the night—Mud's orders. Never you worry, though. I grumbled about it aplenty. He'll never suspect I was grateful for the assignment."

"Hmm, okay then."

The light of dusk was all that was left of this dreadful day. Bernard delivered dinner, giving Brierly a hard roll as well. It must have been their harvest season, because along with the bread came a bruised peach for each of us. I ate lying on my stomach, lifting my head each time I wanted a bite.

The small black cat appeared on the window ledge and let out a mournful cry. Brierly jumped to her feet, beckoning her cat to enter. The animal stepped between the iron bars and leapt soundlessly into the cell. As Brierly scratched the fur behind Twila's ears, the cat purred like the trolling motor on Uncle Steve's boat. The thought of happier days brought a smile to my lips, triggering another bout of painful throbbing in my face.

Brierly wrapped herself in a blanket and went to her own corner of the cell. The black cat curled up next to her, and soon Brierly slept. When I heard the familiar scuffle of rats in the corridor, I lifted my head to catch Twila's reaction. She left Brierly's side and crouched near the cell door to wait for her prey. I fell asleep to the sound of the cat enjoying a well-earned feast.

Brierly was allowed to tend me for the next few days, although Mud seemed to think he forced her. Because of the magic from my counter and whatever poultice she kept smearing on my wounds, I healed quickly. It was both a blessing and a curse—a blessing I didn't suffer with festering sores for weeks, and a curse that I no longer needed Brierly's care so Mud sent her elsewhere.

I continued accumulating tick marks on my wall as the days rolled by. No sooner had I recovered than the whole horrible experience was repeated. I was strung up on the hook, dripping blood after a thorough whipping, and praying for the peace of unconsciousness to take me away, when Arbon said, "You could return to Algonia and collect your counter from Archidus. Once you return to the old world, Legard can bring you back to Shuyle. If you deliver your counter into my possession, I will allow you to live out your days as any normal human. I've waited hundreds of years—I can afford to wait a few more. When the dictates of time summon you to the grave, I will assume my place as Protector's Keeper. What say you? Surely a savvy young lad such as yourself can convince my brother you escaped, that you are once again ready to assume your duties as the Protector."

I shook my head. Archidus would never be fooled. He would see right through me. I groaned. "No."

"I wasn't suggesting you leave at once. No, that would be foolish. There would be no motivation for you to return. But when Legard delivers your girl to me, I think you'll see the light of reason. Unless of course I tire of you and you're already dead." Chuckling, Lord Arbon turned and left. My cell door clanged shut.

"Ellie, no," I whispered in despair. "Why is this happening to me?"

They left me hanging by my wrists. My arms ached from lack of blood, and the pain took me in and out of consciousness.

I didn't know how much time had passed when I heard Mud's grumbling mixed with the high, clear voice of Brierly. "Mud, I've better things to do than tend to some dying prisoner's wounds. It's a waste of my time and you know it, especially with the harvest. You don't think the grapes press themselves into wine, do you? If you want to eat well this winter and enjoy your drink, and I know you do, you'd leave me to my work."

I opened my eyes and turned my head toward the door.

"Get in there and do what yer told," Mud said. One hard shove sent Brierly staggering into my cell.

She swallowed as she glanced at me, then turned back to Mud. "Well, are you going to get him down?" It sounded like it took some effort for her to keep her voice steady and uninterested.

The cell door slammed shut with extra vigor. "Get 'im down yerself."

Brierly came closer and touched my face. "I may have gone a little too far that time."

Guilt shot through me at the realization that I enjoyed her touch, craved it, even. Turning my head to see her face, I mumbled, "It . . . was good."

Hooks had been hung at varying heights on the wall. The idea was to stretch a prisoner's chain high enough that the downward pressure kept it securely in place. Brierly wasn't nearly tall enough to reach the hook that held my chain. Standing on my toes, I worked to get the loop of chain over the top of the hook. The exertion sent sweat trickling down the back of my neck, stinging my bloody wounds. As the loop finally came free of the hook, I collapsed to the floor.

PART II
Ellie

SEVEN
Ellie's Escape

Azalit turned in the saddle and scowled at me. "Ellie, we can't. There's nothing you can do. It's too dangerous."

I glanced over my shoulder. "We have to go back. Stop the horse this instant." The sight of Chase and Garrick rolling in the dirt in agony haunted me. I couldn't keep running away. I had to know what had happened in that grove of trees. But the haughty elf girl ignored me. Annoyed, I reached around her and fought for control of the reins. I wrestled the left rein from her grasp and jerked the horse's head to the side. The exhausted animal needed no more persuasion than that. Pulled into a tight circle, the horse slowed to a trot and then stopped altogether.

"You'll get yourself killed," Azalit said. "'Tis foolishness to return. That rogue was Legard. No one stands a chance against him except Wickliff. He's much too powerful."

I let go of the rein and slid to the ground. "If you'll not come back with me, then go for help."

Hot tears burned my eyes as I lifted my skirt and ran back the way we'd come. Now that I found myself alone, all the pent-up fear and anxiety of the past few days burst forth in a rush of great sobs. I cried so hard I couldn't breathe. Gasping for air, I stopped to walk.

I caught sight of someone running through the trees in the distance and bolted for cover, but it was Davy. With his head bent to the ground, it appeared he was searching the dry dirt for prints. "Davy," I whispered in relief. I ran into his embrace, thankful he was alive. "Where are the others? What happened back there?"

He sucked in a deep breath. "I don't know. Aiton sent me to follow you. Where's Azalit?"

"She didn't want to come with me. I'm going back. I have to know what happened."

Davy frowned, wiping the tears from my cheeks with his callused thumbs. "So do I."

I'd been too distraught over Chase to notice much of anything as we fled, so I was lucky to have found Davy. Otherwise, I'm not sure I could have retraced our path. The ground was heavy with pine needles and so dry there was hardly a visible track to follow.

"We're getting close," Davy whispered. "I don't want to walk into a trap, mind you. Can you stay hidden while I circle around and have a look?"

I nodded. He pointed to a clump of trees and watched until I hid myself. After he slipped silently through the woods, I dropped my head into my hands. I didn't see how Chase and the others could have escaped alive. *Oh, Chase, please don't be dead.*

"Ellie," Davy yelled.

My head snapped up. Was he in trouble? Was it a trap as he feared? Or had he found them all dead? My heart thundered so wildly in my chest I thought it would explode. I stood and peered through the leaves at the trail Davy had taken. There he was, dragging his pa alongside him. The sliver of hope blossomed inside me.

I ran toward Garrick. Behind Davy, Aiton dragged Pellyn, followed by Segur and Wickliff. Barhydt and Marcus dragged an unconscious Falon between them. My eyes took all this in before my lips could formulate a sound.

I knew the answer before the question could be asked, but my heart still hoped for something different. "Chase?" I choked out. Nine weary men stared back at me with pained expressions. "Garrick, tell me what happened?" My raised voice sounded shrill, and not at all like myself.

"Ellie, he—" Garrick seemed too weak to speak, but the slight shake of his head was unmistakable.

Frantic, I hiked up my skirt. I'd see for myself. I ran along the line of men, intent on returning to the grove. When I passed Marcus, he let go of Falon and grabbed my arm, spinning me around to face him. "He's not there. Legard took him. I'm sorry, but we have to keep moving toward Algonia."

"Is he dead?" I whispered.

Marcus hesitated. "He wasn't when they disappeared."

"Then we have to look for him. We can't leave. We—"

"He could have been taken anywhere, and we're in no condition to mount a rescue. Legard's purpose in taking you captive was to ensnare a Keeper. Now that he has one, I don't see any reason they'd keep him alive. I'm sorry, but we can't waste time looking for him."

The bluntness of Marcus's words and the sudden realization that I'd never see my Chase again hit me like a ton of coal. My knees buckled. Before I collapsed, Marcus hoisted me into his arms. "Keep moving," he ordered the men.

The captain cradled me against his chest as we marched at a snail's pace. With half of the men barely able to walk, reaching Algonia seemed liked a lofty goal at best. But what did it matter to me now? I felt numb and detached. Without Chase, there would be no pleasure in a safe return. I felt so tired my eyes wanted to close, but the instant they did, I saw the ghastly attack—Chase and the others writhing in pain, helpless to defend themselves against the Sniffer.

Desperate to think of something else, I studied the thick scar along the base of Marcus's neck and wondered how he got it. No doubt he was fighting some senseless battle. I should have offered to walk. Certainly this soldier was as exhausted as I. But even though I wanted to say something—wanted to walk—nothing came from my lips. I had feared this day each time I watched Chase disappear, and I had dreaded it more than anything else. And now it had happened. He had disappeared and would never return.

My mind was so absorbed with pain that I barely registered the sound of approaching horses. Barhydt, or maybe it was Aiton, called out excitedly in recognition. I raised my head, trying to see, but the blur of tears left everything a smear of colors, like a poorly done watercolor portrait. Lacking the energy to engage myself in the present, I sank back into my own thoughts. Marcus handed me off to someone on horseback, and another set of strong arms encircled me, holding my limp body atop a prancing horse.

In the distance, or least it seemed that way, I heard Marcus say, "Leitner, how did you know?"

"Archidus saw you coming. He sent us into the Borderlands to meet you."

"We needed your skills a few hours earlier," Marcus said sadly.

The soldier he'd addressed as Leitner replied, "I'm sorry, Captain. We came as fast as we could once the order arrived."

"I say that not in criticism, but in despair. We lost a Keeper to Legard not two hours past."

For me, the hours of hard riding were filled with nothingness. I felt like the abandoned shell of a snail—a vacant, hollow remnant of myself. We made camp late that night, safe within the borders of Algonia. There wasn't a fence or anything when we crossed the border, but I lifted my head to look when exclamations of relief sounded around me. I couldn't see what there was about the border that would stop an army from galloping up behind us, but I didn't have the energy to inquire.

The soldier handed me down from the horse. The next set of arms were familiar—Davy. He laid me on a bedroll next to Garrick, saying, "Ellie, drink this."

I wanted nothing, but I hadn't the strength to resist. As I drank cold water from the flask Davy held to my lips, I heard the gurgle of a spring nearby and the rustle of leaves in the trees overhead. "Thank you," I whispered.

"Lie down and rest for a bit. I'll bring you some supper when it's ready."

I obeyed, and he pulled a blanket over my shoulders. From time to time, the sound of Garrick moaning in pain awakened me. Davy's strong hands grasped my shoulders. "Ellie, wake up. It's time to eat."

He held a spoon to my lips, and I opened my mouth. Something warm slid past my tongue—stew. It should have tasted divine, but every bite stuck in my mouth like overcooked porridge. Only with Davy's constant encouragement did I force each bite down my constricted throat. When I thought I'd gag if I tried to eat another bite, I pushed the food away. Smiling, he took the bowl and handed me the flask. "Take another drink then."

The water soothed the burning in my throat. I had never run as hard as I had the day before. I returned the flask and lowered my head onto the bedroll. Davy's gentle hands tucked the blanket under my chin before he left.

I fell into a fitful sleep, tormented by dragons, darkness, and Legard, all of which I faced alone. Chase was painfully absent from every dream. I must have cried out for him in the night, because Davy's hand on my shoulder and his reassuring words woke me from my nightmare. "Ellie, it's only a dream. It's all right," he whispered.

I shook my head. "No, it's not. It will never again be right."

"Hush now and go back to sleep."

I woke to a harshly bright day. The sky through the treetops was a brilliant blue. Around me the birds engaged in a chorus of songs. I pulled the blanket over my head and tried to ignore nature's happiness as the camp came to life. Horses nickered when the soldiers untied them, and the tack jingled as the men saddled their mounts. One of Chase's gray, drizzling Northwest days would have suited my melancholy mood much better.

Garrick groaned as he dragged himself to his feet. Poor Chase, if by some miracle he still lived, would be suffering through the same pains as Garrick. Only Chase was alone.

"Ellie, time to get up," Davy said. "I've got some bread for you."

I felt like telling him to go away. His kindness was more than I deserved—more than I wanted. But guilt nagged at my conscience for hiding under my blanket and ignoring him. I sat up and smoothed back my hair, which I'm certain could have rivaled that of a witch. "Thank you," I muttered.

Davy packed our bedrolls and helped with the horses, while Garrick sat next to me and ate. Poor Garrick. I never fully appreciated what he'd gone through when his beloved wife Rose died. I'd never had much tolerance for his visits to the tavern, but in that moment it all changed for me. I knew how he felt, and I wanted to crawl into a hole and hide from my own painful thoughts. Drowning his sorrows in a bottle of whiskey at the tavern had been Garrick's answer to the same torment I now felt.

"Ellie," he said.

"Yes, Garrick."

"I think he's still alive. I can feel it." Garrick's agony-filled eyes looked deep into my own. "Don't give up until you know he's dead. When we get back to Master Archidus, Harper's counter will tell us if he's alive."

I stared, dumbfounded, at Garrick's simple wisdom. Of course, the counter would tell us if he was alive! All we had to do was open it. If it remained dark, he lived. If it lit up in the hand of another, it was searching for a new Keeper, and I would know Chase was lost to me forever.

The light of reason must have flickered in my lifeless eyes, because a slight smile curved Garrick's lips. After dragging himself to his feet, he extended a weak hand in my direction. "Come on. Let's go see if I'm right about that boyfriend of yours."

A rush of warmth cascaded through me as I took Garrick's hand and stood to face my future. He had given me something I'd been completely void of since Legard's attack. One of the most precious of all commodities. One of the three great virtues spoken of in the Bible. He'd given me hope. "Thank you," I said.

I rode behind Davy that day, and we made good time. By midafternoon we met a large army heading the opposite direction. In hushed tones, Marcus and the captain of our squadron spoke with the captain of the big army. Moments later we moved our horses off the road and let the men pass. The word spread through our ranks that a massive force of Shuylians was on its way to attack Algonia. Master Archidus had summoned every squadron to rally at the front lines. The men with us expected to be sent into battle after delivering us to Master Archidus' fortress.

Garrick and the others afflicted by Legard's magic steadily regained their strength. Wickliff's liquid energy was gone. Segur had administered the last of it to the old elf during Legard's attack, so all the men were forced to recuperate without the aid of medicine. Garrick's recovery seemed to be the quickest. When I commented on it, he said, "It's because I'm a Keeper. The magic from the counter seems to help you heal faster."

I smiled. "Oh, that's good."

He returned my smile, then put into words what I had thought. "That means Chase should be healing up pretty good."

Another ounce of hope to add to my small store. "Thank you. I needed to hear that."

Marcus fell in line next to Garrick. I could tell they'd become fast and loyal friends in the short time they'd known one another.

The woods grew thicker as we rode deeper into Algonia. Every so often we came upon a small village. The inhabitants emptied out of their thatched-roof houses and waved as our procession passed by. A few times, we went through the home village of one of the soldiers who rode with us. He would pull out of the line and dismount. After a hearty greeting from family members, the soldier would gallop his horse back into formation.

At dusk I got my first sight of the fortress. Its towering walls were as magnificent as Chase had described them, and I felt a deep pang of regret that he wasn't with me to see it. He had so looked forward to getting back here and then going home. But now, who knew when or even if we would get home.

EIGHT
Master Archidus

The large double doors of the fortress slowly opened, and our horses' shod hooves clattered loudly against the still of evening. The lamps on the house fronts cast a faint light onto the cobblestone streets. A few people peered out their windows or stepped onto their porches to watch our procession. I wondered if they knew anything about us.

Once the soldiers delivered us to the castle, the squadron that had rescued us went on their way. A woman with fine, graceful features and wearing elegant robes followed two burly guards out the castle door, and Azalit rushed into her embrace. A group of maids and footmen bade us to follow them. Rooms had been made up for each of us.

I soon found myself alone with a kind woman about the age of Chase's mom. She drew a bath for me and scrubbed my hair with something that smelled like lavender and ginger. Then, she dressed me in a fresh-smelling gossamer nightgown and draped a pale green robe over my shoulders. The woman sat me on a stool, chattering all the while about her family and her children. I asked questions where appropriate to keep her talking. Focusing on her stories kept my mind from fretting over my own troubles.

She brushed out my hair and plaited it, then gathered my petticoats, dress, and chemise into her arms. "I'll send these to be washed and bring you something to eat, dear."

"Thank you, Heather." It had taken some persuasion, but she had finally agreed to be on a first-name basis with me. Although the room wasn't cold, a small fire burned in the fireplace. I moved to a plush chair near the hearth and gazed into the flickering orange light. But the dragon's screams seemed to echo out of the flames, and the burning Susack Plain flashed before my eyes. The memory of Chase using his body to shield mine nearly crushed my already breaking heart. He was so good to me. He would have died to protect me. He'd been that way since the first night we met.

Tearing my eyes from the fireplace, I stood suddenly, then walked to the window and pushed open the glass pane. The night breeze swirled past the heat of my sunburned skin, and I breathed in great gulps of the cool air.

More than once Chase had brought the heat of a blush to my cheeks. Often it was simply the nearness of him, or the way he looked at me. I smiled at the thought of him staring at me in nothing but a bath towel when he had unexpectedly appeared in my room. The smoldering, appreciative way he had looked me up and down had not only brought a blush to my cheeks, it had left me speechless. And how could I forget the New Year's Eve Ball in Boston in 1863? I wasn't the only girl who noticed Chase's broad set of shoulders and handsome face.

The flood of memories brought tears to my eyes. When was the last time I told him I loved him? Or had I taken him for granted? I wasn't sure. I couldn't remember. All I recalled now were the opportunities I'd missed. I had seen my share of dying. My mother, my father, my grandfather, and then Aunt Lydia were all gone. But this—this was different. I'd expected all of those people to die before me. But not Chase. We should have grown old and gray together. This was all wrong.

A knock sounded at the open door, and I wiped my fingertips across my cheeks. I had a headache, I noticed, as I turned to face Heather. She carried a tray laden with food. "Dear, will you take your meal in bed or at the table?"

I glanced at the table in front of the fireplace, but had no desire to be near those haunting flames. "I'll take my meal in bed. Thank you."

She set the tray on a small table near the bed, turned down the sheets, and propped up the pillows. "Come now, climb in." I slid my legs between the cool sheets. She offered me a bowl heaped with strawberries, blueberries, and grapes. "Perhaps you'd like some fruit?"

I wasn't sure I could eat, but I knew it would be rude to refuse her hospitality. "Thank you."

"If you need anything, pull this cord to ring the bell and I'll be right up. Sleep tight, dear." She closed the door behind her, leaving me alone again. I ate slowly at first, but after awhile, the delicacies on the tray distracted me. There were tiny bowls of soups—four different varieties, to be exact—and a basket filled with breads of varying colors, shapes, and flavors. Some were sweet, some were sour, and some were filled with nuts or fruit. Some were dense while others were fluffy and light, made almost entirely of air. I used the cold slices of meat from another plate to make little sandwiches. Small, delicate pastries and a variety of custards were neatly arranged on another plate. It was a meal fit for a king, and unlike anything I'd ever eaten. Then again, I'd never set foot in a castle before, either.

After I finished my feast, I yawned. It had been a long time since I'd been this full. I extinguished the bedside candles, and clutching a pillow to my chest, I pulled the covers over my head and cried myself to sleep.

I awoke the next morning surprised I had slept through the night. Someone had laid a gown on the chair. It was a rich green color, accented with golden trim. I dressed myself, leaving my hair in Heather's braid since I didn't see any hairpins, and stepped into the hall. I wandered through several hallways and up a circular staircase. I'd never seen anything like this before, and the grandeur of it nearly caused me to forget why I'd left my room in the first place. It wasn't until I entered the upstairs corridor and heard the sound of familiar voices echoing down the hallway that I remembered. I wanted to find Garrick and the others. I needed them to help me gain an audience with Master Archidus, so I could have a look at Chase's counter.

I turned the corner and saw them standing in a tight circle. "If I'm right, and he's still alive, I'm going back for him," Garrick said.

Marcus's head snapped up. "How will you know if he's alive? 'Tis a fool's errand you suggest—going into Shuyle on merely the hope he's survived."

"His counter will tell us if he's still alive," Garrick said, his voice rising with excitement. "If he's alive after being in Arbon's custody for a few days, then I think it's safe to assume Legard didn't deliver him to be executed. Think about it. Lord Arbon wants the counters, not the Keepers. We are simply one barrier he must get through to have the counter. Since Harper doesn't have his counter with him, there is little benefit in killing him. In fact, if Chase were dead, Archidus would be free to find a new Keeper. Wouldn't that put Arbon even farther from his ultimate goal?"

I paused in the hall and watched Marcus nod. "Yes," he said. "I hadn't thought of it from that perspective. Keeping him alive ties Master Archidus' hands. It forces him to hold the Protector's counter in the new world."

Garrick nodded. The three men seemed absorbed with their conversation, and I hesitated to interrupt.

"If you go, I'll go with you," Marcus said.

"I couldn't ask that of you."

The soldier placed his scarred hand on Garrick's shoulder. "My friend, you don't have to."

With a thankful smile, Garrick returned the gesture of friendship. "Thank you."

At that moment, Davy turned and looked down the hall, directly at me, almost as if he sensed me there. Without hesitation he walked to me and offered his arm, smiling. "You look well this morning. Were your accommodations to your liking?"

"Yes, they were wonderful."

"Come with us? We're waiting to see Master Archidus."

"I will. Thank you."

Within minutes, a short man opened the large door and bade us enter. Two guards, with skin as dark as chocolate, stood watch inside. A long table sat in the center of the great room, and two large fireplaces adorned the walls.

"Good morning, Quirus," Marcus said.

Like an echo Garrick said, "Good morning, Quirus."

The small man they greeted nodded back to them, then turned and addressed Davy. "Welcome, Keeper. As you surely have surmised, I am called Quirus."

"It is a pleasure to make your acquaintance." Davy extended his hand, but Quirus grasped his wrist. Looking perplexed, Davy squeezed the man's wrist in return and said, "I'm Davy Adams, and this is Miss Ellie Williams."

The Algonian bowed in front of me. "Welcome to Cadré Unair, the fortress city of Master Archidus, and the capital of Algonia. It is an honor to meet you, milady."

"Thank you," I said, dropping into a curtsy.

Quirus turned and stood ramrod straight. "You may be seated. Master Archidus will be with you shortly. I shall have the table prepared while you wait."

Garrick and Marcus slumped into two of the oversized chairs surrounding the enormous table. Davy gestured me forward and slid a chair out, seating me between his pa and himself. One of the doors opened, and a procession of servants carried platters of food into the room. A blur of activity ensued as plates and silverware were set before us and a bountiful feast spread on the table.

Garrick stood. "I'm starving." He moved around the table, filling his plate, with Marcus following.

Davy picked up my plate. "What can I get for you?"

Caught off guard by his consideration, I scanned the mounds of food. There were so many varieties. I recognized the delicious rolls I'd eaten the night before. "One of those star-shaped rolls with the sugar on top, some strawberries, and—it all looks delectable. Surprise me."

Davy grinned. "As you wish." He filled my plate with two of my favorite rolls, an egg, a slice of ham, a delicate pastry with cream on top, and generous pile of dark red berries.

"Thank you," I said as he set the plate before me.

I tried to eat, but the anticipation of learning Chase's fate had my nerves on end and my stomach doing flip-flops. A feast such as this should have been fully enjoyed, but I could only pick at my food. After a while, Garrick leaned over and whispered, "Ellie, eat. You've got to keep your strength up." I forced myself to clean up my plate, simply to please him.

Finally, the door opened and Quirus entered, followed by two more guards and a man who I could only assume was Master Archidus himself. Quirus sat next to Marcus, while Master Archidus took his place at the head of the table and said, "First and foremost, I wish to express my gratitude for the safe return of my daughter. The impulsiveness of youth can often be frustrating to a parent."

Garrick and Marcus nodded. "You're welcome," they said in unison.

Archidus looked consumed with worry as I studied him through my lowered lashes. I was dying to inquire regarding Chase, but unsure how to do it properly. A servant filled the Master's goblet, and he took a long drink before settling his eyes on me. With a compassionate smile he answered my unspoken question.

"Yes, the Protector lives."

I raised my head. "Are you certain?" I asked eagerly, then clamped my hand over my mouth in embarrassment. Surely I was the only one foolish enough to have ever asked Master Archidus if he was certain of anything.

With a chuckle he removed a counter from his pocket and passed it to Garrick. "You may see for yourself."

Garrick set the counter in the palm of my hand. A collage of memories passed before my eyes as I looked at the device. How many times had Chase placed it in my hand? He had tried to give it to me before he knew what it was. He had handed it to me to set when we returned to the cabin. Even though he didn't agree with my decision, he had given it to me when I wanted to return to Boston. And then, lastly, while he wore Davy's counter around his neck, Chase had given me his to hold. *Oh, Chase, we had so many memories together.* Tears blurred the counter before my eyes, but I blinked them back.

I slid my thumb across the latch, and the top sprang open. I smiled to find the inside of the counter dark. I shut it, then quickly reopened it—just to make certain. Again, it was dark. The counter awaited Chase's return, as did I.

I looked up at Master Archidus and sighed, clutching the counter to my chest. "Oh, thank you." I hated to give it up and wished to keep it in my possession so I would always know if he lived. However, Master Archidus clearly expected me to return it. Regretfully, I relinquished my hold and passed it back to Garrick, who gave it to the Master.

"Garrick the Guardian, you've earned the right to have this returned to you." Master Archidus set another counter on the table in front of him. Garrick glanced at it, but left it untouched.

Master Archidus stood and looked at Davy. "Perception's Keeper, it is an honor to finally meet you." Davy stood as Master Archidus approached him. The Master clasped Davy's hand in the same manner Quirus had. "I congratulate you on your forethought and quick action. Very few could have kept their counter a secret from Legard as long as you did. For that, I will ever be grateful. It puzzled me that you didn't simply choose to leave when you obviously perceived the danger you were in. However, that's now in the past. It is usually necessary to educate a new Keeper on the dangers of holding a counter, but in your case, I believe your recent experiences leave you well acquainted with the enemy. So, I'll dispense with any further formalities and return this to you for safekeeping." Master Archidus offered Davy a gold counter.

"Thank you," Davy replied. He took the counter and flipped it open. Light emanated from the interior before he closed it.

"For the time being, you and Miss Williams are welcome to be our guests. If there is anything you should require, simply ask, and we will make every effort to ensure your comfort."

"We appreciate the hospitality, sir," Davy replied.

"Yes, thank you," I added softly.

Master Archidus returned to his seat. He added food to his plate, then glanced between Garrick and Marcus. Garrick filled his plate again and returned the Master's gaze. Although Chase lived, I knew he was far from safe, and the thought of eating more food repulsed me. When would Garrick talk to Master Archidus about a rescue? I'd heard his intentions in the hall. Time was wasting. I felt helpless to do anything for Chase, and it was maddening. Garrick and Marcus were his only hope.

Finally, the Master spoke. "No."

What on earth is he talking about?

Garrick leaned forward. "I can't abandon him. Not when we know he's alive somewhere."

They were discussing Chase!

"It's too dangerous," Master Archidus declared. "You and Marcus are too valuable to risk."

"No, we're not. You were willing to risk us last time, and look— here we are, back again," said Garrick.

"But the Protector is not. That was a different situation. This time the captive is being held in the heart of Shuyle—totally inaccessible under the best of conditions."

Marcus folded his arms and lifted his chin. "An army may not be able to get in, but two lone men might."

The Master raised his eyebrows. "Captain Landseer, exactly how do you propose entering Shuyle undetected? Never mind finding which prison camp or dungeon they hold Chase in, freeing him, and then successfully escaping with him."

"We'll disguise ourselves as Shuylian soldiers," Marcus said.

Frowning, Master Archidus stood abruptly. "I have more pressing matters to attend to. You may see me tomorrow for my answer." Quirus and his two guards followed him out of the room.

Garrick lowered his fork to his plate. "That didn't go quite like I'd planned."

"It could have been worse," Marcus said. "We started out with no and ended with 'see me tomorrow for my answer.' 'Tis progress, at least. If the answer be yes, we have much work to do. I say we start our preparations."

Garrick's chair scraped across the stone floor as he stood. Before he left with Marcus, he said, "Davy, you stay out of trouble and take care of Ellie."

"Of course I will, Pa."

NINE
Cadré Unair

After leaving the hall, I spent the day with Davy. We lost ourselves in the maze of cobblestone streets that made up the fortress city. One vendor was kind enough to offer us bread, even though we hadn't anything to pay him with. It neared dusk by the time we found our way back to the castle.

A butler opened the ornate door. "Milady," he said, dipping his head toward me. Davy stepped inside behind me. "Sir, you're both expected for dinner. Come this way, please."

Davy and I exchanged curious glances as we followed the butler to a small dining room. Seated around the table were the soldiers who'd rescued us. As I took the empty seat next to Aiton, I said, "I'm sorry we're late. I didn't know we were expected for supper."

With a twinkle in his eye, Aiton chuckled. "No need to apologize, miss. We Algonians are a bit spontaneous."

I returned his smile and then glanced at the others. Everyone was present except Azalit. Perhaps she would not be allowed to leave the castle for quite some time.

"Miss Ellie, we would like to extend our regrets that Chase isn't with us tonight," Aiton said. "We'd hoped to persuade Master Archidus to allow us to go in search of him, but we were denied.

All except Marcus have been ordered to rejoin their regiments on the morrow. Hence, we called for a feast to say goodbye."

My heart sank. I would have liked a whole army to be sent out to rescue my beau. "That's unfortunate, but I appreciate you trying," I said. I turned to the other soldiers, who were expressing their hope for Chase's safe return. "Thank you all, for everything."

It was late by the time all of the soldiers except Marcus left to go their separate ways. Garrick, Marcus, Davy, and I wished them well on their travels. Then Davy extended his arm in the fashion of a true gentleman and said, "I'll walk you to your room." After we climbed a staircase and walked down one corridor, he turned to me. "Where exactly is your room?"

"You know, I'm so turned about I haven't the foggiest notion."

"Did it have a window?"

"Yes."

"Could you tell which direction it faced?"

"Um . . ."

"Did you see the sun this morning? Could it have been east?"

"No, I don't believe it was east."

He raised his hand to point at one of the doors. "This is my room. It faces east, so let's try a different hall."

Every door looked exactly the same. When I recognized the woman who'd helped me the night before, I called out to her.

"Oh, there you are. I was beginning to worry," she said, turning to face us.

"I'm sorry. There are so many doors and hallways that I got myself turned around and lost." I lowered my arm and looked up at Davy. "Good night. Thank you for your escort today."

"You're welcome. Night, Ellie." Smiling, he turned and walked away.

Heather must have taken it upon herself to mother me, for she asked questions about my day as she ushered me into my room and closed the door. "This gown does look lovely on you. I hoped it would bring out the color in your eyes, and I was right. But now it's late, and I want to get you into bed. After the ordeal you've been through, you need your rest." She unfastened the buttons on the gown and helped me step out of it. *This must be what it feels like to be a rich Southern belle, with oodles of fancy gowns and people waiting on you hand and foot.*

Heather slid the gossamer nightgown over my head and started to brush my hair. "Seems like a fine young man you were keeping company with tonight." The lilt in her voice begged for details.

"Yes, Davy's a good friend."

"I may be past my prime, but I'm not blind. The two of you make a striking couple, and it looks like he's inclined to be more than a friend."

I sighed. "There's already someone else for me."

She continued to brush my hair. "Why so downhearted then? Tell me about him."

"Oh, Heather, he's so wonderful, yet I fear I may never see him again. Legard captured him during our journey here, and he now sits in one of Lord Arbon's prisons." I shuddered at the thought.

"What's his name?"

"Chase Harper, but everyone around here seems to refer to him as the Protector."

"Oh, I see. He's a Keeper."

I sighed. "Yes."

"Tell me how you met him, and what it is about him that strikes your fancy," she said, splitting my hair into three sections to begin the braid.

"It's a bit complicated. You see, I seem to have a predisposition for ending up in trouble. My grandfather was the Protector's Keeper before Chase. One day two men with the vilest of intentions took me captive. They were searching for my grandfather's counter and expected I knew its whereabouts, when from out of nowhere this dashingly handsome young man came to my rescue. But he's so much more than that. He's kindhearted, generous, smart, and so loyal and devoted to me. I have no doubt he loves me—in fact I'm certain he would do anything for me, even die for me." My eyes filled with tears. Would I ever exhaust my supply and be done crying?

"A man like that is a rare find indeed. Now into bed with you. Everything always looks brighter after a good night's sleep." Heather turned down the sheets. "Sleep well, dear," she said before leaving me alone with my thoughts.

That night and for many nights to follow, I didn't sleep well at all.

Our days in Cadré Unair were a brief respite after the chaos of our journey. Garrick and Marcus received permission from Master Archidus to search for Chase, and spent the next two days preparing for their journey. Each evening after dinner, they hunched over maps of Shuyle and the Borderlands, studying out possible routes. Garrick fully recovered from the effects of Legard's attack after a visit to an elf healer.

The Master was quite accommodating. I waited each day for a brief audience with him. Every morning I said, "Master Archidus, sir, I wanted to inquire after Chase. Is he still well?" Thankfully, the Master always responded with "He still lives." After a quick curtsy and expression of gratitude, I'd leave him to his business.

An air of increasing tension filled Cadré Unair. Groups of soldiers gathered and drilled in the large field within the eastern wall. A never-ending flow of supply wagons rolled into and out of the city. Squadrons of soldiers reported to the castle and were outfitted with supplies and given their assignments before marching away. Davy and I spent hours walking the streets of the quaint city. As guests of Master Archidus we were treated as royalty. Heather kept me supplied with elegant gowns, even when I complained that they were much too fancy for someone as ordinary as me.

On the third day, Garrick and Marcus rode through the gates of Cadré Unair dressed as peasants. Davy and I watched the heavy double doors swing closed behind them. Although I was happy someone was trying to help Chase, it was nevertheless a somber day as Davy and his pa shared an emotional farewell. Garrick and Marcus faced a difficult and dangerous task.

The gardens surrounding the castle were immaculately kept and filled with flowers. Large hedges towered above the stone walkways that formed a maze of paths leading to a colorful rose garden and a bubbling water fountain. Two days after Garrick and Marcus left, Davy was escorting me on a tour of the gardens, when Quirus interrupted our meanderings.

"Master Archidus requests a meeting at once."

I frowned. "Is something wrong?"

"Follow me, please," Quirus said.

I removed my hand from Davy's arm, lifted my long skirt, and ran to catch the servant. For someone with short legs, he moved with surprising quickness. "Quirus, tell me, is it about Chase? Is he dead? I have to know, please. Is that what this is about?"

Clearly unaffected by my concern, Quirus said, "Milady, you will be speaking to the Master shortly."

"Yes, but—" *Oh, it's useless.*

Davy walked briskly at my heels. Every few strides I took a running step to catch Quirus and stay ahead of Davy. We entered the castle and hurried up two staircases before walking down the hallway leading to Master Archidus' meeting hall. Quirus knocked twice on the heavy wooden door, and the guards opened it.

I hurried in. Dropping into a curtsy before the Master, I bit my tongue to keep from speaking out of turn.

"Yes, he lives," said Master Archidus, responding to my unanswered question. He then turned his attention to Davy. "I summoned you here because of another concern. Legard is in Algonia, even as we speak. He broke through the magic of our protective barrier at the southern tip of the border. He, along with Shuyle's chief sorcerers, leads the largest army I've seen in the new world. They will be fighting their way through Algonia with their eye set on Cadré Unair. I see them breaching our gates, and I mustn't risk keeping either of you here any longer. I simply cannot guarantee your safety. I leave at dawn to lead our army against the Shuylians. Therefore, I must return you to the old world at once.

"Legard's skill at hiding his intentions and actions from me is impeccable. Presuming I have surmised correctly, his sights are set on the two counters I'm holding. It would not be prudent to have a third here as well. However, should Legard or another Sniffer come looking for you in the old world, take what precautions you can to protect Miss Williams as well as yourself. While they have the Protector, she may yet be in danger. But do not forget, your first priority is the safety of your counter. It cannot fall into Arbon's hands."

With a weary sigh, Master Archidus shook hands with Davy. "The clothes you arrived in are waiting for you in your rooms. Once you change, Quirus will show you to Witches Hollow. From there, I will return you to the old world."

My heart raced, and it felt as if the Master had condemned me to be burned at the stake. "What about Chase? How will we know if Garrick and Marcus are successful?" My life revolved around the daily confirmation of Chase's well-being from Master Archidus. If I left here, I would lose that. I would forever wonder if Chase lived.

Master Archidus turned to look at me. His face softened with compassion and understanding, and I felt as if he completely understood my anguish. "You mustn't rely on his safe return. The odds against him are great. I will promise you this, though. Should Chase one day return to Algonia, I will not return him to his time on Earth, but to the same place and time I send the two of you. Mercifully, regardless of how long he is here, it will be no more than a few hours for you. I wish I could offer you more, but I must excuse myself. I have many preparations to attend to before the morrow."

I stood in stunned silence as the Master and his guards left the room. Davy cleared his throat and offered me his hand, saying, "We should get ready."

Quirus followed as Davy walked me to my room and opened the door for me. "I'll return after I've changed," Davy said.

I entered the beautiful, elegant room that had been mine for a few days. I would be sad to leave it behind—sad to leave Heather, the mother I'd never had. On my bed were my old clothes, scrubbed clean and repaired. I slipped out of today's gown, made of royal-blue chiffon, and fondly touched the silver-colored lace at the bodice. I had been spoiled here—treated like one of the princesses I'd read about as a child in my fairy-tale books. I smiled. What had Chase said? "This is the fairy-tale world, Ellie," or something like that. *It is time to face the real world, I suppose.*

I squared my shoulders and got dressed. A knock sounded as I hooked the buttons on my boots. I opened the door. "I'm ready."

When I paused to glance back, Quirus said, "Come now, milady. We must hurry."

Davy and I followed him out of the castle and through the city streets. The blacksmiths' shops overflowed with activity. Broad-shouldered men with soot-smudged faces bent over the swords and shields they were repairing. The clang of hammer on steel filled the air, and heat radiated from the smithy. A line of horses stood waiting to be shod, and a stack of metal wagon rims needed assembly. Swarms of soldiers mingled in the streets, no doubt anticipating their orders. The capital city felt like a beehive.

The two heavy doors in the fortress wall stood open but heavily guarded. The sentries questioned everyone coming in and searched each wagon, but they simply nodded toward Quirus, and soon we left Cadré Unair behind.

The sun glinted off the spears and shields of a group of soldiers marching toward the fortress. Every man wore a serious expression. What would the peaceful city look like a week from now? The changes we'd witnessed in the past few days were already dramatic, and the enemy hadn't even arrived.

Quirus led us down a hill over heavily wooded terrain. After we walked for some time, he called for a halt in a circular grove of trees.

Large roots protruded out of the ground, and I found a comfortable one to sit on. "We've arrived at Witches Hollow," Quirus said. "Master Archidus will return you shortly. Best of luck to you as—"

I never heard Quirus complete his sentence, for I was suddenly yanked from my perch on the root and plunged into darkness. I had felt this once before, when the Sniffer had clamped his filthy hand around my neck as he pulled me to the new world for the first time. I let out a cry of alarm when I dropped into cold, wet snow. It was a stark contrast from the mild weather of Algonia, and I scrambled to my feet.

TEN
Waiting

Davy moved to my side, brushing the snow from his pants. "Are you all right, Ellie?"

"Yes, I'm fine. Where would you guess we are?"

He grinned back at me. "I don't need to guess. I know where we are."

I looked up from brushing off my skirt. "Where?"

He pointed to the trees behind me. There were odd-shaped boards crudely nailed into the fork of a tree. I looked back at Davy.

"That's my old tree fort, from when I was a child," he explained. "We're in the woods behind my cabin."

"That's good, I suppose. When do you think Chase will get here?"

Davy hesitated. "I reckon Master Archidus didn't want you to set store by Chase's safe return. You heard what he said."

"I know, but I think he'll be fine." A shudder ran down my spine as a gust of cold air swirled through the trees.

"We should wait in the cabin. I'll build you a fire."

I shook my head. "I have to wait here. I can't risk missing him."

Davy tugged on my arm. "You'll freeze out here. The Master said it could be hours."

Lifting my chin, I jerked my arm away. "No! You go ahead, but I'll wait. I could never forgive myself if he appeared and I wasn't here."

Davy shook his head and chuckled. "Have it your way then, but I won't let you freeze to death out here. I'll be back with a coat and a blanket."

I rubbed my fingers and blew on them as Davy marched through the snow, his hands in his pockets. Once he left the stand of trees, I lifted my eyes heavenward. *Please let Chase come back to me,* I prayed. Minute by minute the time ticked by.

Davy returned and put one of his coats over my shoulders and wrapped a blanket around my legs. "Someone ransacked the cabin while we were gone. There's a lot of damage, but it doesn't look like they took anything."

"That's terrible."

"What can we expect when we left our front door open? The bread you made is rock-hard, so it's been days since we were taken, maybe weeks."

"Hmm. Thank you for the coat and the blanket. This is much better."

"Would you like a chair? Or something to eat?" Davy asked.

I smiled. "A chair, if it's not too much trouble."

"It's no trouble at all."

He left the trees again but soon returned, carrying a chair and an armload of firewood. He kicked the snow off to the side, clearing a small area. "Since you're bound and determined to wait it out, I decided I'd build you a fire here."

In spite of my plight, I couldn't help but smile at his thoughtfulness. "Thank you, Davy. I don't know what I'd ever do without you."

He pulled some shavings and a tinderbox from his pocket, and within a few minutes the dry wood crackled as the flame took hold. I was so chilled, the sight of fire didn't trigger flashbacks of the Borderlands.

"I'm gonna check on the animals, and then I'll round us up something for supper. Holler if you need me," Davy said.

"Certainly." I moved closer to the blaze, stretching my hands toward the warmth.

What is taking Chase so long? Master Archidus had promised he'd return him to the same time and place. Closing my eyes, I whispered another prayer for Chase's safe return. The fire had nearly burned itself out by the time Davy returned. He carried another armload of firewood, and in his other hand swung a cast-iron frying pan.

While he built up the fire, he talked. "I ran into Mr. Mortenson. Seems he's been taking care of our animals for the past ten days. He said he saw someone wearing a long cloak snooping around our cabin. By the description he gave, I'd guess it was a Sniffer. When Mr. Mortenson tried to talk to him, the stranger ran behind the cabin and disappeared. That's when he figured out we were gone."

"What did you tell Mr. Mortenson about you and Garrick?" I asked.

"I've not got a quick tongue, but I did manage to come up with a story about Pa and me taking a day trip, which ended with him taking ill. I said my pa sent me back to check on things here, and I had left him in the capable hands of a fine family. It sounded a bit foolish while I was tellin' it."

"Sounds like a fine tale to me. Chase and I certainly told our fair share of stories. Actually, everyone I ever met with him heard a story about me, except his sister Jessica. She heard the truth, but didn't believe it for quite some time. I suppose in my case, the stories are more believable than the truth."

"I remember your stories. Like the one about you being my ma's cousin, and then you being married," Davy said, his tone of voice making it clear he wasn't happy to hear that last one.

I looked down. "Yes." For a while, only the crackle of burning logs filled the air between us as we waited.

Suddenly, Davy stood and said, "I'm hungry. I'll go fetch something from the cellar and fry us up some supper."

The sky had been gray and overcast all afternoon, gradually growing darker. *How long should I wait for him? How could I ever stop waiting? To stop would mean I've given up hope. I can't do that.* Like an old oak tree, I felt rooted to this spot. I couldn't possibly entertain the thought of anything else. Chase simply had to return to me. I couldn't live without him, so I wouldn't move.

It was nearly dark by the time I heard Davy's footstep's crunching through the snow. "You hungry?" he asked.

Not wanting to disappoint him, I lied, "Yes. What can I do?"

"Nothing. It's ready to cook." He dropped his load of firewood next to the fire. In the other arm, he carried a bowl. "Actually, you can hold these for us." He handed me two plates and forks from the top of the bowl.

"Certainly." I watched him drop a dab of butter into the frying pan and position the pan over the hot coals. The butter melted, and he dumped the contents of the bowl into the pan. Thin slices of carrots and potatoes, along with chunks of beef, soon sizzled as he hunched over the pan, diligently turning the meat and vegetables. When the corners of the meat blackened, he slid his coat sleeve over his hand and pulled the pan away from the coals.

"You're certainly quite adept at cooking," I said.

"Uh . . . I have to be, I suppose. I would've gone crazy eatin' the same thing day after day with my pa's cooking."

"Hmm. Do you remember Chase cooking you eggs when you were little?"

Davy rolled his head back and smiled. "How could I forget? He said he knew how to make scrambled eggs, but he took one look around my ma's kitchen and I knew he'd gotten himself into a fix. But I was starving. I was little, too—only five or six. He burned the eggs and then ate almost all of them before I even got started. Funny thing was they actually tasted pretty good once I closed my eyes and didn't look at what I was eating. Harper must have told you that story, huh?"

"Yes, he did."

Davy stood holding the pan. "Supper's ready."

I held the plates while he heaped them with food. After arranging more logs on the fire, he took his plate and started eating.

The smell of hot food under my nose almost had me convinced I might be hungry after all. Two bites into the savory meal I was certain of it. "Davy, this is delicious," I said between bites three and four.

With his mouth full he nodded. "It's not fancy like that castle fare we've been eatin', but it'll fill ya up."

I ate nearly the whole plate of food, then said, "I'm stuffed. Thank you."

In the distance, the mournful cry of a wolf sounded. I glanced up. Not a single star shone through the cloudy darkness overhead. The wind had died down, and the night was cold and still. The front of me had been sufficiently warmed by the fire, but my back increasingly felt the chill in the air. I stood and turned to face away from the fire.

"Are you cold?" Davy asked.

"Half of me is."

"Eventually, you'll need to go inside."

"I know," I said quietly, "but please, not yet."

He stoked the fire until the wood ran out. As the flames died, the darkness crept closer. With nightfall came the chill of despair, and the realization that Chase wasn't coming back today. And if he didn't come back today, he would probably never come back to me.

Unbidden, tears welled up in my eyes. I stood like a statue, staring into the woods, and soon silent tears coursed down my cheeks. When the coals burned to nothing behind me, I heard Davy stand. His silent waiting spoke louder than any words, and I knew it was time. Even wearing his winter coat I felt a shudder run down my spine. With my mind made up, I wiped my eyes and followed him to the cabin.

Davy opened the door for me. "I started a fire earlier this afternoon."

I stepped into the warmth of the cabin. "Thank you."

We walked into a disaster. Feathers from the down pillows were scattered across the floor. Every cupboard had been emptied of its contents. Chairs and tables were overturned. Someone had even ripped up floorboards in places.

I stood numbly and watched Davy put the bed back to rights and clear a path for me. I knew I should help, but I couldn't make myself move. Not when the thought of facing a lifetime without Chase clamped down on my soul, squeezing the life out of me. Suddenly, I felt so tired.

Davy took the oversized coat off my shoulders and hung it next to the door. "I'll get more wood, stoke up the fire for the night."

I sat on the edge of the bed. A thin layer of flour coated the floor, and I mindlessly swirled the toe of my boot through the white powder. I looked up when the door swung open again. Davy stepped in and kicked it closed with his heel. I went back to staring at the pattern I'd made in the flour, while he added wood to the coals in the hearth. The orange glow of the fire spread through the cabin, and shadows moved across the floor.

Davy knelt in front of me. "Let's get you out of these boots." He undid the buttons and slid the boots off. His brow furrowed. "You're cold." Methodically, he rubbed each of my feet, restoring the circulation.

"Thank you. That's much better," I whispered.

"Good night, Ellie." He stood and retreated to the back bedroom. I pulled the quilts over my cold toes and tucked the blanket under my chin. Today hadn't gone quite like I'd hoped, but perchance I'd have better luck tomorrow. I drifted into an uneasy sleep filled with unwanted dreams.

I woke to an empty house. With the door to Davy's room wide open, I noticed it was in the same state of disaster as the main room. I sat back on the edge of the bed and brushed the flour from my socks. I made up my mind to put my boots on and visit the privy before setting to work on this mess. No sooner had I put on both shoes than I heard someone running up the steps and across the porch. I looked at the door, wondering what had Davy in such a hurry.

The door flew open. "Ellie!" Davy's face was pale, like he'd seen a ghost. He burst into the room, panting. "He's here—Legard." Davy ran toward me, leaping a fallen chair and sliding to a stop in the mess of spilled flour. Digging his counter out of his pocket, he kept an eye on the doorway to the cabin.

"Where?" I asked, following his gaze. A sullen-looking Legard materialized just outside the open door.

A scream caught in my throat as Davy grabbed my arm and shuffled us away.

ELEVEN
Running

We reappeared on a beach and began walking. "How did he find us so fast?" I asked.

Davy glanced behind us. "I don't know, but we've got to lose him. Confound it. Run!" We took no more than three steps before Davy touched another button, moving us on to the next shuffle. We reappeared at a dead run, crashing through the underbrush of a forest. Again Legard trailed us as we disappeared. We must have run through over ten shuffles before we finally got ahead of him. A bustling town appeared around us. It was after Davy's time and mine, because a mix of automobiles and horse-drawn carriages moved through the crowded street. I pulled Davy into the road, drawing a few honks as we darted between the cars.

Glancing over his shoulder with wide eyes, Davy asked, "What are those things?"

"Cars. You know, like horseless coaches. These are the early models. You should see what comes later." We hid ourselves in Rodger's Dry Goods Store, behind a rack of fabrics. Peering between the bolts of cloth, we watched the spot where we had appeared. Within no time at all, Legard materialized. My heart raced in fear at the sight of him hunting us. I thought perhaps we'd stumped him when he wandered up the street, lifting his head every so often to test the air.

"What is he looking for?" Davy mumbled.

"Us, of course," I whispered.

"I know that," he said kindly, "but how does he follow us? What tells him where we went?"

"My grandfather said they follow your counter signatures. When you use the counter it leaves a trace behind, which Sniffers can follow. Grandfather said running between shuffles makes it harder for Sniffers to find the signatures. Or I've heard you can stay in the same place and go to multiple times in that location. When you stack so many counter signatures on top of each other, it leaves a garbled mess which is difficult to follow as well."

"Do you think the counter signature stays there forever, or does it disappear after awhile?" Davy asked.

"I'm fairly certain it fades with time."

The store clerk, a big, round man, cleared his throat and stared at us over small, wire-rimmed glasses. "Can I help you two with something?" he asked.

"No thank you, sir. We were just looking," I said as sweetly as I could.

"If you're not buying, best move on then. We've got to make room for the paying customers."

I nodded and stood. "Yes, sir."

Davy and I moved slowly toward the door. "Excuse me, sir. Is there a back door we could use?" he asked. "It is quite important, and it wouldn't be any trouble to you."

The man looked perplexed. "Of course, it wouldn't be any trouble. Right this way."

He led us through the store and unlocked the back door, then held it open for us. Something in his expression told me his response to our request had shocked him. Perhaps his compliance had resulted from the magic Davy possessed as Perception's Keeper.

We walked in the opposite direction from where we'd seen Legard and kept ourselves behind the buildings of the main street.

"Let's shuffle out of here," Davy said.

We ran through another round of shuffles, each time putting as much distance as possible between counter signatures. When we reached the fifth shuffle, we waited. After hiding ourselves, we watched the spot where we had appeared. Sometime later, Davy said, "I think we lost him."

"I hope so, but where are we, and where are we going to go after this? We can't go back to the cabin now."

Davy studied his counter.

"Do you know how to read the symbols?" I asked.

"Yes, I know the date. Pa had me practice while we were in Cadré Unair together. It's June 8, 1808. But I'm trying to remember the last map of the United States I saw when I was in school. I think we're in the Missouri Territory."

"Hmm," I muttered.

We waited for hours with no sign of Legard. Finally, with my empty stomach rumbling, I said to Davy, "Will you take me to Chase's house, please? Perhaps Master Archidus forgot what he said to us and returned him to his own time. Plus, the food there is plentiful."

After a brief pause, Davy said, "I can do that. Where do we go?"

"It was the third week of March when we left. Chase wouldn't get back right away, so let's try March 31, 2012."

Davy carefully set the dials. "This will be a new experience," he muttered. "What part of the country?"

"Oh, Portland, Oregon. Here, I'll show you." I grasped his hand to steady the counter and positioned the pinpoint of light on Portland. "There," I said, smiling. I was weary of shuffling, and hope bubbled up inside me like a fountain at the prospect of finding Chase.

Davy took my hand and pressed Shuffle and then Go. Relief washed over me when we appeared in modern-day Portland. I immediately knew where we were. We stood in Waterfront Park near one of the bridges spanning the Willamette River. Chase and Jessica had brought me here only a month ago when we'd met their parents downtown for dinner.

In the gray of early dawn, a few joggers and homeless people moved along the wide sidewalk next to the river. I tugged on Davy's hand. "Come on."

He stared dumbfounded at the skyscrapers, the mass of cars crossing the bridge, and the strangely dressed people. Everyone who passed us stared right back.

I had a plan—find a phone to borrow, then call every number I knew, starting with Chase's, until I got someone to answer. I was walking across the grass toward the nearest building when Davy mumbled from behind me, "Ellie, I think we may have a problem."

I spun around. "What? Do you see Legard?"

"No," Davy said, looking intently at his counter. "I don't think we're in 2012. The counter says it's March 31, 1991."

I stopped in my tracks and turned slowly. "Are you certain?" The blood drained from my face as anxiety pierced my heart.

"I'm certain the counter says 1991."

I looked around me. It looked like the 2012 I remembered, but I hadn't paid attention to all the details at the time. "Wait here." I ran back to the sidewalk. "Excuse me, sir," I called to a man jogging past.

"Yeah?" he said, jogging in place in front of me.

"Do you know what the date is?" I asked.

"The thirty-first."

"What year is it?"

He raised his eyebrows and chuckled. "What are you on? Is this a trick question?"

Davy had followed me and now stood at my back.

I shook my head. "It's not like that. We're in a play. This is a costume. I know it's a strange question, but I . . . I had a head injury, you see. I forget the silliest things. Please, could you help me remember?"

"It's 1991. I hope you get feeling better," the man said before jogging away.

I turned back to Davy. "You're right. Can I see the counter?"

He humored me and handed it over. I adjusted the dials myself. Although I didn't remember the symbols, I moved the 1 up one notch to a 2, the 9 down one notch to a 0, and so forth. "Does that look right to you?" I asked Davy.

He nodded. "That's how I had it before."

"Let's try again." I handed the counter back to him and watched his every move. He pressed Shuffle and Go. Five more shuffles and we reappeared in Waterfront Park. I spun around, looking in every direction. It looked the same. I waited for the woman who was walking her dog toward us. When I caught her eye, I spoke up.

"Good morning. Can I ask you a question? I recently suffered a head injury and can't recall what year it is."

"I'm sorry to hear that. It's 1991. Cool costumes by the way," she said cheerfully.

"Thank you." Disappointment weighed as heavily on me as the dark clouds gathering over Portland.

"I'm sorry, Ellie. I reckon I ought to do something different, but I'm at a loss. Maybe 2012 is too far in the future."

I pressed my fingertips to my eyes and sank onto a bench. "Perhaps you're right. Let me think. My grandfather did mention a limit to the number of years one could travel."

Davy stood in front of me, shaking his head at the city sprawled out in front of him.

"I have an idea. I need an envelope and a piece of paper," I said.

Davy followed me into two different buildings while I begged for a piece of paper, an envelope, and a pen. Soon, I sat at a stone bench outside one of the buildings and wrote my letter.

Dear Chase,

Once again I find I am alone, writing a letter that I will never be able to mail myself. If these words find their way to you, then I rejoice that you are alive. Nothing would bring me greater happiness. At times I fear you will never escape Lord Arbon's prison. At other times, my heart refuses to believe you may be lost to me forever.

When Algonia fell under attack, Master Archidus forced Davy and me to leave. Please know I would never have left there without you if I had any choice in the matter.

I tried to return to 2012 using Davy's counter, but alas it got me no farther than March 31, 1991. Please come get me at Waterfront Park near Morrison Street. I will wait there all day for you. After that, I don't know where we'll go. Legard hunts for Davy and his counter. Perhaps he hunts for me as well. He seems tireless in his efforts, and I don't know how long we can evade him.

I love you, Chase. Please come back for me. I can't see how I will ever survive a lifetime without you.

With love,
Ellie

Dear Mr. and Mrs. Harper and Jessica,

If we should never return and you have received this letter, please know of my undying gratitude and love for you and your family. Your son had the noblest of hearts and gave the ultimate sacrifice in protecting my life. Unfortunately, he was forced into the middle of a war on another world, from which escape may have proved impossible for him. I feel certain he would have wanted you to know he loved you, and that he is sorry for the pain and worry his disappearance caused you.

Sincerely,
Ellie Williams

"There, it's done," I said, then folded the paper and sealed it in the envelope. I penned Chase's address on the front and wrote, "Please mail March 26, 2012."

"Now I need to find someone whom I can trust to mail this in twenty-one years." I was anxious to get back to Waterfront Park. I didn't want to miss Chase if he was coming. I scanned the crowd of business professionals pouring into the office building behind me. I would ask a woman. I watched for the right person.

Finally, a lady about ten years older than me came into view. She hurried down the sidewalk toward us, a kind look on her face.

"Excuse me, ma'am. I have a favor to ask you," I said. "I need this letter mailed on March 26, 2012. Would you be willing to hold it for the next twenty-one years and then stamp and mail it at that time? I realize it's an odd request, but it is very important to me." My voice cracked with emotion, and the ever-present tears filled my eyes.

The woman stared at my letter and me for a long moment.

"Please?" I choked out.

"This isn't a trick is it?" she asked.

"No, of course not. Please, I simply need it mailed, but the date is crucial. It must be mailed on March 26, no sooner, no later. I'm sorry to make this so difficult, but could you please help me?"

She shrugged her shoulders and put her hand out for the letter. "I'll try to remember, but that's a long time from now." She slipped the envelope into her bag and started to walk away.

"Thank you," I called.

She raised a hand in farewell. "You're welcome."

We kept a constant vigil at Waterfront Park. Davy couldn't stop talking about the bakery we'd smelled while I wrote the letter. He left to beg two hearty wheat rolls from the old lady behind the counter. It took the edge off our hunger but hardly filled us. We were both starving and cold by the time the sun set on the Rose City.

Davy stood in front of me and offered his hand. "Ellie, we have to assume Chase didn't get the letter. The day is past. We should start looking for food and a place to spend the night."

I knew Davy was right, but I hated to admit it. I didn't want to face another failure. My arms were folded, my whole body was shivering, and my teeth were chattering. I gave him my hand and we shuffled away from Portland and my last hope. During our shuffles Davy set the dials on the counter. I didn't look where he was taking me. I didn't care. After our last shuffle, we appeared in the trees behind Rose's boardinghouse—Davy's house as a child. Like a blanket, the humid air wrapped me in its warmth. The heat of a New York summer quickly thawed my frozen fingers and toes.

"What are you doing?" I asked. "What year is this?"

"It's the summer of 1816. I'm four, and my mother just started the boardinghouse. I'm starving, Ellie. Where else are we going to find something to eat?"

"You're going to steal food from your mother?"

"Ellie, it is my house. And I don't think my ma would begrudge her starving son a little food, do you?"

"I suppose not, but—"

"Wait here. I'll be right back." Davy moved to the cellar door but paused with his fingers on the handle. His mother was bound to see him if he didn't hurry. He pulled his hand back and stood up straight. *What is he doing?* I thought. He looked around the yard. Turning, he walked to the back door, knocked, and waited.

When Rose stepped out on the porch looking young and beautiful, Davy stared at her for a moment before stammering something and pointing at a pile of logs. She nodded her agreement to whatever he'd said. As he left to pick up the ax, she shook her head. A smaller version of the Davy I had first met darted around his mother's skirt. He ran on stubby legs, following the newcomer. Rose went back inside and closed the door.

Curiosity drew me out of the trees, and I walked toward the woodpile. Perhaps I shouldn't show my face. I would be here in a couple of years to help bury Rose. Where was Garrick? It wouldn't be wise to let him see us. He would remember.

"Hey, Davy," Davy called to his younger self.

The little boy propped his hands on his hips. "How cum you know my name?"

Davy tapped the side of his head and grinned. "I'm smart."

"What's your name?" little Davy asked.

"Let's see . . . what is my name? I have an idea. You guess, and I'll tell you when you get it right."

"Okay . . . Nathaniel?"

Davy swung the ax while he talked. "Nope."

"Robert?"

"Nope."

"George? Henry? Samuel? John? Joshua?"

Davy gave a quick shake of his head between each name. After "Joshua," he noticed me and paused.

"Who are you?" little Davy asked me.

"I'm his sister, Elizabeth," I said, giving him my middle name.

"Oh, I'm Davy."

I smiled. "It's nice to meet you Davy," I replied.

Little Davy went right back to guessing. "Is it Daniel?"

"No, you got it already. It's Joshua," Davy said. "Don't you have some chores to do? Those chickens are begging for their scratch. Bet the slop bucket needs emptying. On a hot day like today you'll want to get the eggs cooling in the cellar before too long."

"How do you know what my chores are?" little Davy asked.

Davy chuckled. "I told you, I'm smart. I know all sorts of things. Now, you best get chasin' down those eggs and mind yer ma." The little boy walked dejectedly toward the chicken coop.

I looked from one Davy to the other. "That was interesting. I can honestly say I've never seen anyone talking to himself like that before. What made you decide to go to the door?"

"I thought about what you said. If my ma knew it was me, she wouldn't care that I took the food, but she wouldn't know. She might feel like she'd been robbed. It wouldn't be right. I offered to split wood in exchange for some food. She agreed. Garrick must not be here yet. For as long as I can remember, he split her wood. I don't remember much of anything before he came, so I won't remember this."

I stooped and filled my arms with wood, then stacked while Davy split. The mindless work left a lot of time for thinking. Chase was in every memory passing through my conscience. He would be here next year, angry I'd left for Boston. He would be trying to run away from his pain. Maybe that's what I needed—to run away. But I saw no escape for me. My pain was entrenched so deep within my soul I feared I'd never outrun it.

Davy's dark hair dripped with sweat by the time we finished. Rose brought us each a sandwich and handed Davy a knapsack. She smiled. "Thank you. I was fretting over how I'd get that pile of wood split. I lost my husband after the War of 1812, and splitting wood is not a chore I fancy."

Davy and I were both savoring our sandwiches as she talked. "You shouldn't have to worry about it too much longer," he said.

"Why do you say that?" Rose asked.

I looked at Davy, wondering what he was thinking, saying something like that. Looking flustered, he mumbled, "Um . . . a feeling, I suppose. Maybe one of your boarders will help out."

Rose smiled. "Perhaps. But I can't get over how much you look like my late husband. You aren't by chance related to any of the Adams family from up in Portsmouth, are you?"

Davy stared at his mother for a moment, then shook his head as he started backing away. "No, I'm from . . . Virginia. Thank you for the food, ma'am. We best be movin' on."

"Thank you again, and good luck to you both," she called.

Davy tipped his hat toward her, then took my hand and started toward the trees. I leaned into his shoulder and pushed him the other direction. "The road—your ma's watching. She'll find it a bit odd if we wander off into the forest and disappear," I whispered.

He turned. "Right."

We were well on our way out of town before either of us spoke. Davy smiled sadly.

"It was hard seeing my ma, since I know what the future holds for her."

TWELVE
Vandalia

For days we wandered. Lost in my sadness, I mindlessly followed Davy. Each day he found odd jobs in trade for food. We bathed and washed our clothes in rivers, and spent our nights camped under the stars.

One morning, he woke in a foul mood. "I can't have you living like this," he said, pointing to the bed of pine needles we'd slept on. "We have nothing. We're like a couple of vagabonds. I need steady work. We need a place we can put down some roots—try to get ahead."

"I'm sorry—you shouldn't have to care for me. I can go home. I don't know why I didn't think of it before. Take me to Boston, in 1864. Things would be much easier for you then."

Davy paced back and forth, running his fingers through his hair. "Until Legard found you! No, that's not what I'm saying, Ellie. I have no intention of leaving you anywhere, but I do have a mind to settle down someplace where we have work and a roof over our heads. I'd like to at least have a gun and a couple of bedrolls to my name."

I picked a stray leaf out of my hair. "I'll allow that would be nice. But should you change your mind and want to be on your own, I would understand."

"I won't," Davy said softly.

Truly, I had no desire to return to my Boston home. That place held nothing but bittersweet memories—Chase sneaking in to chop wood for Mary and me, or dancing with him at the New Year's Eve ball. They had been sweet memories until I lost him. Now, the thought of being there again, and the realization I'd have to explain his absence should I return without him, left me feeling bitter.

Davy and I spent the next two days in search of a place for him to put down roots. We tried cities and settlements all across the eastern half of the United States. He mustn't have wanted to get too far away from the time he grew up in, because we didn't leave the 1830s. After working on the docks for a day in New York Harbor, he adamantly declared city life wasn't for him.

We were in the spring of 1831 when we happened upon a frontier settlement. A flurry of construction was underway in the small community. The people we met walking through town were friendly.

"Wait here," Davy said. He crossed the street and introduced himself to a group of men loading a wagon. I watched the interaction and couldn't help smiling when he came back grinning. "Welcome to Vandalia, Illinois, the state capital," he said. "I may have found work. They said the blacksmith, Matthew Sweeny, might need a hand. And there's a whole slew of settlers clearing farmland outside of town. Some of 'em have cash money to hire help. First, though, we should find Gibsons' Mercantile. Rumor has it they're in need of some help as well. Mrs. Gibson gave birth to twins a month ago. One of the men I talked with is married to her sister. He said Mrs. Gibson isn't recovering too well and that Mr. Gibson's looking to hire someone to help her. They might trade us room and board. Do you want to do that?"

I couldn't help but smile at the thought of tiny twins. "Of course."

Gibsons' Mercantile wasn't hard to find. The large two-story frame building sat in the center of town. The store clerk, who I assumed was Mr. Gibson, was busy with a customer when we walked in. Davy must have grown impatient because he wandered off to browse the shelves, admiring the new tools, instead of waiting with me.

"Can I help you, miss?" a gentle voice asked.

I turned and met the clerk's gaze. Of medium build and not much taller than me, the studious-looking man seemed tired and overworked.

"Good morning, sir. Are you Mr. Gibson?"

He slid his glasses back into place on his nose. "I am. What can I do for you?"

"I'm Ellie, and that's my brother, Davy. We heard you might be looking for help. We're orphans and need a place to stay. I could help your wife, or work in the store, in exchange for room and board, if you're willing."

He looked me over as he scratched his chin. "I'll have to talk with the missus, but we do have an extra room. I haven't seen you around town before."

"We're new. My brother is apprenticing to be a blacksmith. He's hoping to find work as well."

Davy returned to my side, and Mr. Gibson put out his hand. "You must be Davy. Your sister told me a little about your circumstances. I'm Lyman Gibson."

They shook hands. "That's right. Davy Adams. It's nice to meet you, sir."

"I'd wager old Matt Sweeny could use an extra pair of hands at his shop. Seems he's always complaining about too much work."

Davy smiled. "That's what I'm hoping, sir."

We followed Mr. Gibson through the door at the back of the store. Mrs. Gibson sat sipping tea at the table, looking as if she hadn't slept in weeks. The kitchen and dining area was on the main level, behind the store. There were stairs, most likely leading to bedrooms on the second story.

Mr. Gibson had customers waiting, so after the briefest of introductions, he left the decision to his wife and returned to his business.

She sighed. "We've only got one extra room. If you don't mind sharing, or if one of you doesn't mind sharing a room with the twins, it would be wonderful to have some help around here. I can't seem to get on top of the chores."

"I'll sleep with the twins," I said. "If they don't need feeding, I can tend to them in the night, so you can get your rest."

Mrs. Gibson smiled and let out another sigh. Already the haggard look on her face softened with relief. "Thank you, dear. I love those babies all to pieces, but they plumb tucker me out."

I glanced at Davy, knowing he'd be anxious to get doing something. He didn't seem the type to sit around a kitchen and talk with the womenfolk. "I'll be fine here," I said. "I know you're wanting to see the blacksmith."

Davy looked me in the eyes and then nodded to Mrs. Gibson. "Thank you, ma'am. We're much obliged. I'll be back in a bit."

"Bye, Davy," I said. "Now, Mrs. Gibson what should I do first?"

"Please, dear, call me Carol."

I smiled. "All right, Carol it is—" The sound of a tiny cry came down the stairs.

She chuckled. "See what I mean? No sooner do I start something than one of them beckons."

"I can clean up in here for you." There was a pile of dirty dishes, and the floor begged for a good sweeping.

Carol leaned on the table as she got to her feet. "Thank you, Ellie. Whatever you see that needs doing, I'd be much obliged."

Lyman and Carol Gibson proved to be the most delightful people. After a week, I had their home ticking like a clock. Over the following months, Carol's strength slowly returned. The twins were a joy, and when I held Edgar and Emma, I couldn't help but think of Rose and Garrick's twins. It saddened me to think of Rose and the two little babies she never got to hold—the babies Garrick never got to see. What a miracle the Gibsons' babies were.

Matt Sweeny hired Davy to work Wednesdays and Saturdays at his blacksmith shop. The other days of the week, Davy cleared timber for anyone willing to pay him. On the rare days he didn't have other work, Mr. Gibson sent him on deliveries or had him stocking shelves. Davy was a hard worker and generally always happy. He never rested or took a day off, and it puzzled me that he didn't seem to be mourning the loss of his father like I mourned Chase.

"Davy," I said to him one day, "you always seem so cheerful. Don't you miss your pa?"

"Every day," he said, stopping to look at me. "But spending energy missing him won't bring him back. Before he left he made me promise that whatever happened, I'd keep on living. I gave him my word, and I intend to keep it. Life's too short, Ellie. Look at my ma— she died before I was seven. I understand you're having a mighty hard time about losing your beau, but I hope eventually you'll come to accept it. I reckon it's what Chase would have wanted for you."

I stared back at Davy, tears threatening to burst forth at the mention of Chase. Unable to answer, I dipped my head and turned back to the bread I was kneading.

We had come to live at the Gibsons' home on March 20, 1831. The comfort of my surroundings and the constant companionship of Carol and her twins masked the pain of losing Chase. I tried not to think of him and found the most happiness when I focused on the present. The past held too many painful memories, and the future looked bleak and lonely.

In late August, a heavy thunderstorm rumbled into town. It dumped rain for two days straight, turning the roads into a muddy, sloppy mess. Rivulets of water ran through the ruts left by the wagon wheels. There was no work for Davy that day, and he paced the house like a caged bear. Finally, he retreated to his room. As I walked by after getting a change of clothes for Emma, he called to me. "Ellie, I want to show you something."

I went into his room and sat on the bed across from him. "What is it?" I asked, holding the baby against my hip.

Davy lifted an old tin can and poured a pile of bills and coins onto the quilt.

"That's a lot." I touched the crinkled bills and fingered the heavy pile of gold and silver coins. "What are you going to do with it all?"

"Eventually, I'll have enough to start my own blacksmith shop. But there's a fall social at the church in three weeks, and I thought you might like a new dress."

I smiled back at him, taken completely by surprise. "How did you know?" Carol had passed on a few of her old things to me, but my wardrobe was pitiful.

Davy smiled. "Just a feeling. But I did catch you admiring the new bolt of fabric Mr. Gibson put out last week. Take what you want of the money."

I hesitated. "Are you sure?"

"Of course. You earned it too. If you weren't working for our room and board, more than half of this would already be spent."

"Thank you." I took a few coins, and Davy scooped the rest of the money into his tin can, which he hid behind the bed.

"If you want more, let me know."

I dropped the coins in my apron pocket and smiled. "I'm certain this will be enough. I'd better get Emma down to Carol and go buy my fabric."

As it turned out, Mr. Gibson wouldn't take even a penny for the fabric, and he even threw in some lace to go with it. Carol, an accomplished seamstress, bubbled with excitement over the new dress. She may have been even more excited than I was. We finished the dress within the week and it hung in my room, awaiting the fall social. I took it upon myself to sew a new shirt for Davy, since his were most definitely not fit for an event like that.

On the afternoon of the social, I set the new shirt on Davy's bed. Mr. Sweeny had asked him to work that day. With the harvest, many tools had come into the shop needing repairs, and the blacksmith had fallen behind. I waited by the window, bouncing Edgar on my hip. It was nearly time to go when Davy came running down the street. He went straight to the barn and hitched the horses to the buggy. Lyman Gibson didn't care for horses, or animals in general.

Since Davy and I loved them, we had taken over all aspects of their care, much to Mr. Gibson's delight.

Once Davy completed the hitching, he darted through the kitchen and took the stairs two at a time. "Sorry I'm late. I'll get cleaned up and we'll go."

"Don't worry, we're not in a hurry," Carol called after him. She turned to me. "That boy gets more done in a day than anyone I know."

Lyman glanced up from his newspaper. "Carol, he's hardly a boy anymore."

"I suppose you're right," she said. They were both chuckling when Davy bounded down the stairs.

Our eyes met. "Is this for me?" he asked with a grin as he buttoned the new shirt.

I walked toward him. "Do you like it?"

His attention caught on my new dress, and his gaze ran up and down me. I smiled at the obvious pleasure I saw in his expression when he stammered, "Yes, yes . . . thank you. I do like it. Not as much as I like your dress, though. It looks mighty fine."

"Why, thank you."

Mr. Gibson was gathering up the babies' things, but I caught Carol watching our interaction intently. Embarrassed, I turned away to fuss over baby Edgar.

Davy drove the buggy across town. He pulled the horses to a stop, set the brake, and secured the reins. After he leapt down, he extended his arms to take Edgar from me. "Hey, little man," he said, tickling the baby as he held him. Edgar rewarded him with a slobbery giggle. Davy offered me his hand as I stepped down.

"I can take him," I said.

Edgar tugged on Davy's ear. "That's all right. I've got him. He's sure getting big," Davy said. I slipped my hand under his arm when he offered it, and we walked in together.

The social was a family affair, so when it came time for the dancing, there were dancers of all ages and skills. Davy and I played with Edgar and Emma while Carol and Lyman took a turn around the floor. A few songs later, Carol breathlessly reached for Emma and said, "Why don't you two take our place? Lyman and I need a rest."

We handed over the babies, and Davy whisked me onto the dance floor. It had been so many months since I'd done anything pleasurable that I quite lost myself in the enjoyment of dancing. It wasn't until one of Davy's friends asked to cut in that I thought about what we were doing.

Davy had accumulated a number of friends, and people of all ages were naturally drawn to his likable personality. This particular friend, Peter, was the son of one of the founders of Vandalia. His family owned a well-established and prosperous farm. Peter had hired out as a team with Davy on several occasions. According to Davy, he was saving money to buy his own homestead.

Peter slapped Davy on the back and began to step in. "Mind if I take a turn around the dance floor with your sister?"

Davy was slow to relinquish his hold. I wiggled my hand free and moved into Peter's arms. I smiled at my so-called brother. "You should ask Sylvia Hansen to dance—she's had her eye on you all evening."

I danced my way through several eligible bachelors, listening halfheartedly to their conversation, nodding in agreement or saying "Uh-huh" or "That's interesting" in the appropriate places. But for the most part Davy held my attention. He sat watching me with his arms folded and a scowl on his face. *What has him in a pucker? He should be dancing.* There were plenty of darling girls who would have been swooning for his affections, not to mention he hadn't taken my hint about Sylvia.

I knew Sylvia had set her cap for him because she'd told me so the last time she visited the store. When Mr. Gibson took his lunch with Carol each day, I minded the shop counter for him. Gradually, I'd met most of the townsfolk. Sylvia came in each week for her mother, and she usually came back to the kitchen to talk if I wasn't out front. Other than Carol and Davy, she was the closest friend I had in Vandalia.

At the end of a song, I pled fatigue and left the dance floor to approach Davy. "Why aren't you dancing?" I asked. "Everyone's going to think you a poor excuse for a gentleman, sulking over here like this. I meant it when I suggested you dance with Sylvia. She's very nice, and I think you'd like her. I'll have you know you'll not be served breakfast in the morning if you don't dance with her."

Without a word, Davy crossed the hall and invited Sylvia to dance. She lit up like one of those twenty-first-century light bulbs when he took her in his arms. He danced two songs with her and then returned to where I sat visiting with Carol and Lyman and a group of their friends. "Are you happy now?" he whispered in my ear.

I smiled at him. "Yes, quite."

Davy sat next to Lyman, who turned to him and said, "I have a business proposition for you. There's a load of freight that needs to be fetched from the dock in St. Louis in ten days. My usual hauler is behind schedule and can't deliver it for at least another three weeks. That's too late. I need those dry goods. I'll pay you regular teamster's wages to drive my wagon down there and get my load from the warehouse. You'll need someone to ride shotgun for you, though—maybe Peter or Jared. What say you?"

I didn't miss the worried glance Davy sent in my direction. He would fret over Legard showing up while he was gone—I knew it. But I also knew he would enjoy going. "You should do it, Davy," I said. "You know you'd love the trip."

"Yes, I would," he replied with some hesitation. "When would you want us to leave, Mr. Gibson?"

"Wednesday."

Davy glanced down at his hands before raising his eyes. "I'll do it."

I was gathering the laundry Wednesday morning when the click of his boots coming down the hall caught my attention. "Ellie," he said as he walked into the twins' room. "When Peter gets here I'll be leaving. You'll be careful while I'm gone?"

I looked at Davy. "Of course."

"If you see any sign of Legard, you hide from him, all right?"

"Of course. You be careful as well. I reckon you'll have more to worry about on the road than just Legard."

"I know." Davy wrapped one arm around my shoulder and lightly kissed my forehead. "If all goes well, we'll return in two weeks."

I adjusted the collar on his coat. "Goodbye, Davy."

Holding Mr. Gibson's rifle loosely in his left hand, he looked me in the eyes and said softly, "You take care, Ellie."

THIRTEEN
Courting

Davy had been gone three days before Carol spoke to me about him. We'd been cleaning shelves in the store when William Smith, one of the eligible bachelors I'd danced with at the social, invited me to take a ride with him in his new phaeton on Sunday afternoon. I politely refused, since he didn't remotely interest me.

Once the store emptied a few minutes later, Carol straightened herself up. "Ellie, what are you doing with yourself? A girl your age should be keeping company with half a dozen suitors, and here you turned down Mr. Smith's offer without a second thought. You've slighted every young man in town since the day you got here."

"He's at least twenty-five. That's a might too old for me," I complained. "And I don't like any of the boys in town—not in a courting sort of way."

"Nonsense. My Lyman is five years older than me. But tell me then, what *are* you doing with Davy?"

I froze. "What do you mean? He's my brother."

"If he's your brother, then I'm your mother," Carol said. "You may have the town fooled, but I have three brothers, and you can't pull the wool over my eyes. I've seen the way he looks at you, especially when he doesn't think anyone's watching. That boy's smitten, but you're so preoccupied you never notice him. Why is that? He's certainly handsome enough. I'll bet every girl in town wishes he'd come calling."

Carol had her hands on her hips and her eyes on me. I had lived in avoidance for months. After I cried myself to sleep each night, I shoved my feelings under my pillow and left them there until the next night. But here Carol was, forcing me to face them. I shrugged my shoulders and looked away. "I don't know—"

"What's got you worried, dear? You can tell me."

I paused for a long while. Carol didn't push, but she waited while I pondered what to say. How could I best tell this wonderful woman, who'd become my dearest friend, the painful circumstances I found myself in, without divulging too much information?

I remembered Eliza Benson, a girl at my school in Boston who was three years my senior. In her final year of schooling she became engaged to a navigator, Nathaniel Thomas, who worked on a merchant ship. Before he left on his second voyage, they planned their marriage for the following spring. However, his ship was lost at sea.

I'd thought of Nathaniel many times since Chase's disappearance. Their circumstances, although completely different, left both Eliza and me in a similar state. We didn't know the fate of the men we loved. If they were dead, there was no closure—no funeral, no memorial—nothing. But they could be alive. Perhaps Nathaniel's ship had run aground somewhere and he was stranded, unable to return to Eliza, but still very much alive. Perhaps my Chase still lived, but was held captive by Lord Arbon.

I braced myself for the confession and met Carol's gaze. "You're right. Davy isn't my brother, but a close friend. I recently lost someone very dear to me, someone I hoped to marry." I paused, organizing my thoughts—I would use Eliza's story.

Carol asked, "What was his name?"

"Joseph Chase Harper, but everyone called him Chase," I said quietly. "He was the navigator for a ship, but the ship didn't return from its last voyage. Everyone on board has been presumed dead, but my heart doesn't want to believe it is so. Davy's pa was Chase's older brother. He was on the ship as well."

"Did the two of you run away?"

"No. We are orphans. Davy's ma died in childbirth when he was six. She was expecting twins, but there were complications. My mother died in my infancy, and my father passed away when I was eight. My grandfather raised me, but now he is gone as well. Davy is convinced his pa and my Chase are gone. He thinks the time in which they could have returned has passed, but I'm not so sure."

Carol crossed the room and wrapped me in a hug. "Ellie, I'm sorry. No wonder you've seemed sad. You should have told me sooner."

That brooked no argument from me. I had been feeling guilty about keeping so many secrets. "Yes, I suppose. But what do I do now? I have no interest in courting anyone."

Before Carol could say anything, a woman and her three small children entered the store. Carol moved away from me to greet the customer. She took care of the woman's order, and once we were alone again, Carol took a deep breath and answered me.

"It's fine to grieve. A broken heart takes time to heal. But I promise you eventually it will heal. There may be a scar, but you can learn to love again. Even the bitterest disappointments soften with time. You needn't begin courting right away, but don't wait too long. Life is too precious to waste even a day of it. I've heard of people pining away their entire lives over lost loved ones. And it's foolish when there are so many other people in this world who need our love. I know Davy is a patient man, but you can't expect him to wait forever. If you looked for a hundred years, I don't know that you'd ever find a more likely prospect for a husband. I can tell he's biding his time, waiting for even the slightest encouragement from you. If you've any interest at all, you shouldn't make him wait too long."

Even though my heart still hung onto a fragile hope that Chase lived, Carol's words rang true.

Nearly three weeks later, Davy and Peter returned from St. Louis with the freight. The weather had turned cold and rainy, making their trip longer than originally expected. I felt immense relief to see the mud-splattered wagon pull up in front of the store. While Davy and Peter unloaded the cargo, Carol, Mr. Gibson, and I began restocking the shelves.

Peter added a crate to the pile Carol and I were unpacking. "Afternoon, Miss Ellie," he said.

I smiled. "Good afternoon to you. I trust you had a safe trip."

"Thank you, we did." He tipped his rain-covered hat in my direction before retracing his steps to the wagon. Carol pried open the crate filled with fabric and carried three bolts to the front of the store.

Davy pushed through the door and stooped to set down his load. "Ellie, how are you? Was there any trouble?"

I reached over and touched his wet hand. "There was no trouble. And I'm well, thank you."

"I need to talk to you tonight, all right?"

"Certainly. I'm glad you're home."

Davy spun on his heel and marched out the door when we heard Peter coming in. *What was that all about?* Peter eyed me as he lowered his load. I didn't want to get drawn into a conversation with him, not when I was worrying over what Davy needed to tell me. I turned quickly. "What do you need next, Carol?" I called.

Peter hesitated only a moment before leaving to fetch another load. I kept myself busy while they finished unloading, and after Mr. Gibson paid Peter, he left.

Davy drove the team around back to unhitch and put the wagon away. He looked wet and chilled, and his hand had been ice cold when I'd touched it. He would no doubt appreciate a hot bath, so I set to work warming water while he took care of the team. If he knew about showers, he would have been dreaming of one of those. There were moments when I longed for the conveniences of modern life. I had been spoiled living with Chase. *It was simply too good to be true,* I told myself.

The rain drummed against the windowpane by the time Davy stepped through the door. The twins were napping, and Carol and her husband were still busy unpacking the freight. I had given her advice considerable thought, and when Davy stepped into the kitchen I saw him in a different light. The past six months in Vandalia had matured him. He was no longer Garrick's little boy.

With care, he leaned the rifle against the wall, then let his bedroll and pack slide off his shoulder onto the floor. He hung his oilskin coat on the hook, followed by his dripping hat. I stood quietly by the fireplace, watching as he ran his fingers through his sweaty hair, leaving it a tousled mess. I smiled. He braced himself against the doorframe and stepped on the heel of his left boot with the toe of his right one. Slowly, he worked his foot free. When both muddy boots were off he turned. "How long have you been there?" he asked.

I chuckled. "The whole time."

"I didn't notice. I should get cleaned up," he muttered.

I slid a chair out from the table. "I'm warming water for a bath. Come sit by the fire. You look cold."

Davy took the chair from me, fetched another, and set them in front of the hearth. "Sit with me."

I sat in the chair he offered. He picked up another log and added it to the flames before sitting down and stretching his hands and feet toward the blaze.

"The trip went well, I presume?" I asked.

"Coming back was slow and hard because of the mud, but no other problems. The horses did well, and the steamboat docked on schedule. Peter and I enjoyed our association together on the road. We make a fine team."

"That's good. Can I get you something to eat?"

"Maybe some bread and butter—whatever we have in here. I don't want you to go to the cellar in this downpour."

I smiled. *So thoughtful . . . and courteous.*

The water came to a boil while I buttered two pieces of bread. Davy dumped the heavy kettle into the tub and refilled it. Carol was right. I could look for a hundred years and never find a man as kind and devoted as Davy. I handed the bread to him on a plate.

"Thank you, Ellie."

While Davy chewed, I contemplated him. Finally, I asked, "What did you need to talk to me about? Is something amiss?"

He sat quietly for a while before answering. "Peter asked me for something that I don't think I can give him."

"Well, don't give it to him then," I said, imagining Peter asking Davy for some of his hard-earned money. "What could he possibly want from you anyway?"

Davy chewed the bread, staring into the crackling flames. "You."

"What? Well, he can't have me. No one can have me. I'm my own person."

Davy glanced at me, a slight smile turning up the corners of his mouth. "Believe me, I know." He finished his bread and set his plate on the table.

My curiosity had me hanging on his every word. "What exactly did you two talk about?"

He leaned back and rested his hands on his stomach. "It seems Peter has designs to win your heart. After we made camp last night, he asked for my blessing to start courtin' you once we got back to town. I'll allow that made me right huffy, so I didn't say anything at first. While I was thinking on it, the hobbles came loose on Bud. He turned tail and trotted away. The rest of the team went into a conniption fit with Bud on the run, so Peter and I flew out of our bedrolls, pulled on our boots, and gave chase. We had to catch that horse 'fore he got all the way to Vandalia without the freight and us. After that, Peter didn't bring it up again. Neither did I, because I didn't know what I'd say to him."

Davy dumped the next kettle and started to put up the partition that separated the tub from the rest of the kitchen.

Maybe that's what Peter was working himself up to ask me this afternoon. "Davy, I'm not ready to court anyone right now. I told Carol about Chase and your pa. The story I used was that they were both on a ship that became lost at sea, with everyone presumed dead. Could you please tell Peter I haven't recovered from that loss sufficiently to begin courting someone else?"

"I'll tell him." Davy looked at me intently. "When you are fully recovered, is he the type of fellow you would court?"

"Not really," I answered truthfully. "I'll have to hope he finds someone else before then."

Davy smiled. "Or you could always find someone else," he said, then disappeared behind the partition.

FOURTEEN
The Lake

Because Mr. Gibson was so pleased with Davy's hauling job, he used him exclusively from then on. Davy was careful and meticulous. He covered every crate and box with oilskin tarps and firmly secured them so the contents wouldn't break. Merchants in the neighboring towns began hiring him to run their freight as well. Davy split the earnings with Mr. Gibson, who owned the wagon and team, and Peter frequently rode shotgun with him. One day, I asked Davy if Peter had inquired about me again. To my surprise he said, "Only every time."

In December, Davy returned from St. Louis with Christmas presents for both of us. He showed off his new rifle and powder horn before offering me a package wrapped in brown paper. Inside was a dark blue woolen coat trimmed in white fur. A pang of sadness touched my heart as I remembered the last Christmas present I'd received— also a coat, but from Chase.

The town was abuzz with talk of the treacherous winter Vandalia had endured the year before. Folks feared a repeat of last year, with three feet of snowpack, and drifts as high as six feet. When the first snowfall blanketed the town, everyone who visited the store had his or her own version of the ordeal to tell.

The previous Christmas, snow had begun falling, accumulating over three feet in a few hours. Then came the freezing rain, covering everything with a thick crust of ice, and that was followed by more snow. Some people claimed that for weeks the mercury in their thermometers each morning never rose above twelve degrees below zero. The thick ice could not bear the weight of the deer, so the animals fell through, making them easy prey for the wolves that were light enough to stay on top of the snowpack.

Another teamster passing through town claimed the last of the buffalo east of the Mississippi had been killed off by last year's storm—"Winter of the Deep Snow," as it was called. He said in all his travels he hadn't seen a single buffalo since. Men shuddered as they recalled battling the snow and ice to fetch firewood from the forest. Thankfully, Davy and I hadn't been in Vandalia for that.

When he wasn't hauling freight, he was hunting with Peter in the woods outside of town. Davy kept the Gibsons' table well stocked with wild turkey and venison. During the first week of 1832 the twins learned to walk, and they got into everything. Carol and I were constantly chasing them down. To celebrate Edgar and Emma's first birthday in February, we made a cake and had a party.

I'd turned down a few other suitors over the winter months, and luckily Davy kept Peter at bay for me. Through it all, I found myself increasingly fond of Davy. Certainly Carol had told Lyman that we weren't siblings, but they both seemed agreeable to continue with the present living arrangement and never commented on it.

For Davy and me, finding the Gibsons was a miracle, considering our circumstances when we came to Vandalia. Occasionally, I worried about being an inconvenience or a burden. But truthfully, I didn't see how we could be. If Davy was in town he did the wood splitting, the repairs, and the upkeep of the animals. When he traveled, I took care of the animals, which wasn't very difficult since the four horses were always with Davy. Plus, I was available to tend the children or mind the store for the Gibsons at any time, so it seemed to be a mutually beneficial arrangement. Not to mention, Mr. Gibson's wagon and team were earning him money, and he didn't have to lift a finger for it.

The weather had been warm for the last week of March, and a breeze fanned the curtain over the open window as I sat on the bed on day, dressing Emma. A knock sounded on the open door and Davy said, "Ellie, come take a drive with me. I want to show you something." He stood with his broad shoulders nearly filling the doorway of the room I shared with the twins.

He had just returned from two back-to-back trips. I laughed. "Aren't you tired of driving yet?"

He slipped his hands in his pockets and smiled. "This is different—I'll be with you. So? Can I hitch up the buggy?"

What has him so excited? I feared there'd be no hearing the end of it if I didn't go. "I should check with Carol. She might need—"

Davy quickly cut me off. "Already done. I spoke with her a moment ago. She said you needed to get out of the house and it would do you good to get some fresh air."

I smiled. "Well, in that case, yes."

We went downstairs, where I handed Emma to Carol. Davy made a beeline for the barn. Before I could get a word out, Carol said, "There's a picnic basket for the two of you on the table, and a couple of blankets. The grass will still be damp this time of year."

"Carol, was this your idea?" I asked.

She smiled. "No, dear, but I did think it was a good idea. Now, you go enjoy yourself. It's such a lovely day."

"Thank you," I said, fetching the picnic basket.

When I'd crossed the yard to where Davy was, he took the basket and blankets from me and stowed them in the buggy. I studied his every move as he maneuvered the span of horses into position. He had a soft, calming touch, and the animals stood patiently while he threaded the traces. He had inherited Rose's soft, dark brown eyes and her wavy black hair. His naturally olive complexion already sported a tan from spending so much time out of doors. The past year, filled with hard work and plentiful food, had been good for him. He seemed taller to me, but still not as tall as Chase.

Why did I think that? Can't I enjoy one day without Chase haunting my every thought? Will I forever be tormented by what may have been? I shook my head, vowing to enjoy the picnic and keep my memories in the past where they belonged.

Davy finished with the horses and offered me his hand. I took it and stepped into the buggy. He hopped up beside me and took the reins. "Hah," he called. Both horses moved forward in unison at the sound of his voice. They trotted through town before Davy turned them to the northwest. "Did you notice the capitol building?" he said. "After the first capitol burned down in 1823, they built that one. But they were in such a hurry to build it that they did a poor job. Peter's father says there have been widespread complaints about the safety of the building. There's even talk of tearing it down and building a new one."

I looked at Davy's profile. "Hmm . . . that's interesting. Where is it that you're taking me?"

He grinned back at me. "You'll see. It's a surprise. Peter also told me the original capital of Illinois was Kaskaskia, on the Mississippi River. But when the town kept flooding they sent someone to find a new place to build their state capital. Vandalia was settled with the sole purpose of being Illinois' state capital."

A mischievous thought popped into my head. "Davy, did you know that Vandalia won't always be the capital of Illinois?"

"What do you mean it won't be the capital?"

I knew Davy was fond of Vandalia. He had a bounty of friends here, and I realized he could easily have made it his permanent home. "Well, I don't remember what year it happens, but eventually the capital is moved to Springfield."

Davy shook his head. "What other tidbits of information do you having hiding in that pretty head of yours?"

"All kinds." I impulsively wrapped my arm around his and leaned in toward his shoulder. "What could I tell you about? Let's see, the biggest piece of news for our century is the Civil War. In about thirty years the Northern states will take up arms against the

Southern states over the issue of slavery. The president at the time of the war, Abraham Lincoln, who by the way is from Illinois, will be murdered while in office. I didn't see that in my lifetime, but I read about it."

Davy looked over at me with raised eyebrows. "You're not making that up, are you? Our country will actually fight a war against itself—a real war?"

"Oh, yes," I said. "The Union army, representing the northern states, will fight to preserve the union of the states and abolish slavery. The Confederate army, for the Southern states, will fight to leave the Union so they can maintain the right to own slaves. Believe me, it's a real war. Men I knew enlisted and never returned, while others came home crippled from their injuries. But the war eventually ends and our country is better for it."

"I'll be an old man by the time that war starts."

"Not necessarily. You could live anywhere, anytime you wanted. Just think, I'll still be eighteen when the war starts."

Davy's brow furrowed. "Hmm."

We traveled a dirt road through the woods. He stopped once to point out a deer and her spotted fawn, while the birds serenaded us from the treetops. "Ellie, when we sat in Oregon all day, I saw some peculiar contraptions. Tell me your favorite thing from the modern world, as you called it."

"Other than the food, which was more plentiful than I've ever seen and tasted simply divine, I don't think I could narrow it down to one favorite. Why, there are more high-falutin' inventions than you could count. The toilets were amazing—everything you could imagine needing from a privy, but it's all inside and there's no smell. You flush them, and water washes everything away. I'll warrant the showers were heavenly—oodles of hot water pouring down on you like hot rain. The cars and the roads make traveling so fast. Davy, you can't even imagine how quickly a body can drive from state to state. Oh, and there are phones—only a little bigger than the counter—and you can talk to anyone else who has one. You push the numbers for their phone and it calls them. Your voice goes to their phone and their voice comes to yours. I don't know how that works, but miraculously it does. And if you don't want to talk, you can text. That's when you type letters of the alphabet on your phone, and after you touch the "Send" button, those words appear on the other person's phone so they can read them. Imagine Morse code and the telegraph system, but so much easier and available to everyone."

"What are Morse code and the telegraph system?"

Davy's blank expression nearly made me laugh. "Oh, I suppose they haven't been invented yet either, but I'm certain you'll hear of them soon."

We traveled about four miles before coming to a beautiful lake. The crystal-clear water reflected the surrounding trees and the puffy clouds. "Oh, Davy, this is lovely."

He smiled as he set the brake on the buggy. "Welcome to Lake Vandalia."

He unhitched and hobbled the horses, then turned them loose to graze on the spring grass, while I spread out the blankets. Davy stretched his hand behind his head and lay down.

"I'll have to mark this day on my calendar," I said.

"Why's that?"

"This is most certainly the first time I've seen you take leisure for yourself."

Davy just laughed and patted the blanket next to him. "Come look at the sky."

I laid my head on his outstretched arm. Fluffy clouds decorated the brilliant blue above us. I sighed. "It's beautiful here. How did you find this place?"

"Peter and I hunt here. Game is plentiful, and it's close to town. Watch the clouds. See how fast they're moving."

I turned my eyes heavenward. The clouds rolled across the sky at a steady pace, yet it was calm here, with the trees as a windbreak. "It's been a while since I've enjoyed nature. I've missed it. For a long time I didn't dare leave the safety of the house for fear of seeing Legard."

"Yes, I'd noticed," Davy said. "Peter asked about courting you again."

I didn't say anything as Davy rolled onto his side and propped himself up on his elbow. Gazing into my face, he asked, "Are you ready to start courting him?"

I breathed out my answer. "No." Was Davy thinking what I thought he was? Was I ready to start a new life? Could I finally bury the past? I saw the questions burning in his eyes.

"What about someone else? Are you ready to start courting if it's the right man?"

"Perhaps," I said quietly, "but who would this man be?"

He lifted his rough, calloused hand and gently traced the outline of my cheek. "Might be someone you've known a long time. Someone who's loved you since he was a little boy." He paused, sending my heart racing.

Is this right? I agonized. *Oh, Chase, where are you?* Instantly, my eyes brimmed with tears. I held perfectly still, not wanting them to escape and trickle down my cheek—not wanting them to betray my inner feelings. *Why am I caught in this predicament? Do I move ahead? Keep waiting? I could be everything to this good man if I let myself.* I thought about Carol's wise counsel. If I couldn't have Chase, I doubted I'd ever find someone that suited me more than Davy. Certainly, there wasn't a better man. We worked well together, and although we may never be rich, I wouldn't want for anything.

"What would you say if I told you this man was me?" Davy asked boldly.

It wouldn't hurt to court a bit, see how we felt about each other, would it? "Perchance I could start courting."

He smiled the same crooked grin that had endeared me to him when he was a child. "That's good to know." A loud splash on the lake drew our attention. A beaver skimmed the surface, slapping its wide tail. Davy raised his hand and pointed. "Do you see the geese?"

A goose swam along the water's edge, with a string of gray goslings following her. "How sweet," I said. "This picnic was a wonderful idea."

Lake Vandalia teemed with wildlife, and for the next hour Davy and I sat together, enjoying the beauty of nature. Then he set the picnic basket between us and asked, "Should we eat?"

I opened it and handed him a sandwich. "Can I ask you something?"

"Anything."

"I've often wondered why you didn't disappear when Legard and the other Sniffer attacked us. You obviously knew they were coming, because you hid your counter."

Davy looked straight ahead at the lake as if deep in thought. "Pa told me a little about the counter I have—Perception. He said I'd have increased perception because of its magic. He was right. Sometimes I know things before they happen. Other times, I get a sense for what people are thinking or feeling. I felt them coming that day. I knew they would take you, and I didn't want you to face that alone."

"Thank you. I don't think I would have survived the ordeal without you."

Davy smiled at me. "You're welcome. I wouldn't have wanted you to try."

FIFTEEN
Moving

Davy and I courted subtly, since the townsfolk still thought of us as siblings. Eventually, something would have to change. But for now I felt happier than I'd been in a long time. Matt Sweeny, the blacksmith, had come to count on the work Davy did for him on Wednesdays and Saturdays. With all the traveling for his booming freight business, Davy rarely got his regular days in at Sweeny's place and often tried to make up for it between hauls, working at the smithy from dawn till dark.

One afternoon, Emma was down for a nap but little Edgar was as busy as a beaver. I hefted him onto my hip and said, "Carol, you should go rest and I'll take Edgar out for a walk."

She sighed. "Maybe I will. My stomach is a bit unsettled this afternoon." She had felt ill for several days and thought she was expecting again.

I sat with the little boy in my lap and put his shoes on while his mother went upstairs. Davy was working at Sweeny's, and sometimes it felt as if I never saw him.

"Ed, do you want to go see Davy?" He may not have understood me, but his face lit up anyway. He knew he was going outside, and that was all that mattered. I led him through the store. "Mr. Gibson, I'm taking Edgar for a walk. Carol is resting with Emma."

Mr. Gibson ruffled his son's blond hair as we walked by. "Thank you, Ellie."

The walk to the blacksmith's shop was slow going. I held Edgar's hand as his tiny legs marched alongside mine. The weather was consistently warm now, and soon it would be downright hot. The jingle of tack and the creak of wagons filled the street as a steady flow of settlers moved into the area or passed through on their way farther west.

I looked ahead toward the blacksmith's, smiling when I saw Davy. He was bent over, with the hind leg of a large draft horse resting across his thigh. He pulled a nail from between his lips, carefully positioned it in the horseshoe, and then hammered it into the hoof. After twisting off the sharp point with the claw of the hammer, he repeated the process five more times before the shoe was firmly nailed in place. He straightened up, letting the horse's leg slide off his. Turning his head to the side, Davy caught sight of me. He grinned and set his tools down, then crossed the street and scooped up Edgar.

"This is a surprise. What's the occasion?"

"Emma and Carol are sleeping," I explained, "but Edgar wouldn't go down for a nap."

Davy wiped his forehead with a bandana, then offered me his arm. "I'll walk with you. I haven't seen much of you lately."

I smiled. "Well, I'm always here."

"I know. It's my fault and I'm sorry. I was thinking we should go for a drive again. Are you free tomorrow afternoon? I've got a few things to finish for Sweeny in the morning, and then we could watch the sun set across the lake."

"I'd like that."

Davy listened intently while I talked about the twins, Carol possibly expecting another baby, and the latest news that had passed through the store while he'd been gone. I nodded at Edgar. "I think you put him to sleep." His little head rested comfortably on Davy's broad shoulder, and his eyes were closed tight. "I should take him home and try to get him into his bed," I said.

"I'll carry him for you—he's getting heavy."

Davy walked me home and carried Edgar to the kitchen door. When I put my hand out to turn the knob, Davy caught it in his. Surprised, I looked up at him.

"I'm sorry I've been gone so much. I promise I won't haul freight forever. Right now it's good money, and I'm trying to save for a place of my own."

"I understand."

He looked at me intently for a minute, as if he contemplated saying more, but then glanced away and opened the door for me. "I'll see you later tonight," he said quietly.

I slid Edgar onto my shoulder and stood in the doorway watching Davy hurry back to work.

When the sun set across Vandalia Lake Saturday evening, Davy and I watched it from the comfort of Carol's wool blanket. A brilliant blaze of orange gradually softened to a dark pink. It was firefly season, and swarms of the cheerful bugs danced through the sky and between the trees. I'd never seen anything so magical.

"Oh, what a perfect night. This is beautiful," I said.

I glanced at Davy, but he wasn't looking at the trace of sunset or the hordes of dancing fireflies. He was watching me. His stare caught me, and I gazed back at him. His gentle hand touched my cheek, and my heart thumped wildly in my chest. Slowly, he leaned forward. His eyes darted to my mouth before he kissed me. His lips were soft and inviting, not at all demanding. Slowly he drew me in, and I couldn't help but respond. My fingers slid through the hair at the nape of his neck as I returned his kiss. After a moment, I dropped my hand and lowered my gaze. He turned his head and looked at the fireflies.

"Now it's a perfect night," he said. In the fading light, I caught sight of his contented grin. He sighed. "I should get you home so Carol won't worry."

During the days before Davy left for his next run to St. Louis, he couldn't keep his eyes off me. Carol nagged me about it until I finally confessed to kissing him. She squealed like a schoolgirl at the news.

When he left on his next haul with Peter, I counted the days, excited for his return. The team made good time, and they pulled into the yard a day earlier than I expected. Shading my eyes from the sun, I walked out to meet Davy. When no one was looking, he swept me into a big hug and spun around once before setting me back on my feet, then brushed a quick kiss across my lips.

I smiled. "You're back early."

A grin spread across his face as he turned back to the horses. "Yeah, good roads, good weather, and the steamship docked on schedule. A successful trip overall."

"I'm glad you're home safe."

Davy unhitched the team. "Old Smoke's about to throw a shoe. I've got to fix that first thing tomorrow," he muttered.

I helped him hang the tack and feed the horses. When he pulled his pack and gun from the wagon, he had two of each. He slung both packs over his shoulder and carried a rifle in each hand. I recognized the new rifle he'd got for Christmas, but the other one was older. "What are the extra pack and gun for?"

He glanced away, not making eye contact. "Nothing. I just picked up some extra gear while I was in St. Louis. I'm famished. Let's go inside." I followed him to the back door.

"How about a trip to the lake tomorrow," he said, "after I fix Smoke's shoe?"

"Don't those horses need a rest?"

"Probably, but I want to take you to the lake. Pulling a little buggy to the lake and back is nothing compared to the freight wagon. Plus, Bud and Smoke like taking you to the lake when they get to graze on all that lush grass."

I laughed. "Oh, you think so? Did they tell you this? Your perception allows you to speak with animals now?"

Davy laughed. "Perhaps. We do have a lot of time to talk things through out there on the trail."

Smiling, I opened the door for him. I had really missed him this time. "You win. I'll go with you tomorrow."

He took all of his gear upstairs, rather than dumping it by the door like he usually did.

Davy was uncommonly quiet during our drive to the lake. He made small talk but kept his comments brief, and I began to worry that something was wrong. We were walking hand in hand along the lakeshore when he blurted out, "I'm ready to move on."

Shocked, I stopped and pulled my hand from his. "What do you mean 'move on'? Leave Vandalia?"

"Yes, I want to move."

"But why? You love it here. You have so many friends. Your freight business is thriving. Why would you want to leave now?"

He stopped walking and turned to face me. "Because I love you more." He fished something out of his pocket, and before I realized what he was doing he slid a ring on my left hand and dropped to one knee. "I want to marry you, Ellie. I want us to grow old together, and we can't do that here. You said so yourself—you'll still be eighteen when that big war starts. If we stay here I'll be an old man by then. We've been here for over a year, and I've already aged. But you, why you haven't changed a lick. I know I'm not Chase, but if you give me a chance, I'll devote my life to making you happy."

As I lifted my hand, a diamond glistened in the sunlight. I didn't know what to say as I stood in front of him. I had expected this someday, but not yet. Davy stood, smiling as he pulled me into his arms. "You don't need to decide now. After everything you've been through, I expect it'll take some time."

"Thank you, Davy. I do love you, too. I'll consider your proposal and let you know."

When I looked at him, I feared I'd see disappointment in his expression, but it was kind and understanding. Perhaps his perception allowed him to comprehend the difficulty of this decision for me. There are some courses in life that, once set upon, you didn't turn back from. I considered marriage one of those. If I said yes to Davy, I would have to forever lock Chase out of my heart. That would be a daunting task, one I wasn't sure I wanted to undertake. Secretly, I still prayed for a miracle.

Davy kissed me twice before saying, "Thank you, Ellie. That's more than I dared hope for. I half expected you to give me the mitten and say no."

When he stepped back, I looked closely at the ring he'd put on my finger. "Oh," I gasped, thinking it looked familiar but not able to place the memory. "This is beautiful. Where did you get it?"

"It was my mother's. Last year my pa gave it to me. Told me he wanted it to go to the girl I chose to marry."

"Have you carried this around for the last year?"

"Nah. When I was in St. Louis last week, I went back to the cabin in Ohio and got the ring, my old rifle, and my huntin' knife. That's where the extra gear came from. Before I left, I threw a few other things in one of our packs. I wasn't there long."

"You went back without telling me?" I was so accustomed to Chase's thoughtfulness in always checking in before he left. "Perchance Legard had captured you. What would I have thought if Peter came home saying you had disappeared in St. Louis?"

"I didn't want you to worry. But more importantly, I didn't want to accidentally lead Legard back to you. That's why I left from St. Louis."

"I see." Another question burned inside of me. I had to know. "Then you didn't see any sign of Garrick, or Chase?"

Davy shook his head. "I went back two days after the day Archidus left us in the woods. Everything was as it was before."

I sighed, and Davy wrapped his arms around me. "Ellie, I'm sorry things didn't turn out like you hoped."

I raised my eyes to his. "Thank you for your consideration." He had shaved off the twelve days of stubble that had been there yesterday. I touched his smooth cheek and kissed him. "Are you hungry?"

"Always."

We ate our picnic under the leafy canopy surrounding the lake. Davy lay on the blanket while I finished eating. Never once in the past year had he complained about being tired, but he must have been on that day. Within minutes he slept soundly. I propped myself on my elbow and studied him. Absentmindedly, I spun the gold ring around my finger with my thumb. I owed it to him to make a decision.

Davy worked hard. There was no question he would take care of me. Although a little weather beaten of late, he had handsome features. From what I'd seen he was even-tempered and slow to anger. He would make a good husband and a good father. I had only really seen him angry once—in Cleveland, the day he'd heard the rumor that Chase and I were married. Davy had been furious at the thought of Chase leading me on foot across Ohio in the dead of winter. I smiled sadly. Even now I could picture Chase hustling out of the Red House Tavern, looking to see if I was all right. His devilishly handsome grin had sent my heart racing when he'd called me Mrs. Harper. I had so enjoyed the sound of that. How could I forget the hot flush that spread across my face? I had blatantly bared my deepest desire, but it hadn't rattled Chase. If anything, he'd seemed quite pleased with the idea of us being married. But alas, that didn't seem to be my destiny after all.

I gazed at the ring on my left hand. The gold band delicately swirled around a solitary diamond. The ring was a little big for my finger, but I didn't think it was in danger of falling off. Now that I knew where this ring had come from, I chuckled at the thought of Garrick making Chase take him ring shopping in 1968. He had told me the story. Never in my wildest dreams had I expected the same ring to make its way onto my finger.

I hated to wake Davy, so I lowered my head onto the blanket and closed my eyes. The soothing sounds of birds in the trees and our horses grazing around us nearly put me to sleep as well.

Awhile later, Davy stirred. "Did I fall asleep?" he mumbled.

I opened my eyes. "Yes, you did. Perhaps you work too hard, Mr. Adams."

He smiled. "Maybe."

"When you spoke of moving, did you have a particular place in mind?"

"What year did Harper take you from?"

"It was 1863—December of 1863."

"That means we have to go to a year after that. Do you have a preference?"

"I'll give it some thought."

Our drive home from the lake took a bizarre twist at the edge of town. I had my arm wrapped around Davy's and we were laughing when he leaned over and kissed my cheek. Neither of us had noticed Peter riding toward us. When Davy glanced back at the road, he met his friend's gaze. The look on Peter's face went from the shock of betrayal to fury.

Davy's shoulders slumped as the other man spurred his horse into a gallop. "He knows."

I jerked my arm out of his. "I'm sorry."

Davy held the reins in one hand and picked up my hand, replacing it in the crook of his arm. "Don't fret about it, Ellie. This is my fault. I should have told him sooner. Looks like he's headed toward home. I'll ride out to his place."

The mood was somber after that as we drove through the streets of town, back to the Gibsons' Mercantile. I could tell Davy felt bad about deceiving Peter. They had spent a considerable amount of time together and had developed a close friendship. Since Peter wanted to court me, of course he'd be riled at the sight of Davy kissing me.

I took Bud to the corral, and Davy handed me the basket and blanket. "I'll hurry back. I owe Peter an explanation," he said, hefting a saddle for Smoke in one arm. He gave me a quick kiss. I offered him an encouraging smile before turning to walk inside.

I stepped into an empty kitchen and set the basket on the table. Perhaps Carol and the twins were upstairs. A look there showed me only vacant rooms. She must be helping in the store, which would be a difficult task with both children underfoot. I hurried downstairs and opened the door to the store. What I saw left me frozen in fear.

SIXTEEN
Followed

My heart pounded its way into my throat as I stared at the profile of Legard. Mr. Gibson, bless his heart, was telling him Davy and I had left town several days ago. The Sniffer grunted his thanks and turned toward the store's front door.

The knob on the back door felt slick from the sweat on my palms. Silently, I retreated into the kitchen, afraid to close the door tight and reveal my presence.

Davy! He would pass the front of the store on his way to Peter's. I had to stop him from leaving. As I dashed out the door, Davy mounted up and turned Smoke toward the road. Waving, I ran in front of the horse, causing Davy to jerk back on the reins.

"What's the matter?" he asked.

I grabbed Smoke's bridle and turned him around. "He's here. In the store."

Davy flew off the horse and pulled me into the cover of the barn. Peering out the doorway, he said, "Who? What did you see?" I was breathless, more from fear than the short sprint to the barnyard. He grabbed my shoulders. "Tell me."

"Legard was in the store," I said, "talking to Mr. Gibson. He told him we'd left town. I don't know why Mr. Gibson lied for us. Legard was walking to the front door when I ran to find you."

Davy's face paled. "We're leaving now. Wait for me. I'm getting my rifle and pack. It's not safe here anymore."

He darted away, while I leaned against the barn door and closed my eyes. I didn't want to leave, but we couldn't stay. Legard knew we had been here. Poor Carol—what would she think of our sudden disappearance? The sadness of yet another separation nearly made me sick. Little Edgar and Emma. Oh, how I would miss them.

Minutes later, Davy stepped into the barn, a pack and bedroll on his back, and his new rifle in hand. "What about Carol?" I whispered in agony.

"There's no time," he said. "Legard is in the street, in front of the store. Come on. I want to get farther away from here before we disappear. We shouldn't endanger the Gibsons any more than we already have."

Davy and I ran behind our neighbors' yards toward the woods a short distance away. The houses and trees blocked our view of the street, so it was impossible to watch Legard. Once we hid in the trees, Davy spoke again. "Hold onto me."

I hooked my arm through his and glanced behind us. Through a narrow opening in the trees I saw a flash of gray moving up the street. Davy pulled the counter from his pocket and pressed Shuffle. In the blink of an eye, we left our beloved Vandalia behind.

We appeared in the deep South, in the middle of a cotton field. A group of workers sang in the distance as they moved from plant to plant. We hurried down the row, not wanting to be seen. Davy turned his head to look at me, but suddenly he glanced past me and his eyes widened. He took a sharp breath. "He's here."

Davy pulled me into a run as we escaped to our next shuffle. We reappeared running over flat grassland. "This is no good," he said. "There's no place to hide."

We were still running as he slung the strap of his rifle over his shoulder and again retrieved the counter from his pocket. I looked behind us and there was Legard, dogging our every move. My glimpse of him was brief, however, because Davy pushed Shuffle again.

Suddenly the dark of night surrounded us. We slowed to a walk, unable to see where we were going. "We've got to lose him. We need a throng of people," Davy whispered, touching another button on the counter.

A dense jungle allowed us to momentarily get ahead, but we feared it was only a matter of time before the Sniffer picked up our trail again. During a most unpleasant shuffle through a knee-deep swamp of muddy water, I had a thought. "Davy, it's always crowded on New Year's Eve in New York City. Try a modern date, like the late 1900s."

He spun the dials and pressed Go. As I predicted, it was crowded. The city would have been dark if it weren't for the lights of passing cars and well-lit storefronts. I hoped the crowd of people would swallow us, offering protection against Legard's eagle eyes. We drew stares from everyone who paused to actually look at us. I thought at first the clothing had caught their interest, but quickly realized it was the gun. I knew from my time with Chase that people didn't walk around town carrying their rifles in the modern world.

Davy, although initially caught off guard by the mass of people, forged ahead, intent on evading the Sniffer. He weaved through the crowded space, never once loosening his grip on my hand. After veering off the main sidewalk, we began descending the stairwell into the subway.

"Wait," I said, stopping. There were policemen patrolling the subway station below us. "Davy, I don't think we can go down here with the gun."

He paused. "That shouldn't matter." Obviously, he didn't want to retrace his steps, and neither did I at the thought that Legard might be right behind us. But when the two policemen noticed us in the stairwell, their hands dropped to their gun belts. They moved in our direction, and I knew we had no choice.

I yanked on Davy's arm, compelling him to follow me. "It does matter. Come on." His resistance melted when one of the officers yelled at him, and we ran back up to the street. Thankfully, there was still no sign of Legard, but I'd bet my house in Boston that he was wandering around New York City by now. We slipped into the crowd, crossing the street in front of a line of yellow taxis. I couldn't help but notice the dismayed shake of Davy's head as he took in the sights around him. Random horns honking and the drone of sirens in the distance made up a deafening background noise. "How can people live like this?" he said. "It's complete mayhem."

"I don't think it's always this bad. There's a big celebration in Times Square for the New Year."

"Still, it can't ever be that good—no grass, no dirt, all this rock. And it stinks."

"It's concrete and asphalt, not rock."

He frowned. "Whatever it is, I don't like it."

I smiled, laughing in spite of our precarious predicament. Davy was a true frontiersman—he could never survive city life. We zigzagged through the busy streets, pausing now and then to watch for Legard. I relaxed as more time passed with no sign of him.

Davy steered me out of the crowd and climbed under the scaffolding along the sidewalk. He stepped into the shadow of a doorway and slid the pack off his back, then leaned his rifle against the wall. "Let's wait here and see if we lost him. Are you cold?"

The hem of my skirt and my feet were still wet from the swamp. "Yes, it is chilly."

Davy untied his bedroll and wrapped the wool blanket around my shoulders. Exhausted, I slumped down next to the building. He replaced the pack on his back and picked up his gun, slinging it over his shoulder. Ever vigilant, he stood guard. "Ellie, I'm sorry. I shouldn't have gone back to the cabin. In spite of my best efforts he followed me. I led him right back to you—the one thing I didn't want to do."

My heart went out to Davy at the anguish in his voice. "Don't be angry at yourself," I said. "We'll lose him again."

In the shadows, we were well hidden from passersby on the sidewalk. The hacking cough of a vagrant alerted us to his presence, curled up in a pile of newspapers in the next doorway. The icy cold of the concrete seeped through the blanket, and the moisture along the bottom of my skirt froze. A shudder ran down my spine, and I pulled the blanket tighter around my neck.

By the light of the street lamps, we watched people hurrying down the sidewalk. Rarely did anyone pause to look in our direction. Everyone hurried, probably anxious to get to a party. It seemed like another lifetime since I had sat with Chase on New Year's Eve, watching the ball drop in Times Square on TV. If I weren't so tired, I would have been interested in seeing more of New York City. I would have wanted to find Times Square and see the ball drop for myself. What year were we in, anyway? Davy seemed preoccupied with guard duty, and I was too cold to bother asking. We waited for hours, Davy diligently watching for any sign of Legard.

The roar of a crowd and an explosion of fireworks sounded in the distance—another new year. This one was bound to be an improvement over the dreadful one I'd just endured. Or at least I hoped so. As the minutes turned into hours, I grew numb and climbed to my feet. Davy stood statuesque, with his arms folded across his chest and his jaw set tightly against the cold. I spread the blanket and wrapped my arms around him. His shoulders shivered as he hugged me.

"Davy," I murmured, "I think we lost him. Let's go someplace warm."

His hand left my back and slid into his pocket. "Where?"

"My grandfather's cabin. It's always warm there," I said, dreaming of the desert heat in the Utah territory. Davy held the counter between us, and I positioned the globe for him. The bluish light never looked more inviting to me. "How about September 6, 1863?" I said, picking a date. I didn't want to meet the Mexican vaqueros, yet I didn't want to have left the cabin abandoned too long, either. That would be three months after I'd been there with Chase. "Imagine a two-room cabin near a river with a plank-sided barn," I said.

Davy set the dials. He glanced toward the street in both directions and then pressed Shuffle and Go. Five shuffles later, we appeared at the cabin of Mr. Johnson, the nearest neighbor to my grandfather. The relief of the sudden warmth and the familiar surroundings brought a smile to my lips. It amused me that both Chase and Davy had missed my grandfather's cabin and appeared here instead.

"Is this it?" Davy asked.

"No, but his cabin is just upriver."

"Will your grandfather be there?"

"He died a few months ago, in June of this year. Hopefully no one has taken over the cabin by now."

A half mile up the road, we met the Johnsons returning from church. I waved. "Afternoon, Mr. Johnson, Millie."

Mr. Johnson pulled his wagon alongside us and stopped. "Why, Ellie," his wife Millie said, "we've been worried sick about you. Where have you and your grandfather been? We haven't seen either of you in months."

I improvised. "My grandfather took ill. We were trying to get him some help from the doctors in Salt Lake City. But he recently passed away."

Mr. and Mrs. Johnson expressed their condolences. "Your grandfather, he was a good man," added Mr. Johnson.

I nodded. "Thank you."

I had a thought. Perchance he'd seen something. "Mr. Johnson, do you remember the man I was with in June? Chase Harper? He was helping me look for our animals that got loose. Have you seen him since then? Was he ever here looking for me?"

Mr. Johnson scratched his beard. "No, I don't reckon I've seen him. Why? Did you lose him or something?" The man laughed at his own joke.

Yes, I did, actually. Davy's expression darkened at the mention of Chase. I'm sure it hurt him that I so hopefully inquired regarding my previous beau. With Davy's ring on my finger it had been thoughtless of me to ask in front of him, but he never would have left me alone long enough to visit the Johnsons on my own. I had no choice but to ask.

"I had something to give to him," I said, "but he was called away suddenly. I hoped he would have returned by now."

"Nope, sorry I haven't seen him." Mr. Johnson nodded toward Davy. "And you are?"

Davy stepped forward and shook Mr. Johnson's hand. "I'm Davy Adams, the man that's hoping to marry Miss Williams," he said curtly.

Millie clapped her hands together. "Wouldn't that be delightful? The two of you make a handsome couple."

"It's nice to meet you," said Mr. Johnson.

Davy smiled and said in a softer tone, "Thank you. It's a pleasure to make your acquaintance as well."

Mr. Johnson picked up his reins. In an effort to avoid leaving more of my friends in a state of worry over my sudden disappearances, I added, "If you don't see us around, we are considering heading back East. With my grandfather gone, perhaps I'll return to Boston."

"All right, Miss Ellie. Best of luck to both of you. If you need anything while you're here, you let us know," Mr. Johnson said.

"Thank you," I called.

They both glanced over their shoulders as they drove away. I hoped Millie wasn't the gossiping type, or I'd find myself the star of the next scandalous story everyone passed along in hushed tones. I could hear it now: *Did you know Miss Williams was seen walking to a vacant cabin with the man she's engaged to be married to— unchaperoned, of all things?*

Davy interrupted my musing. "Ellie, I thought you'd finally put Chase to rest."

"I'm sorry. I couldn't help myself."

Davy's eyebrows knit together in disapproval. But he took a deep breath and nodded, accepting my apology. We made good time walking to the cabin. It stood in the same pitiful state I'd left it, with the front door splintered and ripped from its hinges. The animals were gone. No doubt they were either taken by predators or wandered to a barnyard where someone actually took care of them. A thick layer of dust coated everything. It must have rained heavily at least once, because the water had come through the open doorway, rivulets carving paths across the dirty floorboards.

My eyes were drawn to the center of the floor. Even through the grime I saw the dark brown stain—Chase's blood. After fleeing with him to 2011, I'd insisted we return to the cabin to fetch my grandfather's journal. It detailed the history of the counter and the meanings of the symbols. While here we had been attacked by one of the vaqueros. The flood of memories that accompanied the sight of that stain nearly toppled my already exhausted frame. I bent to brush the dust away. This was all I had left of him, but at least it proved he had been real. There were times when it seemed as if he had only been a dream. But here he had shed blood for me. He had been my protector.

Davy quietly set his pack and rifle by the bed, unaware of the journey my memories had sent me on. He picked up the pitcher. "I'm gonna fetch some water."

I couldn't answer him. My eyes were brimming with tears. If I tried to speak, I would most certainly start crying and he would discover the truth. I hadn't put Chase to rest. But I must. After Davy left the cabin, I kissed the tip of my finger and gently touched the stained floorboard. "Goodbye, Chase darling. I loved you more than life itself, but it's time for me to move on."

When I heard Davy, I stood and squared my shoulders. I took a deep breath, wiped the tears from my eyes, and put a smile on my face.

Davy set the pitcher on the table. "Are you thirsty? Hungry?"

I avoided looking at him. "Mostly tired."

He pulled some hardtack and jerky out of his pack. "You should eat something." I took the hard biscuit from his hand. He used part of the water to rinse out two cups before filling them. We drank the entire pitcher of water, and Davy left to fill it again. I ate the hardtack and some jerky. My jaw ached from chewing by the time I finished, but it seemed to please Davy that I'd eaten.

"Can I get you anything else?" he asked.

"No. Thank you. I think I need some rest."

He watched me as I rose from the table and retreated to the room I'd slept in as a child. After giving the quilt on my bed a good shake, I removed my boots and lay down.

Unbidden, my thoughts again returned to Chase. But dreaming of him was hopeless. If he had lived, Archidus would have sent him back to me. When the Master had looked into my eyes, it was as if he'd seen my soul and knew how important Chase was to me, and I did not doubt the Master's word. Since Chase hadn't appeared in the Ohio woods as promised, I held little hope of him surviving. He could not have brought himself back to my world alone, and the only other place Archidus would have sent Chase was his home in Portland. But for reasons I didn't understand, Davy's counter couldn't get me there. I would have to accept life without Chase. I had waited well over a year.

Furthermore, I had seen the compassion in Archidus' expression when he looked at Garrick and Davy together. He would know where Davy was and would have sent Garrick back to his son. I could only assume that if Garrick hadn't returned, neither would Chase. After all, Garrick and Marcus had been Chase's only chance for rescue. I rolled over onto my stomach, muffling my mournful sobs with a pillow.

SEVENTEEN
Fiancé

We hid ourselves at the cabin for over two weeks. Davy never left me alone. He kept his pack ready to go and close at hand. We ate the food my grandfather had stored in his cellar, along with whatever game Davy shot. One day a lone chicken pecked its way into the barnyard. I threw food out for her, and soon she was back to laying her eggs in the henhouse. It was heavenly once we'd saved enough of them to make a meal.

Davy carried his pack and insisted I tag along whenever he hunted. He feared Legard would track us here and didn't want to be caught unawares. Neither of us brought up the subject of his proposal, but Rose's wedding ring never left my finger. I did enjoy seeing it there. Subconsciously, I had made up my mind. I couldn't see myself leaving Davy and realized I already thought of him as my fiancé. However, I hadn't found the courage to say it yet—to commit myself.

Gradually, we grew more at ease. We both felt if Legard had successfully followed us he would have been here by now. One morning after filling the water pitcher, Davy said, "Ellie, where do you go for supplies around here?"

I smiled. "Why? My roast rabbit and cracked-wheat cereal don't suit you?"

He laughed. "I only wish to supplement your excellent cooking with a little variety."

"St. George is the nearest town. But it's about eighteen miles southwest of here. I wish the horses weren't gone. We used to have two of them, you know."

Davy shook his head. "I can't believe I'm going to ask this of you, but I don't see any way around it. Would you walk to town with me? I know I'm a poor example of a gentleman for even asking, but with Legard tracking us, I don't dare use the counter or leave you alone."

My smile widened. "You're so sweet, Davy. Of course I'll walk to town. I think it'll be quite enjoyable, actually."

Even after two weeks, he still marveled at the dramatic landscape of the southern Utah Territory. It was unlike anything he'd encountered growing up in Ohio. As we walked the dusty road to town, he commented on it again.

Miles later, I stood in the sparse shade of a juniper tree and drank from the canteen Davy handed me. After I returned it to him, he took a long drink, then replaced the lid and stowed the canteen in his pack. He moved closer to me and slid his hand around the small of my back.

"Ellie, have you given my proposal some consideration?"

I placed my hands on his shoulders and felt his muscles tighten. "I have. Quite a bit, actually." Why was it so hard for me to decide what to do? I suppose that despite my best efforts I still mourned Chase. But, undoubtedly, I would mourn him until the day I died. I may as well face that fact and get on with living.

I looked up at Davy's face—so hopeful and handsome—and smiled. "Yes, I will marry you."

I ran my fingernails through the back of his hair as he leaned forward to kiss me. "I love you, Ellie Williams."

"I love you, too," I echoed, all the while pushing away the haunting memory of saying those same words to Chase.

PART III
Chase

EIGHTEEN
Candlelight

My moaning filled the vacancy in my cell, but the voice didn't sound at all like me. Lord Arbon had spent another hour toying with my pain—the inflicting of it bringing him obvious pleasure. He had taunted me with his promises and threats, which included torturing Ellie to force my compliance. He had it stuck in his head that I could get Protector's counter back from Archidus and bring it to him. As with every other time, before Arbon left, he always finished with "Unless, of course, I tire of you."

Along with the physical pain of his razor-sharp whip, his mental torture featured tales of Algonia's imminent destruction. His victory claims included breaching the magical barrier guarding the heart of Algonia, and an attack on the capital city of Cadré Unair. Arbon seemed serious enough, and I wondered what would happen if he did overrun Algonia. At other times I doubted the truthfulness of his claims. Certainly, he would say anything to break me and bring me to despair. I hoped since he had never produced Garrick, Davy, or Ellie, they had indeed reached the safety of Algonia's borders. But Arbon assured me Legard would stop at nothing. Even now the Sniffer scoured the land for Ellie, who they perceived as my weakness. And they were right. My resolve would shatter once they had her.

Where was Brierly? I needed her. I lay in a pool of my own blood on the cold stone floor. I was weak and tired. I'd lost count of how many times I'd passed out. It would certainly happen again before it got better. I wanted to look at my window and guess at how much time had passed, but my right eye was swollen shut. I forced my left eye open, but what I saw wouldn't come into focus. My situation was downright appalling. The prisoner in the next cell banged his tin plate against the iron bars. "Shut yer trap."

I did shut my mouth. I clenched my jaw—my teeth grinding with each throb of fresh pain. The longer I was imprisoned, the less interested they seemed in keeping me alive.

Finally, someone sent blessed Brierly to put me back together. My angel of mercy was shoved through the door with her bowl of herbs and her clean water. "I was waiting for you," I grumbled.

"Were you now?" she teased, sounding as if she forced a cheerful tone into her voice. I figured she put on her happiest front when she came into my cell, but I didn't mind.

"What took you so long?" My weak attempt at humor came out in a painful slur, making me sound angry.

She choked back a sob. "I'm sorry."

I was sorry, too. Sorry to be stuck in this forsaken place, and sorry she had to see the heinous things men did to each other. "Why can't I just die?" I asked.

"Shh . . . don't say that. As long as you're alive there's still hope."

I raised my torso and my voice. "Hope for what? More pain? More torture? You know I'll never get out of here."

Brierly shrank back like she expected me to hit her, and as soon as I'd spoken I regretted it. But I couldn't bring myself to take back the words. She worked quietly and swiftly, doctoring my flayed-open back and bruised face. The big guard had been on duty today, and he had a fist like a hammer. I liked Mud better. At least he didn't add his own brutality on top of what Arbon had in store for me.

Brierly was nearly finished when the sounds of confrontation descended the stairwell. I had only heard one of the voices a few times before, but I recognized it instantly. "Where's the prisoner?" yelled Legard.

"What prisoner?" stammered Mud.

"You fool! The Keeper." The rustle of Legard's cloak was all I heard as he flew down the stairs. The jangle of keys and the heavy thud of Mud's boots followed.

"In 'is cell, of course," Mud said.

By this time Legard stood at my door. "What's she doing in there?"

"Lord Arbon sends her in to clean up the mess when he's done."

"She's Algonian. Get her out. Now!" Legard ordered.

Mud fumbled with the keys before finally opening the lock. I raised my head. Squinting my left eye, I saw a disheveled-looking Legard.

What a sight for sore eyes. A low chuckle escaped my throat. So things weren't going so great for Lord Arbon after all.

I weakly dropped my head onto the stone floor as Mud yanked Brierly from my cell. Thankfully, she had already applied her miracle poultice to my back. Its soothing warmth would ease the pain, and I would eventually heal. The same as every other cursed time.

"Who has keys to this cell?" Legard asked.

"I do, Bernard, and the other guard—Bartimus." Mud's voice quivered.

"Get them back. I want no one holding keys to this cell except you. And you better make sure he stays in here or I'll have your head. From now on, no one but you goes in or out of here unless Lord Arbon or I are here. Do I make myself clear?"

Mud stammered, "Yes, sir."

"Now get those keys."

As the guard hustled down the corridor, I forced open my good eye. Legard watched me, a concerned expression clouding his face. What had he seen? And how did it involve me?

In the weeks that followed, Mud kept me under close scrutiny. He constantly grumbled about it, too. No one was allowed in my cell for any reason, and Mud became personally responsible for me. Thankfully, Bernard still passed me food as part of his rotation. Without that I would have starved. The head guard wasn't all that great of a caretaker. To put it mildly, my cell now reeked of sewage.

The mild temperatures of early fall turned cold, particularly at night, and the flimsy, flea-ridden blanket did little to keep out the chill. After Lord Arbon's initial torture session, a guard had unlocked one of the shackles on my wrist long enough for Brierly to get my arms into a shirt. It was long sleeved and loose fitting. Although old and threadbare, it provided welcomed protection for the healing mass of ever-present wounds on my back. Without it the flies would have been unbearable. But with the recent drop in temperature, there were nights I shivered for hours.

Days passed, and I again stood in front of my wall full of tick marks. "Fifty-seven, fifty-eight, fifty-nine. I've been in here fifty-nine days." I was talking to myself, which happened often. Perhaps that was the first step in going crazy. At times I felt so restless and claustrophobic I thought I would go insane. Other times despair weighed so heavily on my heart, I simply sat in the corner for hours, my knees drawn up to my chest.

One day, I couldn't sit still. My wounds had healed, and with the harvest season, the food from Bernard had been relatively plentiful. He frequently tossed in a wormy apple or pear and even on a few occasions a scrap of meat. I had never been full, but at least the excruciating hunger pains I'd had at the beginning didn't plague me. Without thinking, I said, "I've lost weight, but if I can get out of here soon, I shouldn't have any trouble getting back to where I was." My optimism shocked me. It would take a miracle to get me out of here, especially now. Most likely Lord Arbon would be back soon.

A shudder ran through my body. I feared Arbon and dreaded his appearance. I hated feeling that way—reduced to living in constant, gripping fear. I shook my head, forcing away the thought of him. I would think about him when he walked through my door—no sooner.

I raised both hands to the top of my head and scratched. I'd bet money I had lice. What else would make a person's head itch so bad? In the state I was in, it was good I didn't have to see anyone I knew. By now I must look like all of the other filthy, hollow-cheeked prisoners down the corridor. I bent to retrieve the jagged rock from where it lay in the crevice between the wall and the stones of the floor. "Sixty," I muttered, scratching the crosshatch line across the most recent set of marks.

I sat below the window. *What should I think about today?* I filled the long hours of each day by visiting my memories. My favorite ones were of Ellie. Reliving the night I first found her was the most entertaining. Discovering the magical counter buried in a cave at Zion National Park last summer had propelled me into this fatal mess. But it had also taken me to Ellie Williams in 1863, a fact I didn't regret.

Memories from the weeks she and I had spent together in 1818 with Garrick and young Davy were easily the most bittersweet. Dealing with Rose's tragic death had nearly been too much for Garrick. For weeks, he'd drowned his sorrows in a whiskey bottle at the tavern, leaving Ellie and me to take care of Davy and the boardinghouse. During that time, I'd glimpsed the future I wanted— go to work and come home each night to the girl I loved. I'd watched her with young Davy and wondered what it would be like to see her with a son of mine someday. I'd dreamed of marrying her. It seemed like a simple request, and I thought it wouldn't be asking too much out of life. But I guess I was wrong. I'd been denied everything, including my freedom, and it made me angry.

I scratched my scalp again—this itching was maddening. The day ended, and Bernard dropped a stale loaf in my hands. Halfway through the meager meal, I noticed a splotch of fuzzy green mold on the bread. *Well, Mom always said to eat your greens.* With a smile,

I clamped down on the moldy spot with my teeth, then yanked the piece off and chewed it. If I were lucky, it would kill me.

Dusk soon gave way to nightfall. Twila regularly visited my cell, and the rat population in Lord Arbon's dungeon had suffered. Tonight was no exception. From the window ledge, she greeted me with a meow. "Hi, Twila girl," I whispered. She padded over and nuzzled me with her small head. "Where's Brierly tonight, huh? Why haven't I seen her around?" Meow. "Every night you say the same thing, and it doesn't tell me a whole lot," I muttered. I scratched behind her ears and along her back—all her favorite places. I had nothing better to do. When Twila had her fill of me, she set off to hunt.

I stretched out on the floor. In spite of my permanent backache from sleeping on stones, I had faith my tiredness would eventually outweigh my discomfort and I would drift off to sleep. At least that had been the case for the past sixty nights, and I expected tonight would be no different.

By the faint moonlight, I saw Twila return sometime later, a rat dangling from her jaws. She gnawed on her kill across the cell from me. After her meal, the small cat curled up next to me and I rested my hand on her furry back, grateful when sleep finally welcomed me.

Suddenly, a sharp hiss sounded. The palm of my hand hit the cold floor when Twila jumped to her feet. My eyes flew open. Bolting upright, I listened. "What you lookin' at?" grumbled the prisoner two cells away.

A flicker of candlelight appeared. Whoever advanced down the corridor kept silent. It wasn't Mud, who had a loud walk. It wasn't Bernard, who shuffled. It couldn't have been Bartimus, since he would have answered the prisoner's question with a harsh rebuke. Plus, they would have lit the torches. Legard would move quietly, but he would have no need to visit the dungeon under the cover of darkness.

The beating of my racing heart filled my eardrums as I sat up in the corner and waited. I watched the advancing light. Two Shuylian soldiers stopped at my door. One of them extended the candle into the cell. They were dirty and bearded. Their battle helmets sat low on their foreheads, shadowing their faces. I remained in the corner adjacent to the door, out of the reach of their weak light.

They peered into my apparently empty cell before turning away. One of the soldiers sighed as if disappointed. What were they looking for? Why did they move with such stealth? I cautiously stood and crossed my cell, holding the chains between my wrists to keep them quiet. I pressed my forehead to the bars and watched the men walk away. There was something familiar about the one carrying the candle. The way he moved, the set of his broad, square shoulders. I'd followed that swagger before. "Garrick?" I whispered, my eyes filling with tears, even as I realized my mind must be playing tricks on me.

The soldiers continued down the hallway. I wanted to see them now, especially the one who reminded me of my brother. Although it couldn't be Garrick, maybe for a moment I could pretend it was. Either way, I wanted to know what these men were doing in the dungeon. "Wait," I said, but my voice came out as a croak. I tried again. "Wait."

The two soldiers turned. The candle bearer hurried toward me. "Harper?"

I stretched my chained hands through the iron bars, willing this apparition to stay—to be real. I wanted to touch him. This had to be my imagination. Surely, if not that, it was a dream, or a nightmare of what would never be. "Garrick, is that you?"

He passed the candle to the other soldier, pulled off his helmet, and grabbed my shoulder. He pressed his forehead to mine between the bars. "Little brother, I thought I'd lost you."

"You're here." I couldn't say more. My hand squeezed Garrick's forearm. Every resolve I'd made and every emotion I'd suppressed seemed to explode within me. Tears flowed down my cheeks, and I fought the urge to sob like a baby.

The other soldier watched the corridor. Suddenly, he extinguished the light. "Keeper, it is well that we found you alive, but quickly, tell us everything you know. Where are the keys to the cell? When do the guards patrol the dungeon?"

I sniffed and swallowed, trying to gain control of my voice. "Marcus?" I mumbled, recognizing the voice of the other soldier.

"Speak," he urged.

"Mud, the head guard, has the keys—no one else. I don't know where he keeps them except on his belt. They seem to always be with him. Bernard, a servant, feeds us every morning and night. Mud is sporadic. There's no set schedule he follows during the day, and I rarely see him in here at night."

"Who's Mud? How will we know him?" Marcus questioned.

"He's fat, ornery, and has a light brown beard and receding hairline. The other dungeon guard is Bartimus. He's tall and built like an ox. But he doesn't have keys to my cell."

Marcus's hand gripped my arm through the bars. "Keeper, stay strong. We shall return for you."

"Thank you," I said. "Wait, there's more. It's Brierly. She's here. She's a slave somewhere in the castle . . . or at least she was."

Marcus turned back. "My sister Brierly? Are you certain?"

"Yeah, I'm sure. We've talked a bunch, but I haven't seen her in awhile."

"I will find her. Thank you, Keeper," Marcus whispered. Turning to Garrick he said, "We can't stay. It's too dangerous."

"No, Garrick, don't leave me. Get me out of here. Please!"

"Wait for me. I'll be back, little brother," Garrick said before slipping through my fingers to follow Marcus.

The loneliness of the pitch-black night closed in on me as they retreated down the corridor. Of course I'd wait for him. Where else could I go?

NINETEEN
Wait

With Garrick and Marcus gone, the deathly silence enveloped me. I stood at the door, gripping the iron bars as the minutes turned into hours. Were they not coming back tonight? I eventually retreated to my corner and sat. There hadn't been enough time to ask my questions. I had barely gotten over the shock of seeing them and they'd gone. Did they know of Ellie? Was she safe? What were they planning?

The first light of dawn seeped through the window of my cell. Garrick and Marcus couldn't come back now, at least until it was dark again. With that realization came the weight of tiredness, and I slipped into a restless sleep. The dreams filling my slumber were full of escape, running, and hiding. I woke to the rattle of keys in my lock. My sleepy mind jumped to the conclusion that I was rescued— free at last. I shot awake only to discover Bartimus crossing my cell, flanked by Mud and Lord Arbon. Behind them stood a line of Arbon's personal guards. My shock at this unexpected intrusion must have shown on my face.

"Wake up, you lazy lout," Bartimus shouted.

I was climbing to my feet when he kicked me. His heavy boot sent me into the wall and knocked the wind out me. I gasped for air and scrambled to get to my feet, out of the reach of his next kick. His iron fist rattled my head like a bobble-head doll before Mud yanked me across the room by my shackles.

I pulled back, groaning. "No, no, no." I knew what was coming. My pulse quickened, and I couldn't breathe. Bartimus yanked my shirt over my head and down my arms so it hung at my elbows, and then Mud fastened my iron chain to the hook in the wall. All the while I struggled.

"Since you so obviously disdain my visits, give me something I can work with," Lord Arbon demanded. "Where in your world would Perception's Keeper be hiding? A time, a place—something. That can't be too difficult. Surely you don't hold any fondness for him. Point me toward any Keeper, for that matter. Wisdom's Keeper has fled France. Where would he go? Who is Illusion's Keeper? Male or female? Dark or fair? Surely as Protector you know them all by now."

Davy. Had he gone back? Wisdom's Keeper was Raoul. He must have gotten wind of the chaos and gone into hiding. Luckily, Arbon and his ilk hadn't yet discovered the karate lady in San Francisco— Illusion's Keeper. I ground my teeth in anticipation of the pain. With help coming, I couldn't speak now. *Please don't let me die after Garrick and Marcus finally found me.*

A hiss escaped Lord Arbon's lips. "I see you are still as defiant as ever."

With a crack, the lash of his invisible whip tore open my right shoulder blade. I couldn't stifle my cry of agony. I counted—it gave my mind something to do. *One . . . two . . . three . . . four.* "I had an interesting visit from Legard," Arbon said. "It seems he saw you in the old world and thought you had escaped. But I assured him that no one leaves my dungeon alive without my blessing. I find solace in the hope that perhaps you will soon decide to join me in my efforts. Together we could accomplish great things. You would live like royalty in my kingdom."

Five . . . six . . . seven. Not wanting to give Arbon the satisfaction of hearing me scream again, I had clenched my teeth, and now my jaw ached. How did I even notice that over the searing pain in my back? *Eight . . . nine.*

A voice interrupted. "Milord, an urgent message from the front." There was a rustle of paper and then nothing. No crack of the whip. No movement behind me. A trickle of warm blood ran down my spine.

"I have other matters to attend to," Lord Arbon said. "Give my questions serious consideration, Keeper. I expect answers next time, or you won't find me so lenient. Get him down, but no one tends to him. I'll see the door locked before I leave."

Bartimus yanked my hands off the hook and sent me sprawling across my cell. The heavy door slammed closed and the key turned the lock before Lord Arbon's entourage marched up the stairs. On my hands and knees, I dropped my forehead to the stone floor. Comparatively speaking, he'd let me off easy. But if Garrick and Marcus couldn't get those keys, I didn't hold out much hope for the next time. Arbon was a man of his word when it came to my torture.

Blood oozed down my side and dripped onto the floor. This time there would be no one to share my pain and doctor my wounds. I would miss Brierly's soft touch and kind words. I had a pang of guilt at the thought of her. Why had I been so mean the last time we spoke? Maybe Legard had suspected she would be the means by which I would escape someday. Is that why I hadn't seen her? Had she been punished? *Please let Marcus find her before it's too late.* I stayed on my knees, praying as I waited for the blood to dry. If my shirt stuck to the open wounds it would only make it worse.

Bernard delivered food and water. I wanted to ask him about Brierly. But although I knew he was fond of her, I couldn't be sure where his true loyalties lay. I hobbled to the doorway and took my food without saying a word. My chest hurt from Bartimus' kick, and walking sent a fresh wave of nauseating pain through my back. I sat cross-legged in the center of my cell and slowly ate. Might as well make it last, since there would be nothing else to do for hours. Eventually, I pulled the shirt back over my head and covered my wounds. I eased myself onto my side and tried to sleep off the pain.

Three days passed, and still no sign of Garrick and Marcus. Had they been discovered, or killed? I took some comfort in the fact that nothing out of the ordinary occurred within the scope of my senses. Plus, I hadn't heard the crows cawing outside my window. I'd learned the gallows were just beyond the dungeons on the other side of the castle wall. After a hanging, the crows fought over the corpse. The fact they'd been absent meant no one had been executed in the last week.

I mourned the loss of Brierly's care when I felt the pain of infection for the first time. Until now, I hadn't fully appreciated the value of that sticky poultice she always smeared in my wounds.

I became nocturnal, watching for Garrick every night. Tonight was no different. I had slept away most of the day. My neighbor had died during the previous night, but to my knowledge no one had removed his body. He'd had a hacking cough, so some respiratory illness was probably to blame. With his passing, the corridor became much quieter. A few other prisoners coughed, but none sounded as bad as my neighbor had. I needed to get out of here before I developed the cough of death. I dropped my head into my hands and set to work scratching the lice off my scalp.

I had no shortage of time, and I spent every minute of it thinking about leaving. The thought of returning to Ellie, of holding her in my arms again, tantalized me. I dared to hope for it now, whereas days before it had seemed impossible. The deep longing for it made the fear of failing to escape intense.

Legard already hunted Davy, and after Arbon's confession of what his Sniffer had seen, I assumed I would get free. I would see Legard in the old world again, and I would be hunted. If Ellie were with me, she would be hunted. We would never truly be free as long as Arbon lived. This tangled web of thoughts dampened my excitement about escaping.

Kelly Nelson

At the sound of metal on metal, I snapped my head up. There was no moon visible through my window, and darkness filled the corridor, making it impossible to distinguish between the walls of my cell and the door. The click of the lock releasing its hold drew me to my feet. The chain between my wrists jangled, and I grabbed a section of it with each hand to keep it quiet as I walked toward where I knew the door to be.

"Chase?" Brierly whispered.

"I'm right here," I whispered back, smiling. Her outstretched hand bumped into my chest. She clutched onto me and we stepped out. Slowly, and as silently as possible, she pulled the cell door closed behind me. With one hand fisted around my shirtsleeve, she felt her way across the corridor. Once her fingertips grazed the wall, she propelled me forward. I had so much I wanted to say, but now wasn't the time. I silently followed her.

We had almost reached the stairwell leading to the outside courtyard when someone moved ahead of us. I stopped, pulling back on Brierly. The person hurried down the stairs in the pitch black. I flattened myself against the wall, knowing any second he or she would pass us.

Suddenly, Brierly whispered, "Marcus?"

"Someone's coming. Back to the cell!" Marcus said in the faintest whisper.

We retraced our steps as the door to the outside banged shut and the orange glow of a torch slowly descended the stairwell. Garrick was there too, and we all filed into my cell. Marcus pulled the door shut behind us as the guard entered the corridor. The squeak of the rusty hinges and the click of the lock sounded like a fire alarm in the quiet darkness. I heard Marcus and Garrick draw their swords, inch by inch, out of their scabbards. As the glow of the torch advanced, I lay down where I usually slept and closed my eyes.

The irony of the situation didn't escape me. They had set out to free me, yet here we all were, locked in my cell. If the guard noticed something amiss, my freedom would have been short lived.

170

Narrowly opening my eyes, I saw the glow of the torch illuminating my cell. On a typical night, I opened my eyes and looked at whoever made the rounds. No reason to act any different tonight. I fluttered my eyes open and took in the sight of Bartimus, peering into my cell by torchlight.

"What you lookin' at?"

Garrick, Marcus, and Brierly were plastered against the wall in the corner. I closed my eyes and pretended to sleep.

Listening intently, I heard Bartimus climb the stairs into the castle. At least I assumed they led there, since Arbon and Legard always entered from that stairwell, never the one coming from the courtyard.

I climbed to my feet and walked to the door. Out of the dark a hand touched my back. "Harper—" Garrick started to whisper.

I cringed away from him. "Ahh . . . don't touch my back."

"Shh!" Marcus ordered.

I heard the familiar click of my lock opening, and the four of us left the cell. We walked down the dark corridor. "Somebody there?" mumbled a prisoner. We didn't answer, but I feared he could hear my thundering heart. "Who goes there? Cursed rats! The devil take 'em all."

We finally reached the stairwell. There were two things I knew about Bartimus. He was mean, and he was unpredictable. I broke out in a sweat at the thought of him opening the door in front of us. He'd been known to immediately circle around for another pass through the dungeon, and if he was in a foul mood he dragged his sword across the bars of each cell, making sure everyone knew he was there. Marcus pushed open the door, and the four of us stepped into the crisp, clear night. I scanned the courtyard—not another soul in sight.

I sucked in my first breath of fresh air in over two months and raised my eyes heavenward. Tears wet my cheeks at my first taste of freedom.

There was no moon, but the stars were as brilliant as I'd ever seen. I would have relished it for a moment, but Garrick pulled me along behind him. Marcus led the way to the outer wall, then scaled it, searching out handholds. Soon, a section of rope sailed through the air and dropped to the ground next to us. One at a time, we followed Marcus over the wall. Then we all ran along a road that flanked the exterior of the courtyard, ducking behind bushes when two mounted guards trotted past. The road soon veered between rows of cottages, and we headed away from the castle.

A low growl from one of the porches sent us scurrying in another direction. We didn't need a Shuylian guard dog to blow our cover. The community of cottages changed the farther we went, becoming more rural. We followed the road, holding close to the trees and ever watchful for any sign of someone approaching. Soon, farms, orchards, and dairies spread out before us.

We hadn't gone far before my labored breathing changed to ragged gasps. Weak from lack of exercise and proper food, I was sucking wind like a freshman on the first day of track. Marcus offered no mercy, and I didn't ask for any. I knew better than anyone the consequences of getting caught.

The slow progression of light over the eastern horizon revealed Marcus and Garrick dressed as picture-perfect Shuylian soldiers. Marcus carried a longbow and had a quiver slung across his back. Tarnished metal breastplates sporting a plethora of dings and dents adorned his and Marcus's chests, and Shuylian sword scabbards were strapped to their waists.

At the sight of a dairy farmer driving a wagon filled with what looked like barrels of milk, we darted off the road. Once he passed, Marcus whispered, "There's an abandoned farm ahead. It's not more than a mile farther. We'll hide there until nightfall."

My legs cramped as I forced them to keep pace with the others. Finally, Marcus turned off the main road and jogged down an overgrown drive. Nearly buried underneath the climbing vines of a blackberry bramble was a small cottage. Trees and bushes had overgrown the farm, but Garrick and Marcus seemed right at home.

As the captain drew water from an old well, Garrick pushed open the broken door to the cottage and retrieved two packs from inside. Dying of thirst, I watched Marcus. The rope he pulled on was so badly frayed, it was a miracle it didn't snap under the weight of the liquid. But the bucket leaked all the way up and was no more than half full by the time it reached our hands. The water was cool and lacked the foul aftertaste I'd grown accustomed to in the dungeon.

I wiped the moisture from my lips with the back of my hand and smiled. Although afraid I would collapse at any moment from exhaustion, I'd never felt better. I was free. I could get a drink of water when I wanted, breathe fresh air, and look at the sky.

My thoughts turned to America. Until that moment, I hadn't fully appreciated the Declaration of Independence. The phrase so often quoted, "Life, liberty, and the pursuit of happiness," now meant something to me. For over two months I'd been denied even the most basic rights. I would never again allow myself to take my country for granted. I said a prayer of gratitude as I stood leaning against the crumbling well, watching Marcus draw up the bucket again.

"Harper, you're bleeding," Garrick said. "I take it life's not been kind to you lately."

I lifted my head. "No, it hasn't."

"Follow me, little brother. Let's do something about those handcuffs."

He picked up a Shuylian battle-ax and led the way to an old stump behind the cottage. Taking his wood-chopping stance, he rested the heavy ax blade on top of the stump. "Spread your hands— right here—and I'll try to break that chain."

I knelt in front of the stump and balled each hand into a fist, then stretched the chain across the spot Garrick indicated. With my eyes closed, I turned my head. The impact of the ax blade vibrated through the iron shackles, but my hands didn't separate. I opened my eyes. The blade had damaged the chain on the second link from my right hand.

"Again, Harper," Garrick said, swinging the ax over his head. I closed my eyes as he brought the ax down. On the fifth try, my wrists flew apart at impact and the blade sat buried in the top of the stump.

Stretching my arms to the side, I smiled. It seemed like an eternity since I'd had full range of motion.

"Pull the chain tight and let's try to get rid of it."

Four swift strikes of his ax and again my hands flew apart, one busted link of chain ricocheting off my chest. Garrick tossed the chain into the bushes, then offered me his hand. Clasping my wrist in true Algonian style, he pulled me to my feet. I wrapped my arm around his shoulder, and he returned the embrace. The safety of his presence broke the last of my emotional resolve. With tears in my eyes and choking back a sob, I said, "Thank you. I couldn't have asked for a better brother."

"I had to get you back." Garrick's voice was also filled with emotion. "I wouldn't want a life without you in it."

We stepped away from each other. I wiped my eyes, trying to pull myself together.

Brierly walked around the side of the old cottage, smiling. "Chase, I brought some medicine. I can look after your wounds, if you'd like. I heard Arbon had visited you, but I wasn't allowed in the dungeon."

I stepped toward her. "It wasn't as bad this time."

The four of us sat on old logs while Brierly mixed her medicinal herbs into a poultice. Garrick pulled Shuylian soldier gear out of their packs. We ate jerky and some fruit they had gleaned from the abandoned orchard behind the cottage.

Marcus bit off half of the undersized apple in one bite. After tossing the core into the brambles, he looked at Brierly and me. "Both of you will need to dress like soldiers. Our cover for the trip back is we're Shuylian militia with orders to report to the front. We should make better time getting home that way. Coming here, Garrick and I had to skirt the main roads and take lengthy detours to avoid being picked up as deserters, since we were going the wrong direction." He nodded to his sister. "We'll have to cut your hair."

She lifted the braid off her shoulder, letting her fingers slide down its length before nodding.

Brierly tugged at my shirt, and I pulled it off for her. Garrick winced at the sight of my wounds and turned his head away. "How did you get the keys from Mud?" I asked Brierly.

"Marcus found me doing laundry outside the courtyard the day after he talked with you. We waited until Mud sent for me, and then Marcus followed. He took care of Mud while I got the keys."

I glanced at Marcus. He raised his finger and slid it across his throat. "Nobody touches my sister."

Grinning, Garrick looked from Marcus to Brierly, then winked at her. "That's good to know," he muttered, ripping off a chunk of jerky with his teeth.

Marcus raised his eyebrows at Garrick and shook his head. A blush colored Brierly's cheeks as she laughed lightly. The sound was music to my ears. I hadn't heard laughter in a long time, and never from her. She finished treating the wounds on my back while I ate. Garrick set me up with a Shuylian soldier uniform, and I replaced my filthy Algonian breeches with the Shuylian-style black leather ones. Marcus pulled out his dagger, probably the one that had slit Mud's throat, and sawed off Brierly's long auburn braid.

While dressing, I glanced at Garrick. "How's Ellie?"

He handed me a sword and a helmet. "She took it pretty hard when they captured you, and Archidus didn't offer her much hope for your safe return. But he did let her see your counter so she knew you were alive. Three days after returning to Algonia, Marcus and I rode out to look for you. I don't know anything after that. Ellie and Davy were both waiting at the fortress when we left. She really cares for you, though."

I nodded. "Thanks, Garrick. Davy might be back in the old world now. Arbon pushed me for information on where he could be. Legard is there, searching for the Keepers."

"With the war going on here, I guess that doesn't surprise me."
I set the helmet on my head. "How do I look?"

Garrick smiled. "You look like a dirty, rotten Shuylian soldier. You stink like one, too."

"Arbon didn't exactly provide shower facilities." I pulled off my helmet to scratch my head. "I think I have lice."

"Then don't you dare use my helmet, and whatever you do, keep those shackles on your wrists hidden. That would be a dead giveaway."

The sight of Brierly exiting the cottage in her soldier garb caught our attention. "Well?" she said shyly. She sported a jagged haircut and clothes that were way too big. Her soft eyes and clear complexion looked dramatically out of place.

Frowning, Marcus folded his arms. "You're the smallest, youngest-looking soldier I've ever seen, but it'll have to do. Dirty up your hands and face—maybe that'll help. You let us do the talking, and don't make eye contact with anyone. I'll take the first watch. The rest of you try to get some sleep."

With a belly full of food and water, I was sleepy. I followed Garrick into the dim cottage and dropped onto my side. The last thing I saw before sinking into sleep was Brierly lowering herself to the floor next to me.

TWENTY
Bloodbath

"Marcus! Soldiers coming," Garrick called.

I must be dreaming, I thought, too tired to move. I couldn't escape anyway—Arbon had me trapped in his dungeon. I would wake up soon enough, when the torture began. No need to hasten its coming. I let myself keep sleeping.

A rough hand shook my shoulder, but I ignored it. If it was Bartimus, I would get up when he kicked me. Mud would drag me to my feet, so there was no need to expend any energy yet. With an iron grip, someone grabbed my arm and yanked me to my feet.

"Keeper, wake up," Marcus hissed. My heavy eyes blinked open. I scrambled to get my feet under me, relieved to see the captain instead of a prison guard. "Take cover in the brambles until we see how many," he said.

I staggered after him with my helmet and sword. Marcus guided Brierly into the orchard, pulling his pack onto his back. Garrick brought up the rear, carrying another loaded pack. The sound of horses approaching the cottage sent us scurrying in three directions. Marcus and Brierly advanced the farthest before hiding. Garrick pulled ahead of me and crouched behind a dead apple tree overgrown with blackberries. I shoved some thorny vines aside with my sword and climbed into a bramble. The vines fell back into place, hopefully disguising my location. Every inch of me felt the prick of thorns. The slightest movement drove them deeper into my skin, bringing me fully awake.

The leaves had begun to change color but still clung to the vines. Through them I watched two soldiers dismount. One kicked the door to the run-down cottage off of its hinges and walked in. "Someone's been here," he yelled to the other soldier. "Check the orchard."

Scowling, the other man scanned the rows of trees and walked toward our hiding places. I dropped my gaze, fearful he'd see the glint of my eyes through the shallow maze of blackberry vines.

The leaves rustled not twenty feet away from me, and I glanced to the side. The soldier raised a long spear and drove it into the brambles. The sight sent my heart racing. Randomly he stabbed the thicket, working his way closer. I should have stayed with Garrick or Marcus, who had both gone deeper into the orchard. At the rate this soldier was moving, he'd run me through within the next minute. I needed a plan, and fast.

Soon he stood close enough that I saw the breadcrumbs stuck in his beard. His beady black eyes looked hard and mean. He paused and leaned the spear against his shoulder, then relaxed his stance and took a leak while I hunched, unmoving, not six feet away. I breathed shallowly, worried he'd hear me. If I would have been thinking clearly, I could have pulled my breastplate over my face when he had first plunged his spear into the bramble, but it was too late now. Any movement on my part was certain to be seen, if not heard as well. My mind raced through my options—gamble that his spear missed me, or try to free myself from the thorny vines so I could climb out and fight. Either way, it didn't look good for me.

He fastened his pants and hefted his weapon in front of him. I heard it rattle through the dead vines as he thrust it into the brambles again. If I moved now, he'd stab me through before I could escape my thorny hideout. I'd waited too long. Now I had no choice but to stay put and play Russian roulette with his spear. I lowered my helmeted head, closed my eyes, and prayed.

The other soldier had continued kicking around the cottage. "The woman and the prisoner are long gone, if it even was them. Probably some locals or young 'uns playing is all. Let's go. The captain's waitin' for our report, and I want to see Colette before we leave for the front."

"Be right there." The soldier in front of me grunted, and I chanced a glance at him. To my horror he raised his spear, his arm poised for the next thrust. I clenched my eyes and gritted my teeth, preparing to be impaled by the razor-sharp point. The tip sank into the ground next to my feet. A quiet sigh escaped my lips as only thorns pierced my skin. He pulled his weapon back, raking the thorns across my shirtsleeves. I opened my eyes and watched the two soldiers mount their horses and gallop out of sight. With my sword, I pushed the vines aside and crawled into the open.

Garrick emerged from hiding and brushed the dead leaves off his head. "That was close. You okay, little brother?"

"I'm fine," I said, picking a thorn out of my pant leg.

"Let's leave. I don't want to be here if their captain orders a more thorough search," Marcus said as he walked out of the orchard with Brierly. We'll go across country for a day or two before we risk traveling the road."

With my pain, exhaustion, and fatigue, I had to turn off my brain and numbly follow him, thinking about nothing except what he ordered me to do. I marched when he marched, I slept when he said sleep, and I ate when he handed me food. I became so driven by my need to simply survive each day that I didn't think of anything else. After two days of traversing the Shuylian countryside, we again intersected the road leading to the Valley of Tierran.

Still, we only moved at night. I'm not sure any of us were fully convinced our Shuylian uniforms would fool anyone, especially with troops of soldiers searching for Brierly and me. One evening, we happened upon a large contingent of Shuylian soldiers camped along the road. The chorus of crows cawing in the sky should have tipped us off, but I think we were all too tired to notice them. Marcus attempted to skirt the camp, but it was much larger than expected, and we soon found ourselves in the midst of the Shuylian army. Marcus pulled his sister behind him and motioned for Garrick and me to flank her. With Brierly positioned between us, we marched through the camp. I tried to keep my eyes on the ground, but my heart raced each time a soldier gave us more than a cursory glance.

An oversized tent had been pitched ahead of us, and a roaring fire blazed beneath a boar's carcass.

"Wait," Brierly whispered. Marcus hesitated in the shadows at the edge of the clearing. "Those are Lord Arbon's personal guards," she said. "That must be his private quarters. Rumors floating around the castle said he would be heading to the front. The Shuylian army is losing ground, and he fears Archidus will again secure his border. For the first time in hundreds of years, Arbon will personally lead his army against his brother."

A mixture of anger and fear flooded my veins as Lord Arbon himself stepped out of his tent and barked an order to his cook. His elaborate robes swirled around his boots as he turned to disappear between the tent flaps. I muttered the first thing that came to mind. "We should kill him."

The eyes of my three companions turned to me. My gaze locked onto the tent. He was so close and had caused me so much pain. Would he not continue to hunt me, as well as everyone I loved, until he got what he wanted? As long as Arbon lived, there would be no peace in my life and no escaping this ever-present foreboding.

"We should," Brierly agreed.

"No," Marcus said. "My responsibility is to see you safely back to Algonia. I'll not risk that for anything."

"I'm tired of hiding from him!" I said. "I don't want the fear of him catching me to haunt every minute of my life. And I can't let him get Ellie, ever." A knot of fear twisted my gut at the thought of what he might do to her, or anyone else I cared about. "We could sneak in when he sleeps. We don't stand a chance against him if he's awake." My mind flashed back to the invisible whip Arbon had wielded from across the cell with only the flick of his finger. I could just imagine the horrible pain he might inflict on soldiers like Marcus if he made it to the front lines.

Garrick leaned toward Marcus. "You've got to admit, we stand a better chance than anyone else. He'll only wreak havoc on your army if he makes it to the battlefield. Should he be allowed to continue inflicting his atrocities on the innocent? If we're successful, we might save thousands of Algonian lives."

Marcus met his gaze. "And if we're not?"

None of us had an answer to that. We backed away from the clearing. Marcus crouched beneath the trees and dropped his head into his hands. I leaned against a thick trunk and waited for him to decide what we'd do next. The food on the trail had been a vast improvement over Arbon's dungeon menu. A few henhouses had donated eggs, and the Shuylian garden plots we raided had yielded carrots, squash, and overripe ears of corn. Although I was gaining my strength back, I hadn't eaten enough to put on weight yet, and fatigue still tackled me on a regular basis.

Marcus stared at the tent. "It does need to be done, and there may never be an opportunity like this again. He's not left the safety of Shuyle since before I was born." The large man paused as if deep in thought, and Brierly and Garrick sat down as well.

The captain rose and paced in front of us. With our eyes fully adjusted to the dark, we watched his silhouette against the distant glow of Arbon's fire. Marcus pulled a wallet-sized leather bag from under his shirt, then dug out a sealed pouch and shook it. He knelt before Garrick and gripped his shoulder. "I'll not risk the life of a Keeper or that of my sister. Swear an oath that, should I fail, you will protect my sister's life with your own and hasten your way back to Algonia. Do you remember the way we came? The northern route?"

"Yes, I remember it," Garrick said.

"Very well. Do you swear to bind yourself with the oath I propose?" Marcus demanded.

Garrick hesitated only a moment. "Yes, I swear."

"Give me your hand." They clasped wrists and sealed the oath with an Algonian handshake.

Marcus turned to me. "Do you swear an oath to protect my sister and return to Algonia with no interference, should I fail?"

"I swear," I replied, extending my hand to meet his. I doubted I had the courage to face Arbon. The sight of him sent a crippling fear through me. But Marcus—I did not doubt him. If anyone could achieve the impossible it was the captain. "What will you do?" I asked.

He held the pouch in front of him. "Poison," he whispered. "Tasteless. Odorless. I got this when they made me captain. It's an easy out for someone wishing to escape the tortures inflicted upon prisoners of war. It's also a guarantee we won't divulge military secrets to the enemy. Ingesting the whole packet results in death. A partial dose renders the victim paralyzed in sleep. I'll try to get this in Arbon's food. Once the camp sleeps, I'll enter his tent and finish him off."

Brierly reached to touch his arm affectionately. "Arbon's a winebibber. You've the best chance of him taking it if it's in his drink."

Marcus nodded to his sister. He shrugged out of his pack and handed it to me before turning to pass the longbow and quiver to Garrick. "You can leave now, or wait for me. If you stay, be ready to clear out of here at the first sign of trouble, but no later than the beginning of the third watch. Good luck, my friend."

The captain turned to leave. "Wait," Garrick said. "Arbon holds two counters. To truly succeed, we must return them to Master Archidus."

Marcus nodded. "Yes, I'd thought of that. I will hope he carries them on his person."

He disappeared into the darkness. Garrick, Brierly, and I crept to a stand of trees that offered better protection from Shuylian eyes and a side view of Arbon's tent. Then we watched the clearing in front of us. Moments later, Marcus sauntered into camp from the opposite direction. The cook set a tray on a makeshift table. A bottle of wine reflected the flickering firelight. Marcus bent to adjust his boot. When the cook set to work carving slices of meat off the boar, Marcus strode to the table and uncorked the bottle. He emptied the contents of the small pouch and replaced the cork. With his back to the fire, he failed to see the cook turning toward him with a thick slab of meat.

"What you doin'? That's the Lord's drink. Move on with ya!" roared the cook. "I'll have ya strung up for stealin' a sip of wine." Marcus lifted his hands, feigning innocence and backing away as the cook jabbed at him with the butcher's knife. The yelling brought three of Arbon's guards rushing to the scene. They beat Marcus into submission and dragged him into the woods.

"Report to yer regiment and stay there. You show yer face in the Lord's camp again, and I'll slit yer throat," one of the guards yelled.

"Should we go check on him?" I whispered to Garrick.

He shook his head. "We can't, little brother. We swore an oath."

"I know, but—"

"He'll be fine. They think he's one of them."

There wasn't much to see after that. The cook delivered the tray of food and wine to Arbon's tent, and the fire died down. The guards served themselves generous portions of roast boar, and the cook sent the remainder of the pig to be devoured by the other soldiers. My stomach ached at the sight and smell of all that meat. I couldn't even remember what it felt like to sink my teeth into a thick steak or a juicy burger. I hugged my empty stomach and waited. Not meaning to, I drifted off to sleep.

Garrick's sudden movement woke me. I bolted upright and peered through the darkness. Thirty or more soldiers lay on the ground in front our hiding place. The tent sat on the opposite side of the clearing. With a side view of the tent, we could see the two night guards—one at the tent entrance, the other at the back. And to the left were the glowing embers of the dying fire. Garrick raised his hand and pointed to the right side of the camp. By the faint moonlight we watched Marcus move behind a tree.

The guard stationed in front of the tent gazed at the quarter moon moving across the sky, then walked to the guard standing behind and gave a whispered order. The second guard left and woke two replacements. On their way to guard duty, both of the newly awakened guards entered the trees, one of them near where Marcus hid. One came out, fastening his breeches as he walked, and took his place. The main guard paced impatiently, waiting for the other.

Finally, the second guard emerged from the trees and walked to the front of the tent. He dropped his head as he walked, looking at his feet.

"What took you so long?" grumbled the guard.

"Sorry, sir," Marcus mumbled in response. He took the spot in front of Arbon's tent flap. The off-duty guards laid out their bedrolls and soon added their snoring to that of the other soldiers.

Brierly had given in to exhaustion and slept curled up on a bed of pine needles. Garrick and I kept a constant vigil as the night progressed. Marcus stood stone still—the picture of a perfect guard. Again I thought, *What is he waiting for?* More than an hour later he finally moved.

Silently, he crept along the wall of the tent. The rear guardsman leaned against his spear, as if sleeping standing up. Marcus was three feet away when the man stiffened and turned. Like a cat Marcus leapt forward, pulling the guard's head back and slitting his throat before he could draw another breath. Marcus held the man's limp body in his arms. His gaze panned the sleeping soldiers as he slowly lowered the body onto the ground.

Marcus returned to the front of the tent and pulled the flap aside. After glancing over his shoulder, he disappeared. The thud of my pounding heart drowned out every other sound. I no longer heard the owls or the crickets, and my ears lost track of the steady hum of snoring as I focused on the tent. After what seemed an eternity,

Marcus emerged. He staggered toward the trees, his left arm hanging limp at his side. Before he made it to cover, he stumbled and fell to the dirt. I started to rise.

Garrick held out his hand. "Wait."

Marcus held his knife in his right hand. It didn't reflect the glint of the moonlight, and I hoped Arbon's blood had darkened the blade. Marcus dragged himself into the trees, while not a soul in the camp stirred.

"Now we go. But we'll leave the camp via that direction," Garrick whispered, pointing to where we had last seen Marcus.

I laid one hand on Brierly's shoulder and brought the other to my lips. "Shh. It's done. Let's go."

She took my hand, and we followed Garrick around the perimeter of the camp. In the dark of the woods we nearly stepped on Marcus's prostrate form. Dirt and dried leaves clung to his sticky, blood-soaked clothes and hands. In the dark and this close to danger, it was impossible to determine the extent of his wounds.

Brierly took the quiver and bow, and Garrick and I pulled Marcus to his feet. Entwined in his left hand was a leather string from which dangled two counters. There were no pockets in my pants, so I wound the string between my fingers and held Marcus's wrist. With an arm wrapped around each of our necks, we dragged him away from his bloodbath.

TWENTY-ONE
Escape

The pack rubbing my back reopened my wounds, and at times the weight of Marcus nearly dropped me to my knees. We had no idea what had happened at the camp. Since Arbon hadn't emerged from the tent or cried out a warning, we hoped he had died. But with Marcus unconscious we couldn't confirm it.

I felt something drip onto my boot. "We're leaving a blood trail."

Garrick looked at me across the captain's drooping head. "I know. If I remember right there's a river around here."

"We'll lead them right to us if we're not careful."

Brierly stepped next to Garrick and put her hand on his arm. "Please, let's stop. There are supplies in the pack. If I bandage his wounds, our trail won't be so visible."

She sounded worried. I was too. Marcus had been unconscious since we'd found him, and my neck and shoulder were slick with his blood. It trickled down my back and mingled with my own. I agreed with Brierly, plus I needed a rest. Stopping in my tracks, I started to lay Marcus down. Garrick had no choice but to comply.

Once Marcus hit the ground, I collapsed next to him. Brierly pulled the pack off my back and rifled through it. I uncorked the water flask and drank my fill, still holding the bloody leather string between my fingers. The two counters tapped together whenever

I moved my hand. I tied the cut string in a knot, pulled on it to ensure it would hold, and then clicked one of the counters open. The familiar bluish light illuminated a look of wonder on Brierly's face. I smiled. "Looks like your brother did his job."

Garrick stood looking back the way we'd come. "We've gotta hurry."

I turned the light toward Brierly and Marcus. "He has the guard's uniform over his other clothes," Brierly said. "Help me get it off."

Garrick and I rolled Marcus over and removed the loose-fitting red-and-black jacket. Both the sleeve and the side were sliced open. Garrick rolled the jacket into ball, saying, "I'll get rid of this."

Brierly removed her brother's breastplate and opened his shirt. I looked at the breastplate. It had saved his life—assuming he lived. A crack ran through the metal. Where the breastplate ended, the flesh of his side bore a deep gash. It continued across the bicep muscle of his left arm. What looked like black blood oozed from both wounds.

Brierly pulled a needle from her medicine bag. "Help me hold the skin together." The skin around the wound looked blackened in the light of the counter. I pinched Marcus's torn flesh together while his sister worked.

Garrick returned and watched Brierly. Once Marcus's wounds were stitched closed and tightly bound, we dragged him to his feet between us. We weren't leaving a blood trail, but it would be easy for a tracker to follow us.

An hour before first light, we found the river. Downstream would take us closer to the Valley of Tierran, but Garrick led us upstream. "I think they'll expect us to go down," he said. "But the woods are denser upstream, and if I remember right there are some caves in the side hills."

As we dragged Marcus against the current, the rocks rolling underfoot made it difficult going. "We need to hide," Garrick said after a while. "Those guards will be waking up soon. On horseback, it won't take them long to catch us."

The first light of dawn signaled the coming day as we headed for the hills. When we got closer, Garrick stopped and lowered Marcus to the ground. "Somewhere around here Marcus and I saw caves on our way into Shuyle. Stay here. I'll scout ahead."

Garrick soon returned, grinning with excitement. "Come on, I found something."

We dragged Marcus through the trees and partway up the hill. Camouflaged by an array of large boulders was a narrow opening. *How ironic that my journey into this supernatural world began in a cave and now may end in one,* I thought.

We could barely squeeze Marcus's broad shoulders through the opening. "Harper, come with me. We've got to hide our tracks."

Garrick and I found downed pine branches and ran back to where we'd exited the river. With painstaking care we fluffed up the blades of grass and smoothed any disturbance in the dirt. We were backing our way up the hill toward the cave when we heard horses galloping up the river, their shod hooves clattering over the rocks.

I moved to the mouth of the cave and tossed my branch into the darkness. "Hurry, Garrick." Waiting for him, I glanced from side to side and my eyes widened. Like a signal flare, a smear of blood marred the light gray rock's surface next to me. I spit into the palm of my hand and furiously rubbed at the stain, recalling leaning my back against the rock as I helped Marcus through. By the time Garrick shoved me inside, the stain was mostly gone.

"Help me hide the gap with rocks," he said. We felt around in the darkness and located three boulders to roll across the opening. The sound of soldiers scouring the hillside below drove us farther into the cave. We dragged Marcus behind us as we felt our way along the rock wall.

A distinct rattle stopped us in our tracks.

"Rattler," Garrick whispered.

"What now?" I said.

The scrape of his sword exiting its scabbard was the only other sound in the cave. "Everybody stay behind me. I'd trade my Camaro for a flashlight right now." I knew he was fond of his car, so he must have been feeling desperate.

"Your sword's not going to do you any good if you can't see what you're swinging at."

"You got a better idea? I'm hoping maybe I'll get lucky."

"With Arbon's army hunting us we're probably goners either way, but that snake can see better than you. If you take a swing at it, you'll be the one to get struck."

"You think you're pretty smart, don't you, little brother?" Garrick said, but I heard him put his sword back into the scabbard. The threatening shake of the rattlesnake's tail held us rooted in place. My arm cramped from holding onto Marcus, and my legs and back ached from the miles of carrying him.

"Duh, the counters," I muttered, reaching into my shirt and pulling on the string.

"What?" Garrick asked.

I clicked one open and turned it toward the sound. The radius of the weak light revealed a mass of boulders piled in front of us—no snake in sight, but there were a dozen shaded crevices where one could be lurking. "What if we back away, slowly," I said. But the sound of soldiers approaching kept us from moving anywhere. I clicked the counter shut and looked over my shoulder. With the boulders we had placed over the opening, only a sliver of light entered the cavern, and we were well into the darkest recesses of the cave.

Metal clanged against the rock face. "I may have found something," a Shuylian said.

"What'd ya find?" said another.

"Cave of sorts," the first answered, blocking the opening with his body. One shove and a boulder toppled into the cave. Brierly, Garrick, and I stood paralyzed, holding our breath, the darkness our only hope. I lowered my lashes, not wanting my eyes to reflect the light. At the sound of the next boulder falling, a second snake picked up rattling.

"Let's have us a look-see," said the second soldier.

"Nah, listen—rattlers in there. You go if you want, but I ain't riskin' a snakebite."

One of the soldiers shoved the other one out of the way and peered in, but the rattler's incessant warning must have kept him at bay as well. "Nothin' in there but snakes," he said, then turned and left.

As the sounds of their search moved upriver, I said, "Should we back up?"

"Yeah," Garrick whispered.

I chuckled. "See? The snake wasn't so bad after all. It saved your life. Aren't you glad you didn't kill it?"

Garrick grunted.

We dragged Marcus away from the rattlers and retreated to where we'd started. Stalemate—we couldn't advance into the cave for fear of the snakes, and we couldn't leave. The sounds of soldiers searching the woods drifted up the hillside as the three of us hunkered around Marcus. Eventually, the rattlers rested their tails. I wondered if they had crawled away or simply grown tired of sounding their warning.

We stayed holed up in the cave until nightfall. Marcus still lay unconscious and unresponsive. The only sign of life was his shallow, ragged breathing and an occasional groan. Searchers had twice climbed our hillside and passed by our cave. With each passing we held our breath and prayed Marcus wouldn't choose that moment to make a noise.

With the soldiers gone for the night, Garrick and I discussed our options. If we had to carry Marcus, we couldn't move quickly enough to put the necessary distance between the Shuylian army and us before sunrise, and to move him would cause him to lose more blood. The soldiers seemed satisfied we weren't in the rattlesnake cave, so we decided to remain hidden.

That night Garrick went for water, but he didn't come back as soon as I anticipated. Agitated, I paced the small space between Marcus and the exit. Had Garrick run into trouble? Should I leave to look for him, or stay to help Brierly and Marcus? The stress was maddening.

I jerked around at the sound of a rock tumbling down the hillside. After a moment of silence, Garrick whispered from the opening, "Look what I found."

"Crap, Garrick! What took so long? You sure know how to give a guy a heart attack."

"Take these," he ordered, handing me the water flasks. Each felt heavy with cold river water.

I took the flasks and offered one to Brierly, then said, "Okay, brother, what did you find? After all the anxiety you just put me through, it better be good."

"Nuts. I got us a whole passel of walnuts." Garrick stepped closer. "Feel this. My shirt front's full of 'em."

"You've got to be kidding me. You were late for that?" I grumbled. "Here I worried about you, and you were picking nuts?"

Garrick laughed. "You worried about me, little brother? I didn't know you cared so much."

I shoved his shoulder. He spent half the night cracking the nuts by the faint light of a counter, then feeling around for the centers. We took turns sleeping and watching Marcus. I walked with Brierly to the river and we cleaned the blood off our clothes and hands. I had dreaded the thought of another day holed up in that cave without at least stretching my legs. A handful of Garrick's raw nuts, some jerky, and hard rolls filled my belly that night.

A smaller contingent of soldiers rode the woods the next day. They seemed to have expanded their search radius. Midmorning they passed the hillside on their way upstream, and what looked like the same group returned in the afternoon, riding past at a gallop.

Marcus came to that night. The first words out of his mouth were "Did you not swear an oath to me that you'd leave for Algonia?"

Smart-aleck Garrick said, "Yes, we did swear an oath and we kept it, too. Soon as you left Arbon's tent we started walking, but I practically fell over you. If you didn't want me pickin' you up, you shouldn't go passing out on the trail I'm plannin' to take. You were a real pain in butt, you know that? You're heavy and you were bleedin' like a stuck pig. Plus, what kind of captain doesn't return and report?"

Once Garrick's mock tirade ended, Marcus's weak laugh joined his friend's hearty chuckle.

"So . . . what happened?" Brierly asked. "How did you get hurt?"

"It looks like Arbon is dead," I said.

"Unless he can put his head back on, he is," Marcus replied.

Brierly leaned closer to her brother. "Tell me everything."

"I got the poison in the wine before they ran me out of their camp. Then during the second watch, I took the guard's place at his tent door. I could hear Arbon snoring while I stood guard. When I entered his tent, I moved to his bedside and smote off his head, a fatal wound by all counts. I began searching his robes for the counters. At first I didn't find them and feared they were hidden at his castle. But when I felt a string across his chest, I pulled on it and the counters slid from under his arm. As I raised my knife and cut the string, something happened. Maybe his nerves made him jerk, I don't know. But his hand moved and from out of nowhere I was flayed open, the force of the blow throwing me to the ground. He held no weapon, and there was no one but Arbon in that tent with me, and he was dead—or so I thought. 'Twas his ghost, or some black magic at work. The shock of the attack and the mass of blood I was losing sent me running for my life. I intended to come back for you, but I couldn't see straight. Everything blurred and spun around me. I don't recollect what happened after I left the tent."

Garrick cleared his throat. "You nearly made it to the woods before you collapsed. We skirted their camp, and Harper and I dragged you out of there. That night we crossed the same river you and I traveled on our way into Shuyle, then angled upstream to the caves. This is our second day in this cave. Arbon's soldiers have been looking for us, but they might finally be losing interest."

"So this is day two?" Marcus asked.

"The tail end of it."

"If they haven't found us yet, I'd guess it's safest to stay put. I propose we wait until they give up searching before we leave. If they don't find us soon, they're bound to assume we've left the area."

Garrick and I nodded. Although still weak, Marcus ventured out of the cave that night and bathed in the river with Brierly's help. We warned him of the rattlesnakes. After religiously staying on our side of the cave, we hadn't heard them since that first day. We thought they'd left, but no one cared enough to risk walking deeper into the cave to find out.

That night Garrick gathered walnuts again. He collected mounds of them, which he cracked and stowed in his pack. Brierly went with him on his gathering expedition, returning with wild lettuce leaves and sour crabapples. All things considered, this seemed like a feast. After living in Arbon's dungeon, I had acclimated to sleeping on rock-hard ground. Each day and into the night I slept soundly, giving my body time to recover.

Our third day in the cave was uneventful. Not a single horseman passed our hillside. When night fell Marcus said, "Although my wound feels like it's on fire, I think I'm well enough to travel. It's already late in the year, and we'll encounter snow over the pass if we don't make haste."

"You don't think we can make it through the Valley of Tierran?" Garrick asked.

"After what I did, I don't dare risk it. We have no idea what the repercussions of Arbon's death will be. I'd rather take my chances against the elements than the wrath of the Shuylian army. Arbon's chief sorcerers are among the most skilled, and I fear they would discover me among their ranks."

We left the cave that night. Thanks to Brierly's poultice and three days of rest, my back had nearly healed. I hoped the tender skin wouldn't again crack open when I carried a pack. Marcus's wound still oozed black pus, and the loss of blood left him able to travel only short distances before he needed rest. For three days we traveled at night, concealing ourselves from any prying Shuylian eyes as soon as the sun rose. During that time we skirted a small mining camp and a crude timber settlement. By the fourth day we were so far from any sign of civilization that we reverted to day travel. Our route took us due north along the backside of the Shuylian Mountains.

On their way into Shuyle, Marcus and Garrick had commandeered one longbow and a quiver of arrows, along with the soldier uniforms. Because of Marcus's injured arm, Garrick and I took turns hunting while we traveled. Rabbits were plentiful in the foothills. On a good day we could bag two or three of them. Other than Garrick's walnuts, we had exhausted the supply of food in our packs. What I'd learned about the Donner Party made me worried about ascending a mountain range with only a sack of nuts and a quiver of arrows.

According to Marcus, springs bubbling with clear water were plentiful, but the game across the top was limited to bighorn sheep, a few deer, and an occasional game bird. Plus, you had a pack of wolves for competition. As a result, our last evening in the lowlands was spent hunting. We bagged five rabbits and two grouse. Marcus thought if we rationed the meat and hurried, that should be enough to get us over the pass.

The Shuylian Mountains were high and rugged, but fortunately not wide. Each mountain peak was stacked in a single-file line, and often one peak blended into the next. The tops of these peaks were snow covered almost year-round. In only a few places was there a low swell between peaks, allowing for travel between one side of the mountain range to the other. The mountains made an ideal natural border.

Many miles north of the Valley of Tierran lay Saddle Pass, one of the few places to cross the mountains. This rocky, narrow gap was one of the few weaknesses in the Shuylian border, yet according to Marcus, its distance from any other Shuylian military target made it impractical for regular use by the Algonian army. All the same, an outpost of Shuylian soldiers guarded it day and night.

Marcus and Garrick had traversed this pass coming into Shuyle. They said that at the time, no more than a dozen soldiers occupied the Shuylian fort, located at the highest point in the pass. With frigid nighttime temperatures near the summit, every guard had been inside when Garrick and Marcus slipped over the summit, unseen. It was through this frigid pass that we intended to return to Algonia.

After making good progress up the mountain the first day, we stopped for the night. Marcus and I went in one direction to collect firewood, while Garrick and Brierly went in another. They took their sweet time, then came back with a small armful of sticks. Garrick laughed at the pile of dead logs we'd accumulated.

"What are you two building? A signal fire? You haven't turned Shuylian on me, have you?" He winked at Brierly, smiling all the while.

Marcus waved him off. "Bah. You're nothing but a worthless rogue."

After cooking our meat and wrapping it for the journey, we bedded down near a spring, under the shelter of an overhanging cliff. This shallow cave sure beat being out in the open. The four of us slept next to each other to conserve body heat.

I awoke the next morning wedged between Brierly and Garrick. I shoved the wool blankets off my face, and a blast of cold wind took my breath away. Snowflakes blew past our meager shelter.

I elbowed Garrick. "Wake up—this doesn't look good."

We all sat and stared into a wall of swirling white snow. Garrick tugged the blanket up to his chin. "No . . . it doesn't look good."

Marcus placed his helmet on his head and stood. "Now who thinks I hauled too much wood? We won't be going anywhere until this clears." He coaxed the remaining coals into a flame, but kept the fire small. After thawing some of our meat, we ate. We spent the entire day huddled together in the corner of our rocky shelter. That night Marcus again built a fire, but he refused to use all the wood. We gathered around the blaze, absorbing every precious wisp of heat at the expense of breathing in smoky air. When the fire burned out, we lay down to sleep, all of us reeking of smoke. When we had the blankets covering our heads, it was like living with a bunch of chain smokers, but the frigid air outside was worse.

We had all expected the weather to clear by morning, so when we again woke to a raging blizzard, I just sat and stared into the storm.

Marcus scraped his knife across the flint, sending a shower of sparks into the tinder. "This will be our last fire." When the sparks didn't catch, Garrick and I hovered over where he worked, blocking the wind. Once Marcus had a flame, we passed him small sticks with our numb fingers. The remaining wood gave enough warmth to take the chill off before we faced the long day ahead. Huddling in our blankets, we watched the last of the coals burn out.

The bitter cold aggravated the painful gnawing in my stomach. Marcus strictly rationed our meat and nuts, and what we ate wasn't nearly enough to compensate for the calories we burned trying to stay warm. The meat had frozen solid, so Marcus hacked at it with the battle ax until it cracked into bite-sized pieces. Before we went to bed on the second day of the blizzard, we each ate a handful of nuts and two chunks of rabbit. In the morning, there were a few walnuts and some grouse meat for each of us.

The cold was getting to Brierly, so we always put her in the middle. Last night Garrick had taken the other middle spot. On this night, I slept in the middle. Brierly had started shaking, and even wrapped in Marcus's arms, she shivered uncontrollably.

I still wore the elfish boots I'd been given in Algonia. I was wearing them when Arbon's guards threw me into the dungeon, and I'd walked out of there with them on my feet. They were indeed magic, as Theobald had promised. My feet and the part of my legs covered by the boots were comfortably warm. Both Garrick and Marcus wore the same quality boots. Brierly, on the other hand, had thin-soled, slave-issue boots from her time of servitude. Once we realized she was too cold, we traded our boots around, always keeping a pair on her feet. During the day, we sat with our fingers shoved into the tops of the boots to warm them, then we'd hold our warm fingers to our faces and ears. Tonight, since I lay in the middle, Brierly wore my boots. My stocking feet already felt the chill. Halfway through the night I'd get Marcus's boots. Sleep was hard to come by in such miserable conditions.

Morning finally dawned, and to our dismay we looked out into a flurry of falling snowflakes. The wind had died, but the clouds were dumping quarter-sized pieces of fluffy snow. The visibility had improved, but was hardly adequate. We were all weak from lack of food, and stiff from the cold.

I pulled Marcus aside. "I hate the thought of walking through that snow," I said through chattering teeth, "but at some point we have to leave. It's only getting deeper while we're getting weaker. If we stay here we'll freeze to death, starting with Brierly. I didn't come all this way to die sittin' under a rock ledge on the side of a stinkin' Shuylian mountain."

Marcus shook his head, an anguished look on his face. "This wasn't how I planned it. By day five we should have been descending the Borderland side of the pass, not trapped near the top in a blizzard. I can't lose my sister now—not before my mother sees her safe. I pray I didn't make a fatal error. But with snowfall like this, we'll be soaked through in no time. Let's give it until midday. The worst of it might be blowing over."

I feared it was already too late for us. Weak and tired, I had nothing more to say and returned to the shelter of our blankets. Garrick had Brierly sitting in front of him, with both of his arms wrapped around her. Her petite hands fit into the top of his boots. Once her hands warmed, she'd cover her face, nose, or ears. I watched them while I paced our tiny shelter, trying to generate some body heat. Brierly's teeth chattered, and her lips had a bluish tint. It took a full-time effort to keep oneself from getting frostbite.

Garrick must have taken it upon himself to help Brierly stay warm, because he devoted all of his energy to making her comfortable. He kept her water flask near his body to keep it from freezing. He let her wear his boots so often that she finally insisted he take them back before he lost his toes to frostbite. Marcus's threat regarding touching his sister obviously didn't apply to Garrick's efforts to keep her warm—instead, her brother appeared grateful. Rough and tough Garrick had a tender, attentive side I had only seen when he'd been with Rose. I didn't know if he had any feelings for Brierly other than the same friendship and compassion I felt toward her, but he always seemed to know how to help her.

Marcus distributed the last of the walnuts and a few chunks of meat. We held the frozen meat in our mouths until it thawed enough that we could chew it. "We'll never make it all the way over the pass now," Marcus said. "Without all this snow, it would have been one hard day of hiking from here to the summit. I'd hoped to bypass the guard station undetected during the night, but that's not going to happen. We need to take provisions or we'll never make it off the mountain alive. When we're finished eating we'll leave. We'll hike through the day and all night if we have to, but we'll not stop until we reach the outpost. It should be nearly a full moon tonight, so if the clouds clear we can see where we're going. If not—"

Marcus never finished his sentence. He didn't have to. None of us were under any illusions. If we lost our way in the snow, it would be the end.

TWENTY-TWO
Summit

The snowpack was a good two feet deep, drifting to four feet in places. We walked single file, so whoever led worked the hardest. Garrick, Marcus, and I took turns breaking the trail. My knees and thighs stung from the cold, wet snow, and the icy air burned a path down my throat and into my lungs. As we hiked, the snowfall lessened and then stopped completely. The heavy cloud cover blew off to the south, and by nightfall a radiant moon appeared on the horizon. The brilliant white snow reflected the moonlight, making it easy for us to see, but with the clearing skies the temperature plummeted.

Our packs were nearly empty, since we had no food and wore every spare piece of clothing. Our blankets were wrapped around our heads and shoulders. Garrick and Marcus each carried a pack, with Marcus leading the way, followed by me, carrying the bow and arrows. Garrick brought up the rear with Brierly. The two of them frequently fell behind, so Marcus and I had to stop and wait.

The exertion of hiking through deep snow had me pouring sweat in spite of the cold. I finally felt warm, but now that I'd worked up a sweat, I couldn't stop moving. In temperatures like this, if we stopped for the night without shelter and warmth, we would freeze to death.

Brierly's weak voice caught my attention. "I can't take another step. You go on—I'll follow your trail and catch up later."

"No, you can do it," Garrick said. "Put one foot in front of the other and don't think about it. I'm not leaving you."

I turned to look. He walked behind Brierly with his hand on her back, propelling her up terrain that felt like a treadmill on high incline. "I can't," she sobbed, falling to her knees.

Garrick shrugged the pack off his shoulders. "Harper, take this." I walked back down the trail and took his pack. "Hold my blanket," he said. My burning throat made talking difficult so I just followed his orders. He pulled Brierly to her feet. "Help me get her on my back and put my blanket over her."

Brierly clung to Garrick's shoulders, her face next to his. I put his blanket over her. "Can you hang on to this?" I held the ends next to her pale hands. She opened her shaking fingers and clutched the blanket. I pulled it over both their heads, and we left to catch Marcus.

The captain seemed prone to tunnel vision at times. It was a while later before he stopped to make sure we still followed him, and by then we had almost caught up. He turned and marched back down the mountain, his eyes trained on Garrick. "What are you doing? Put her down. She needs to keep moving to stay warm."

Garrick was breathing so heavily he couldn't answer at first. Finally, he said, "She's too weak. Plus, we're traveling faster this way. She needs shelter and a fire, not a hike in the mountains."

Marcus raised his voice. "Well, that's where I'm taking her, and I say she needs to walk. She's got to be moving or she'll fall asleep and freeze to death."

"We'll get there twice as fast if I carry her. And I say we need to get there sooner, rather than later," Garrick yelled back.

Marcus moved threateningly toward Garrick. "I'm her brother, and I disagree."

I held out my hands. "Guys—"

Brierly choked out a sob. "Stop it, you two. Marcus, I cannot take another step. Leave me be."

With an angry grunt, Marcus whirled around and hiked off at a furious pace. The hunger and cold were getting to everyone, and once again my thoughts turned to the Donner Party and the deadly Sierra Nevada mountains.

The captain pulled ahead while I stayed back with Garrick. We kept moving through the night. By the light of early morning we crested the summit and saw the outpost in the distance.

Marcus ducked behind a drift of snow and waited for us. Garrick set Brierly on her feet, and we watched the outpost while we caught our breath. The shelter for the animals was crudely built, but the two cottages looked cozy, and smoke exited one of the chimneys. From what we could see, there wasn't a guard posted outside. Tracks in the snow led from the cottage to the barn. Other than that, it was clear the Shuylian soldiers hadn't left the cottage since the storm hit.

"There are only six horses in the corral," Marcus said.

"Where do you think the others went?" Garrick asked.

Marcus's cracked lips formed a smile, and I could see tiny icicles dangling from his beard. "I don't know, but if their riders are with them that evens up our odds a bit."

Now that we were at the outpost, Garrick and Marcus seemed to forget their earlier disagreement. Garrick reached into the pack on my back and pulled out a piece of oilskin cloth tied closed with twine. He unfolded it and handed me a pistol and two clips.

I pocketed one clip and loaded the other. "I didn't know you had guns."

"For emergencies."

Marcus pointed to the cottage. "We have the element of surprise on our side. So, the three of us will barge in, take out the enemy, and then come back for my sister."

I looked up as I slid a bullet into the chamber. "Shouldn't we give them a chance to surrender first?"

Marcus shrugged and drew his sword. "We could offer, but they wouldn't accept. Follow me."

With her eyes on Garrick, Brierly whispered, "Be careful."

Marcus darted through the snow, the battle-ax swinging loosely in one hand and his sword poised for action in the other. Garrick left his sword in its scabbard and loaded his pistol. It was reassuring to know the soldiers wouldn't have guns. But they most certainly had swords and bows.

Marcus zigzagged to the cottage and pressed his back against the wall. The sound of the soldiers' voices drifted out as Garrick and I joined our friend. We crept forward, the crunch of the snow underfoot sounding thunderous in the early morning stillness. I repositioned my fingers around the cold steel of the handgun. I hated fighting, and the only way I could do it was to think of Brierly freezing to death today if we didn't succeed.

We stepped onto the porch, placing each footstep with care. Garrick moved next to Marcus. Standing before the door, Marcus raised three fingers from his sword hilt and mouthed, "On three." Garrick nodded, and Marcus began counting with his fingers. *One, two.* A low growl sounded on the other side of the door, followed by angry barking. Marcus quickly put down his third finger. He and Garrick kicked the door open, sending two dogs sprawling across the room. Instantly, we were under attack. The dogs lunged for our legs, while six men scrambled out of their chairs or off their bunks and lunged for their weapons. Marcus stabbed one dog through the back of the head when its jaws clamped down on his leg. Garrick fired two shots at the other.

"Attack," the Shuylians' leader yelled. A wall of soldiers ran toward us. When a hatchet flew at my head I ducked, and it lodged into the doorframe next to me. With a yell Marcus jumped forward, swinging his sword and the ax. Garrick and I stood side by side in the doorway with our pistols. One by one we picked off four of the Shuylians as they ran toward us with swords raised. Marcus beheaded the first soldier he encountered and now dueled with the second. Garrick took aim, and when Marcus moved clear of the line of fire, Garrick finished off the last soldier. Within seconds, we'd taken the pass. Sickened, I turned and left the cottage.

I walked back to Brierly and pulled her to her feet. Shaking from the cold, she could hardly walk. I swept her into my arms and carried her down to the outpost. Garrick stood waiting at the door. I stepped over the dead dogs and entered. The smell of blood in the warm air turned my stomach. I stepped over the soldiers' bodies and set Brierly in the chair Garrick had placed before the fire.

Marcus filled a cup with steaming liquid and handed it to her. "Drink this."

Wide-eyed, she looked around the room. "I can't stay in here . . . with them."

Marcus pointed at Garrick and me. "Get the bodies out of here."

We started with the dogs, dragging their carcasses through the snow, away from the cottage. The vacant eyes of the soldiers bored holes in my soul. I pulled the corpses by their ankles, trying not to look at their faces.

We spent the day warming ourselves and cooking food. Garrick massaged Brierly's feet and hands in warm water, while Marcus fried some pork and potatoes he found in the cellar. Even with Garrick's warning, I ate too much. An hour later I was throwing it up outside. Garrick and Marcus both felt ill, but neither of them threw up. Brierly helped Garrick make a soup for dinner. It was mostly broth and easier on our stomachs.

In the middle of the night, howling wolves awakened me. Probably, the scent of blood had lured them to the pile of dead bodies. The Shuylian horses were secured within a sturdy fence, but their agitated neighing only added to the restlessness of the night.

Dawn broke with the wolves gone and the horses still alive in their paddock. I fed them and milked the cow. I failed to milk her dry—I didn't have the patience for that—but I got enough for us to drink with breakfast. All the while I thought of Ellie teaching me to milk her cow. That was so long ago—it almost seemed like another lifetime. *Where is she now?* Surely she had waited for me at Archidus' fortress.

We rested for two days and ate the soldiers' food. But as the time passed, Marcus grew restless. On the second afternoon, Garrick busied himself teaching Brierly how to play poker with the Shuylians' version of face cards. I lay on one of the cots, my hands tucked under my head, enjoying my full stomach and a soft bunk. Marcus paced across the room and rifled through the stack of parchment he'd already read a hundred times.

"Marcus, what's bothering you?" I asked him.

He tossed the Shuylian papers on the floor. "There are no orders for this fort. No schedule. I don't like wasting time like this, especially when we're holed up in the enemy's outpost."

"We needed the rest and we needed the food. There was no way we could have gone on."

"I agree, but I'd like to get off this mountain, and the sooner the better. There were twelve horses here last time. Maybe the other six men pulled out for the winter, but maybe they went for supplies and are on their way back."

Garrick turned his head from his game. "We're rested and we're full. So when do you want to leave?"

"At first light tomorrow," Marcus answered.

Garrick nodded. "Now that we got that settled, sit down and relax for a minute." He looked at Brierly, and taking a handful of almonds from a sack, he said, "I'll see your five and raise you another five." He counted out ten nuts for the game, then tossed the rest into his mouth.

I took a deep breath. Nothing could beat the comfort of a warm fire and hanging out with friends.

At first light we saddled the Shuylian horses, packing two of them with a tent, blankets, food, and other supplies for the trail. We took the men's fur-lined coats and hats from the cottage, plus anything else we thought we might need.

Riding down the Algonian side of Saddle Pass on horses sure beat hiking up the Shuylian side on foot. We made camp late that night and ate salted pork, hard biscuits, and almonds. Tied to trees, the horses probably weren't as comfortable. They pawed the ground, looking for grass, and by morning they had gnawed the bark off the trees.

The snow thinned as we descended the mountain. A second Shuylian outpost lay at the base of Saddle Pass. With the frigid temperatures, they weren't any more diligent in guarding the pass than the soldiers on top.

Although only a skiff of snow covered the valley, it was bitter cold. Three cottages and a larger barnyard made up the outpost. When we skirted the place at midnight, all of the buildings were dark, and every window had been shuttered against the cold. A lone horse whinnied as we walked past, but no one came out. We traveled well into the night to put a safe distance between us and the Shuylians, then made a crude tent out of an oilskin tarp. Our horses had left a trail in the snow leading right to our camp, so we posted a guard in case we were followed. I took the first watch, followed by Marcus, then Garrick.

When I stretched and opened my eyes the next morning, Garrick sat at the tent's opening, grinning back at me. "What?" I grumbled, still half asleep.

"It's snowing, little brother," he whispered excitedly.

"I hate snow. I'm going back to sleep."

Marcus and Brierly stirred next to me. There would be no going back to sleep if the captain awoke. Once he was up, everyone was up. But now that I was awake, I realized the value of those thick snowflakes. Our tracks were rapidly disappearing.

The Borderlands were socked in with heavy cloud cover, and the temperature felt milder. We ate quickly and packed up camp.

"The Borderland this far north is much wider than where we crossed last time," Marcus said once we were ready to go.

I rolled my eyes and grunted in disappointment.

"But bear in mind the advantages. Dragons aren't fond of the cold and rarely patrol these lands."

I smiled. "That does make me feel better."

TWENTY-THREE
Gatekeeper

Crossing the northern end of the Susack Plain took five days of hard travel. There wasn't a soul in sight, as far as the eye could see. We were able to keep Brierly dry and relatively warm. She wore a Shuylian fur hat and coat, and as usual, Garrick attended to her every need. They often rode side by side, chatting with each other, while Marcus and I were content to travel in the company of our own thoughts.

My mind was on Ellie and my family. What were they thinking right now? Did my parents assume I'd run away with her? I couldn't remember what I had told Jessica about Master Archidus, and I wondered if there was any chance she could accurately guess my fate. Maybe my family thought I was dead. I still had a long road to travel before I found any answers.

The horrors of the past few months haunted my dreams. Brierly or Garrick reached out to comfort me many times when my screams awoke them in the night. Even in the light of day, the dead eyes of the soldiers I'd killed hung at the forefront of my memory, and when they weren't haunting me, flashbacks of Arbon's torture sent my heart racing.

"We're getting closer now," Marcus said on the sixth day.

We had left the plain and plunged into the woods. Icicles hung from tree branches, and crusty snow covered the ground. Marcus seemed to relax once we crossed the border into Algonia. We were plodding along, feeling a sense of safety at being so far away from the enemy, when angry Algonian soldiers suddenly surrounded us. Caught unawares, we were yanked off our horses. Two soldiers threw me face first into the snow and seized my weapon.

"What the—" yelled Garrick.

"Halt! I demand to see a Gatekeeper," Marcus shouted.

The Algonian leader laughed at him. "That's what you all say, but you're nothing but a pack of thieving liars. Think you can fool the Gatekeeper, do ya? There'll be no leniency for Shuylian scum in these parts."

"What?" I said. But running on the heels of that question was the distinct thought, *We're dressed as Shuylian soldiers, riding Shuylian horses, and we're far from the fortress city of Master Archidus.* "I can explain. I'm a Keeper. If you'll take us to Master Archidus, he can—"

The soldier brought the hilt of his sword down on the back of my head and laughed. "Keeper, my eye. You're a filthy Shuylian deserter. Look at yerself. We got us a whole passel of 'em locked up already, and you'll be joining 'em."

With a sword pressed to his throat, Marcus's hands were secured behind his back. "I'm Marcus Landseer, captain of Algonia's twenty-fifth regiment. If there is any question regarding the identity of any individual crossing the border, Algonian law dictates that person has the right to an immediate audience with a Gatekeeper."

The Algonian leader spat in the snow. "Ain't no question in my mind what you are, but I'll see if the Gatekeeper's available. For now, you'll sit in prison like every other Shuylian soldier who dared step foot in Algonia."

The soldier tying Brierly tried to look at her but she dropped her head. "You're a young 'un. Them Shuylians must be getting desperate."

Again Marcus attempted to change their minds. "We're all Algonian. We stole the clothes and the horses to flee Shuyle. The young one is my little brother. He was kidnapped as a youth and forced into servitude by the Shuylians. The other two are Keepers, as they say—the Guardian and the Protector. Master Archidus awaits their return in Cadré Unair. You cannot afford to detain us. We must speak with a Gatekeeper."

Marcus's words were ignored, and the soldiers marched us at sword point past the outskirts of their village. The gate to a heavily guarded enclosure opened, and the four of us were shoved inside. We turned to see over a hundred true Shuylian soldiers staring back at us.

Algonian bowmen stood guard on the corner watchtowers. The walls, made of vertical logs filed to sharp points, stood at least ten feet high. "Untie me," Marcus said, turning his hands toward Garrick and me.

With our hands tied behind our backs, Garrick turned around and worked on it while Brierly and I watched. "I can't get my fingers between the knots," he muttered.

"Let me try," Brierly whispered. "My fingers are smaller."

She turned and felt for the rope. I watched her, wondering how the Algonian soldier who tied her wrists had failed to notice her long fingernails and the feminine quality of her delicate hands. She wedged her nails between the knots and worked them free.

"Thank you," Marcus said. He quickly rubbed his wrists before untying Garrick and me. Garrick untied Brierly. He wrapped his arm around her shoulder, ushering her to a seat on a vacant log. Marcus and I followed and dropped to our haunches in front of them. A pile of firewood lay near the door, and a handful of fires burned around the outdoor enclosure, each crowded with soldiers trying to stay warm. In our fur coats, we were dressed warmer than most. While the majority of the soldiers ignored us, a few glared in our direction.

Marcus took off his hat and ran his fingers through his hair. "We should have been taken to the Gatekeeper posthaste, not thrown in prison. When I get out of here, I'll have that captain court-martialed." Marcus stood and paced in front of us.

"What's a Gatekeeper?" I asked.

"A sorcerer who can discern the truth of one's words. We have them stationed at intervals along our border. If we're lucky there'll be one nearby, and—"

Brierly dropped her gaze, twisting her fingers in her lap. "Hush, brother. They're coming."

At the sound of someone behind us, Marcus stiffened. He and I turned. "Where you from?" demanded the biggest of the five soldiers standing before us.

"Caldor," Marcus said.

"They don't make them fur coats in Caldor."

"We deliver supplies to the outpost in Saddle Pass, but we were caught in a blizzard—whiteout conditions. We found ourselves on the Algonian side of the Susack Plain once the weather cleared." Marcus paused, then slowly turned away, saying, "But if you don't mind we'd like to keep to ourselves."

The soldier leered at Brierly. "I do mind. Who's the pretty boy? Maybe he'd like to warm himself by our fire."

The muscles in Marcus's jaw tightened, and Garrick leapt to his feet. The Shuylian laughed. "You're friend here must like pretty boys."

Garrick lunged forward, throwing a quick jab into the soldier's face. A spurt of blood erupted from the man's nose. An arrow whizzed past my face and stuck in the ground between the two men.

"Stand down, soldiers," yelled the Algonian guard, "or my next arrow finds its way to your heart."

Both Marcus and I pulled Garrick back. "Relax or you're gonna get yourself killed," I whispered.

Marcus yanked the arrow out of the ground and held it next to his leg as the Shuylians backed away. "Sit down, you fool," Marcus said, pushing Garrick onto the log next to Brierly. "We'll not be sleeping tonight if the Gatekeeper doesn't send for us soon."

The minutes of our imprisonment turned to hours. At dusk the gate opened, and Algonian guards carried in two large pots and several baskets of bread. "Form a line and wait yer turn," one of them yelled.

Prisoners were allowed to approach the food four at a time. When our turn arrived, we walked forward and received a scoop of rice in one hand and a slice of wheat bread in the other.

Garrick and Brierly went through in the group before us and were walking away as Marcus and I approached the guards. When Marcus got his bread he stopped. "Move on then," ordered the guard.

"Cabot?" Marcus said.

The guard narrowed his gaze. "How do you know me by name?"

Marcus paused, letting the other two Shuylians get their bread and rice and leave. "It's Marcus Landseer. We served together in the Fourteenth, under Captain Andarton—"

"What are you doing with the Shuylians? I wouldn't have figured you for a turncoat."

"I'm no traitor," Marcus whispered. "I was in Shuyle on a special mission for Master Archidus. This was my disguise to get out of there. I need to talk with a Gatekeeper. I've got two Keepers with me. I didn't rescue them from Arbon so they could die in an Algonian prison camp."

A shove in the back from the dull end of the other guard's spear propelled Marcus forward. "Quit your talking and move along."

The captain turned to walk backward. "Cabot, you know me. See that man there, the one with the young soldier? He's a Keeper. He has enemies in here. Mark my words he'll be dead by morning if somebody doesn't let me talk to the Gatekeeper."

"I'll see what I can do," Cabot said.

"What took you so long?" Garrick asked when Marcus and I sat down. Garrick and Brierly were almost finished eating.

Marcus bit into his bread. "I know that guard. We served together ten years ago, before I made captain."

"Will he help us?" Brierly asked.

"I hope so."

It was fully dark before a group of guards with torches entered the enclosure and sought out Marcus. When we all stood to follow him, two guards flashed their swords in our faces. "Until we sort this out, your friends stay here."

We turned and sat down. Marcus's words regarding Garrick were foremost in my mind, and I intently watched the shadowy figures of the Shuylians. A group of them had congregated around one of the fires. The oversized man Garrick had hit looked like he was working to rile up a mob. I slid my fingers around the arrow— our only weapon.

When he left the fire, only three men accompanied him. Garrick was busy talking to Brierly. "Brother, your friend's coming back for round two," I said softly.

Garrick looked up at the four soldiers. "Brierly, stay back."

I stood, my nerves on edge, rolling the arrow between my fingers. "Let's hope the bowman can't find our hearts in the dark."

Garrick rose next to me. "We can always hope."

The four Shuylians stopped in front of us. "No one makes a fool of me and lives to tell about it," the big man said.

Garrick raised his hands in surrender. "Look, I'm sorry about that. I've had a rough day. Maybe we can start—"

The man lunged at him. Grunting in pain, Garrick doubled over while his nemesis pummeled him in the head.

The first soldier to reach me got the arrow through the heart. I yanked on the shaft as the man fell, but it snapped off in my hand. I moved lightly on my feet, trying to remember everything I'd learned about hand-to-hand combat. I held my own against my next opponent, trying to move closer to Garrick as I fought. Something wasn't right. He'd finally begun fighting back, but he wasn't himself.

Like kids on a playground, a mob of Shuylians gathered to gawk at the fight. I was so focused on the battle, I forgot about Brierly until she screamed behind me. There was no mistaking her feminine voice. I lunged at my opponent, raking the splintered end of the arrow shaft across his throat. Clutching his neck, he backed away from me, blood oozing between his fingers.

Where to go next? Something was definitely wrong with Garrick, but a burly Shuylian had shoved Brierly against the wall, and she struggled futilely against him. He was laughing wickedly when I tackled him. We hit the ground as a chorus of shouts echoed through the enclosure.

"Halt! Halt! Stand down!" Guards carrying torches rushed through the gate, and the crowd of bystanders faded into the shadows. Marcus rushed into the fray, wielding a sword. In one motion, he yanked me off the Shuylian and drove his sword through the man's heart.

Brierly screamed. "Garrick."

I looked behind me in time to see my brother crumple onto the frozen dirt. I scrambled across the ground and rolled him onto his back. Imbedded in his thigh was a knife-sized splinter of wood. The Algonian guards took care of Garrick's attacker and the one I'd wounded, dropping them to the ground in a dead heap.

"Marcus, we need a doctor . . . a healer . . . whatever they're called," I yelled.

Garrick lay unconscious but still breathing, and blood saturated his whole leg. With the amount of blood he was losing, the wood splinter must have severed a major artery. Brierly and I tore a strip off his pant leg and fastened a tourniquet. The guards brought a board in and carried Garrick out of the prison, then laid him in a wagon. I helped Brierly in and jumped on the back just before the horses galloped away. Marcus had barked orders, and everyone in the vicinity had obeyed him. His meeting with the Gatekeeper had obviously gone well.

We traveled about a mile before we entered the village. The wagon jerked to a stop in front of an ancient apothecary shop. Marcus vaulted from the wagon seat and banged on the door. A tall woman with silver-gray hair cracked the door. Marcus bowed in respect. "I have an injured man—a Keeper—can you please heal him?"

The door opened wider. "A Keeper, you say?" she asked in a melodic voice. "This I must see for myself. Bring him in."

We carried Garrick through the shop and set him on a table in a cluttered back room. The dim candlelight cast eerie shadows across the walls. Stacks of dusty bottles lined the shelves, and books lay open on chairs.

"He's Shuylian?" she questioned.

"No, he is not. We've just escaped from Shuyle and haven't anything else to wear," Marcus said.

She raised her slender hand and waved us away. "Well, then, out with you so I can be about my business."

Marcus spun around and left. Before I turned, I watched the woman as she bent to study Garrick's wound. She slid a lock of her silver hair behind a delicately pointed elf ear. I exited the apothecary shop, leaving my brother in what I hoped were the capable hands of a healer.

I found Marcus and Brierly sitting on the back of the wagon and joined them to wait for word on Garrick's condition. "It must have gone good with the Gatekeeper," I said.

Marcus sighed. "Once I got in to see him, there was no question of my integrity and identity. This should never have happened. It's maddening that we weren't taken directly to him."

I shook my head, thinking about what might be happening in the dusty old apothecary shop. If Garrick were in a modern-day hospital, I would feel more confident about a full recovery. But here . . . I had no clue what his chances were with magic medicine.

The three of us, along with the driver of the wagon, sat in silence. Brierly pulled her knees up under her oversized coat and lowered her head. I could tell she was worried sick about Garrick.

I jerked around at the sound of a carriage approaching. It rolled to a stop next to the wagon. A dignified old man in a fur-trimmed black cloak stepped out to greet us. "Good evening."

"Evening, sir," Marcus said. "Protector Chase Harper, I'd like to present you to Lampaigne, the northern Gatekeeper."

I hopped off the wagon and extended my hand. "It's a pleasure to meet you, sir."

Lampaigne clasped my wrist, his fingers wrapping around the iron shackle. He raised an eyebrow at me and smiled. His gaze penetrated into my soul. "The greatest pleasure of this acquaintance is most certainly mine. I see life's journey has not been an easy one, but do not let that discourage you. Etched in your heart is worry for your brother. Was he alive upon entrance to Madam Sabina's shop?"

"Yes."

The Gatekeeper's smiled broadened. "Ahh, then you have nothing to fear. Madam Sabina is one of the finest healers in Algonia. Your brother won't escape this life once she is watching over him."

I smiled, trusting Lampaigne instantly, and a rush of hot tears filled my eyes. "Thank you." I began to pull back my hand but he held it firmly.

"Perhaps you wish me to remove these shackles? Or do you desire to wear them as a token of your great feat? For I know of no other who has seen the inside of Lord Arbon's dungeon and lived to tell the tale."

I chuckled. "That's one great feat I'd actually rather forget." The shackle on my right wrist clicked open and fell into Lampaigne's hand.

Smiling, I rubbed the calluses around my wrist. At one pressure point the skin was still raw and cracked. "Thank you." I extended my left hand, and the Gatekeeper wrapped his fingers around that shackle. It too fell away.

He offered them back to me. "Would you care to keep them?"

I looked at the shackles, each marked with the roaring dragon—Shuyle's national symbol. "Absolutely not. I hope I never see them again. You can have them. Now you know someone who escaped the dungeon, and you have the shackles to prove it."

"Thank you, Keeper. Good luck to you in your upcoming journey. Please give my well wishes to the Guardian."

Lampaigne turned to face Marcus. "Captain Landseer, your services to Algonia will forever be remembered, and your name will be had for good throughout the annals of the Algonian nation. As a people we are deeply indebted to you."

The Gatekeeper and the captain bowed to each other. "Thank you, sir," Marcus said.

The old sorcerer climbed into his carriage, and his matched pair of white horses trotted into the darkness.

TWENTY-FOUR
Fortress City

A few hours later, the door to Madam Sabina's Apothecary opened. The graceful elf exited her shop, and to my astonishment, Garrick followed in her footsteps, with nothing more than a slight limp. I jumped from the wagon and rushed toward them.

"He's okay?" I asked her.

"Your friend suffered a great loss of blood. You were fortunate to get him to me when you did. I have regenerated his blood supply and mended the wound. However, the new tissue needs time to strengthen. He'll not be fit for battle until the passing of two weeks' time. I administered a dose of liquid energy, so he'll have the strength to travel. I hear both of you are anxious to return to the fortress city."

"Yes, we are. Thank you, Madam Sabina."

She nodded once. "You are most welcome."

We were given lodging in the military barracks on the edge of town, which Marcus called the Village of Lewknor. The barracks consisted of a circle of small cottages with thatched roofs.

The driver of the wagon stopped beside one. "Hopefully someone started a fire to warm the place up for ya. If not, firewood's 'round back."

Marcus reached over and clasped his wrist. "Thank you, soldier."

Garrick limped into the cottage, leaning on Brierly.

"Keeper," Marcus said to me, "we should take in wood." The two of us loaded our arms with firewood. When we entered the cottage, Brierly had located and lit a candle off the glowing embers in the fireplace. The one-room cottage contained four cots, a table and chairs, and a stone fireplace.

Marcus added fresh logs to the coals, and soon the crackle of a roaring blaze filled the room. Someone had unloaded our packs from the Shuylian horses and leaned them against the wall next to the door. Garrick lowered himself onto a cot, and Brierly spread a blanket over him as I pulled out a chair.

A small table in the center of the room held food. There were four pewter mugs and an earthenware jug with a large cork in the top. Famished, I bit into an apple while surveying the selection of breads and cheeses. After eating our fill, my friends and I fell asleep, warm in our beds. Only once during the night did I wake up—in a sweat, panicking over what had happened in my nightmare. Everyone else remained asleep when I bolted out of bed in terror.

As usual Marcus was the first to rise in the morning. He was nowhere to be found when the rest of us awoke. Garrick was moving stiffly, and by the gray light of dawn I saw an assortment of bruises across his face. Unable to defend himself, he'd taken a beating as a result of the wooden splinter lodged in his leg. Although I had a tender spot on my cheek, I'd fared much better. The ache in my once-cracked rib flared up whenever it got hit, and this morning was no exception.

"I wonder where my brother is," Brierly said.

"Hopefully getting us a ride out of here," I replied.

I stoked the fire to take off the morning chill, and we finished the remainder of the food from the night before. The door opened and Marcus stepped in. After settling himself in front of the blaze, he said, "We've got a choice. We can lay over here for a week while Garrick recovers and travel in the company of a regiment heading south. Or we can leave immediately for the fortress city with a small escort of Algonian soldiers."

"Are we riding or walking?" Garrick asked.

"Riding. We have the six Shuylian horses at our disposal."

"I can ride. Let's press on."

"The northern region is one of the poorest in Algonia. They've offered us a few provisions for the journey, but I don't feel we can ask for more than that. We'll have to endure the shame of these Shuylian clothes a bit longer, I'm afraid. Thankfully, we'll have an escort to vouch for our identities, as well as two Algonian messengers who carry reports to and from Cadré Unair."

Traveling from the Village of Lewknor to Cadré Unair took six days. We were viewed with scorn in the villages we passed through. But if the people only realized the rough-looking man in the dirty Shuylian soldier uniform was none other than the Algonian captain who'd destroyed the hated Lord Arbon, I'm sure their reaction would have been much different. The Algonian messengers handled questions relating to our identities, and any delays were brief.

On the evening of the sixth day, we exited the dense forest surrounding the fortress city and followed the gray wall to its entrance. A mounted guard raised his spear and yelled, "Halt!"

We stopped our horses. What had been heavy double doors was now a charred mess of splintered planks. Sections of the stone wall had crumbled under what must have been a mighty attack. The Algonian flag, charred on one corner and torn on another, hung at a crooked angle. Our messengers spent a lengthy amount of time discussing us with the guards patrolling the destroyed entrance.

My horse pranced underneath me, no doubt feeding off my agitation. If the city had been attacked, where was Ellie? Killed, or taken captive? Was she even now on her way into Shuyle, or did she wait for me in the castle as I had expected? The relief I felt at arriving had quickly disappeared.

Up on the catwalk, a line of bowmen, standing at full draw with their arrows trained on our hearts, forced us to keep our distance.

After some time, one of the messengers returned to report. "The fortress city is strictly limiting access to only those who live in Cadré Unair or those with official business."

Marcus leaned forward and said in a raised voice, "Where's the king? Did you not tell him who I am? If anyone has official business in Cadré Unair, it is I."

"I told the guards, but they refused you an audience with the king and failed to give me any indication of the current state of affairs. They ordered me to leave my report at the gate and return on the morrow for the return reply. The four of you are to stay put. This protocol is quite unusual."

While the sun set we waited. The diligent bowmen never once relaxed their stance. It was unnerving. *Wouldn't that be my luck—make it this far and then have one of those archers flinch and send his arrow through my heart?* I finally had to turn my horse and look away.

The air grew chill, and a dense fog rolled into the valley below. I longed to take Ellie by the hand and walk the few miles through that forest and enter Witches Hollow on a one-way ticket to Oregon.

"Marcus, my friend, is that you?" called an elderly voice. I yanked on my reins, spinning my horse to again face the fortress.

Wickliff, flanked by four guards, walked toward us. As they picked their way through the rubble, I smiled at the familiar and beloved face of the ancient elf. Marcus vaulted off his horse and strode forward. I glanced at the bowmen before dismounting. They were lowering their weapons. Marcus and Wickliff embraced, and then the old elf looked at me and spread his arms wide. With misty eyes and an emotional voice, he said, "My young Keeper, it is indeed a miracle you found your way back to us."

I stepped forward and wrapped my arms around him. "Wickliff, you have no idea how glad I am to see you again. But Ellie—is she here?"

"No, I'm afraid not. She and Perception's Keeper were at the castle when I left for my home. I was called back a week later to attend to the affairs of the nation while Archidus led the army south to face Legard and the Shuylians. The urgency of the situation prevented us from discussing anything more than the most pressing of matters. It was sometime later that I thought to inquire as to their whereabouts. A woman in the castle informed me that Ellie left to return to the old world with Perception's Keeper. Unfortunately, that seems to be the only information available."

I stared back at him. I had expected to find Ellie here, waiting for me. "Can you send me back through Witches Hollow?" I asked, beginning to turn in that direction.

"I can, but now?" Wickliff said. "Keeper, come, you must be tired . . . hungry? Let us eat. I want to hear of what transpired since we were last in each other's company."

"But I don't want her waiting," I muttered.

"My young friend, remember what I said? Use your counter and her wait can be mercifully shortened. There is no need to rush off."

Garrick stepped next to me and placed a hand on my shoulder. "Little brother, you go back lookin' like that—smellin' like that— your girlfriend's gonna be doin' the rushing off."

I glanced at my filthy hands and jagged nails, then brushed my fingers across my beard. Now that I was thinking about myself, the lice on my head started squirming, sending me into a frenzy of scratching. "Yeah, maybe you're right."

We led our horses through the opening and entered the fortress city. Thankfully the destruction seemed limited to the courtyard area and the entrance. A few buildings had burned, including the guard station, but the inner city appeared untouched by the battle.

Wickliff pointed to a group of soldiers marching toward us. "Although we have driven the enemy out of our lands, as a precaution the city is patrolled by soldiers, and only a few civilians are allowed to travel the streets, especially after dark."

I spent an hour with two servants. They provided an oversized tub full of hot, soapy water, and I soaked and cleaned every square inch of my body. When I mentioned the lice, one of the servants left, promising he had something to take care of that. He soon returned with a bottle of foul-smelling liquid, which he lathered into my scalp. The scent burned my nose and made my eyes water. I put a towel over my face to breathe. "This reeks!" I said. "What is it?"

The servant laughed. "It's good potion. Lice don't like it either. They'll leave you be now." He washed and dried his hands. "Let it soak in till I return." The servant gathered up my filthy Shuylian clothes and motioned for the other guy to follow him.

"How long—" I began, but they were already out the door. "Smelling like this, everybody will leave me be."

It didn't take long before the stench started suffocating me. With one towel over my face and one around my waist, I shoved open the window and sucked in the cool air. I stayed by the window even after goosebumps raised along my arms.

Finally, the servant returned, carrying a stack of clean clothes in one arm and a large bucket in the other. "Come, rinse your head," he ordered, placing the bucket on a stool in the center of the room.

I dunked my head into his bucket and gasped. "Dude, that water's freezing cold."

He chuckled, pushing my head toward the bucket again. "Better to kill the lice with. Back in you go. Takes some scrubbing to get the potion out."

I surrendered my head to the icy water, and the servant set to work scrubbing my scalp. I had a throbbing headache from the cold by the time he finished. He set the bucket on the floor and touched the stool. "Come now. Sit here."

I shook my head in disbelief. I'd thought servants were supposed to serve you, not order you around. I sat on his stool and he cut my hair. Next, he shaved me. I sat motionless as the straight razor scraped across my face. "You need a healer," he said.

What is he talking about? "I feel fine." Other than the lice, which had better be gone after what this guy put me through, nothing was wrong with me. Since the Shuylian outpost, in spite of being on the trail for the past couple of weeks, I'd eaten more food than I had in months. My strength was returning, and I was gaining weight.

The servant finished shaving me and wiped my face clean. "Wait here for me to return with the healer," he said.

I stood, grabbing the towel at my waist so it didn't drop to my ankles. "I'm fine, really. I want to see Wickliff." But the servant was gone before I finished the sentence. I'd had it with all the pampering and put on the clothes he'd left for me—white linen shirt and brown leather breeches. The elfish boots were still in mint condition, so they went back on my feet. The counters we'd taken from Arbon were lying next to the boots. I'd kept them hidden under my clothes since that fateful night. The burden of knowing they were there weighed on me, and I wanted to return them to Master Archidus before all else. I slipped the leather string over my neck and dropped the counters below the loose-fitting shirt.

I wasn't about to wait around for a healer. I ran my hand over my hair as I opened the door. It felt strange—too short. Then I felt my cheeks, which were smooth for the first time in months, except for a ridge of skin where Arbon's whip had caught my face. With my beard I hadn't noticed the scar before. There wasn't a mirror in sight, so I'd have to look at it later. I left the room in search of Wickliff and my comrades.

Other servants saw me wandering the corridors and pointed me in the direction of the dining hall. Marcus, Garrick, and Wickliff sat in soft-backed chairs around the fireplace, and I joined them.

"My young Keeper, you must see the healer before you depart," Wickliff said.

"Why do people keep telling me that? I feel fine."

"I'm certain you feel fine, but—" Wickliff raised his eyebrows and shrugged his shoulders.

"But what?"

Garrick took a drink from his goblet, then said, "For Ellie's sake, you might consider it. You're not so nice to look at anymore, what with that four-inch scar across your cheek."

My hand flew to my face. The scar went from below my cheekbone across my jaw to below my ear. If I could feel it this distinctly with my fingers, what did it look like? "What can a healer do?"

"They have procedures where the old skin is removed and new skin is grown," Wickliff explained. "It's all done with magic, of course, and is quite painless, but it does take a few days. Or they have potions, which take even longer, but don't require the constant ministrations of the healer."

"Maybe I'll see the healer then."

Wickliff smiled. "Good. I'll arrange for it first thing in the morning."

Marcus jumped to his feet, scraping his chair loudly across the stone floor. Brierly walked through the doorway in an elegant, medieval-style dress. The bad haircut her brother had given her was covered with a fancy bonnet made of the same silk as her dress. She crossed the room and gave him a hug. "Doesn't it feel wonderful to be clean?"

"It does, Sister," Marcus agreed softly.

Garrick stood and nodded in her direction. "You look lovely this evening, Miss Brierly."

A smile lit her face as she curtsied in front of him. "Thank you for your assistance in returning me to my homeland," she said through misty eyes.

"You're welcome. I'm glad to see you safely in Algonia."

We enjoyed a feast that evening, after which Brierly excused herself to go to bed. The rest of us sat around the fire until the wee hours of the morning. Wickliff insisted we share the entire story, and for the first time I heard the tale of Marcus and Garrick's adventures getting into Shuyle and finding me. We recounted the trials we'd faced getting back to Algonia. And once again, Marcus replayed the course of events leading to Lord Arbon's demise. The Algonians finally had retribution for all the wrongs inflicted on them.

"I shall write it down as you have recounted it," Wickliff said. "Your story will live on, even after you have passed away. For these are the doings that will become the legends of tomorrow."

"Where are Archidus or Quirus?" I asked, realizing I'd not seen them since entering the castle.

"Alas, that is why I am still here," Wickliff replied. "A great misfortune befell them during the battle of the southern border. The Shuylians killed Quirus, and Master Archidus was gravely wounded. For a time we feared he wouldn't live. He is currently with a healer in our southern region and cannot be moved. It was there the battle raged most fiercely. The Shuylians broke through our defenses, and a portion of their army entered Algonia and advanced to the fortress city. Archidus led the offensive, which retook the border and drove the majority of the Shuylian army out of Algonia. Before he left, the Master charged me with guarding Cadré Unair . . . and these."

Wickliff paused, and with a smile, he removed two counters from the pocket of his robes and handed one to each of us. I looked at the gold object in the firelight. The etching on the case featured a sword, not a shield.

"I think this one's yours," Garrick said.

We exchanged counters. My eyes took in the familiar markings of Protector, and I smiled as I slid my thumb over the latch on the side. It clicked open, and the friendly bluish light greeted me. I snapped the counter shut and nodded. "Thank you."

I leaned back and worked the counter into the pocket of the leather breeches. "Now we have something for you." After pulling Arbon's counters from under my shirt, I held them by the string and dangled them in front of Wickliff. "The two counters Lord Arbon held—your daughter's and his own."

The elf extended his hand and received the counters. "It has been a long time that these have been separated from the virtues of Algonia. They are a welcome sight indeed. I shall hold them in safekeeping until such time as Master Archidus is able to take possession of them. It grows late, my friends. Perhaps we should retire."

That night I slept soundly. Whether because of the late hour, my full stomach, or the relative safety and comfort of my surroundings, I didn't know. But it was refreshing to awaken to the light of dawn without having relived the dungeon ordeal in my dreams.

A servant girl delivered breakfast to my room. Delicate pastries, juice, eggs, and hearty slices of meat filled the platter set before me. Not wanting Ellie to find me looking like a skinny runt, I ate nearly everything on the tray. When I was completely stuffed, I lay back on my bed until a knock sounded at my door. "Come in," I called.

One of the servants from the night before opened the door. "Come with me, Keeper. The healer awaits."

I rolled off the bed and followed him through the labyrinth of passageways until he opened a large oak door and ushered me in.

A familiar voice greeted me. "Although surprising, it's certainly pleasant to see you again." From the shadows of the dimly lit room walked Azalit, the Master's daughter.

I raised my eyebrows, suddenly skeptical. "You're the healer?"

She tossed her blond hair over her shoulder. "No, Keeper. I'm the assistant."

"Sorry, I didn't mean it that way."

She ignored my apology. "You can take your shirt off and hang it on the hook behind the door."

"I don't think that's necessary. The scar is on my face."

"Wickliff seems to think your back needs tending to, so I'll be the judge of what's necessary. Are you going to take your shirt off, or do I need to cut it off of you?"

I looked at the five-inch knife blade Azalit held in her hand. She was clearly enjoying her position of power and probably trying to get back at me for tackling her in the woods near the Shuylian border.

"All right. You don't need to get so uptight about it." I pulled my shirt over my head and turned to hang it on the hook.

"Oh my!" Azalit's sharp intake of breath stopped me in my tracks, and when I glanced over my shoulder, her face softened. "I'm sorry," she said.

Remembering the mass of torn flesh Brierly had dealt with, I hung up my shirt and said, "That's okay. It's a lot better than it was."

A middle-aged woman with dark brown hair and fine features stepped through the door. "Good morning, Keeper. I am Madam Catherine." Her long hair was fastened at the nape of her slender neck with a silver clasp, and she moved with the same stately grace as Garrick's healer.

Smiling, she motioned to a wooden table. "Please sit down."

I hopped on the table and she stepped forward, her fingers tracing the outline of my jaw. Without a word she moved behind me. "What have we here?" Her light touch seemed to skim across my back, and I wondered if I'd lost the feeling in my skin where the scars were the thickest.

"I can repair this," she said softly. "However, it will take some time."

"What if I don't have time?" I asked. "Wickliff mentioned a potion or something?"

She moved to stand in front of me. "You'll get a better result if I repair the tissue. It will take a week, but I can guarantee your skin will have no memory of the torture. The potion is usually adequate. It will most certainly restore your face, but I fear there may be too many layers of scarring on your back. The choice is yours, however."

"What do I do if I choose the potion?"

She lifted her head. "Azalit, get me a bottle of skin restorative, please."

"What size, Madam Catherine?" Azalit said.

"Large."

She returned with a blue glass vial no bigger than a travel-sized shampoo bottle. I raised my eyebrows in disbelief. Surely, Azalit didn't consider that large.

Madam Catherine took the vial and turned to me. "Rub the contents of this vial over the scar tissue at least once a day, but no more often than twice a day. You will see marked improvement within the first dozen applications, but you will need to continue treatment for sixty days to achieve the full benefit of the potion. I recommend applying it twice a day for the first week, and once a day thereafter."

I chuckled. "I don't mean to sound rude or anything, but that's not a large bottle. I'll be lucky if it covers my back once."

"It is only meant to cover your back once. 'Tis a refilling vial," she said, as if that explained everything.

Grinning, Azalit said, "Use the full contents of the bottle with each application, and it will refill once the cork is replaced."

I took the vial. "Twice a day for one week. Once a day for the rest of the sixty days, right?"

"Yes, Keeper, that is correct," Madam Catherine said in her sing-song voice. "Is there any other way I may be of service?"

"I had lice from the dungeon. Last night a servant put this disgusting stuff on my head. Do you think it got rid of it?"

"I know the potion. That's military-grade lice control. Fairly effective, but you should have been brought to me. We have much more civilized methods of dealing with that sort of inconvenience." She bustled around the room while she talked, and returned with two small vials—one red and one colorless. "Lie down and I'll treat your head again before you leave. I'd hate for you to deal with a reinfestation after you've left Algonia."

I pulled my feet up and lay down. "I'd hate that too."

She lifted my head and spread a towel beneath it. Gently, she massaged cinnamon-smelling oil into my scalp. "While we let this sit, I'll have Azalit apply your first restorative treatment."

I sat up, the aroma reminding me of Mom's cinnamon rolls on Christmas morning. Azalit rubbed the oil from the vial across my back, then moved in front of me to massage the last of it into the scar on my cheek. "Thank you," I said.

She lowered her gaze as she placed the cork in the vial and set it next to me. "You're welcome."

I watched her. "I'm sorry to hear about your father."

"Mother and I hope he is soon well enough to return. As much as he inconveniences my freedom at times, I miss him greatly."

I reached up, feeling the gritty oil that covered my scalp. "Yeah, I know what you mean. I really miss my dad, even though he can be a pain sometimes."

Madam Catherine came back into the room. "Lie down now, and I'll apply the neutralizing oil." I pulled my feet back up and lay down. The next oil had no scent, and after giving me a relaxing head massage, the healer said, "Your treatment is complete."

I sat up and touched my head. The hair was soft, dry, and clean—not a trace of the gritty oil remained.

I smiled and hopped off the table. "Thank you both." I walked to where I'd hung my shirt.

"Keeper Chase, aren't you forgetting something?" Azalit called. When I turned, she waved the potion bottle in front of her face.

"Oh yeah." I returned to take the bottle from her. "Thanks."

I shook it—full again, just like she'd said. I yanked my shirt over my head and went to search for Garrick.

TWENTY-FIVE
2012

It took over an hour to locate Garrick. The head butler said he'd left in Brierly's company while I was with the healer. I finally found them walking through the gardens behind the castle. I imagined it was spectacular in the summer, but now water saturated the grass, leaving it soggy, and the trees and rose bushes were bare of foliage. Everywhere I walked, rotting brown leaves cluttered the rock paths.

Garrick must have heard me approaching from behind because he turned and said, "Hey, little brother."

"Hi, Garrick, Brierly. What's up?"

"Just saying goodbye," Garrick said. "Marcus and Brierly leave within the hour to return home."

I stopped next to him and slid my hands into my pockets. "When are we leaving?"

"Wickliff's agreed to take us through Witches Hollow when we're ready."

"I'm ready now."

Garrick nodded. "I'd like to see my son again." His attention caught on something, and I followed his gaze. Marcus, dressed to travel, walked briskly in our direction. Garrick turned to Brierly and chuckled. "Time's up. You take care of yourself, Brierly." He pulled her into a bear hug and kissed her forehead.

Kelly Nelson

She smiled at him. "Thank you, Garrick the Guardian. May the sun rise up before you, and the wind be always at your back." She touched his cheek before stepping in front of me.

"Keeper Chase, I wish the same for you. And may your counter speed you to the girl who lays claim to your heart."

Wrapping my arms around her, I dropped my head next to her ear. "Thank you." I was choking up at the thought of saying goodbye. I expected this one would be forever, and I had to say something. I needed her to know what she'd meant to me. "Brierly, you were an angel of mercy in my darkest hour. I will never forget you as long as I live. Meeting you and now seeing you free was worth every lash of Arbon's whip." I held her longer than I'd intended, not wanting to raise my teary eyes for Garrick and Marcus to see.

I blinked back the tears and was about to let Brierly go when the shudder of a sob shook her shoulders. Her arms tightened around my neck. "Making your acquaintance was the first ray of sunshine in my time of servitude," she said. "I'm only sorry that meeting you happened at the expense of your suffering."

"Don't cry. It's okay," I said softly. We stood that way while Garrick walked over to Marcus and said farewell.

Brierly pulled away and dried her eyes, then smiled up at me. "I'll miss you."

"I'll miss you too."

Marcus cleared his throat, and his mouth turned up in a half smile. "You forget so soon my threat about touching my sister."

I sniffled back the last of my emotions and swallowed, then said loudly, "Surely there's an exception for old friends saying goodbye?"

Marcus laughed. "For you, perhaps I will make an exception." We clasped wrists and pulled each other into a quick embrace.

"Thank you for coming for me," I said. "Thank you for helping rescue Ellie. And thank you for taking care of Arbon so he can't terrorize me or anyone else again. You're my hero."

"It's what I do, Keeper. But it is I who must thank you. You brought my sister and me back together. My family owes you a debt that can never be repaid."

"I assure you the debt has more than been paid."

Marcus stepped back and raised his hand in farewell. "Then Godspeed on your journey, my friends. Brierly, come. The horses await."

Within the hour, Wickliff, Garrick, and I walked toward Witches Hollow. We wore our Shuylian fur coats to fend off the cold, wet fog. Garrick rested his hand on his sword—the one given him by Archidus. It amazed me that he hadn't lost it in all of his travels. I still wore the Shuylian sword given to me by Marcus and Garrick at the run-down cottage.

"You may be interested to know," Wickliff said, "that I received word from the southern front this morning. It seems the largest part of Arbon's army has surrendered. Word of his death continues to spread through the ranks of the Shuylian army. Arbon's heir, Lord Dolosus, has not come forward to claim his place at the peace talk, and with Legard absent from the new world, the Shuylians find themselves leaderless. Our Gatekeepers are negotiating a treaty with their chief sorcerers. The absence of Lord Dolosus is of some concern, but perhaps he is among those who have fallen in battle. Based on my experiences, in due time every question is answered."

"That's good news," Garrick said.

"Yeah, it sure is," I added.

As we entered Witches Hollow, Wickliff put a hand on each of us. "Where are we off to, my young friends?"

"Wherever Archidus sent Ellie and Davy," I answered.

"Ah, that would be ideal, but unfortunately we aren't privy to that information. You're welcome to await the return of Master Archidus. I would relish your company a while longer."

"I don't want to wait," I said.

"Archidus would send Davy back to our cabin in Ohio," Garrick said. "But I don't know about Ellie. Maybe Archidus sent her home. It can't be that hard to find them once we're back in the old world."

Hoping the Master had sent her to 2012, I said, "Let's go to my house."

Wickliff closed his eyes. "Concentrate on the time and place you wish to appear, and I'll tap into your thoughts."

I closed my eyes and pictured my room as I'd left it. From talking with Wickliff I knew Ellie had left the new world about nine days after being taken by Legard. I imagined my room on March 29, 2012.

A woman's scream sent my eyes flying open.

"Mom?" I said in surprise. "What are you doing in my room?"

She shook her head. Her eyes opened wider as she took in the sight of Garrick and Wickliff. "Waiting for you. But this isn't quite . . . what I expected."

Wickliff let go of my arm and took a step back. "Well, my young Keepers, I'll let you get on with your homecoming. Farewell, and may we meet again."

I turned and shook hands with him in Algonian style. "Thank you, Wickliff." Garrick shook his hand and thanked him as well before the elf disappeared.

In the warmth of my house, I was sweating bullets in the Shuylian coat. I shrugged it off my shoulders and let it slide to the floor, then hugged my mom. She just stared at me, barely lifting her arms to hug me back at first. "It's so good to see you again, Mom."

Tears streamed down her cheeks as she finally pulled me closer. "Are you okay? Where were you?" When I didn't answer right away, she stepped back and looked me over.

"Oh my," she said, turning my face toward the light of the window. "How did that happen?"

In that moment, I decided there would be no more hiding the truth. I was done keeping secrets from my family. My parents deserved to know. Whether they believed me or not would be up to them. "A bullwhip."

Her brows furrowed. "A whip?"

"Yeah, but don't worry about it. I've got this potion, and the scar will be gone in sixty days." I moved toward my door. "Where's Ellie?"

Mom shook her head. "Ellie? Wasn't she with you? We all assumed you were together."

"She didn't come back already? How many days have I been gone?"

"Maybe ten."

"Did we get here first? Maybe she's not back yet," I muttered.

"Jennifer," my dad called. I heard him walking down the hall, but before my mom could answer, he stepped into my doorway.

"Dad," I said.

My father crossed the room, glancing at Garrick on his way, and wrapped his arms around me. "Son, thank you for coming home."

"Dad, I'm sorry," I choked out. "I never would have left like that on purpose. I've been trying to get home for a long time."

"Where were you?" he demanded. "Your mother's been worried sick. You owe us an explanation."

"I was stuck in a dungeon in another world. I can tell you the long version later. But right now I have to find Ellie." I looked at my dresser. "Where's my phone?" Obviously my mother had cleaned my room, and nothing was where I'd left it.

She opened a drawer. "In here."

I pulled out the phone and called Adam. "Hey, dude, this is Chase. Have you seen Ellie in the last ten days?"

"Where the heck have you two been?" Adam asked.

"Dude, answer my question."

"No, of course not. Didn't she leave with you?"

"She left with me, but we got separated. I hoped she had come home. Look, I've got to go. Bye." I slid my phone shut and set it on my dresser. Garrick picked it up and studied it.

"Who's your friend?" my dad asked.

I looked up. "This is Garrick Eastman. He's the man who risked his life to save mine. He's like a brother."

Garrick extended his hand. "It's nice to meet you, Mr. Harper."

My dad shook his hand, but didn't return the smile. "I'm Joe."

I retrieved my counter from my pocket and spun the dials. "What are you doing?" my mom asked. "I've read the journal, Chase. Please don't go."

"I'm hopping ten days into the future to see if Ellie came back," I said.

Panic crossed my mom's face. "No, you can't leave already."

My dad stepped closer. "Chase, sit down. We need to talk. I don't know where you've been, but I don't think you should be running around playing dungeons and dragons with your friend here. Your mother and Jessica seem to believe all this nonsense, but it has got to stop."

After everything I'd been through, he had the nerve to think he knew it all. He should've trusted me. Granted, I hadn't explained anything, but this was a crisis. I opened my arms and stepped back, smiling. "Seeing is believing, Dad. I'll see you tomorrow."

I pushed Shuffle and Go. I had one focus, and that was Ellie. I reappeared in Jessica's room at midnight. I had jumped ahead ten days. This put me at twenty days after our disaster in the new world began. According to Wickliff, she'd been long gone by then, and the fortress city was under attack by the Shuylians.

I woke Jessica. She tried to ask a million questions, but I forced her to answer my one. "Have you seen Ellie in the past twenty days?"

"No, but that's what you—"

I disappeared before she finished her sentence. While shuffling, I set the dials to one day after I'd originally gone home and pushed Go. Hopefully, my dad would be more receptive to the truth after thinking on it for twenty-four hours. I tried to see things from his perspective and realized I needed to take the time to explain what had happened.

Ellie obviously hadn't been sent back to the modern world, which left Davy's home in Ohio 1829 as the most logical alternative. Archidus must have sent Davy back to his home, and Ellie had been with him. Whether I spent a little time here with my dad or not, it would make no difference to Ellie now. If I set the counter for 1829 today or tomorrow, I'd still get there in 1829.

I'd forgotten to take Garrick with me and wondered what he'd done for a day at my house, or if he'd left on his own to look for Davy. I reappeared in my bedroom. The bed had been slept in, and Garrick's sword lay on my dresser. I glanced at the clock— dinnertime. I unstrapped the Shuylian sword and tossed it on the bed. After a deep breath, I left to face my dad.

Every eye followed me as I entered the kitchen. "Dad, I need you to believe me. I'm not making this stuff up," I said.

The expression on his face had softened, and he no longer looked like he was about to strangle me. "I know. Garrick and I talked until 2:00 AM. He explained a lot of things, and I'm sorry I was so hard on you. Son, this whole concept is difficult for me to swallow, but be patient with me and I'll get it down."

"Thanks." I paused. "I will have to leave again. I really do need to find Ellie. But this time I'll come right back."

My dad nodded. "I understand."

I joined Garrick and my family at the dinner table. My mom never took her eyes off me.

"Have you lost weight?" she asked. "You look thin."

"Yeah. They don't feed you too good in a dungeon, Mom." She grimaced. Quoting one of her favorite lines, I said, "But don't worry. Doesn't it always come back on a lot easier than it goes off?"

She smiled. "Yes, it does."

After dinner, I talked with my parents on the couch for over three hours. My mom had an endless string of questions regarding the counter and what I'd been doing for the past few months. Garrick spent the evening in front of the computer with Jessica.

When it was time for bed, I gave my dad a hug. My mom wrapped her arms around me and whispered, "Be careful, Chase. I hope you find her."

"I will. I love you, Mom."

"I love you too."

I looked around the living room. I wouldn't come back here until I had Ellie with me. "Garrick, you ready?" I called.

"Yup." He stood and pushed his chair back from the desk. "Thanks for showing me around your computer."

"Oh, you're welcome," Jessica said. "Will you come back?"

"I'm not sure."

"Well, I hope you do. But if not, it was fun meeting you." She threw her arms around his neck for a quick hug.

I smiled. The hug had caught Garrick off guard, but he didn't know Jessica—she hugged everybody.

My sister moved on to me and put her arms around me. "Chase, I'm so glad you're okay. You have no idea what a mess Mom and Dad were when they couldn't find you. Be careful next time."

TWENTY-SIX
Chasing Ellie

I closed the door to my room. Garrick strapped his sword on while I opened my closet. My mom had been in there, too. Everything was organized, including my assortment of weapons. They were laid out on the shelf, and the Nazi trench coat now hung from a hanger. I grabbed my Algonian sword and buckled it around my waist.

"You want to take us home?" I asked Garrick.

He pulled out his counter, and I set my hand on his shoulder. We walked through our shuffle zones, attracting attention whenever we appeared in a populated area. With our Algonian clothes and swords we stood out like zebras in a herd of horses. But I didn't care. These people would never see us again.

We appeared in Garrick's cabin. The front door creaked as it swung in the wind. Someone had torn the place apart. Food littered the floor, and every cupboard had been emptied.

Garrick picked up a broken chair. "Legard. Archidus predicted he'd come looking for Davy's counter."

"Sorry, Garrick," I said. So much of his hard work had been destroyed. We walked through the cabin. Ellie and Davy weren't there.

"This is only five days after we left. Let's jump ahead," Garrick said. I rested my hand on his shoulder. "I'm setting it for ten days from now." He pressed Go. A shimmer appeared in front of my eyes, but when it cleared everything was as it was before, except the flour on the floor had been disturbed.

"There are tracks," Garrick mumbled.

"Probably just raccoons that wandered in."

Garrick bent down. "No, these are boot tracks."

"You! How?" Legard's voice boomed from behind me.

I spun around. He stood in the doorway to the back room. Panic seized me, and for the briefest second, I froze. But I wasn't in Shuyle anymore, and his deadly magic pulse wouldn't work on me here. I drew my sword and took my fencing stance. Garrick drew his sword and moved next to me.

Legard stared at me with a look of utter disbelief. "It can't be you. I left you in the dungeon." With a swish of his gray cloak he disappeared.

In that instant, I remembered. "Legard is going back to the dungeon. He'll find me there, but he'll restrict who has access to my cell. I won't see Brierly again until the night you rescue me."

Garrick and I stood, swords raised, waiting, but Legard didn't return.

Finally, my friend took a deep breath and lowered his weapon. "If Ellie and Davy ever were here, it wasn't for long, with Legard hanging around. Let's ask some folks in town. Maybe someone saw them."

I followed Garrick to his neighbor's house. The door opened. "Mrs. Mortenson—" he started to say. The woman looked like she had been crying. "What happened?" Garrick asked.

"It's my husband—he was killed! Be careful, Mr. Eastman. An evil man's been lurking about your homestead. When I came home last night after spending several days with my daughter, the Robertsons from down the street brought word that my husband was injured. Someone had stabbed him. He and Mr. Robertson had been feeding your animals. Over the past week, both of them saw that strange man. My husband was so weak when I got there, all he could say was he was sorry. He passed on a short while later." Mrs.

Mortenson paused, clearly having a hard time remaining composed. "I am glad you're well, though. We feared the worst when we noticed you were missing."

Garrick looked like he'd had the wind knocked out of him. "I'm so sorry. I—"

I stepped forward. "Ma'am, have you seen Davy at all?"

"No, I haven't, but like I said, I've been at my daughter's house all week. She just had her baby, you know. Maybe my husband did, but—" Mrs. Mortenson couldn't finish her sentence because she started crying.

I nudged Garrick to get him moving. "Thank you, ma'am. I'm sorry for your loss. We'll get out of your way," I said.

We walked back to Garrick's cabin and sat on the porch. The temperature was pleasant for a winter's day. "He was a good man— Mr. Mortenson," Garrick said. "He was always helping someone. If he saw a need, he took care of it. The Mortensons were like a second family to Davy. They have a son a year older than him. There were some days Davy spent more time at their house than he did at ours."

I let out a sigh. "I'm sorry."

Garrick sat in silence for a long time. When a chill wind blew in off the lake, I started pacing in front of him.

He stood and joined me. "If the Mortensons haven't seen Davy, I don't know who would have. If he was here, where would he go? If he was never here, where would Archidus have sent him?"

"I don't know, Garrick. But let's go look for them. Sitting here isn't getting us anywhere."

He set his hand on my shoulder, and I set my counter for Boston, January 12, 1864. Thinking of the hedge I'd hidden behind so many times before, I pressed Shuffle and Go. Surely Ellie would realize I'd look for her here. I left Garrick, crossed the street, and knocked on the door. A woman I'd never seen before answered.

"Is Mary here?" I asked.

"No, she ain't. Mary's done gone into town. You gots to come back later," the woman said in a strong Southern accent.

I put my hand on the door to stop her from closing it. "Is Ellie here? She has curly blond hair, and she's about this tall. Really pretty."

The woman shook her head, her wiry black hair bouncing on her shoulders. "No, sir."

"I'll try her later then," I said, turning to leave.

I returned to the hedge. "She's not here yet," I told Garrick. On my counter I rolled the day forward one notch, then put my hand on Garrick and pressed Go. When the shimmer cleared, I left the hedge. I ran up the porch steps and knocked.

This time a familiar face appeared at the door. "Mr. Joseph, what you doin' back here so soon?" Mary asked, calling me by my rarely used first name. She glanced toward the road. "Where's my Miss Ellie?"

My shoulders sagged at her words. "I was going to ask you the same thing. I hoped to find her here."

"Why, I don't understand. She left here with you not two weeks past. Where is she?"

"I'm sorry, but we got separated. I lost her."

Mary propped her hands on her hips and pursed her lips. "Well, you best get back out there and find her."

"I will find her. I promise."

I hurried back to the hedge and told Garrick it was time to go again. I set my counter for Zion Canyon, June 28, 1863. Thinking of Ellie's grandfather's cabin, I pressed Shuffle and Go.

The bloodstain I'd left on the wood floor was the first thing I saw as I reappeared. Like a slide show, the memories flashed before my eyes as if it had all happened yesterday. Appearing in Ellie's neighbor's barnyard. Her dusty fingertips brushing my face and my chest. Her cheek next to mine as she taught me how to milk her cow. The look on her face at the sight of the spider on my arm when I pulled the moneybag from under the floorboards. And finally, her worried expression when she looked at my wounded hand. I shook my head, pushing the memories away so I could focus on finding her.

The front door was still a splintered mess, and the cabin was empty. I walked to the corral. A few chickens pecked in the dust, but there was no sign of Ellie.

"I'm going to ask her neighbor if they've seen anything," I told Garrick.

He set his hand on my shoulder, and I pressed Go. We reappeared at the Johnson's cabin. I must have knocked for five minutes before Garrick said, "Harper, no one's home."

Dejectedly, I walked away, Garrick following. "Let's get some sleep. We'll try again in the morning," he said.

"I don't want to go home until I find her."

"We'll go to my place then." He set his counter, and we appeared in the bedroom of his one-room apartment near Texas A&M University. "You can have the bed, little brother," he said.

"Give me a pillow and a blanket. I'll take the couch."

The despair at not finding Ellie in the three most logical places I could think of left me exhausted. The feeling I was missing something nagged at me. During the night I awoke in a sweat from a Shuylian nightmare. In the hazy moment before I was fully awake, I realized what had been bothering me the night before. Regardless of where Archidus had sent Ellie and Davy, why didn't she return to 2012? That was home, for both of us. She had made her decision—she didn't want to live in 1863. Davy had a counter. If he took her away from the cabin in 1829, why hadn't he taken her home?

I was brooding on the subject while we ate breakfast. I knew Davy had a thing for Ellie, and it was no secret he didn't think I was good enough for her. Would he purposely not take her home? I sat stirring my eggs as I thought about this, when the phone rang. Garrick stood and answered it. *No caller ID, no answering machine,* I reminded myself.

"Hello," Garrick said. "Shelly?" He sounded surprised. "Actually, it's not a good time. I've got a lot of work to finish up today." Pause. "Yeah, of course I'm feeling good. Why do you ask?" Pause. "Oh, the gunshot wound. Yeah, it's much better." Another pause. "Thanks, you have a good day too. Bye."

He hung up the phone and shoveled a bite of food into his mouth. "I've got to work up the courage to break it off with that girl." He looked at me. "What?"

I set my fork on the table. "Davy has his counter, so why didn't he take Ellie home? I know her. She would have asked him to take her back to my house. And she wouldn't have left there without talking to Jessica. They're best friends. You know as well as I do that Davy likes Ellie. He doesn't think I'm good enough for her—he practically said so himself in the cabin the night before we gave him the counter. What if he's hiding her from me?"

Garrick set his fork down and folded his hands under his chin. "Davy may like Ellie, but he is a man of integrity. If she asked him to take her somewhere, I'm certain he would try."

"Then why wasn't she there?"

Garrick appeared to be deep in thought. "What if he tried, but couldn't get there?"

"What do you mean?"

"Have you tried to go into the future with your counter?"

"No," I answered.

"Other than the night I lost Rose, neither have I. Archidus discouraged me from going to the future, but said my counter had the ability to go about fifty years forward. Think about it, Harper. Davy is from 1829. Ellie would have been asking him to take her nearly two hundred years forward. He could have tried, but it may have been impossible for him."

I thought about that. "Davy might be from 1829, but his counter isn't that old."

"Where did the counter come from?"

"I got it from Ruth during World War II—in 1939, I think."

"There's your answer then. If anyone knows the capabilities of a counter it would be Archidus, and he said fifty years into the future. Fifty years from 1939 would only be 1989."

"I wasn't even born then," I mumbled.

"Don't be so critical of Davy until you know the whole story. For all we know he may have really tried."

"I'm sorry, but I don't know what to do. Legard is hunting for them. Arbon said as much in the dungeon. I need to find her before he does." I ran my fingers through my hair and let out a sigh. "What if Legard already found them and she's on her way back to Shuyle?"

"Harper, don't borrow trouble," Garrick said. "If we don't find them first, we'll figure it out then. For now, let's keep looking. Ohio is still the most logical in my mind. I say we go back there and try again."

"Okay," I mumbled.

We left our dishes on the table and disappeared with Garrick's counter. After our shuffle zones, we landed in the ransacked cabin. I sat down dejectedly on the bed and ran the toe of my elfish boot across the dusting of flour on the floor, adding my prints to those of Legard and the critters who'd scavenged the spilled food.

"Maybe we're trying the right places but have the wrong times," Garrick said. "If Ellie couldn't get to you, where would she think you would look for her?"

"Boston first, and maybe her grandfather's cabin second. Those are the only two places Ellie and I've been together, other than visiting you."

"Davy would have to assume I'd look here at the cabin, but Legard has been here. I want to check more times in the future, see if he comes back to the cabin later, after Legard moves on."

Garrick's optimism never ceased to amaze me. I sat unmoving on the edge of the bed. "You want to wait for me here?" he asked.

"Sure." I needed time to think—time alone. After everything I'd been through, this was a bitter blow. I hadn't prepared for this. I'd braced myself for death. I'd mentally geared up to endure countless years of Arbon's torture. Once I'd escaped the dungeon, I'd even resigned myself to the fact that I might never make it back to Algonia—or home, for that matter. But never in my wildest dreams did I imagine Ellie would disappear with Davy. Where were they? What was he telling her? He was Perception's Keeper, after all. Hadn't Garrick said that Perception's Keeper could skew the perceptions of those around them? Had Davy convinced Ellie not to look for me? Convinced her I'd died?

A flash of gray in the doorway brought my head up with a jerk. Legard. I jumped to my feet and drew my sword, then reached my hand in my pocket and felt my counter. My thumb rested on the small latch as I backed myself toward the corner. I didn't need him spontaneously reappearing behind me. That was how he'd captured me in the first place. I couldn't let him get his hands on me, or I had no doubt I'd find myself at the Dragon's Lair on a one-way ticket into Shuyle.

"So, even after my warning to Mud you managed to escape," Legard said. "How? Do we have a traitor in the castle?"

A slight smile turned my mouth. I hadn't answered his questions in prison, so it was funny that he wasted breath asking them now. Slowly he drew his sword and put the wall of the cabin at his back. He too was wary. Maybe he didn't know the truth.

"The war's over. Arbon's dead," I said. "The Shuylian army surrendered at the southern front, and the Algonian Gatekeepers are negotiating a peace treaty. It's finished."

Legard's eyes flashed. "You lie, Keeper!"

He tried to hide that I'd rattled him, but I saw it. He looked tired, like he'd been hunting a long time without success. I smiled. Regardless of what else Davy was doing, he'd kept Ellie safe from Legard, and for that I'd forever be grateful.

I held my voice as even as I could. "Believe me or not. It's your choice. But maybe you should see for yourself before you waste more time looking for the Keepers. You've lost your leader and any advantage you may have had. The Algonians now hold all the counters."

In the center of the room the air shimmered—Garrick. I left the safety of my corner and ran to my friend. Pointing my sword at the Sniffer, I yelled, "Legard."

Garrick drew his sword in the settling shimmer, and ever the bold one, he charged. The Sniffer brought his sword down to meet the attack, and the clang of metal filled the cabin. I followed Garrick—someone needed to watch his back since Legard could reappear anywhere in the room at any moment.

Garrick stumbled forward when his next swing struck air. Back to back, we spun, searching the empty room. "Where'd he go?" Garrick said.

"Shuyle, I think. I told him about Arbon and the surrender." Garrick and I relaxed our stance. "Did you find anything?"

"During the next year, no one I talked with in Cleveland has heard or seen anything from Davy," Garrick replied.

"I thought about what you said. Maybe I should try Ellie's grandfather's cabin a year later."

"Wouldn't hurt."

Not trusting Legard, Garrick and I kept our swords ready until after we disappeared. We hit the Shuffle button twice to minimize the risk of the Sniffer following us if he came back.

When we appeared in Utah Territory in June 1864, everything had changed. A covered wagon sat near the cabin. The corral was full of animals, and the front door had been repaired. Chickens ranged around the yard. Had Davy and Ellie settled here sometime in the past year? I ran to the door and pounded my fist. "Ellie! Davy!" I yelled.

No one answered, so I tried turning the knob. Locked. I ran my fingers through my hair and faced Garrick. "They aren't here, I guess."

"Looks like they're bound to come back soon, though. Let's wait."

We pumped water from the well to quench our thirst, then sat in the shade of the porch. Garrick chewed on a piece of hay, while I tapped my foot on the wooden step, wondering how long Ellie and Davy had been here. The house and yard were well kept, so it had to have been awhile. My imagination went a little crazy at the thought of my girlfriend living here with another man. What was she thinking?

The sun was beginning to set when a wagon rumbled into the yard and a round-bellied man asked, "Can I help you?"

"We're waiting for the owners to return?" Garrick said.

The man adjusted the spectacles on the bridge of his nose, blinking his eyes rapidly, and glanced at the woman sitting next to him. Five kids peered at us from the back of the wagon.

"That would be me. What can I do for you?"

I jumped to my feet. "You're not the owner. Who did you get this cabin from?"

The man was sweating profusely and wiped his forehead with a bandana. "It was abandoned over a year ago, or so I was told."

"This property belonged to Amyot Williams," I explained, "and he had a granddaughter named Ellie. She's tall, pretty, about my age, and has curly blond hair. Have you ever seen her around here?"

"No, I can't say as I have. We came down from Salt Lake City in March. My family and I have been here only a few months."

I let out a sigh and turned to leave. "Thanks anyway," I mumbled.

Garrick stood and followed me. The man kept his eye on us, so we had to walk away rather than disappear right there. At the end of the drive, I jumped us to the Johnsons' house with my counter. If they hadn't seen Ellie, I didn't know who around here would have.

I raised my fist to knock, but the door opened. "What can I help you boys with?" Mr. Johnson asked. He gave our Algonian clothes a once-over but didn't comment.

"Mr. Johnson, I don't know if you remember me. I'm Chase Harper. I was here about a year ago with Ellie Williams. We were looking for her animals that got loose."

He scratched his chin. "Come to think of it, I do remember you."

"I'm trying to find Ellie—I mean Miss Williams. Have you seen her since then? At any time in the past year, have you seen her?"

By this time his wife had joined him at the door with a baby balanced on her hip. She smiled. "Yes, we saw her last fall. Remember, Ben? On our way home from church. We met them walking down the road to the Williams's cabin. She was with her fiancé. He looked like a fine catch for a husband. And what a handsome-looking couple they made, too."

A bombshell hit my world. *Did I hear her right?* "Fiancé? Are you sure?"

Mrs. Johnson nodded. "Oh, yes, I'm certain that's what he said."

My brain stalled out, and I stood dumbfounded.

When I didn't speak, Garrick piped in. "Do you know where they are now?"

Mr. Johnson was looking right at me. "Haven't seen them since. But the funny thing is, Mr. Harper, Miss Williams asked me if I'd seen you. Then, before they left, she made a point of telling me she wouldn't be here long because they may be returning to Boston."

I finally got myself back in the conversation. "Do you remember what date you saw them?"

"I don't recollect. It's been so long. End of summer, maybe early fall. Sorry, but I'm not sure."

I took a step back. "Thank you for your help, Mr. Johnson."

Garrick nodded. "Good day, sir."

I walked up the dusty road in a trance. Was I too late? Had Davy married her somewhere, in some time I couldn't find. Why had Ellie done that? How could she give up on me when I'd promised her I'd always come back to her? Did she fall in love with Davy? What did he have, anyway? Obviously something she liked.

"Where are we going?" Garrick asked, pulling me out of my thoughts. We had walked nearly a half mile back up the road toward the Williams's cabin.

I stopped and shook my head. "I don't know. How could she do that?"

"Worry about that when we find them. At least for the first time we have a solid lead. The way I see it, we have two choices. We can go back to last summer and wait for them at the cabin. Or we can go to Boston and try to intercept them there. What do you want to do?"

I thought about it for a minute. I didn't relish the idea of sitting in the southern Utah heat waiting for weeks on end for Ellie and Davy to come walking up the road. Undoubtedly, Ellie would go home once they arrived in Boston. Mary could give Ellie a message for me, or at least tell me the exact date she was there if I asked her to. If Boston didn't pan out like I thought, we could always come back here.

TWENTY-SEVEN
Boston

Garrick and I appeared behind the hedge. Snow fell from the gray sky as I marched across the street. I climbed the steps to Mary's front door and knocked.

She pulled open the door and gave me a white-toothed smile. "Why Mr. Joseph, you back already?"

"Yeah, have you seen her yet?"

Mary peered behind me. "You still haven't found her!"

"No, but—"

"Mr. Joseph, has some ill befallen her? I don't understand how you can lose a body."

"Mary, please listen to me. I think she's coming back here. I don't know what she's thinking, but I heard she's engaged to someone else. If you see her, promise me you'll tell her I'm looking for her. And don't let her leave, okay? I'll come back on the fifteenth, I promise."

Mary shook her head and frowned. "Engaged? That don't make no sense when I know she's sweet on you."

I backed off the porch. "I'll see you in fifteen days, and remember to tell her I'm looking for her."

I walked down the street, keeping my eye on Mary. Once she closed the door, I darted behind the hedge. "Not here yet," I said. I jumped ahead another fifteen days—February 15, 1864.

Soot-covered snow crunched underfoot, but the streets were slushy from the churning of horse's hooves and wagon wheels. I knocked on Mary's door and waited.

She frowned at the sight of me. "Look at you. Back on the fifteenth, just like you said. But still no Miss Ellie with ya, I see."

"No, and you haven't seen her either, huh?"

"Ain't been no sign of her since you was here last."

"Okay, I'll come back on the first of March."

Again, Mary watched me walked away. I backtracked to Garrick behind the hedge and reset my counter for March 1, 1864. When I moved to leave the hedge, he said, "I'll come with you this time."

When Mary answered the door, she threw it wide open. "You come on in now. I fixed you some dinner. I'll not be sending you away hungry again. I can't believe my manners—I shoulda offered you something last time you was here." The warm air coming out her door and the smell of her home cooking drew us in. "Who's this yer with today, Mr. Joseph?"

"Oh, sorry. This is my brother, Garrick. Garrick, this is Mary."

Garrick offered his hand to Mary, who hesitated a moment before giving it a quick shake. "It's nice to meet you, Mary. We appreciate your hospitality."

"It's a pleasure, sir," she said.

We sat at her kitchen table, and she served us dinner. "You've not seen Ellie, I assume," I said between bites of food.

"No, and I been watchin', too."

Once we finished our meal, Garrick slid his chair back. "That was a mighty fine meal, Mary. You need our help with anything before we leave?"

She cleared away his empty plate. "I could use a man to split my wood pile."

Garrick smiled. "We can certainly take care of that, can't we, little brother? It's the least we can do after filling our bellies at your table."

I slid off my chair and stood. "Thanks, Mary. This way, Garrick." I led him out the back door and retrieved the ax from the shed. The wood I'd stacked on New Year's Eve was nearly gone, and a load of logs had been delivered. "There's only one ax," I said.

"Here, I'll split. You stack."

Garrick got halfway through the pile before he stopped to survey my work. "Harper, that's the sloppiest stacking job I've seen since Davy was ten years old. Those logs will come down on Mary's foot if you leave it like that. You split." Garrick handed off the ax and went to work fixing my stack. When we were done he surveyed his work and smiled. "That's much better."

I stowed the ax in the shed. Stepping in the back door, I yelled, "Mary, we're done. I'll see you on the fifteenth."

"Thank you, and you tell your brother thanks for me," she called back.

On March 15, 1864, there was no change. It was a repeat of every other trip to Mary's door. Again, Mary fed Garrick and me. The last of the snow had melted, and the first buds of spring were opening. A recent windstorm had taken down a tree in the yard, so we cleaned that up for Mary after we ate. When were Ellie and Davy returning to Boston? They had left Utah in the fall of 1863. She was here with me on New Year's Day 1864. I had been checking for her over a two-and-a-half-month time frame. Why hadn't we found them yet? Did Davy persuade her to go somewhere else? This not knowing would kill me.

Once we finished the chores and were safely behind the hedge, I let out a sigh. "April 1, 1864," I muttered. Garrick dropped his hand on my shoulder and gave it a squeeze. He smiled. "We'll find them." I pressed Shuffle and Go.

Immature leaves now covered the trees. The blossoms were in full bloom, and the day was warm. I strode across the street to the front door and raised my hand to knock. Mary had the windows open and her voice carried to the porch.

"I'm tellin' you, Miss Ellie, Mr. Joseph's alive. And he's like clockwork, he is. Every first and fifteenth of the month he comes a knockin' on my door askin' for you. Should be here any time now."

"That can't be. He didn't come back. I don't understand. I waited—I waited all day. He said he'd send him back to me if he lived."

At the sound of her voice, my heart raced and I hesitated, unsure of myself. I pulled my hand away from the door and touched the jagged scar on my face. I had looked in the mirror at my house—hideous, that's what it was. Maybe I should have taken Madam Catherine's other option. But it was too late now.

I leaned against the doorframe and closed my eyes. Ellie and I had been separated for a long time. Had things changed? Was I too late? Maybe she had already married Davy.

"Who's Mr. Joseph?" I heard Davy ask.

"It's Chase," Ellie said.

Silence followed. Garrick gave me a nudge in the back, and I straightened myself. I ran my hand over my short hair and then knocked. Ellie swung the door open. She looked at me for a split second before throwing her arms around my neck. As her left hand flew past my face, I didn't miss the flash of gold and the sparkle of a diamond.

"Chase, I can't believe you're really here. We thought you had died."

Tentatively, I wrapped my arms around her. Was I hugging another man's wife? Ellie choked back a sob, and I felt her quiver as if she had started to cry.

Davy took a step forward. His disapproving glare was too much. I couldn't do this in front of everyone. I didn't know if I could hold myself together. I needed to talk with Ellie—alone.

I put my hand in my pocket and pulled out my counter. Davy moved quickly. "Harper, no!"

Startled, Ellie turned to look at him. Without a word, I clicked my counter open and pressed Shuffle. Once we were gone, I waited patiently to get through the shuffle zones.

On our last shuffle, an emerald-green hillside, I pulled Ellie's hands off my neck and looked at her left hand. "Huh." I shook my head as I recognized the ring. It was the one Garrick had bought at the jewelers in 1968. It was Rose's ring. Never in my wildest dreams did I imagine I'd see it on Ellie's finger one day. I stared at her lovely hands and felt mad. Had she betrayed me? If she was his wife . . . I couldn't stomach the thought of that.

"How could you? You didn't wait for me? Are you already some other guy's wife?" I asked, my voice sounding harsh even to me. She stood quietly, tears streaming down her cheeks. In my anger, I was probably squeezing her wrists too tight. She stared at me with pity and sadness. *Why won't she answer me?*

"Say something, Ellie," I said, dropping her hands.

She sobbed. "No. I'm so sorry, Chase."

I shook my head. She stepped closer and I moved back. "What do you mean, Ellie? What are you sorry about?"

She moved toward me again, crying. "Hold me, please."

I couldn't say no to that and pulled her to me, then buried my face in her curls. Alone, on this breezy hillside in the middle of nowhere, I released my own anguish in one great sob.

I let her cry on my shoulder for a minute, but I had to get a straight answer out of her. "Ellie, tell me one thing. Did you marry Davy?"

"I haven't yet."

I sighed in relief. "Oh, thank you."

"But Chase, I did tell him I would."

I wiped the back of my hand across my eyes and looked at her. "Do you love him?"

"I did when I thought you were dead. But now I'm so confused."

"Ellie tell me, please. Tell me everything that happened from the time Legard took me."

She sucked in a breath and began. "When they told me you had been taken, I was devastated. I thought Legard had killed you, and I wanted to die. I couldn't even walk. Marcus carried me for hours. Finally, Garrick convinced me not to give up on you until I could see your counter. The Algonian army came out to meet us. Most of the soldiers rode to confront the Shuylians, but a group of them escorted us to the fortress city. Archidus let me hold your counter, and thankfully, it was still dark in my hand. For the first time I dared to hope. Garrick and Marcus vowed to go into Shuyle and look for you, but Archidus warned me not to get my hopes up. He was certain that escape was impossible."

"For a seer he sure doesn't see things all that great," I grumbled.

"After nearly a week at his castle, Archidus sent for us. He said they were under attack and he couldn't guarantee our safety. He told me you were still alive, and he promised he would send you back to me if you ever returned." Ellie's voice rose in intensity and emotion. "Chase, he assured me that if you lived he would send you back to the same time and place he sent me and Davy. He told me I wouldn't have to wait long—that you'd be right behind me. Davy and I appeared in the woods behind his cabin in Ohio. I never left that spot once. All day I waited for you, and into the night. It got dark and late, and I was freezing cold. We finally went inside the cabin. The next morning I'd intended to go back to the woods. I would've kept waiting, but Legard came. He was following us. Davy and I ran from him for days. Did the Master not send you back to the woods in Ohio?"

"I never saw Master Archidus. He was wounded in battle, and Quirus was killed. Wickliff brought us back. I had him take us to my house."

"I see."

"Go on, Ellie. What happened next?"

"Once we lost Legard, I asked Davy to take me to your house. Chase, he tried. I don't know why, but his counter wouldn't get us any closer than 1991. I even insisted on setting it myself. But when I was there, in 1991, I wrote you a letter. I asked a lady to save it and mail it for me. You didn't get a letter?"

"No, but I was only home for a day, and then I left to find you. No one said anything about a letter to me."

"In the letter I told you where I was. I hoped you would get it and know where to come for me. I waited at Waterfront Park in 1991 all day until it got dark. You can't imagine my disappointment when Davy said we needed to leave. We had nothing, Chase. No food, no supplies—nothing but the clothes on our backs and Davy's counter. He insisted he needed to find work and a place where we could have a roof over our heads. We found ourselves in Vandalia, Illinois, in 1831. The Gibsons took us into their home in exchange for me doing housework and helping with their twins. I was so lonely without you. If it weren't for the twins, I would have lost my mind.

"We were there for over a year. Davy's quite industrious. He worked for the blacksmith and started his own freight business. He was doing very well for himself when Legard found us. Again we ran from him. Davy had asked me to marry him before we left Vandalia, but I hadn't given him an answer. I still didn't want to believe you were gone. We spent a couple of weeks at my grandfather's cabin. When I asked Mr. Johnson if he'd ever seen you since the day we appeared in his yard, he said no. I guess at that point I gave up. I had waited so long. For me it's been a year and a half! What was I supposed to think, Chase? Archidus was very specific. He said if you didn't come back within a few hours, I was to assume you had perished. I tried everything I could think of. At the cabin I agreed to Davy's proposal. We came to Boston to get married."

It took me a minute to process the information, but I understood. Would I have done any differently in her situation? If I thought I was forever trapped in Algonia, would I have returned Brierly's affections rather than remain alone? I couldn't say for sure.

Ellie raised her hand and touched the scar on my face. "I've told you my story. Now please tell me what happened to you. I've spent countless hours worrying, wondering where you were and what you were thinking."

"I was thinking only of you."

When I didn't say more, she encouraged me. "What else? Where did Legard take you?"

"It's not a pretty story, Ellie."

"I don't care. I have to know."

"When Legard disappeared with me from our camp, we reappeared on the Shuylian side of the Susack Plain. They locked me in a prison wagon and took me into Shuyle. At Lord Arbon's castle my wrists were shackled, and I was thrown into his dungeon."

I stopped and took a deep breath, rubbing the calluses on my wrists. *How much should I say about what happened in that dungeon? I'd rather forget about it, but that's unlikely.* The horrors of that experience regularly visited my nightmares, and I did want to tell someone.

"An attack by Legard left me paralyzed in the corner of my cell, with blood gushing from the back of my head. Arbon didn't want me to die yet, so he sent a slave girl to patch me up. He was so wicked. He would have killed her if she had failed to keep me alive. As it turns out, that girl—Brierly is her name—is Marcus's little sister. Day after day I sat in that dank cell. I was there for over two months. Arbon liked—" I turned my head, cringing at what I would say next. "He liked to torture people. The scar on my face is from his whip."

Tears again sprang to Ellie's eyes, and she buried her head in my chest. "Oh, Chase, I'm so sorry."

"It's okay. It's over now," I whispered.

"Please keep going. What happened next?"

"One night Garrick and Marcus entered the dungeon looking for me. I told Marcus about Brierly, and she helped them get the keys to my cell. The four of us escaped a few nights later dressed as Shuylian soldiers. By this time a massive war was underway. We came across Lord Arbon camped with his army, and Marcus poisoned Arbon's wine and then beheaded him. That single event shifted the course of the war and gave the Algonians the advantage. After what Marcus had done we didn't dare travel the main roads. It took weeks to return to Algonia by the northern route, and we nearly froze in a blizzard going over the mountain pass. Eventually we made it back to Algonia. That's it, I guess."

"What a terrible ordeal," Ellie said softly.

"At least it wasn't as long as yours," I said with a grin, trying to make light of it. "I want to forget it ever happened."

"Compared to your ordeal, mine wasn't much of one. It was more of an inconvenience." Her face darkened. "But Chase, I've gotten myself into an awful fix. It's hopeless. Regardless of what I do now, I hurt someone."

She had stopped crying, but her cheeks were still wet with tears. I held her face and brushed them away with my thumbs. "I'm sorry. Believe me, this wasn't what I intended. I love you, and I always will." I smiled sadly. I knew what I should say, but it would be difficult if the answer weren't what I hoped. "As for what you should do, it's impossible to make both Davy and me happy. You need to worry about you. Don't think about him. Don't think about me. Just think about you and what makes you happy."

As she looked into my face, her luminous, tear-filled eyes mesmerized me. I leaned closer, glancing between her sad eyes and her beautiful lips. It had been so long. If this was goodbye, I didn't want any regrets. I kissed her, and she seemed to melt in my arms. Returning my kisses, she wrapped her fingers around the back of my head, pulling me closer.

The thought of her kissing Davy like that fired me up faster than a blowtorch. I pulled away and stepped back, trying to suppress my anger. I had to allow her the space and time to decide for herself.

Tears again filled her eyes as she looked into mine. A soft breeze blew a strand of hair across her face until she pushed it behind her ear. "Chase, you make me happy. But what do I say to Davy? He spent the last year taking care of me, waiting for me to get over you. What a devastating blow for him. But if I honor my word and marry him, look at you."

I turned and walked a circle in front of her, running my fingers over my head. "Yeah, that would be bad for me. But Ellie, you still haven't told me what you want to do. Who would you rather be with? Don't think about honoring your word or Davy's time taking care of you. That crap doesn't matter anymore. Do you love him more than me? Tell me the honest truth. I can take it."

"No!" Her eyes brightened, and a smile turned her lips. "Even Davy knows that. When he proposed he made reference to you. Sort of apologized for not being you. Everyone knows I love you."

I smiled. "Then it shouldn't be a big shock to Davy if you tell him you can't go through with the marriage."

"I suppose you're right."

I let out a huge sigh. "So you'll come home with me?"

"Yes, I'll come home with you."

I pulled out the counter and offered Ellie my hand. "Thank goodness we got that settled."

She smiled. "It's so nice to be traveling with you again."

I laughed. "What? It wasn't so great with a different Keeper?"

Her laughter joined mine. "It wasn't the same." She leaned her head against my shoulder, and we walked into our first shuffle.

"Should we give Davy a chance to cool down and talk to Garrick, or do you want to return at the same time we left?" I asked.

"Hmm . . . perhaps we should give them a little time."

After setting the counter for Boston on April 1, 1864, I pressed Shuffle, then Go. "Don't let Davy try to change your mind. I hear Perception's Keeper can be very persuasive."

"Don't worry, Chase darling. After I thought I'd lost you, it took over a year of his persuasions before I finally succumbed. I'll not be persuaded now that I know you live."

We appeared behind the hedge, and I led her to the front porch. I gave her an encouraging smile as I opened the door and we stepped in.

TWENTY-EIGHT
Coming Home

Davy jumped up from the kitchen table and rushed toward the door. "Ellie, are you well?"

"I'm fine," she said.

"Harper, you had no right—"

"Look, I'm sorry," I said.

Ellie let go of my hand and stepped forward. "Davy, can I talk with you privately?"

"Of course," he said.

Ellie turned to leave the house with him close behind her. A moment of panic seized me when he placed his hand on her back. *What if he disappears with her?*

Garrick gripped my shoulder. "How'd it go, little brother?"

"Davy's not going to be happy."

"We talked. He expected as much. He'll be okay."

"I hope so," I said. "I owe him, for keeping her safe from Legard. How do you say 'thank you' when you're stealing somebody's fiancé?"

"I'll guarantee Davy's not happy about it, but he freely admitted she's never stopped loving you. He's young, Harper. I'm sure he'll find someone else." Garrick shook his head. "What a crazy, mixed-up life we're leading here."

"Yeah, I'm ready to be normal again. I want to wake up in my own bed, go to school, play some sports, and complain about homework. I've had my fill of dragons, dungeons, sorcerers, and swords."

"Me too."

"Where you goin' after this?" I asked Garrick.

"I'll see what Davy wants to do. It won't be Ohio, though. I don't want to be anywhere near there if Legard decides to come back for revenge."

"You ready for dinner?" Mary called to me from the kitchen. "I already fed Mr. Garrick and Mr. Davy. You wanna eat now, or wait on Miss Ellie?"

"I'll wait for Ellie," I said.

Mary walked into the living room. "What is she doin' now?"

"I hope she's telling Davy she can't marry him," I said.

Mary smiled. "Now she knows you still be alive, how could a body do anything but? I've never seen her face light up like it does when you walk in the room."

I smiled back at Mary. "Thanks."

When Davy opened the door, immense relief washed over me at the disappointed look on his face—and the fact his ring was absent from Ellie's finger. I stepped forward, offering to shake his hand. He hesitated a moment before accepting my handshake.

"Thank you for taking care of her," I said. "I'll forever be in your debt for that, and I'm sorry it didn't work out like you wanted."

A halfhearted smile turned the corners of Davy's mouth. "You're welcome, Harper. All I can say is, you better make her happy."

"I'll dedicate every minute to it."

He tipped his hat to Ellie. "Best of luck to the both of you. I'll be on my way."

A look of concern filled Ellie's eyes. "Where will you go?"

He picked up his rifle and shouldered his pack. "Back to work, I suppose." He walked out the door. "Pa, you comin' with me?"

"You bet, Son." Garrick hustled past me, slapping me on the back. "Take care, little brother."

I'd traveled with him for so long, I dreaded the thought of him leaving. "Garrick, when will I see you again?"

"I'll come to your room in a few months and tell you where we are." He pulled Ellie into a hug. "Take care of this boy for me. He's had a rough go of it lately."

She glanced at Davy as he left. "I will. I'm so sorry to have hurt your son."

Garrick smiled. "He'll get over it. You did the right thing."

Ellie wrapped her arm around my waist, and we watched from the doorway as Garrick ran after Davy.

"Don't forget to come see me. I don't want another ten years to pass by," I yelled.

Garrick waved back at me. "I won't."

Mary threw up her hands and marched into the kitchen. "I ain't sure what all this talk is about, but I do know your dinner's gettin' cold and the both o' you is too thin. You need ol' Mary to fatten you up. Still don't know how two lovebirds can go losin' each other, but somehow you done it. Young man, I 'spect you'll be takin' better care from here on out, won't you now?"

I looked at Ellie and laughed. "You bet I will, Mary. I'll definitely be taking better care."

"That's good. I'd expect nothing less from a fine gentleman like yerself."

"I think I'll go change before we eat. These clothes are embarrassingly dirty," Ellie said.

I smiled and looked her over from top to bottom. For the first time, I noticed her dust-covered dress, with cockleburs and mud lining the hem, and the sleeves, which showed wear at the elbows.

"It doesn't bother me," I said, not wanting to let go of her.

She smiled. "But it does bother me."

I brushed my thumb across her lips and kissed her once before I relinquished my hold.

I couldn't keep my eyes off of Ellie as we ate together in Mary's kitchen. To simply be in her presence and see her smiling back at me was more than I'd dreamed possible during my days in the dungeon. After I practically inhaled the first half of my dinner, I realized there was no need to hurry. Finally, I was home. I was where I wanted to be—with Ellie.

While we finished eating, Mary shared the latest Civil War news. After a lull in the conversation, she asked, "Will you two be stayin' on for a few days?" I shrugged my shoulders and glanced at Ellie. Now that I'd found her, I didn't care where I was or what we did, as long as we were together.

"I think we'll be going home. It's been an awfully long time. Perchance we'll be back this way again, though." She glanced in my direction.

I nodded. "We'll come visit.

"You sure you wanna leave?" Mary asked. "The day's about spent."

I slid off my chair and offered Ellie my hand. "We'll be fine, Mary. Trust me."

Ellie and I said our farewells and walked hand in hand down the street. I breathed in the smell of blossoms on the warm spring air. "It's a good day to be alive."

She smiled and squeezed my arm. "Yes, it is."

We walked longer than necessary, savoring the simple beauties of nature. It had been a long winter. With my counter in my hand, I said, "Well, Ellie, are you ready for modern-day Oregon?"

"Most certainly."

Chuckling, I made sure we were alone before pressing Shuffle and Go. I kept my counter in the palm of my hand, once again enjoying every shuffle. "Welcome to Ireland, Miss Williams. I mean England." I laughed. "No wait, it is Ireland."

She smiled. "I fear you've been out of school too long, Mr. Harper."

"You can say that again."

While leading her through some sagebrush and cacti, I said, "Looks like we're in Mexico, 1651. What do you want to do when we get home?"

"Take a shower and shave my legs."

"Come to think of it, I probably should do that too. Not the legs part, though." That brought a ripple of laughter from her.

"New York, 1801," I said a moment later. The dense forest made moving anywhere difficult, so Ellie stepped in front of me. "I'm so happy you found me. This was the life I wanted, not—" She trailed off her sentence, and I touched my lips to hers as we disappeared.

The sound of horses and wagons pulled me out of the kiss. I opened my eyes and glanced around. It looked like a mid-1800s town with people bustling up and down the street—kind of familiar. With my hand on the side of Ellie's face, mesmerized by her beauty, I leaned down to kiss her again.

"Young man, who's your father?" I spun around and stood facing a preacher. "Where's the sense of propriety in you young people these days?" he asked.

I'd seen him before. I looked over his shoulder to where a spinster lady with a hawkish nose and a sour expression stood watching. Then I smiled as I remembered being here on a previous shuffle. I must have run from this very preacher just a moment ago. My counter had put us in front of the very mercantile I'd run behind with Ellie. I snapped the counter shut and shoved it into my pocket. With my head down, I didn't see the preacher's hand dart toward me.

"Ow," I yelled. "Let go of me." He twisted my ear and pulled, dragging me up the street. An assortment of curious spectators flocked to the scene. The spinster folded her arms and smiled at my predicament.

"Young lady, where are your parents?" the preacher asked.

Ellie held tightly onto to my arm. "I'm an orphan, sir. If you'll leave us be, we're actually leaving town."

"Not before I have a talk with this young man." He had my head bent down to his shoulder level. I grabbed his wrist, trying to pry him off of me. But pulling on his hand just made him squeeze harder, digging his fingernails into my ear.

"Sir, it isn't safe for you to be touching me. Let go, or it's not going to be pretty."

"I'll not have couples flaunting themselves in public, especially the young, unmarried ones." This shuffle had to be nearly over. I released my hold on his wrist. Resorting to desperate measures, I drew my sword and flicked the tip toward his chest. I applied enough pressure to get his attention. "Let go of me, now."

The onlookers gasped. A few of them pointed at my sword. The preacher dropped his hand to his side, and we backed away. I spied a clear path to the dim interior of the livery, and we darted for cover.

No sooner had we stepped into the shadows of the barn than we disappeared. A desolate mountain region and a gust of icy wind welcomed us to our next shuffle. "Brrr, it's cold," Ellie said as I returned my sword to its scabbard.

"Come here," I whispered, pulling her next to me. "What are the odds of running into that guy twice in one lifetime? After that trick, I half expected to land in the ocean next. I was beginning to think my counter had it in for me."

"Not the ocean," Ellie moaned. "Anywhere but the ocean."

I was still laughing when we appeared in the quiet darkness of my room. The glowing numbers on my clock said 10:30. I blew out a breath. "Home at last."

Ellie let go of my hand and turned on the light. She smiled contentedly as she looked around my room.

I unbuckled my sword and tossed it onto the bed. "What do you think about staying here with Jessica tonight?"

Ellie smiled. "I think that sounds wonderful."

"Do you want to use the shower first?"

"Thank you. I'll go see—"

"Oh my gosh, you're back! I can't believe it," Jessica screamed as she burst into my room and threw her arms around Ellie. "You've got to tell me everything. I about died when Chase came home without you."

Ellie hugged her. "It's good to see you. It's been so long. I'll tell you everything, but I've got to take a shower first." The two of them left my room arm in arm, with my sister chattering up a storm. Deciding to do the responsible thing, I left my room and went downstairs.

I knocked on my parents' bedroom door. "Mom?"

"Come in. Is something wrong?" she called.

I opened the door and stepped into their room. "No, I'm home. Just thought you'd want to know I found Ellie."

"That's great. Where was she?"

"A lot of places, but I found her in Boston."

"You were in Boston tonight?"

I chuckled. "Yeah, I was. Along with Utah, Ohio, and Texas, not to mention layovers in Ireland, Mexico, New York, and a few other places I don't remember."

"That's amazing," my mom said. "I still can hardly believe it."

"I'm glad it worked out for you," my dad put in, sounding less enthusiastic about my time travel.

"Thanks, Dad. Good night. Hey, Mom, what day is it? I know the date, but what day of the week is it?"

"Honey, it's Friday."

"I guess I missed spring break."

"Yes, you did."

I closed their door behind me as I left. Even with eating regular meals, it seemed like I was always hungry. I stopped by the kitchen and found a carton of ice cream. Since it was almost gone, I got a spoon and threw the lid away. The shower was running upstairs, so I plopped myself on the couch and turned on ESPN. A contented chuckle escaped my lips as the first bite of Tillamook Mudslide melted in my mouth and the announcer's voice rattled off the top ten plays of the week.

When the shower stopped, I turned off the television and tossed the empty ice-cream carton into the trash. I crossed paths with Ellie when she left the bathroom, steamy air billowing out the door. Her radiant smile stopped me in my tracks. Wearing a pair of Jessica's pajama pants and a T-shirt, she ran her fingers through her wet hair and sighed. "That felt divine."

"You're beautiful," I said. She dropped her gaze, but I could tell she was smiling. Did I make her blush? I couldn't tell, with her face in the shadow. "In all my travels, I've never seen anything as beautiful as you."

She raised her eyes to meet mine. "You always make me feel special. Thank you," she whispered back. Stepping forward she placed her hand on my cheek. I slid my fingers through her wet hair and pulled her mouth to mine.

"Hey, none of that, you two," my sister teased.

I jerked my head back. Jessica had left her room and was walking down the hall, wagging her finger at me.

"Can't a guy get a little privacy around here?"

Ellie's laughter filled the hall as she walked away. "I hope I left you enough hot water."

Jessica gave my shoulder a shove as she passed me in the hall. "Snap out of it. You look like a lovesick puppy dog."

"I missed you too, Sis."

I stepped into the bathroom and locked the door behind me. One hot shower later, I stood in front of the mirror, looking at my back with a towel around my waist. What I could see was a mass of ugly scars. I needed to get Madam Catherine's potion on my back and face. I couldn't show up in the locker room looking like this. I picked up my Algonian clothes, thankful I could retire them. I darted from the bathroom to my room and pulled on some shorts.

I found Madam Catherine's restorative potion in the pocket of the Shuylian fur coat. Time to enlist some help. No need to put a shirt on—it would only make the scars seem more dramatic if I had to take it off later. I couldn't ask my mom. Her pained expression at simply hearing about the whippings was almost too much, so I didn't want her to see the brutal effect with her own eyes. I didn't relish the thought of Ellie seeing it either, so I'd ask Jessica.

I knocked on her door. Ellie opened it. "Yes?"

I had expected Jessica to answer her door. *Did Ellie just check me out? I swear she did.* I realized I hadn't said a thing when she asked, "Is something wrong?"

"I'm fine. Where's Jess?"

"She's in the bathroom. Do you need something?"

I took a step backward and wished I had a shirt on. "Yeah . . . I . . . no." I couldn't very well turn and walk away now, or she would see my scars.

"Chase, what is it? What's bothering you?"

What's taking Jessica so long? "I'll just wait. I was going to ask her to help me with this medicine," I finally said, showing Ellie the potion bottle in my hand.

She laughed. "Why didn't you just say so? Give it to me. I'll help you." She took the potion from my hand. "What is it?"

I touched the scar on my cheek. "It's a skin restorative potion I got from the elf healers."

"For your face?"

"That and—"

When I paused, Ellie grabbed my elbow and turned me sideways. She groaned. "Your back. Oh, I can't imagine you going through that! It makes me sick to think of it."

"I know it looks bad. Don't think about it, though. That's why I wanted to ask Jessica. I didn't want you or my mom to see it." I tried to back away.

Ellie held me firmly in place. "I've seen this once before—on a runaway slave. Come in and tell me what we do with this."

"We rub it on the scars. It's okay to use the whole bottle. It magically refills itself."

Ellie raised her eyebrows and uncorked the glass vial. "It does?"

I shrugged my shoulders. "It did last time."

She slid her arm through mine and propelled me into the room. "Sit down and I'll put it on for you." I sat on the edge of Jessica's bed and rested my elbows on my knees. The cool liquid trickled across my back before Ellie massaged it into the scars. The potion smelled like the lavender candle my mom always lit in the kitchen. I felt myself relax as Ellie's hand ran over every inch of my back.

"What exactly is this supposed to do?" she asked.

"If I put it on twice a day for a week and then once a day for the next sixty days, the scars should disappear."

"That would be a miracle."

"Yup, it would."

"Now look at me," she said. I turned my head and smiled back at her. The last bit of potion dropped onto her fingertips, and she spread it over my scarred cheek. "What are these?" She touched below my eye and the ridge of my cheekbone.

"I don't know," I said, and I didn't care. The beautiful girl in front of me absorbed all of my attention.

She looked closer. "They're tiny scars."

"I got hit in the face a lot. But it's nothing."

She coaxed one more drop out of the bottle and traced each scar. "We'll put some on anyway."

"Thank you, Ellie."

I stood to leave as Jessica bounced into the room. "Time to go to bed. I have a swim meet tomorrow," she said.

"Hey, Jess, in a week or so I'm going to come in here in the middle of the night and ask you if you've seen Ellie. Just tell me no. Don't say anything except no. Okay?"

"Why?" my sister asked.

"Because I went ten days into the future when I first started looking for Ellie, and I asked you if you'd seen her in the last ten days. You told me no, so I kept looking and eventually found her. Now that I've got her back, I don't want anything to get messed up. Don't forget. Please, just say no."

Jessica shrugged her shoulders. "All right, I'll say no."

I took the blue vial from Ellie's hand. "Good night, you two."

I shook the bottle once, and sure enough, it had refilled. I went to my room, and for the first time in months, I climbed into my own bed.

TWENTY-NINE
Explanations

The sound of Ellie playing the piano woke me. I slapped myself once to make certain I wasn't dreaming in Lord Arbon's dungeon, then opened my door and sat on my bed, listening. I was home. I had found Ellie, and I was free to do as I pleased. Today I wouldn't be marching under Marcus's orders from dawn till dark. Never before had I climbed out of bed on a Saturday morning to such an overwhelming appreciation for something as basic as freedom. When the music stopped, I put on a T-shirt and slipped my counter into my pocket.

Ellie was rummaging around in the kitchen when I got downstairs. "Anything good to eat?" I asked, walking into the room.

She turned to look at me. "Oh, I didn't know you were awake."

"I just got up. Did you sleep okay?"

"Yes, and you?"

"For the first time in a long while I slept great. Were you looking for the Cheerios?" I said, remembering they were her favorite.

"Actually, I was."

"I'll check the pantry." I found a box of Honey Nut Cheerios and opened it for her. "Here you go. What do you want to do? I've got the whole day free."

"Your father asked me to tell you to go outside as soon as you woke up. And your mother left a note about the horses on the table."

Kelly Nelson

I picked up the note and read it. Maybe I wasn't as free as I thought.

Ellie smiled. "I can do the horses and stalls for you."

"What does my dad want?"

"He's doing yard work, but I got the feeling he wanted to talk to you."

I poured a bowl of cereal and sat next to her at the table. "I guess I'd better go help him then."

When we finished breakfast, I changed my clothes and walked outside. My dad was raking underneath the fir trees. He had accumulated piles of branches and pinecones around the yard. I pulled on gloves and got a pitchfork and the wheelbarrow from the shop. "Hey, Dad, what's up?"

He looked at me and smiled. "Morning, Chase."

I set to work scooping up his piles and adding them to our burn pile. It took him so long to bring up what he wanted to discuss that I'd begun to wonder if Ellie was mistaken.

"Son, after talking with Garrick, I realize this counter business isn't something you can get out of," he finally said.

"No, Dad. It isn't."

"I can't say I like it, but I guess I'll try to be supportive."

"Thanks."

"There is something else I wanted to talk about."

Here it comes. I stopped working and leaned on my pitchfork. "Yeah, Dad."

"Now that you found Ellie, what are your plans?"

I doubted he'd be happy with the fact I wanted to marry her and spend every minute of my life with her. I also knew that wasn't realistic right now. Although determined to stick to my resolution of full disclosure, I'd start with something safe. Before realizing I liked Ellie, my parents had agreed to let her stay with us, but that all changed once the truth came out. Since we had told them she was an orphan and her only living relative was in Massachusetts, they had made arrangements for her to live with my dad's brother, Steve.

"I'm planning on driving her back to Uncle Steve's house today. Last night it was late, and she hadn't seen Jessica in a long time."

"That's good. But what's your long-term plan? If Ellie's from the 1800s, as everyone claims, what happens if you break up?"

I shook my head. *As everyone claims.* "Dad, I'm not breaking up with her, ever."

"What if she breaks up with you?"

"She's had plenty of opportunities to leave me. She even broke off her engagement to come back here. I don't think you have to worry about her."

"Marriage engagement? To whom?"

"She almost married Garrick's adopted son, Davy Adams, who is also a Keeper. While I was stuck in that other world, she was with Davy for over a year. Since she thought I'd died, she had agreed to marry him."

My dad nodded. "Hmm. What will you do after graduation?"

I filled my pitchfork with branches. "Work construction again this summer, save money, go to college in the fall, then find a good time to ask Ellie to marry me. After that I'll try to give her a happily ever after."

Dad kept quiet for a minute before starting to chuckle. "That's some plan. Isn't it too soon to make a decision about marriage, though? You haven't even dated that long."

"Trust me, Dad. It's been longer than you think, and there's no one else for me. I know that for sure."

"I'd like to change your mind about the proposal part. It's not that I don't like her—I do, actually. But I think you're awfully young to decide something like that."

We worked side by side, moving on to the next pile of debris. "I've thought about it a lot, and I'm sure it's the best thing for me."

"I guess you're old enough to make your own decisions. I only hope you'll make them wisely."

We finished the yard work while Ellie took care of the horses, and by midafternoon I sat behind the wheel of the truck. It felt weird to be driving again after so long. I parked in front of Adam's house, and then stood at their front door while Ellie knocked.

"Ellie, Chase, you don't need to knock. You know that," Aunt Marianne said when she opened the door. "I'm so happy to see you both safely back. We were worried about you."

"I'm sorry, Marianne," Ellie replied. "We ran into a little trouble and—" Her voice trailed off, and I could tell she didn't know what to say.

I had given it some thought while working in the yard. There were bound to be questions after we had disappeared for days with no explanation. Thankfully our absence spanned spring break, so we had only missed a few days of school. But people undoubtedly had talked about it. Gambling that my parents hadn't told Marianne about the counter, I plunged into my fictitious explanation. This would be the trial run.

"It was stupid, really. We took a road trip with my uncle Roy to Reno, Nevada. He was in a hurry to get going, so we left without talking to anyone. I figured since we're both adults now, we could do what we wanted. I had no idea my parents would freak out. I guess I learned that lesson the hard way." Uncle Roy was my mother's rebellious brother, so it would be like him to suggest a trip like that.

Aunt Marianne stepped aside and we followed her into the house. "Well, luckily for you and your parents it turned out okay," she said. When I came out of the shadow of the front porch into her brightly lit kitchen, she reached out and touched the scar on my cheek. "Chase, what happened?"

"Motorcycle accident. The first day we got to Reno."

She winced. "Ouch!" The phone rang. "I'd better get that. I'm waiting for someone to call me back." She darted for the phone, and Ellie and I were free to go upstairs.

"So that's the story, huh?" Ellie whispered.

"Did that sound okay?" I asked.

"It makes us sound like immature and irresponsible teenagers, but considering the circumstances, I suppose that's necessary. It's not like anyone would believe the truth."

I smiled. "I'm afraid a motorcycle accident in Reno is as good as it's going to get."

Adam—my cousin and best friend—walked out of his room. "Dude, you're back. Where the heck have you two been?"

I repeated my explanation and didn't miss the curious glance he sent between Ellie and me. From his expression, it was clear people had been gossiping. After that many days, rumors would have made their way through the entire student body of Hilhi. Ellie had been sensitive to her reputation when we'd visited Boston in 1863 together, so I needed to warn her before she faced her friends. Now, wanting to change the subject, I asked Adam, "How was your spring break?"

"It was awesome. We missed you and your dad on the steelhead fishing trip. It was really good this year."

"My dad didn't go?"

"No, he wouldn't go without you. You're going to the party tonight, right?"

"What party?"

"At Kim's. The end-of-spring-break party. How could you forget? We just talked about it last week. You've got to come, especially now that you're back. Everyone's dying to know where you guys went."

I looked at Ellie. I did seem to recall hearing about this a long time ago. The thought of a party seemed so trivial after the ordeal we'd come through.

Ellie's face brightened. "Oh, yes, I remember. We were going to go to Kim's party."

I shrugged and smiled. "Then maybe we'll see you there. It's good to see you, Cousin."

Adam laughed. "Good to have you back. We were afraid you died somewhere."

"Yeah, me too," I muttered as I walked away.

In Ellie's room, with the door closed behind us, I asked, "Are we really going to Kim's?"

She smiled. "Well, darling, what else is there to do? We don't want people to get suspicious. Shouldn't we act as if nothing has changed?"

"But a lot has changed. I've changed."

She touched my arm. "You'll change back, but I reckon it will take some time."

I nodded, hoping she was right. I wanted to feel normal and get excited about normal things again.

Ellie's phone vibrated on her dresser. "Oh, I completely forgot I had a phone. That's not you, is it?"

I raised my hands. "It's not me."

She picked up her phone and looked at it. "Twenty three new messages, it says. Now what do I do? I can't remember."

I chuckled and crossed the room to wrap my arms around her. Standing behind her with my head over her shoulder, I looked at the phone I'd given her for Valentine's Day. "Slide it open, then press this button to see your messages." I helped her scroll through all the old messages from Jessica and Adam, asking where she was. A few other curious people had sent texts as well. I had already gone through the same thing on my phone and deleted over thirty messages from concerned friends and family members. "Here's the text you just got," I explained. "It's from Lauren: 'I talked 2 Jess. Ha ha, glad ur back. Ur still coming 2 the party, right? I have 2 c u. I have news.'"

I put my thumbs on Ellie's keyboard and typed, "Yes! Sorry I didn't return ur messages. Forgot my phone, lol. C u 2nite." Ellie said each word as I typed it.

"Thank you, Chase. It's been so long since I've gone to a party." She turned around in my arms and gave me a hug. "What time do we leave?"

"I'll find out," I answered. I texted Adam to ask what time the party started. Seconds later Ellie's phone buzzed in my hand. I slid it open and read, "7 r u going?"

"Yes. C u there," I texted in reply.

As soon as I set the phone in Ellie's hand it buzzed again. She slid it open and we read, "Do u want a ride or is Chase taking u?"

Ellie glanced at me, and I took the phone back. "Chase is picking me up," I typed, then kissed her and stepped away. "I guess I'll go home and let you get ready."

THIRTY
Soldier's Heart

That evening, I again knocked on Adam's door. This time his younger sister opened it. "Hey, Chase, I'll tell Ellie you're here." I stepped inside and closed the door behind me.

Amanda came back a minute later. "She's almost ready."

Adam bounded down the stairs and stopped in the entryway. "Are you picking up Rachel?" I asked him.

"No, she's driving tonight. I'm waiting for her to get here."

I nodded but my mind wandered off into a tangled mess of memories. I must have started scowling or something, because Adam said, "Dude, what the heck's wrong with you? Is it Ellie? You're not having lady troubles, are you?"

I shook my head. "No, we're fine." I pulled myself into the present and returned his concerned stare. "The whole motorcycle accident freaked me out," I said. "I could have died. I can't stop thinking about that. I'll get over it, though." I forced myself to smile.

Ellie hurried down the stairs. "Sorry to keep you waiting."

"No problem." We started to leave, but I glanced back at Adam. He was a good friend. Maybe someday I'd tell him what had happened. "Thanks, bro. I'll see you there."

We were almost to Kim's before I got up the nerve to mention the gossip I suspected was circulating about Ellie and me. "So, you know we were gone for ten days and everybody thinks we were together the whole time, right?"

"Yes, I am aware of that," Ellie said.

"Well, they're going to think . . . you know."

She lifted her chin. "I know. But I've heard the things some of those girls say, and they've got no room to talk after what they've done."

I started laughing.

"Pray tell, what do you find so funny?" she said.

"You. After the sermon you gave me on preserving your reputation at the New Year's Eve ball in Boston, I thought you'd be at least a little upset that the gossip might tarnish your perfect reputation."

"Well, that was Boston, where everyone works to maintain their impeccable reputations. Here, I find it is quite the contrary. People put on airs, boasting of things that no lady in polite society should even know about, let alone mention. I shan't let what someone like that says bother me, when it is the truth that really matters."

I chuckled again. "Good. I won't let it bother me either then."

I pulled into Kim's driveway and walked around to open the car door for Ellie. She'd never been here before.

"Goodness, that is the largest house I've ever seen," she exclaimed. "Only Kim's family lives here? No live-in servants?"

"Just her family."

Ellie hadn't left the side of the car. She stared at the manicured lawns and elaborate flower beds illuminated by extensive outdoor lighting. "I can't believe you left a girl with all of this for me, who has nothing."

I put my arm on the hood of the car, trapping Ellie there. "Trust me, you have more than you think. This is all superficial—it means nothing. It's what's inside that makes a person beautiful and desirable. And you're both."

"I hope you don't ever have to leave me alone again," she whispered.

"I won't." I leaned forward and would have kissed her, but the glare of headlights coming up the driveway nearly blinded me. I pulled away and took Ellie's hand.

As always, Kim was the perfect hostess. Ellie and I told and retold the motorcycle-accident-while-in-Reno-with-my-uncle-Roy story. To my surprise the explanation was readily accepted, and people were more anxious to talk about themselves than us anyway. Lauren pulled Ellie aside and shared her news—something trivial about her latest crush, no doubt.

Jared and Adam cornered me around 10:00. "Chase, we need you. We're taking on Randy, Tyler, and Ben—three on three out on the sport court."

Adam pushed me forward. "Dude, let's go."

I hesitated, glancing back at Ellie.

"Go ahead," she said.

Lauren put her arm through Ellie's and smiled. "If Ben's playing, let's go watch."

When we got to the sport court, the opposing threesome was already warming up. Randy was one of my least favorite people at Hilhi. He'd had a crush on Ellie last fall and never got over it. He had officially moved to my "do not like" list when he jumped me outside Adam's house a couple of months ago. Ben was Hilhi's basketball superstar, and by Lauren's comment I guessed he was also her latest fling. I didn't know Tyler. He had transferred from another school in November and was a junior, playing on the varsity team.

Adam tossed me a basketball. Lauren and Ellie joined Kim and some other girls on the sidelines. "We're skins," Adam said.

"No, we're not. We're shirts," I yelled.

"You always go skins," Adam said.

"Not tonight. We're shirts."

"Okay, we're shirts," Jared said.

I breathed a sigh of relief when Randy, Ben, and Tyler pulled their shirts over their heads and tossed them under the basket. The thought of everyone gawking at my scarred back didn't sound fun.

I faced off with Tyler for the tip-off. We played to 20. Their team was up 16 to 14 when I drained a 3-pointer. Before they could score, I stole the ball from Randy and passed it to Adam, who drained another 3. We won 20 to 16.

Randy and Ben called for a rematch. All of us were highly competitive, and to say it was a heated match would be an understatement. I didn't get as worked up about it as I would have a few months ago. I guess after fighting Shuylian soldiers, this was nothing. Win or lose, it didn't matter—I'd walk away from it just the same. I still played a physical game and we won again. I thought Randy would lose his temper with me, but maybe having all the girls watching kept him in line.

Later that night, standing on Adam's porch, I slid my hands around Ellie's waist. "Call me if you need anything. I'm number 2 on your speed dial—hold down the 2 and your phone will call me."

"Certainly, Chase. I'll remember." She wrapped her arms around my neck.

"You have a good night," I whispered, kissing her before she could answer. I was still kissing her when she wiggled out of my grasp and put her hand on the doorknob.

"I should go in. Good night, darling."

The door closed, and I stood alone on the porch. I shoved my hands in my pockets and left deep in thought. Had I been home only one day? My experiences in Algonia and Shuyle, although still vivid in my mind, already seemed like a distant memory. It was odd how I would go through phases of feeling completely normal, like during the basketball game tonight. But at other times what happened in Shuyle haunted me in a way that nearly prevented me from functioning.

That night the ghost soldiers visited me. I saw the dying faces of the Shuylians from the Saddle Pass outpost, only they weren't dead. They were grabbing at my clothes while the eerie howls of the wolf pack echoed around me. I shot awake at 3:00 in the morning. Most likely my own screaming had woken me. I waited for Jessica or my mom to come in, but no one did. My whole body felt sticky with sweat, and it didn't take long before I began to think of Ellie.

I left my room to check on her that night, more because I could than because I was worried. I had spent numerous sleepless nights in Arbon's dungeon thinking about her, unable to see for myself that she was safe. Tonight there were no iron bars stopping me. I threw on a sweatshirt and shoes before pressing Shuffle, then Go.

I stood silently in the center of Ellie's room, waiting for my eyes to adjust to the darkness. She was sleeping, her hair fanned across the pillow, framing her perfect face. I walked to the rocking chair in the corner and sat. Watching her sleep in the peace of her room helped me escape the haunting images of my nightmare. The ghosts had fled the moment I saw her. The minutes ticked by on the clock, and when I felt tired again I lay down on the floor. After the dungeon accommodations, the warm carpet was a treat, and in no time at all I fell asleep.

My first waking sensation was someone kneeling next to me, touching my face. Still half asleep, I tried to sort out what was happening. Had Brierly touched me? I wanted it to be Ellie, but maybe I'd only been dreaming of her. Why was Brierly here today? I didn't feel any pain, and I didn't think Arbon had visited me. I felt carpet with my fingertips, and my eyes flew open. It all came back to me—the nightmare, then coming to Ellie's room. I sat up with a start and must have looked lost.

Ellie laughed. "What are you doing on my floor?" The morning sunlight streamed through the slats in the blinds, leaving bright streaks of light across her face.

I rubbed my eyes and yawned. "Sleeping," I said, then climbed to my feet. I offered my hand and pulled her up next to me. "What are you doing?"

She smiled. "Waking up and wondering why you're on the floor in my bedroom."

"I don't know. I think something's wrong with me." I turned away from her and retreated to the rocking chair.

Her brow furrowed. "Why do you say that?"

"Because I have nightmares, and I can't sleep sometimes. It's crazy the things I saw and did. I shot people, then I dragged their bodies into the snow and left them for the wolves. I can't get their faces out of my mind. Those scenes play themselves back in my head over and over. It's like I'm going insane."

Ellie sat on her bed and looked at me. "Anything else?"

"I can't get over the torture. I wake up scared for no reason. But it's over. Arbon's dead. If I've got nothing to worry about, why does my mind play tricks on me? Why does my heart race in fear, for no reason?" I dropped my head into my hands. "I don't know how to fix this."

"I think you have a soldier's heart."

I raised my eyes. "What's that?"

"A friend of mine, Ann Wright in Boston, had an older brother. At the outbreak of the war he joined the Union army. He was gone for over a year before he returned home. When he came back he wasn't the same. After being shot in the ankle, he'd lost his leg to gangrene. Ann said he endured two amputations before the wound finally healed. His whole leg was gone by the time they discharged him. He slept in the bedroom next to Ann's, and she would hear him crying at night. There were times when he'd wake up screaming or madly searching for his rifle in the darkness. Often the crash of him falling awoke her. Night after night he dreamed he was still fighting the war. The doctor told Ann's mother her son suffered from soldier's heart, a consequence of the battles he'd fought."

"How did he get over it?" I asked. The guy's symptoms sounded familiar. I relived my battles through my nightmares. Regularly, I saw Arbon's wicked grin before I'd wake up cringing in terror from the anticipated lash of his whip.

"I don't know." Ellie paused. "I left for Utah shortly after that, and I haven't talked with her about it since. It was still very much a problem for him at the time I left."

"Well, that's encouraging," I said with some sarcasm.

Ellie flashed me an optimistic smile. "Darling, I'm certain it will go away with time. You must be patient with yourself. It's only been a couple of days."

I stood and pulled out my counter. "I hope so. I'd better get home before someone thinks I've gone off and disappeared again. I'll call you later."

THIRTY-ONE
Graduation

It was the second week of June—graduation week. I had Googled "soldier's heart" the day I woke up on Ellie's floor. During the Civil War, the term was used to describe what is now called post-traumatic stress disorder. The symptoms fit me perfectly— nightmares, flashbacks, insomnia, and depression. Symptoms of PTSD usually fade with time, and for me that proved to be true. I'd now been home from Algonia for two and a half months. If my parents ever noticed the times I'd left my room to go sleep on Ellie's floor, they had never mentioned it. My nightmare- filled, sleepless nights became less frequent, and I hoped they'd eventually disappear altogether.

Thanks to Ellie's diligence, Madam Catherine's potion did its job. It left the skin on my face perfectly smooth. As predicted, my back still bore traces of the abuse. I would carry those scars forever as a reminder of my time in prison. However, I felt no shame in taking my shirt off. The scars were faint enough that most people didn't notice. I told those who did notice and bothered to ask about it, "That's what happens when you crash a motorcycle and slide across the asphalt in a T-shirt." Although typically drawing a cringe from the recipient, the explanation was readily accepted.

When I came home from school on Wednesday, my mom called my name and said there was a letter for me on the kitchen counter.

I hung up the keys to the truck and picked up a yellowed envelope, stained brown on one corner. It was addressed to me in Ellie's handwriting. I turned it over. Scribbled across the flap of the envelope were the words "Oops, sorry this is late! I forgot to mail it in March."

Interesting. I ripped open the letter and read.

Dear Chase,

Once again I find I am alone, writing a letter that I will never be able to mail myself. If these words find their way to you, then I rejoice that you are alive. Nothing would bring me greater happiness. At times I fear you will never escape Lord Arbon's prison. At other times, my heart refuses to believe you may be lost to me forever. When Algonia fell under attack, Master Archidus forced Davy and me to leave. Please know I would never have left there without you if I had any choice in the matter.

I tried to return to 2012 using Davy's counter, but alas it got me no farther than March 31, 1991. Please come get me at Waterfront Park, near Morrison Street. I will wait there all day for you. After that, I don't know where we'll go. Legard hunts for Davy and his counter. Perhaps he hunts for me as well. He seems tireless in his efforts, and I don't know how long we can evade him.

I love you, Chase. Please come back for me. I can't see how I will ever survive a lifetime without you.

With love,
Ellie

Dear Mr. & Mrs. Harper and Jessica,

   *If we should never return and you have received
this letter, please know of my undying gratitude
and love for you and your family. Your son had the
noblest of hearts and gave the ultimate sacrifice
in protecting my life. Unfortunately, he was forced
into the middle of a war on another world, from
which escape may have proved impossible for him.
I feel certain he would have wanted you to know
he loved you, and that he is sorry for the pain and
worry his disappearance caused you.*

*Sincerely,
Ellie Williams*

Her cry for help nearly compelled me to pull out my counter and go to her in 1991, but I knew she was now safely at Adam's. Still, I hated the thought of her suffering. I pocketed the letter and retrieved my keys. It seemed like a waste of gas to drive, but my mother panicked if she knew I was leaving with my counter.

Ellie answered the door when I knocked. I held out my hand. "Come take a walk with me?"

She slipped her hand in mine and closed the door. "Is something amiss?"

We started walking, and soon I pulled out the letter and handed it to her. "I'm sorry I didn't come for you like you asked."

She looked at the letter. "I was so distraught that day."

"I could go back. I could take the letter to myself in March— leave it somewhere I was sure to find it. Then I would know to come for you. I could save you all that waiting and worrying."

While Ellie contemplated my offer, we continued down the sidewalk. Finally, she said, "Chase, that's thoughtful of you, but if we did that I would miss meeting the Gibsons and their sweet twins. They were desperately in need of our help at the time. If you came back it would not only change our lives, but theirs and Davy's. There is no way we can know all the future ramifications of changing that one day in our past. It turned out well for me in the end. Because I suffered the agony of thinking I'd lost you, I now fully appreciate every moment we spend together. You can't imagine how satisfying it is for me to see you alive and well. I'm not sure I want to lose that feeling of gratitude."

I hadn't thought about the ripple effect. "I only want you to be happy."

She smiled. "I am happy. And I don't see any reason to change a thing now that I am."

"Then I guess we don't need the letter."

"No, I suppose we don't," Ellie said, crumpling it in her hands.

I wrapped my arms around her. "By the way, beautiful, what are we doing tonight?"

She looked into my eyes and laughed. "I haven't the faintest idea."

"How about a movie? Tomorrow is the last day of school, and we don't have any homework."

A brilliant sunrise lit the sky the next morning as I did the barn chores. Oregon perched on the brink of summer. The horses, fat from grazing on lush spring grass, stood sleeping in a group. While I was eating breakfast, the doorbell rang. I heard someone talking to my mom, but the words were indistinguishable.

"Chase?" she called from the front door.

"Yeah?"

"I think you need to come here."

I left my half-eaten bowl of cereal. A man stood smiling on the porch as he handed my mom a Chevrolet dealership business card.

"You must be Chase Harper," he said, offering his hand.

Eyeing him with curiosity, I shook his hand. "Yeah, I am."

"So you're graduating from high school this week, huh?"

I wondered where he planned to go with this conversation and why he was at my house. "That's right."

He grinned. "I have a graduation present for you."

My eyebrows shot up. "You do?"

"I do." He handed me two keyless-entry remotes. "I need to get your signature on the DMV registration forms." He retrieved a pen from his pocket and slid some papers out of the Chevrolet folder in his hand.

I pushed the silver button on the remote, and the key shot out like a switchblade.

"What is this all about?" my mom questioned.

The man passed the paperwork to her. "Someone bought your son a car as a graduation present. Everything is paid for. All we need is your son's signature on these forms for the DMV."

"Who? What car?" I asked.

With a smile, the man pointed behind him and chuckled. "In the driveway. Take a look." I stepped onto the porch and walked to where I could see the far side of the driveway. A shiny new Camaro was parked next to Jessica's car. It was blue with white rally stripes down the hood.

I stood, open-mouthed, staring at the vehicle. "No way, dude. Who bought the car?"

He rifled through his folder. "Let me see. I think the name was Eastman."

"Garrick? Was it Garrick Eastman?"

The man finally found the answer and looked up. "Yes, that's who it was. Is he some rich relative or something?"

"He's sort of a relative, but I didn't think he was rich," I answered. "Where is he? Did he buy the car himself? Was he here?"

"No, he made the purchase over the phone. But I do have his contact information. It's listed on your paperwork. After you sign the forms, I'll give you a tour of your new car before I leave."

I shook my head in amazement. Who but Garrick would buy me a blue Camaro? But my mind was spinning. Hadn't he promised to tell me where he ended up when he left with Davy? Yet I hadn't heard a thing from him. And how could he afford to buy me a car at today's prices?

My mom finished her thorough inspection of the paperwork and handed me a pen to sign with. I signed each line the dealership guy pointed to, anxious to get on my phone and call the number he'd given me for Garrick. The guy walked me through the car's features before he climbed into the dealership's shuttle van and left.

I pocketed the keys to my new Camaro and left my mom and Jessica admiring the car. While sitting on the porch, I looked through the folder and located the number listed for Garrick Eastman. It had an area code I didn't recognize. I punched the number into my cell phone and waited while it rang.

"Hello," a man's voice answered.

"Is this Garrick?"

"Little brother, did you get my present?" an older version of Garrick's voice asked.

"Yeah, thank you. It's so sick—a Camaro like you had! But how old are you? Where are you?"

"Slow down, Harper. I don't move as fast as I used to. I turned sixty-eight this year, and I'm living in Dallas, Texas."

A sick feeling hit my stomach—my friend, my brother, was an old man. All of those years were gone. I suddenly missed the Garrick I'd come to love as a brother. "You promised you'd tell me where you were. Why didn't you come back? Do I ever see you again?"

He laughed. "Oh, don't worry about that. We'll definitely see a lot more of each other. I'll get there soon. If I remember correctly, Davy and I were mighty busy at first, getting our freight business going."

"When did you go home?"

"Little brother, I'll not go tellin' you the future. You'll know for yourself soon enough."

"Okay, but how did you get the money for something as expensive as a Camaro. That's too nice a present."

"Remember the day you left me alone at your house?"

"Yeah, I remember," I said, wondering what that had to do with anything.

"I'll just say it's amazing what you can do with a glimpse into the future," Garrick replied. "As I recall, your sister introduced me to the personal computer, the Internet, the Google search engine, and the cell phone that day. A few, well-placed investments and a career in the computer industry has left me more than financially secure. A car's the least I can do to show my appreciation for you."

"Isn't that like cheating?"

He laughed. "Depends on how you look at it."

I sat on the porch, stunned. The car parked in my driveway had to be sweetest thing I'd ever seen—next to Ellie, of course. "I don't know what to say, Garrick. Thank you. It's awesome."

"You're welcome. They ride nice, too. I got me one a few months ago, to try it out. Hey, before I forget, remember to thank me in person next time you see me. Otherwise, I might not think about getting the car for you."

"Okay," I said. "But when will I see you?"

"I can't remember exactly. It's the end of summer or something. Don't worry, though—I'll be there to invite you to Davy's wedding."

Now I was really curious. "Davy is getting married?"

Garrick chuckled. "That's all I'm saying. Harper, you'd better get to school. Tell Ellie hello for me, and congratulations, little brother. I'll see you soon."

"Bye, Garrick. Thanks again, bro."

I tossed the truck keys on the kitchen counter. Wouldn't need those. While dialing Ellie's number, I walked to my new Camaro. "This is Chase. Can I pick you up for school today? I've got something I want to show you. No, nothing's wrong. I'll see you in a minute."

Fifteen minutes later I pulled into Adam's driveway. *My cousin has got to see this.* I slid my phone open and texted, "R u home?

Come outside if u r." Not ten seconds later Adam walked out his front door, as I waited next to my new car.

His jaw dropped. "Dude, is that yours?"

"Yeah. Graduation present."

"Dang, you are so lucky. Did your dad get you this?"

"No, a friend."

"Rich friend," Adam muttered. "This is so sick." He opened the door, sat in the driver's seat, and ran his fingers over the leather steering wheel and gearshift. "Dude, you've got to let me drive this sometime." He pulled the latch to pop the hood. "Is it a V-6 or V-8?"

I leaned next to the door, watching him. "V-8. You can drive it later, bro. I'm taking my girlfriend to school."

He sighed. "Okay, but I'm not going to let you change your mind." He lifted the hood, and we were admiring the engine when Ellie walked out the door.

"Good morning, Chase. How are you?"

I smiled proudly. "I'm great."

"Is this what you wanted to show me?"

"Yeah, how do you like my new ride?"

Ellie walked around the car. "It's nice—a lot smaller than your truck."

"Nice, Ellie?" Adam said. "That's all you can say? It's only one of the hottest cars of the year. Don't tell me it's not the sickest thing you've ever seen."

I could feel myself grinning as I took Ellie's backpack and opened the passenger door for her. "Adam, we're gonna be late. I'll see you at school."

I closed the hood and put the backpack behind the front seat, then got in and turned the key. The engine fired to life, and I revved it twice for Adam's benefit before backing onto the street. I felt like a kid on Christmas morning. I hadn't been this lighthearted in months.

Ellie watched me with an interesting expression as I slid the gearshift into first. She looked irresistible, so I wrapped my fingers around the back of her head and kissed her. "Happy graduation, Ellie." I laughed. The tires squealed as I popped the clutch and zipped down the road.

Her head snapped back against the seat and she giggled. "My, aren't you excited today. But where did this come from?"

"Garrick bought it for me—for graduation. He also wanted me to tell you he said hello."

"Is he here?"

"Nope, he ordered the car from his house in Dallas, Texas."

"It's very kind of him, but isn't it a big thing to give someone?"

"Yeah, it's a dang expensive gift. But according to Garrick, he's pretty well off. He was sixty-eight years old when I talked to him."

"That's awful," Ellie said. "We've nearly missed his whole life then. And what about Davy?"

"I was worried at first too, but Garrick said we'd see a lot of him. He promised he was coming to see me at the end of the summer to invite us to Davy's wedding." I turned to watch Ellie's reaction. I'd often wondered if she ever regretted her decision to come with me. If Davy had been raised to be anything like his father, I knew he was a good man.

She put her hand to her heart and sighed. "Oh, thank goodness he's getting married. I would have felt terrible if he'd never found someone else. Whom is he marrying, and where did they go?"

I shrugged. "I don't know yet—Garrick wouldn't tell me. I guess we've got to wait until he shows up."

Epilogue

My fingers tightened around the small plastic bag in my hand. I left the store with a bizarre mix of emotions—excitement, anxiety, and the weight of responsibility. The day was August 23. I'd worked construction all summer and saved every penny for this purchase. After building barns from dawn till dark for the last two and a half months, I sported a suntan and my T-shirts fit a little tighter than they used to. The weight I'd lost in the dungeon was back, and I'd never felt better. It was a good job. The only thing that would have made it better was if Garrick had been there. There was no one I liked working with more.

I wouldn't be seeing Ellie tonight since she planned to go to a movie with Lauren, Jessica, and some other friends. I'd made her promise the next evening to me, though. While I lay in bed stewing about what I'd say to her, a hand touched my shoulder. "What the heck?" I yelled, grabbing the arm above me.

Garrick laughed. "Did I scare you, little brother?"

"No," I lied. "What are you doing sneaking around here?"

"I've got good news. You want to come to a wedding?"

"Sure. Who's Davy marrying?"

"What? You didn't even think it could possibly be me getting married?"

"You told me yourself you were coming to invite me to Davy's wedding."

"What are you talking about? I haven't seen you since Boston. I haven't told anyone about the wedding. You're the first."

I chuckled. "I guess you wouldn't know about that yet. But, hey, thanks for the new Camaro you sent me for graduation," I said, enunciating each word.

"The what?"

I got out of bed. "Come on, I'll show you." I picked up the keys off my dresser. "In your future you give me a new car. Maybe it's in memory of your 1968 Camaro we drove around together." I led him through my darkened house and out the front door. I clicked the automatic unlock on the keyless entry, and the halogen headlights lit up like snake eyes.

"Would you look at that?" Garrick said. "So this is the new Camaro, huh? It's different, but I like it."

"Good, because you're going to get one too. It's a great car, Garrick. You'll love it."

He shook his head, then climbed into the driver's seat and ran his hand over the gearshift. He clicked the radio on. "I really gave you this? How did I afford one of these? How did I ever afford two of these?"

I smiled as I sat in the passenger seat. This was my chance to keep the future a secret from him. "Don't worry about that now, brother. You'll figure it out when the time is right. Tell me this great news you have. Actually, tell me everything from the time you and Davy left us in Boston."

Garrick turned his head to look at me over the middle console. "Davy and I were at a loss as to where we should go. Neither one of us liked the idea of heading back to the cabin in Ohio. Legard had been there too many times. I had no idea how many dates in the future he'd tried while looking for Davy and Ellie, so we never went back. Davy had a stash of money saved in hopes of buying land and building Ellie a house. He'd earned most of it running freight from the dock in St. Louis to the settlements up north. He liked the travel, liked being with the horses. So, we decided to settle in Illinois and start our own freight business. He took me to the town he and Ellie had stayed in.

"We formed a partnership with a man named Lyman Gibson. Lyman put in his team and wagon, and we used Davy's money to purchase a second wagon and team. For the past year we've had two wagons running regular routes. Steamships carry freight up the Mississippi to St. Louis, and then we take it from there. Davy found him a cute girl named Sylvia. Supposedly, Ellie was friends with her. Losing Ellie left Davy feeling disappointed, but once he started looking at someone else, he saw something he really liked. He's smitten with her, and he'd like both of you to come to the wedding."

I smiled. "We'll be there. Tell me when and where."

"Vandalia, Illinois. He gets married on June 28, 1834, but you should come a little early. Get there on June 19 and you can ride shotgun for me on my next freight run. Ellie could spend time with Sylvia and the Gibsons. They're mighty fond of her, you know."

"I'm overdue for a trip with my counter. We'll be there."

"Thanks, little brother. Oh, one more thing. We've told everyone I'm Davy's brother. He's twenty now, so it's impossible to pass him off as my son." Garrick laughed. "Another four years and he'll catch up to me."

We got out of the car and stood face to face. "It sure is good to see you again," I said. I hadn't enjoyed imagining Garrick as an old-timer.

"It's good to see you too, little brother. Enjoy those new wheels. I'm glad I do something nice in the future." He gave me an affectionate slap on the back. "I'll see you soon," he said before he disappeared.

I locked my Camaro and went back to bed. Now there were two things to talk to Ellie about.

August 24—I'd specifically chosen this date for what I had planned. I had been worthless at work. Distracted as I was, I'd wasted two boards cutting the wrong measurement, not to mention the number of nails I'd bent over.

When I got home, I showered in record time, then put on one of the frontier shirts Ellie had made me, along with the Algonian pants and boots. I pulled out my cell phone and composed a text to her. "Wear 1 of ur dresses and pack what u need for a trip to 1834."

I dropped my phone next to my car keys and tucked my shirt in. My phone vibrated with an incoming message. "My, u r full of surprises. I'll get ready."

I took my purchase from the plastic sack and stuffed it in my pocket, then typed, "I'm ready when u r." I sat on my bed, waiting for Ellie to reply. *Come to think of it, where is Vandalia, Illinois, anyway?* I left my room to Google it. Ellie had lived there with Davy for over a year, so all I had to do was get her to the right place and she could take it from there. Even though it would be summer, I didn't like the thought of hiking around the backwoods of Illinois in search of the town.

I studied a map and compared it to my counter. Posted on the Internet were pictures of an old statehouse. Although I'd never been there, I hoped the photos would help me imagine my intended destination.

My mom interrupted my concentration. "Chase, what are you doing in those clothes?"

I turned to look at her. *Busted.* She didn't look happy, and I figured she had already guessed my intentions. "I'm taking Ellie on a date."

"With the counter?"

"Yeah," I muttered, closing the webpage.

"Where?"

"Vandalia, Illinois, in 1834."

"Can't you just stay here? Do something normal for a change. Like take her to a movie, or out to dinner. I'll even give you the money for it. You could go into Portland and find a nice restaurant, walk along the waterfront—anything but disappearing with magic. You know that scares me. I couldn't stand it if I lost you again."

"Mom, don't worry. It's totally safe. I'll be back before you know it, I promise. Plus, this is important. Garrick's son is getting married, and they want us there for the wedding. We're, like, the only family they have."

She sighed, shaking her head. "How long will you be gone?"

"Not long, maybe a half an hour, an hour tops," I said, taking into account the time I might spend at Ellie's.

My mom sighed. "I still don't like it."

"It's fine, Mom." My phone vibrated next to the computer. I slid it open and read, "I'm ready." I closed it and handed it to my mom, smiling. "I don't need a cell phone where I'm going." I gave her a quick hug and backed away. "Bye, Mom. Love you." I spun the dials to today's date and imagined Ellie's bedroom, before shuffling away from my mother's watchful gaze.

I appeared in Ellie's room in time to see her set her phone on the dresser. Her small satchel lay on the bed. She looked stunning in a blue blouse and tan skirt, with her hair piled on her head. As usual, a few wayward curls escaped her neat bun.

"Hello, Ellie."

She spun around. "That was quick." I picked up her bag and tucked it under my arm. She held my hand and leaned against my shoulder. My thumb hovered over the Shuffle button as I thought of where I wanted to take her. I had one detour to make on the way to Vandalia.

"Chase, darling, what's happening in 1834? You've piqued my curiosity."

"I'll tell you that in a minute, but first I've got something else I need to do." I pressed Shuffle then Go. She asked about eight questions during our shuffle zones, finally dragging it out of me that we would be seeing Garrick and Davy. She guessed the occasion was Davy's wedding, but I successfully kept the location a secret.

We appeared on the grassy knoll—the place Master Archidus had taken me from on my first visit to Algonia almost a year ago. Towering pine trees surrounded the small meadow, and sunlight streamed through the branches, decorating the ground with a collage of shadows.

"Where are we?" Ellie asked.

I shoved the counter into my pocket. "We're on the other side of the ravine near my house—where we went horseback riding a year ago."

She smiled, and I thought how beautiful and perfect she was.

"Oh, yes, I remember. What's the date?" she said.

I grinned. "It's still today. Ellie, I've never been a fancy-speeches kind of guy, but here it goes. A year ago today, I met the most incredible, intriguing, and beautiful girl I'd ever seen. And now, a year later—or maybe 149 years later, depending on how you look at it—I couldn't imagine being more in love with her than I am right now."

I fished the small black box out of my pocket and dropped to one knee in front of her. Glancing down, I lifted a white-gold ring with three princess-cut diamonds out of the box and raised my head to look at her. "Miss Ellie Williams, will you marry me?"

She clapped her hands over her mouth. "Yes! Chase, of course I will." She grabbed my arm, pulled me to my feet, and flung her arms around my neck. "You can't imagine how long I've waited to hear those words coming from your lips. I've dreamed of nothing else for years."

My arms circled her waist and I tipped my head to kiss her tenderly. "Thank you for saying yes, and thank you for loving me," I said, still holding the ring in my hand. Ellie seemed so excited she hadn't even looked at it. I chuckled. "Do you want the ring I bought you?"

"Oh, I'm so happy you proposed that I forgot all about it," she exclaimed. "After making me wait 149 years, you can hardly blame me for being a bit overwhelmed."

Kelly Nelson

Smiling, I leaned back and held the ring in front of her.

"What an elegant ring," she said. "It's beautiful."

"See if it fits. Jessica helped me with the size."

Ellie took the ring and slid it on her left hand. "Well, it's no wonder Jessica wanted to try on jewelry the last time we were at the mall." It appeared to fit perfectly, and I smiled at the sight of my ring, instead of someone else's, on Ellie's finger. She admired the ring while I admired her. "It looks lovely on my hand, don't you think?" she said softly.

"Uh-huh, it does look good on you. All I can say is, it's a relief to see my ring instead of Davy's on that finger." I kissed my way from the ear I'd whispered in, back to her mouth.

She leaned away from me and slipped her finger between my lips and hers. "Speaking of Davy, when are you going to tell me exactly what's happening in 1834? You've nearly killed me with suspense, Mr. Harper."

"I already told you—Davy's getting married. That's it." I grabbed her wrist and moved her hand out of my way, again covering her mouth with mine. I didn't get in more than three kisses before she placed her hands on my chest and pushed me back. I laughed at the intense look on her face.

"What do you mean that's it? Whom is he marrying, and where?"

"I don't remember her name, but I'll show you where." I stuffed Ellie's bag under my arm and set the counter, imagining the side of the old statehouse building in the picture I'd seen. Before she could ask another question, I wrapped my arm around her and pressed Shuffle, then Go.

I laughed through each shuffle zone as she peppered me with more questions. "Trust me—you'll see for yourself in a minute. I want it to be a surprise."

We appeared next to the statehouse in the middle of a downpour. I'd imagined appearing in the early evening, but thick, ominous storm clouds blocked the last of the sun's rays, leaving the town prematurely dark. "Crap," I muttered as a deluge of rain dumped on my head. Ellie and I ran for cover, splashing through puddles of water as we rounded the building. When we ducked under the eaves near the door, her eyes widened in recognition.

"Are we in Vandalia?"

I chuckled. "We sure are. You recognize this place?"

Her face lit up. "Most certainly. I lived here for over a year. Goodness, I can't wait to see Edgar and Emma. They'll be three years old now. They probably won't even remember me. Oh, I wish this rain would let up."

We stood by the door of the statehouse, waiting until the storm front passed. A few people traveled the muddy road, but like us, most sought cover and waited for a break in the weather. "Okay, Ellie, I've got no idea where we go from here. Garrick said their partner in the freight business is Lyman Gibson. I thought we'd start there."

"Yes, we should see the Gibsons first thing. The mercantile isn't more than a half mile from here."

The rain let up a bit, so I asked, "You want to make run for it, or wait out the storm?"

"I don't think I can bear to wait another minute. Let's go." Ellie lifted her skirt and dashed into the street. I followed her as she weaved her way between the puddles, careful to avoid the muddiest sections of road. Despite the rain letting up, we were still wet by the time I saw Gibsons' Mercantile. Ellie went directly to the back door and knocked.

The woman who opened the door had a young child on her hip and looked to be in her late twenties. Her jaw dropped when she saw us. "Ellie! My goodness, dear, you're soaked through. Come in, come in. What a pleasant surprise. I didn't know you were in town."

We stepped inside. "Carol, it's so good to see you," Ellie said, hugging the woman. "Who's this?" She touched the tiny fingers of the baby.

"This is William. He will be two on his next birthday."

"I want to hold him, but I've got to dry off first."

Ellie moved farther into the kitchen. I closed the door behind me and quietly followed, worried about tracking mud into the house. Ellie seemed completely at ease and sat in a chair to remove her muddy boots. "We're here for Davy's wedding, but I've not heard who the lucky bride is," she said.

"Sylvia Hansen. And though I had my hopes set on you, they make a delightful couple," Carol said.

Ellie clapped her hands together. "Oh, I'm so happy for them. Sylvia always did have her eye on Davy."

Ellie must have noticed Carol gazing in my direction. "Goodness, where are my manners? Carol, this is Chase Harper—the one I told you about. He came back." Her voice cracked with emotion as she spoke, and she swallowed before continuing. "Chase, this is Carol Gibson. She and her husband Lyman were kind enough to let Davy and me live with them."

She shook my rain-soaked hand. "It's nice to make your acquaintance, Mr. Harper."

"It's nice to meet you too, ma'am. Thank you for all you did for Ellie. I appreciate it."

"Tell me, Mr. Harper, however did you survive being lost at sea for so long?"

The question caught me off guard, and I glanced at Ellie. This had to be the story she'd used to explain my disappearance. I smiled at Carol. "I simply never stopped thinking of Ellie, and I was lucky to have a brother who never gave up looking for me."

"What a tender—" Carol started to say, but two little kids ran into the kitchen and clamored for her attention. These had to be the twins Ellie had talked so much about—a little boy and a little girl, both towheads. Carol motioned us closer. "Come sit by the fire, you two. We'll get you dried off and feed you supper."

Once the twins became reacquainted with Ellie, they didn't leave her alone, and I noticed again how good she was with kids. Tiny William climbed onto my lap and was sitting there when I asked Carol, "Do you know where we could find Garrick Eastman?"

"He and Davy have a place of their own now. They're west of town. Haven't had much of an opportunity to clear their land, though, with all the traveling those two do."

Later that evening, when Ellie announced our engagement, both Carol and Lyman seemed genuinely pleased. They insisted Ellie stay with them while we were in town. After eating and visiting, it was too late for me to find Garrick's house, so I slept on one of Carol's quilts in front of the fireplace.

The next morning, Lyman loaned us his buggy for the trip to Garrick's. Being familiar with the area, Ellie guided me to their cabin with the help of Mr. Gibson's directions. The cabin was patterned after the one Garrick and Davy had in Ohio, with two rooms and a neat stack of wood along one side. The partially dug cellar was full of rainwater. Around the cabin were piles of branches to be burned and stumps to be removed. It was definitely a work in progress, and they needed a backhoe in the worst way. Hearing someone working, we walked around back.

"Garrick," I called.

"Little brother, you found me." He buried his ax in a stump, then rushed over to greet us. Davy followed him, looking more mature than I remembered. Strangely, he was now older than I was.

"Hey, Davy, congratulations," I said, hoping there wouldn't be any hard feelings between us.

He smiled. "Thanks, Harper. I'm glad you came. I'm going to be a married man soon." His excitement was contagious. "I can't wait for you to meet her. Ellie, you were right about Sylvia."

Ellie smiled up at him. "I'm so happy for you. You deserve the best."

Davy settled his gaze on her. "Thank you. You look well and happy."

Her face lit up as she glanced in my direction. "I am. Chase proposed marriage, and I've accepted."

Garrick gave me a hearty slap on the back. "It's about time. Congratulations, you two."

"Congratulations." Davy smiled at Ellie. "I know that's all you ever hoped for. I'm glad you got your beau."

"Thank you," she said.

I was relieved to find there was no awkwardness between the four of us. Ellie and Davy's ordeal had left them with an enduring friendship, and fortunately, their bond had only strengthened when they'd gone their separate ways. I would forever be grateful for the protection and care he'd given her when I couldn't.

In all we spent two weeks with them. Davy and Sylvia were married on a beautiful Saturday afternoon. Ellie thoroughly enjoyed renewing her friendships with everyone she'd come to love in Vandalia.

When it was time to leave, Garrick pulled Davy and me aside and proposed a plan. "Harper, Davy, we could find ourselves anywhere, at any time. I'd like the three of us to get together again. What do you say we meet here in Vandalia next year for the Fourth of July? We'll have us a picnic."

"That's a good idea. I'll be here July 4, 1835," I said.

Davy smiled cheerfully. "I don't plan on being anywhere else."

Garrick nodded. "Good. It's a plan then."

Ellie said her goodbyes and took hold of my hand. Smiling at the other Keepers, I set my counter and pressed Shuffle, then Go.

We appeared in my bedroom. "Should we announce our engagement?" I asked her. "I don't know about my dad, but I'm sure my mom will be excited to hear the news."

Ellie smiled. "Yes, and I've got to tell Jessica."

Holding my fiancée's hand, I led her downstairs. My mother sat on the couch, nervously tapping her foot. I'd forgotten I left her waiting for me. "Hey, Mom," I called.

She sighed. "Thank goodness you're back."

Ellie and Carol had made me new clothes to wear to the wedding. Garrick had given me an old hat of his. So, I was returning home looking like an authentic frontiersman.

"Just look at you two. You look like you stepped out of a western movie," my mom said, moving toward us.

"You're close, Mom, but we walked out of 1834. Ellie has something to tell you."

She looked at me, surprised. "I do? You should tell her."

"No, I'll let you do the honors."

"Well, come on. Somebody tell me," my mom said.

Ellie extended her left hand, the diamonds sparkling on her finger. "We're engaged."

My mom's eyes widened, and her hand flew to her mouth. "I can't believe it. Chase, really?"

I grinned back. "Yup."

"When?" She flung her arms around me, then stepped over to hug Ellie.

Ellie and I looked at each other. "I don't know," she said. "We haven't talked about that yet. Maybe Christmas?"

I grinned. "What about Thanksgiving?"

"No sooner than Thanksgiving, Chase," my mom said. "There are a million things we need to do. Ellie, we've got to go dress shopping, schedule the venue, and order invitations. Then there's the catering. Oh, I'd better start a list." Mom headed for her desk in the kitchen.

I laughed while Ellie smiled at my mother's excitement. The love Ellie and I'd found had withstood the test of time and the trial of separation. The Shuylian dungeon had refined me—made me a simple man. All I needed was the girl standing next to me, and enough food to eat. Fancy wedding or not, it didn't matter to me as long as Ellie was the one saying "I do."

The End

Dear Reader,

Thank you for sharing this amazing journey with me. I began writing the first draft of *The Keeper's Calling* in January and finished the final page of *The Keeper's Defiance* over Thanksgiving weekend. When I typed the last sentence I thought, *I'm done.* I closed my laptop and had no intention of revisiting the story until I had a publishing contract. However, my mom had other plans for me, and you know how persuasive mothers can be.

She read *The Keeper's Defiance* over the Christmas holidays, and in January she called me to make a special request. "I want to see Chase and Ellie get married. Could you write me another chapter for my birthday?" At the time, I was really excited about a contemporary Christian romance I had begun writing and didn't want to set that aside, but how could I say no to my mom? I switched gears and revisited Chase and Ellie.

The "extra chapter" or extended epilogue, as I called it, ended up being 38,000 words, and I really liked what I'd discovered about Garrick. Plus, it was so fun to see Chase head off to college. And, yes, they all end up back in Algonia.

When I mentioned this to my publisher, they asked me to consider expanding my extended epilogue into a fourth book. I hadn't dealt with Legard yet, and knew I needed to take care of him, or Chase would never truly be free. I began the "what if" daydreaming, and one thing led to another. So, although The Keeper's Saga started out as a trilogy, I hope you'll join me in thanking my mom Kris for one more adventure—*The Keepers' Council.*

Please visit my website kellynelsonauthor.com for an update on *The Keepers' Council,* and if you aren't already on my email list, you can add your name by emailing me at kellynelsonauthor@gmail.com.

Happy reading,
Kelly Nelson

About the Author

Kelly Nelson was raised in Orem, Utah, and now resides in Cornelius, Oregon, in the heart of the beautiful Pacific Northwest. She enjoys life on a ten-acre horse property with her husband, four children, and, of course, lots of horses. Kelly has a bachelor's degree from Brigham Young University. She worked as a certified public accountant for several years before opting to stay home and raise a family. As a young girl, she was an avid reader and had a passion for creative writing. Her travels to England, France, Egypt, Israel, West Indies, Mexico, Canada, and across the United States sparked her love of history, adventure, and exotic places, inspiring her to write *The Keeper's Calling, The Keeper's Quest,* and *The Keeper's Defiance.* Learn more about Kelly and the upcoming sequel at kellynelsonauthor.com, or follow her at facebook.com/ TheKeepersSaga, or on Twitter at @kellynelsonauth. She likes hearing from readers and can be contacted at kellynelsonauthor@ gmail.com.